Praise for *The W...*

"In Billie Walker, Moss has conjured up one kick-ass 1940s heroine: a tough-talking, glamorous feminist who's as adept with a pistol as she is on the dance floor, haunted by a tragic past, and unafraid to take on the darkest of foes. An artful, original take on noir suspense that resonates in today's times."

—Fiona Davis, *New York Times*
bestselling author of *The Lions of Fifth Avenue*

"Brilliantly atmospheric and completely immersive—this stylishly fierce adventure into postwar darkness will hold you captive on every page. The amazing Tara Moss has created a cinematic and important feminist noir—dark as midnight velvet and tough as steel. Do not miss this!"

—Hank Phillippi Ryan, *USA Today*
bestselling author of *The First to Lie*

"Billie Walker is the type of heroine I'd love to befriend: resourceful, clever, adventurous, and a true fashionista. With a gripping plot and the perfect dose of history and intrigue, *The War Widow* has all the elements of a great page-turner."

—Ellen Keith, nationally
bestselling author of *The Dutch Wife*

"With a crackling plot and vibrant prose, Tara Moss concocts a first-rate noir detective mystery." —*Christian Science Monitor*

"*The War Widow* is poised to be Tara Moss's breakout novel in the United States, especially given the book's saucy leading lady, Billie Walker. She's a war reporter–turned–private investigator in post–WWII Australia who—much like Moss herself—refuses to be defined or held back by any man on her quest for justice."

—*The Boston Herald*

ALSO BY TARA MOSS

The War Widow

A Novel

Tara Moss

DUTTON

DUTTON

An imprint of Penguin Random House LLC
penguinrandomhouse.com

Previously published in a Dutton hardcover edition in December 2020

First Dutton trade paperback printing: November 2021

Copyright © 2020 by Tara Moss
Excerpt from *The Ghosts of Paris* copyright © 2022 by Tara Moss

First published as *Dead Man Switch* in 2019 by HarperCollins Publishers Australia

THE LIBRARY OF CONGRESS HAS CATALOGED THE
HARDCOVER EDITION OF THIS BOOK AS FOLLOWS:

Names: Moss, Tara, author.
Title: The war widow : a novel / Tara Moss.
Other titles: Dead man switch
Identifiers: LCCN 2019045177 | ISBN 9780593182659 (hardback) |
ISBN 9780593182666 (ebook)
Subjects: GSAFD: Mystery fiction.
Classification: LCC PR9199.4.M6755 D43 2020 | DDC 813/.6—dc23
LC record available at https://lccn.loc.gov/2019045177

Dutton trade paperback ISBN: 9780593182673

Printed in the United States of America
1st Printing

BOOK DESIGN BY ELKE SIGAL

For Oma and Opa

The War Widow

—◦—

Prologue

—⁓—

The night was starless pitch, enveloping him as in the feathered wings of a giant black raven.

Everything ached: his body, his head, the stifling darkness itself, and that darkness was spinning off-kilter, moving unpredictably and leaving him nauseous. His eyes felt warm and wet, and he opened them, strained them wide, but still he could not see. He was not a fighter by nature; nonetheless, his survival instincts had been awakened and the boy struck out—once, twice—hitting nothing but air. Sharp blows came back out of that unpredictable, impenetrable inky blanket, returning his unsuccessful strikes with hard and unforgiving ones. Pain shot through him again in white-hot flashes—his cheekbone, his ribs, his gut—and then the blows stopped. He curled into a ball once more, protecting his head, and he breathed uneasily, his ears ringing. His face felt hot. Something warm and salty dripped into his mouth.

Barely past his seventeenth birthday, he'd already traveled across the seas, seen injustice and violence, but he had never been so scared in his life as he was in that moment, there in the darkness, huddled and blind. Yes, he was scared. Scared as a fly in a web. If it was shameful to feel scared he'd have to think on that another time—if there was anything after this, any time to come at all. For now there was only room for one emotion.

Fear.

"Didn't nobody tell you about curiosity and the cat?" came a voice, and then the earth was moving beneath him; he was pulled by his arms, the ground scraping against his face, his shoulder. He was lifted into the air like a rag doll and dropped. The ground beneath him gave and swayed. It was not ground; it was wool. A blanket. It smelled horribly of damp and carried the metallic tang of blood.

He tried again to speak. "But—"

Another blow. Somewhere in the close distance, just beyond the ringing in his ears, he heard a boot close and an engine start. The dark black bird of oblivion reached for him again and he was gone.

One

—⁓—

Billie Walker was right back in the moment.

The sun was warming her face, a world of abstract Technicolor
behind her eyes as she closed her lids against a brief gust of wind,
turning the corner on Stephansplatz. Each detail was so clear, so
present, even now. There was the smell of something baked in the
air. A shop's delicious daily offerings of Sachertorte and Apfelstrudel.
She'd laughed at something Jack had said. She could feel his large,
reassuring hand in hers as they walked, their world a bubble of new
love and the excitement of foreign soil and the thrill of a story. No
caution. No fear. Their leather shoes clicked on the cobblestones
and she could hear voices beyond the corner, then a shouting that
pulled her from her reverie. Her reporter's notepad was in her hand
in an instant, and she broke from Jack and looked down to catch the
pencil that was slipping.

When she looked up, she saw it. She stopped in her tracks, as
Jack already had. The world came rushing in, shattering the illusion
of safety. A dozen women were on their knees in the large square,

surrounded by men in uniform. They were weeping quietly as their heads were shaved. She saw blood and hair, naked skin and tears. A man was in his underthings on the street beside them, cowering, his back bloodied, his beard shaved, his yarmulke crushed on the ground beside him. A crowd watched. Some of them were shouting, their fists raised. Billie couldn't hear what they were saying through the sound of the blood pumping in her ears. Just as the urge to run forward and intervene struck her, one of the storm troopers turned, caught her eye. She looked away in an instant, as if the gaze would burn her.

She closed her eyes.

What they saw in Vienna was always there, just waiting for her lids to close. One day in 1938 she'd opened her eyes to find it, and now it was there each time she closed them—a kind of reversal. Why those memories? Why that weekend? It was all wrapped up in Jack, in the war, in everything she had to somehow leave behind now, everything that her head told her was over but her heart still clung to.

Billie shook herself gently and gathered up her things. There was no sense in lingering on memories, even if they wouldn't let her go just yet. She wasn't in Europe anymore. She was back in Australia. It was 1946, a new world, and she had to make a new life in it. She had to, and she would. The tram was slowing, pulling up next to Central. She removed a small gilded compact and lipstick from her handbag and reapplied a touch of Tussy's Fighting Red. This was her stop. It was time to rise.

—⏻—

"Morning, John," Billie called as she strode into the foyer of Daking House, moving swiftly on long, graceful legs, yet as quietly as a cat, her crepe-soled oxfords making only the softest sound on the hardwood floor. It was to here that she took the tram most days of the week, for this was where she rented an office.

On hearing Billie's voice the lift attendant stood to attention, roused by the presence of his oft-claimed "favorite customer" in the building. There was no reason to disbelieve him on that score. When Billie arrived in the morning it was always past ten, well after the delivery boys had stocked the ground-floor shops and left again in their trucks, and the silver-haired businessmen had moved through the lobby and disappeared into their various offices, frowning and shuffling, plenty of them already stinking of cigars by nine. Billie never shuffled. She preferred the smell of French perfume to cigar smoke, and if she knew anything about reading the body language of quiet men, the lift attendant did, too. Other tenants like the Roberts Dancing School, the Sydney Single Tax Club, the United Jewish Overseas Relief Fund, the players who frequented the billiards room downstairs, and the like, well, they came and went at odd hours, a bit like Billie often did, but the accountants and legal types and those men from the New South Wales Kennel Control Board kept strict schedules and at this hour were hunched at their desks in their professional chambers, applying themselves to the type of work that was simply not in her blood. Few clients in her trade could be expected to knock at nine A.M. Midnight, however—well, that was not entirely unheard of. Her trade might have a mixed reputation, but the ways of the world demanded it. As did her purse.

"Good morning, Ms. Walker . . . Always a pleasure," the lift operator said.

When he'd started at the building in August, replacing a kind-faced, gray-haired woman who had held the position during the war years, this new lift operator had insisted that she call him by his first name, John. But just what to call Billie was no small question these days. Those in his line of work customarily used formal titles and, new to his job, John Wilson was reluctant to accept her invitation to refer to her simply as "Billie," as the previous attendant had come to. Not just yet, anyway. But every time someone referred to Billie as "Mrs." it reminded her of the uncertainty of her personal life. It reminded her of loss and set her on edge. "Miss" wasn't quite right, either, she felt, and she could hardly be called that after all that had gone on in the past few years, including a wartime wedding, albeit a makeshift one with no ring and few witnesses. In the end she had requested "Ms.," the term sitting better. It had its roots in the old titles, as Billie understood it, and was coined at the turn of the century as a more neutral honorific for women, but was little used. She had seen it mentioned in a *New York Times* article some years previous and at the time of reading hadn't any inkling how well it would later suit her. John Wilson had accepted the request without comment, and now Billie got to hear "Ms. Walker" every working day of the week. In the wider world, well, there was always the tripping over "Miss," "Mrs.," "Madam," "Mademoiselle"—the whole complicated matter of a woman of marriageable age but uncertain status. Strangely, with all that the war had taught the world about the inherent precariousness of life, such details seemed to have gained more, not less, prominence, as if the years of darkness had been prompted by a title, by a woman, rather than by National-sozialismus and the sinister edges of the will to power. It was part of a grasp for stability, Billie supposed, a nostalgic turning back to something simpler, more rigid and readily understood. But Billie didn't want to turn back. That wasn't her style. And, besides, there was no undoing what the war had done.

Wilson dutifully stepped back to usher her into the nearest of the building's four lifts—two for passengers, two for cargo. Only one of the passenger lifts was currently running, and they'd just started operating it from the ground floor again in recent months; previously the tenants had climbed the stairs to the first level to conserve power. It still felt a touch luxurious to go up from the lobby. Billie stepped inside the cab and Wilson slid the outer and inner metal doors closed with his strong left hand, the grille unfolding like a wall of opening scissors. His right hand, once his dominant hand, had not survived the war, and neither had that full arm. His suit was pinned on the side—not so unusual a sight in Sydney these days. His hair was neat and short, but the hairline was uneven on one side. His face, once conventionally handsome, Billie guessed, was marked by burns, though both his eyes, his nose, and most of his mouth were unscathed. For more than a year now the city had filled with broken men returning from overseas. Many were shunned for the disfigurements they could not hide, and the Australian bush was filling with such men, just as it had after the Great War—men who preferred lonely solitude to the stares they were met with on city streets, the pointing of children, the constant reminders. But John had returned to a relieved family and was already well liked by those in the building. He'd made it back, while many had not.

They rode up, the cab rattling.

"How is June?" Billie, as she often did, inquired after Wilson's wife. "And the children?"

"Very well. Thank you for asking," he said, and his mouth moved

into an uneven smile, his eyes crinkling warmly. He slowed the lift
at the sixth floor, jogging the lever up and down a couple of times to
line it up with the hallway outside. He let go of the handle too suddenly and the elevator lurched, the dead man switch kicking in.
"Apologies, Ms. Walker. Just as well we've got the switch to, uh, stop
us, if my hand slips," he said, reddening slightly beneath his scars. If
you didn't keep your hands continuously on the lift control, you
could activate the mechanism—the actual death of the man operating it wasn't necessary to set it off. Wilson was new to his certificate, but it happened to those with more experience, too. He pulled
the grille doors open. "Watch your step."

"Always," Billie replied and flashed him a smile.

She walked along the hall, passing offices already humming with
activity, until she arrived at a wooden door fitted with a frosted glass
window, a simple title painted in black across it:

B. WALKER, PRIVATE INQUIRIES

This was where her late father had spent so much of his life,
where so many of the stories he'd told her at the dinner table had
been born. She'd changed the space very little since taking over;
the setup, furniture, and pictures were largely the same, but of necessity she'd sublet two of the office spaces he'd used to accommodate
his employees. Hers was a smaller agency and she liked that just fine.
Office spaces were at a premium, more than seven pounds eight
shillings per week for a single, and revenue aside, there was some
considerable animosity aimed at those who didn't do their best to
make room for the returned men and their needs. Keeping more of
the office space than absolutely needed would not have aided her

socially or professionally, and as it was, acceptance of Billie and her work was still at best uneven. After Victory in the Pacific Day women were expected to walk out of the aviation plants and munitions factories and news offices and hospitals they'd run successfully during the war and abandon the independence of a wage to return to their kitchens, but Billie had never been one of those women, hadn't been raised that way, and she certainly wasn't going to bow to the pressure now.

The door was unlocked, her secretary already seated in the outer office, where clients sometimes waited. Billie unbelted her double-breasted trench coat and cast a glance at the line of four neat walnut chairs placed before the low table she kept stocked with an assortment of respectable, somewhat bland magazines and a couple of the more fashionable women's journals. The chairs were distinctly unoccupied. The magazines were neatly spread out, untouched. There was no one waiting today, no appointments set. Hadn't been for more than a week. This was another solid reason to sublet the two office spaces.

"Good morning, Ms. Walker. Your mail is on your desk," Samuel Baker informed her, standing as if at attention.

She slid out of her coat and he took it and hung it on the coat rack. She removed her round sunglasses, adjusted the hatpin in the small green topper that sat over her left ear, smoothed down the lines of her fitted summer-weight skirt suit, thanked her secretary-cum-assistant, and strode into the inner office, settling down behind her desk and leaving the communicating door open. Her office had a rust-red carpet, a couple of fading hunter-green filing cabinets, a globe of the world, and a wide wooden desk, blotter, pen set, and telephone that had belonged to her father and had graced the room for at least two decades. On the wall was a large map of Sydney in a slightly battered wooden frame. It had been there for as long as she'd known the office and she suspected that if it was ever moved, the wall beneath would likely be a startlingly different color. It wasn't a fancy space. It didn't need to be. Clients didn't come to her for interior decorating tips.

Her father's ashtray sat on the far edge of Billie's desk, positioned for clients' convenience. Most women now smoked, but Billie had never liked it as a daily habit. There were smoking days, yes, indeed, but this wasn't one of them. The ashtray was cleaned out and empty. The daily newspapers sat on her desk—*The Sydney Morning Herald*, the scandal sheet the *Truth*, and the most recently available *Paris Herald Tribune*—all neatly folded. It paid to know what was being said in the world. Two framed pictures faced Billie. One was a formal portrait of her mother and father on their wedding day, her father in tails with white tie and a black shining top hat tucked under his arm (probably the only time he'd ever touched one) and her mother in a glittering headpiece, a waved bob hairstyle she hadn't changed since, and a scandalously short gown that showed her ankles above low-heeled shoes tied with glossy ribbons. Ella held a bouquet that trailed to the floor, and on her dark lips was the grin of the cat that got the cream. The other frame was smaller and held a more recent image, one of Jack Rake, taken by Billie in Vienna. It was mostly in focus and it caught him smiling that weekend before the world crashed in around them. That weekend they'd fallen in love.

Billie's breath caught in her throat. Jack was just as he looked in those flashes that haunted her each time she closed her eyes. That smile. And the seriousness that followed. Those earnest, searching hazel eyes. "Blast," she murmured, and looked away. She needed work to keep her occupied.

Her ivory blouse had been tied in a pussy bow at her throat but had begun to loosen, and with neatly kept, unvarnished fingers Billie fixed the knot, then picked up the top envelope on her wide wooden desktop. Her eyes narrowed. It was addressed to Mr. B. Walker, and not for the first time. This might be mail for her late father, but well over a year after his death that was unlikely to be the case. Billie Walker was not what many people expected. Perhaps foremost, Billie was not a Mr. But then, what was the fun in doing or being what was expected? She slit open the envelope and glanced through a solicitor's dull note about a previous case involving marital disharmony. The day's mail brought little to be excited about and she soon turned to the newspapers, flicking through them before committing to a more thorough reading with a fresh cup of tea on the way. A shipyard lockout was causing havoc at the Sydney docks. A series of pictures showed Chifley with the governor-general, Prince Henry, Duke of Gloucester, at an official function. Sydney auction houses were busy moving valuables, some of which appeared to be major estate pieces. In world news, two-piece swimming costumes were being modeled in Paris. There was a large-scale withdrawal of Russian troops from Germany. Belgium, the Netherlands, and Luxembourg agreed to repatriate German war prisoners as soon as possible. France had still not signed any agreement.

Billie looked up from the papers as Samuel came in with the tea tray, a morning routine that was always a pleasant distraction. Broadshouldered and lanky, wearing a lightly pin-striped suit and a pleasing burgundy and sky-blue tie of the current style, he sprawled out in one of the two chairs opposite Billie's desk and dropped a sugar cube into her tea, most of his professional formality evaporating when he left the outer office that was his guard post. His tea making was surprisingly good, something he'd mastered either in the army or at the urging of a mother with good English sensibilities. He pushed her teacup across to her.

"What's doing?" he asked, absentmindedly rubbing some irritation under the glove that covered his left hand.

"Very little, Sam, I have to say," Billie responded. She pushed her deep brunette curls back behind her ear and sipped her tea.

Sam was one of those earnest Aussie lads who had enrolled in the army young and had worked in a secretarial role for some time before war broke out and he was needed for more exciting work in the 2/23rd Battalion—exciting work in the war being the kind that set you up as cannon fodder if you didn't have the right connections. Sam wasn't a connected bloke, and had he been rich, he likely wouldn't be working as a second to a PI now. He had many skills as a secretary, but truthfully he wasn't a great typist. Anyone could see why, and clients had good-naturedly joked about it more than once. In Tobruk an Italian thermos bomb had finished off many of his comrades-in-arms and he'd come away with a few less fingers and some terrible scarring on his hands—defensive wounds, Billie had surmised. His left hand was wrapped in a leather glove, filled in the necessary places with wooden prosthetic fingers. His right, though scarred, was whole and as steady as you could want on a trigger hand.

Typing aside, Sam's role was varied. Sometimes it paid for Billie to have a strong arm around. Sometimes it paid to have a tall man in the outer office to run interference if a disgruntled husband came in, angry that she'd helped his wife divorce him. And sometimes it simply paid to have a man for added cover when Billie was in the field, or to compensate for the fact that she was a woman working in a predominantly male business. It helped matters that Sam looked passingly like Alan Ladd, though much taller, which made him easy on the eyes, and realistic as a partner for Billie when such a masquerade was required during an investigation. Most of the grizzled gents in her profession wouldn't pass convincingly as a match for her, but she and Sam made an attractive pair, and that went a long way in certain circumstances. He didn't know much about detective work yet, having been on the job only a few months, but he was great with orders, and unlike some other men he didn't mind taking them from a woman—decent work being rather scarce even for able-bodied men, after all. And by some measure, working as a secretary for Billie was probably more exciting than being in the forces, or at least that's what Sam claimed. It wasn't all filing cabinets and administrative work. He was getting to know all the bars, hotels, doss-houses, and back alleys in the city. Not glamorous, exactly, but not dull, either. And if he couldn't type with ten fingers, well, that was just fine.

"How was *The Overlanders* last night?" Billie asked him. She hadn't seen a lot of pictures lately, but it was something Sam enjoyed spending his paychecks on. "Did Eunice like it?" she added. He'd only just started dating Eunice, though he didn't talk about her much.

Sam was expounding upon Chips Rafferty's portrayal of a Western Australian drover when the telephone rang. He put down his cup, cleared his throat, and answered in a professional tone. "B. Walker, Private Inquiries, how may I . . ."

Sam trailed off and Billie raised an eyebrow, watching.

"They hung up," he said, puzzled, and replaced the receiver in its cradle. "Or they were cut off."

"You didn't hear anything?"

He shook his head. "The street, perhaps."

—m—

It was just past three in the afternoon, only minutes after Billie had suggested Sam might leave early, when she heard a polite knock on the door of the outer office and the sound of him letting someone in.

"I . . . I understood it was a lady detective," said a small, panicked voice in the next room, emphasizing the word "lady" as if it were terribly important. Not everyone knocked on that outer door. In fact, most people came walking straight in with their troubles and needs, so Billie deduced that this was someone either especially polite or especially nervous. She rose swiftly from her desk and made her way to the open doorway of her inner office before Sam could explain. No sense in losing a customer who might skedaddle through nervousness, especially when business was a little too slow for comfort.

A tense woman in her late thirties or early forties stood in the outer office, giving the impression of a spooked deer, her feet planted slightly apart as if she might bolt at any moment. Billie took her appearance in quickly: she stood roughly five foot three and wore an impressive chocolate-brown fur stole clasped at the bust, probably mink or musquash, and fine quality at that. Beneath that was a brown suit of a light summer weight, a little drab and conservative in its design. Probably tailor-made, but not recently. Her Peter Pan hat was prewar in style, not the latest fashion. It was a slightly lighter brown than the suit and was finished with a chocolate-brown feather. The woman wore very little makeup, and a pair of round, plain cheaters made her brown eyes seem huge, adding to the impression of a startled doe. Like her attire, the woman's hair was brown. Her shoes were good-quality reptile skin to match her handbag, but not flashy. The heels were low, sensible. A little worn, but nicely kept. Her gloved hands were clasped tightly over the handle of her small handbag, and both seemed as sealed shut as her mouth, which looked to have lately sucked a lemon.

Billie imagined her wearing a darker, heavier suit of similar utilitarian cut and color in autumn and winter and this one throughout spring and summer, but her fur . . . now, that was special, almost out of place on a person like this. For an antipodean November, Sydney wasn't too hot yet, but this accessory was by no means worn to ward off the cold. The hairs on the stole were gleaming and brushed down evenly. It seemed new and Billie wondered about the story behind it.

"I'm Ms. Walker, the principal here. This is my secretary and assistant, Mr. Baker," Billie explained with a wave of her hand, and the woman's eyes widened for a moment. "Would you like to come into my office, Mrs. . . . ?" The woman did not complete the question with a name. Nonetheless, Billie stepped smoothly back into her office and pulled a chair out for the woman before making her way around the wide wooden desk and waiting by her seat.

It took a moment for the woman to follow her from the outer office. Sam offered to take the woman's stole, but she mumbled a thank-you and refused. After an awkward silence, during which it seemed even odds whether the woman would sit down or bolt, she finally entered and took the offered seat across from Billie.

"Please, make yourself comfortable," Billie said gently. "Samuel, would you please bring some tea?" Billie hoped it might help settle her flighty companion.

Sam tactfully closed the inner office door.

"How may I be of service to you?" Billie asked, watching as the woman's eyes went to the floor, then the globe on the filing cabinet, before finally settling on the big map of Sydney on the wall. Her lips remained sealed throughout.

Billie was used to this initial process sometimes taking a while. She was patient and she didn't press for names or personal information before it was necessary. Many people who came to see her were upset by their circumstances, and for some the mere prospect of dealing with a private inquiry agent about any matter was distressing enough on its own. As Billie well knew, PIs had a mixed reputation. This fact hadn't escaped her, growing up with a PI dad, and little had changed on that score. She suspected that the American detective pictures that were currently popular did not help—they were full of ultramasculine shady types, handy with their fists, who said "sweetheart" while their eyes said something else. Some female clients intentionally sought out private inquiry agents of their own sex, particularly if their problem was a domestic matter that they would find awkward to discuss with a man, or perhaps simply because the prospect of dealing with a Sam Spade type did little to comfort them. This was the bread-and-butter work of a woman like Billie Walker, and she wondered what story the potential client before her would tell. Cheating husband?

The Bakelite wall clock above the doorway ticked away the minutes until eventually Sam returned with a tray assembled with a teapot, milk jug, two cups, sugar, and spoons. He slipped away again without a sound, and the door closed with a soft click. For a big man, he knew how to achieve strategic invisibility. After several more ticks of the clock, her tea sitting untouched, the stranger finally spoke.

"I wanted to see you because . . ." She was finding something difficult to say. "I need . . . a woman's intuition."

Billie let that one lie. She didn't believe in what was often called "women's intuition," even if it was what some people came to her for. Men's intuition was simply called knowledge, or at the very least an informed and rational guess. When the little woman in her stomach told her something was wrong, it was informed by a thousand tiny signals and observations of human behavior. It was deduction at work—some of it conscious, some subconscious, though no less rational than a man's reasoning. Billie did believe in paying attention to the knowledge in that lifesaving gut of hers, but not because she thought it was some mysterious and almost mystical feminine ability. Listening to her gut had been vital in getting her through the war, and it was put to good use in her business. It was something her father, Barry, had done before her. Such instincts were about being observant, about listening—something many women happened to do very well, which was probably where the term had come from. But there was no sense in breaking down the notion of women's intuition now. In fact, for the moment there was no sense in speaking at all. The stranger in her office was now wringing her hands. Billie watched and waited for her to open up. She was like a kettle building up steam.

"My son . . . is missing," the woman finally said. The words sounded heavy and hard to say. Billie noted a light accent slipping in—was it European?

Not a divorce number, then, Billie thought. She'd only just wrapped a rather unfortunate case that had required her to hop four fences to chase a man down, ripping a good pair of silk trousers. She was tempted to swear off divorce cases for however long she could—which likely wouldn't be long at all if she wanted any paying business before 1947 rolled around.

"I see," Billie responded in a level tone. "How old is your boy?"

"He turned seventeen in August."

The jury was out on whether his age was in his favor or against it, but Billie was secretly relieved she wouldn't be looking for a toddler. "Has anything like this happened before?"

"No." The woman shook her head adamantly. "Adin is a good boy. He's just . . . gone. He had dinner, went to bed as usual, but then he was gone. His bed hadn't been slept in."

No one was ever *just gone*. There was always a story. He went to bed, but his bed wasn't slept in. It was unlikely to be abduction, though of course that wasn't completely out of the question. Had he climbed out a window, gone out on the town, and decided not to come back? Or could he have walked out the front door without being detected, perhaps?

"How long ago was this?" Billie asked.

"Two days ago. Well, I knew on Thursday morning that he was gone."

Billie nodded. It was Friday now, so if he went missing on Wednesday after dinner, that was almost two days. A lot could have happened in that time, but it wasn't terrible odds. "Have you spoken to anyone else about this? The police, perhaps?"

The woman nodded, and her mouth cracked a little, turning down. "Yes. I checked with his friends and when they hadn't seen him I went to see the police. They were not helpful . . ." Again the voice strained a touch. There was something there. "I was at the police station yesterday, and when I was leaving, a Miss Primrose recommended I see you."

Constable Primrose. She was good like that. Billie had connections all over Sydney. She passed the woman, now quietly crying, a handkerchief embroidered with the initials *B.W.* It was received with a murmured thank-you. The woman dabbed the corners of her eyes and then placed it on the desk, took off her gloves, and put them in her lap, her pale hands kneading and turning. She wore a gold ring on her left hand, Billie noted. The spooked impression had not left her entirely, but she was opening up now, easing herself into Billie's care. Still, Billie gave her time. Finally the woman took a sip of her tea with a not-so-steady hand, added a lump of sugar, and took another sip. After a minute some color came back into her face and her shoulders dropped an inch.

"So you would characterize this situation as unusual?" Billie asked. Teenagers did have a habit of running away.

The woman nodded adamantly again, her eyes still wet. "Yes." Her tone implied a degree of personal offense.

"I'm sorry to have to ask you these questions," Billie said soothingly, "but it is important to get as much of the story as possible in order for me to help you. If we are to find your son promptly, I can make no assumptions." She didn't know what it was like to be a mother, but she imagined losing a child or having one unaccounted for would be very nearly unbearable. It was bad enough with a missing adult, as she knew too well. "Where do you think your son might be, if you had to guess? Does he have a girlfriend perhaps?" Billie's even-featured face was a picture of care and restraint. A good, compassionate listening face, but there was a veneer of professional composure as well. She'd learned from the best.

"There is no girlfriend. He's a good boy. None of his friends have seen him."

Not when his mother is asking, anyway, Billie thought. She considered things. Missing about two days. No girlfriend the mother knew about. Friends claiming not to have seen him. "If I accept this case," she said, "perhaps you could write down their details for me just the same. I'd like to speak with them myself."

The "if" hung in the air. "Oh, of course." The woman fiddled with her reptile bag for a moment, then opened a small fabric purse and pushed a folded ten-pound note across the desk toward Billie. "Will this be enough for a retainer?"

"If you like I can begin inquiries today. The retainer is suitable. I charge ten pounds a day plus expenses."

The woman didn't seem sure what to make of that. The sucked-lemon look returned. She sat with her knees pressed together, un-moving. "That's a lot," she protested.

Billie had heard that before, more than once. She leaned back in her chair, crossed one leg over the other, and let the tension in the office sit for a while before responding. Once the air was so still it could almost have suffocated a small bird, she gave a tight-lipped smile and said, "Frankly, no, it isn't a lot. I give cases my full at-tention, full-time and at all hours, and I need to pay a decent wage to my assistant, who is also worth every shilling, I assure you. My day is not nine to five. In fact, I may get furthest from nine at night to daybreak. Sometimes the work becomes dangerous." When the woman opened her mouth to object, Billie cut her off, not finished yet. "I can't know whether cases will turn that way until I am further in, and neither can my clients. There are frequently disgruntled hus-bands and jilted lovers and betrayed friends or business colleagues to contend with—and sometimes far worse. People come to me with things they can't do or don't want to do themselves, and often for good reason. And perhaps you haven't employed a private inquiry agent recently, but you'll find a lot in my trade who'd happily charge you one hundred pounds or more if they thought they could get it out of you, for a simple case that could be resolved in just a couple of days." She crossed her legs the other way and gave the woman a level look. "No, ten pounds a day is not a lot," she concluded, and waited.

One PI Billie knew of had taken a client for a staggering five hundred pounds, but you couldn't get that kind of cash out of many clients, and Billie had no interest in working like that in any event. Attempts to regulate the industry had thus far been unsuccessful, though Billie was not totally unsympathetic to the idea, despite the red tape it would doubtless bring. For every one of them who left a client disgruntled and without a shilling to their name, the same shilling-less condition caught two investigators like a virus. Shonky investigators were bad for the industry, bad for Billie. And though she was no angel, it also made Billie sick to think of robbing people in their most vulnerable moments.

At least, the ones who didn't deserve it.

The woman's face had softened slightly, the sucked-lemon look vanishing and the hands on the reptile handbag loosening a touch. The monologue had worked. "What kind of expenses?" she ventured, now trying even to smile a little as if to appease the investigator across from her.

"Anything extra that comes up, travel, for example, if required, but you'll be informed first and can give your approval. I like everything on the level and up front." Billie still hadn't touched the ten pounds, and it sat there between them, a symbol of uncertainty. "Do you have a clear photograph of your son? If I am to proceed I would need an up-to-date photograph and his full name."

The woman took an envelope from her handbag and passed it over. She seemed to have accepted the terms. Inside was a photograph, bent slightly in the upper corner. "His name is Adin Brown. This was taken about a year ago."

Billie studied the picture. Adin was a good-looking boy, and certainly a healthy enough lad to get into trouble, by the looks of it. His hair was distinctive and curly, with a bit of height at the front. He wore his cotton shirt open a touch, just enough to suggest there were a couple of hairs he wanted to show off. There might be a girlfriend. But then, the mother could be right, too.

The woman, still not having given her name, let out a long sigh, seeming unaware she was even doing it. "I never thought I'd hire a lady detective," she remarked.

Billie shifted forward in her chair again. "Well . . . Mrs. Brown, I presume?" Her visitor nodded. "Mrs. Brown, life takes us to interesting places. You've done the right thing if the police aren't showing any initiative. When a person goes missing, every hour counts. Though I must stress that I am not a detective."

The woman looked panicked again for a moment, shoulders high, mouth tight, and those dark brown eyes showing their whites. "You're not . . . ?"

"Oh, don't worry, you've come to the right place," Billie assured her. "It's just that private inquiry agents in this country are prevented by law from using the word 'detective' regarding their work." It was, in fact, practically the only legislation pertaining particularly to the trade. The Australian police were more protective of the term than their North American counterparts evidently were. "If you could write me that list, that would be a good start. May I ask, does Adin have a place of work?"

"He works for the fur company, yes." She pushed a business card across the table and Billie leaned forward and picked it up:

Mrs. Netanya Brown
Brown & Co. Fine Furs
Strand Arcade, Sydney

Billie turned the card over a couple of times. That explained the fur all right. The Strand Arcade was north of Billie's office, but not far. She recognized the company name, though she had never been inside the shop. It was downstairs at the Strand, from memory. There were a handful of successful fur companies in Sydney, the largest of which was a shop on George Street. She wondered how business was after the war. Had the restrictions been fully lifted?

"It's a family company," Mrs. Brown added. "Adin works the floor, sometimes does stocktake, looks after the odd jobs."

"Do you have a lot of staff on this time of year?" Though winter sales would probably be more substantial, considering the goods, it was likely to be getting busy not so long before Christmas.

"Around Christmas we sometimes get one or two temporary salespersons, part-time, but we can't afford any extra staff at the moment. There is just myself, my husband, and Adin."

"And where is your husband today?"

"At the shop." She looked at the thin watch on her wrist. "He'll be closing soon. Oh, it's been such a distressing couple of days."

"I understand. Mrs. Brown, I'd like to drop into the shop this weekend, if that is acceptable. Perhaps tomorrow in the late morning? I can be discreet."

She nodded and Billie got her to describe her son's appearance in detail, run through his usual routines, and write down the names and addresses of his close friends.

"Would I be able to speak with your husband also?"

Mrs. Brown hesitated a little but nodded. Billie took a mental note.

"Does your son own a passport?"

Mrs. Brown's eyebrows shot up. "No. Are you suggesting he might have left the country?"

"I'm not suggesting anything; I'm narrowing our search. Does he have access to any money, Mrs. Brown? His own, or someone else's he might use?"

"Well . . . no. He's a good boy, I told you." Billie noticed she was now gripping the bag in her lap like a woman on a roller coaster. When it came to these initial meetings, clients were an even split in Billie's experience—half of them loved pouring out every sordid detail of their lives and their traumas, and the other half were something like this, finding every detail painful or embarrassing to share with a total stranger, paid or otherwise. Mrs. Brown didn't like this conversation.

Billie ignored the constant reinforcement of Adin Brown's high moral standards. People did not come in just two kinds—good and bad—and in any event Billie wasn't there to judge. "How much would he keep on him, normally?" she asked.

"Only a few pounds for snacks and the tram."

You couldn't get far on that. Billie leaned back in her chair again. The woman had barely touched her tea. "Is there anything else you think I ought to know?" she asked.

"What do you mean?" The tone was almost accusing.

"I don't mean anything by it. The more I have to go on, the better," she explained.

"He's a good boy, Miss Walker. I . . ." She trailed off, unable to finish her sentence, and looked down, her brow creased. The large brown eyes looked wet again.

"I'll do my best to find your son for you, Mrs. Brown, and quickly. We'll start right away."

"Tonight?" It was now after four.

Billie nodded. "Yes. Normal business hours don't apply to this work. And we'll work through the weekend."

Mrs. Brown's features perked up a little, her mouth relaxing, the sense of immediacy seeming to put her more at ease. Or perhaps it was that Billie had accepted the retainer and something was being done. Billie stood and opened the communicating door for her, and bade her new client good day. Sam was sitting at his desk, pretending he hadn't been doing his best to listen through the door. He opened the office door and stepped back to allow Mrs. Brown into the hallway.

"Thank you, Miss Walker," Netanya Brown said again, and disappeared toward the lift as they watched, that fur stole having never left her shoulders.

Sam shut the door gently. "Nervy one," he commented.

Billie nodded thoughtfully and wondered if she was the one who had called that morning. She was just nervy enough to hang up on Sam when she heard a male voice.

"She is quite anxious. Not without reason, perhaps," she mused. "How much of that *didn't* you catch?"

He smiled. "The amount of the retainer."

Billie laughed out loud. "Ten pounds, Sam. Ten. We won't have to close up shop just yet. I could have pressed her for more, but that will do for now. There isn't exactly a stampede rushing the door today.

"I want you to head to the hospitals as soon as you're ready," she continued. He was good with the nurses, she'd noticed, and it wasn't necessary for her to go with him. He knew that drill well enough by now. "Take this photograph with you. We're looking for an Adin Brown, age seventeen. Five foot nine, slim build, no tattoos or identifying scars." She handed over the photo. "Check out the main city hospitals: Sydney, RPA, Prince of Wales, Prince Henry, and St. Vinnie's. Royal South Sydney, too. Have a good chat and find out about any male patient who came in during the past two days—since Wednesday night—and might vaguely fit the description of our boy. Don't bother heading across the bridge yet, but I might send you out there tomorrow, and to the smaller hospitals if we must, though a ring around might suffice for some of them. I'll make a visit to some of his friends, and tonight I'll drop in to see if he's—"

"In the death house," he said, completing her sentence.

She nodded. "Yes. Let's hope not."

The first ports of call for missing persons were always the places you hoped you wouldn't find them. Billie would make a visit to the Sydney City Morgue, but not until well after dark, when she knew she would be welcomed by the man at the desk. It was all about who was on the shift, and if she was right, the best timing would be after eleven, when everyone else was gone. But if Adin was lucky he'd be with one of his friends, or perhaps being harbored by a ladylove his mother wouldn't approve of. If Netanya Brown was right—there was no girlfriend, his friends hadn't seen him, and he only had a few pounds to his name—that did indeed spell trouble.

"You're sure you don't want me to tag along?" Sam asked.

Billie looked at the list of friends. "I can handle these boys," she said. "Much as I like having a case to pay our rent, time is of the essence with something like this." Stretching it out was no good. Billie glanced at the clock again. "When you're finished I want you to have a good meal, but give me a call at eight o'clock sharp—try the office and then my flat—and tell me what you've found. Hopefully then you'll be able to knock off, but I can't promise you'll have much time off this weekend. If there's no dice tonight, we'll be visiting the fur company tomorrow."

She grabbed her trench coat off the rack. "You've enough petrol coupons for your motorcar?" she asked. The rationing allowance was around fifteen gallons each month. They could share coupons normally, but Billie was out for the month.

He nodded, not seeming overly disappointed that his workday had not ended early after all, or that his weekend would be busy. An hour's wage was an hour's wage. They locked up and set off.

Two

———✺———

Billie stepped off the tram on Parramatta Road in Stanmore and took in the sounds of the summer evening: cicadas singing, dogs barking, children playing.

Her trench coat was over her arm. The breeze was refreshing, and she stood for a moment as it gently lifted her wavy hair from her neckline, wondering if Sam had already found the missing boy, Adin Brown, laid up in one of the city hospitals. This was her last stop before a reheated dinner and a date with the death house. It might sound grim on paper, but in fact she felt quite buoyed untangling the pieces of this new puzzle. She liked puzzles. Particularly the paid kind.

Since Netanya Brown walked out of her office some hours earlier, she'd been working through the list of Adin's close friends. So far the work had been singularly uneventful, yet Billie was rarely happier than when embarking on a new investigation, hunting down the answers to a mystery or the hidden details of some story she knew she could break open. It was true that her cases were often frustratingly small, involving domestic and sometimes depressing issues, but she was her own boss and that counted for a lot. The banality of much of the work did not dampen her spirits. And as for returning to work as a reporter—something she'd given considerable thought to before taking over her father's inquiry agency—the Sydney newspapers had dismissed most of their women reporters home once the men started to return from the war, or else confined them to the social pages, or covering the Easter Show, which was a bit too steep a downgrade for Billie after she'd chased Nazi activity across Europe, built a good portfolio of published articles, and worked alongside the likes of Lee Miller and Clare Hollingworth. No, she wouldn't last in that kind of work. It was an imperfect world, and her chosen profession was decidedly imperfect, but for now she had a hint of that spark again, that sense of doing something that mattered to someone. In these moments she felt that answers could be just around the next corner. This had been true whenever she'd been assigned a new story in Europe, and it was true now that she was funneling those skills into her work as a private investigator in the city of her birth. Perhaps it was something in the blood, but launching into a case excited her more than any ticket to the pictures. In that respect she was her father's daughter.

Let's hope this kid knows something.

In the past two hours Billie had ticked off the first two friends on the list Mrs. Brown had given her. One boy had convincingly sworn that he hadn't seen Adin in more than a week, and the other friend hadn't seen him since Saturday. Neither had thought anything was amiss until Adin's mother had rung them and asked if they'd seen him. With Billie's arrival, they seemed genuinely concerned. Having a PI on the case made it more real, more pressing. So far, everything she'd learned had confirmed what Mrs. Brown had told her, and that left this third friend, Maurice, who she hoped would have something helpful to say and would not already be out on the town this early Friday evening.

She turned a corner, then checked the leather-bound notebook in her hand. Yes, this was it—a narrow two-story brick terrace just a couple of blocks from the tramline on the main road. The homes on this stretch of Corunna Road were crammed together, as if they had been constructed in the middle of space-poor London. Still, the overall effect was charming. As Billie approached the house where Adin's friend Maurice lived, she could see that plenty of work went into keeping the small front garden neat, sweeping the steps, and keeping up the potted plants by the door, but the exterior was in dire need of a fresh coat of white paint, and the balcony railings looked unstable. She moved slowly up the little path and knocked on the front door with a gloved hand. A dog barked somewhere, and Billie adjusted a hairpin, listening for movement inside the house.

After a moment, she heard footsteps. It was a young man who opened the door. He was no more than twenty, long-lashed, and lean, almost skinny, and he wore his trousers rolled at the cuff to show white socks above his loafers. His single-pocket shirt was unbuttoned at the top. Billie guessed that he'd spent a fair bit of time on his hair, which was side parted in the standard way, but a bit wavy and long on top, while short at the back and sides. It was the latest style for a certain kind of Sydney boy, some of whom liked the top to sit up even higher. The style was no good for wearing hats, and Billie imagined he didn't don one often. Doubtless he had a comb in his back pocket, because he'd need it.

"Maurice?" He looked her up and down, surprised that she

wanted him. "I'm Billie Walker." She flashed him a business card. "Glad to know you. I'd like to speak to you about your friend Adin Brown," she explained, pushing the card into his palm.

He looked panicked for a moment, his deep brown eyes wide, and he drifted back from the door a touch and then read her card and nodded, as if having decided something. "Mum, I'm heading out to the shop. Be back shortly," he called loudly and stepped outside onto the path, shutting the door behind him.

"I don't want any trouble. My ma's a bit deaf but she's not stupid."

Billie followed him, intrigued, keeping pace as he led her toward the street corner at Northumberland, out of the line of sight of the house. The sun was still up, but the shadows were lengthening and the shadows had eyes, she sensed. A group of boys was watching from the side of a terrace home on the opposite side of the street, their faces stacked like a totem pole, and when she turned her gaze in their direction they vanished like apparitions. Billie turned her attention back to her subject but thought fleetingly about how she'd sent Sam off to check the hospitals, leaving her without a strong arm in a neighborhood that was now feeling less tame than she remembered before the war. All those absent fathers and tales of war seemed to have done the local boys little good, and she was pleased with her last-minute decision to slip her little Colt 1908 pocket semi-automatic into her garter. It was hand-size and factory nickel-plated, with shining mother-of-pearl grips, and came with a sweet little soft suede change-purse pouch, which was attractive but not easy to access if one was in a hurry. The thigh garter she had sewn herself for the purpose of holding the diminutive thirteen-ounce pistol worked nicely by comparison and could be worn under most of her clothes, as it was today. The gun had been a gift from her mother, who was not stupid, either. It would take Billie only a few seconds to have it comfortably in her hand.

"I'm not trouble," she said soothingly to the boy as they neared the corner, trying to ease his nerves, or perhaps her own, though the statement wasn't strictly true if history was anything to go by. She and trouble knew each other pretty well. "I know you told Mrs. Brown that you haven't seen Adin, but I wanted to ask you personally to hear your side of things."

"Why do I have to have a side?"

"Surely you absorb information and form views like any thinking young man in this state," she answered.

Her interview subject narrowed his eyes. "You're not a cop?" he asked accusingly, slowing down to scowl prettily and dart his eyes from side to side to see if they were being watched, which of course they were. Billie wasn't sure if he wanted to be seen with her or not; it seemed even odds.

"Do I look like a police officer to you?" she asked him, in response to which he looked her over from heel to hat, and took his time about it. Yes, he knew he was pretty. This boy was different from the other two. He was older and had more edge.

"No, lady, I can't say as you do," he finally decided, having finished his appraisal at her expressionless red lips. He paused, eyes still fixed on her mouth. "But they've been recruiting them lately. I read about it in the paper."

At this, Billie had to resist rolling her eyes. In '41, when the panic set in about a lack of able men, the New South Wales Police had added six women officers to the force, bringing the grand total to a mere fourteen in the state. But now Premier McKell had ap-

proved an increase in the number of female cops to thirty-six, and
the papers were going mad with the idea, as if the fairer sex might
suddenly take over the entire force, leaving men out of work or even,
heaven forbid, waiting for their dinners, despite the fact that married
women weren't being accepted anyhow. Billie was on a first-name
basis with the famous Special Sergeant (First Class) Lillian Armfield, who had joined the force in 1915, and through her knew well
enough the struggle. The female recruits hadn't even uniforms and
weren't paid overtime like the men; nor were they entitled to a
pension. They had to sign contracts stating that they wouldn't be
compensated for any injuries suffered in the line of duty, couldn't
join the police association, and had to resign if they married—one
of the reasons Lillian never had. With all that, it was a wonder so
many women were keen to sign up, but the applications always far
outnumbered the spaces allotted. The relationship between the police
and private inquiry agents was sometimes fraught, but Billie had her
contacts, as her father had before her. But a cop? No, a cop she was
certainly not.

"I assure you I'm not a newly recruited officer of the law," Billie
said, placing a hand on her hip as his eyes followed the movement,
"and if you're a good boy I suspect you'll never meet one of those fine
women." If he was a good boy, he at least wanted to be bad; that
much was clear.

"You look more like you could be in the pictures," he said.

"Well, we're not shooting any Hollywood pictures in Stanmore
today," she said flatly, not interested in his flattery.

They walked on for another minute or two, their route taking
them almost in a loop. Curtains parted in a house across the street
and a silver-haired lady looked out at them, her nose to the window

glass. One more block and Maurice finally stopped. Billie noticed a milk bar farther along the street, close to where she'd stepped off the tram, and saw a small group of children who seemed to be sharing a treat of some kind. Another set of curtains rippled; this time a dark-haired youth poked his head out of a window to stare at them. They might have been far from where Maurice's mother could see them, but plenty of others were having a gander. Billie suspected Maurice was enjoying the scrutiny, and her patience was wearing thin, but she needed patience if she was to get anything out of this boy.

"When did you last see Adin, Maurice? Can you remember what he said, what he was doing, and how you parted company?" She stopped and flashed one of her professional smiles. He seemed to like that. "It's important."

He considered something for a long time, hands in his pockets. His brown eyes flicked from place to place. "I don't know . . ." he finally mumbled.

Billie waited out an awkward minute, the boy now staring at his shoes. With an inward sigh, she slipped him a shilling—did it as smoothly as a magician. He recognized the feel of it immediately and it seemed to jog his memory. Funny that.

"Look, lady, I haven't seen Adin, just like I told Mrs. Brown. But I think I might know where he's been."

"Go on," she encouraged him, offering another smile.

"Last time I saw him, he was hanging around The Dancers."

The Dancers? That was a club off George Street, near the Trocadero. It was a far smaller and more exclusive joint than the Troc, and the cream of Sydney society liked to wine and dine there and catch the acts that came through. They had some international performers and a nice little dance floor, and there was a fair bit of glamour about the place. It had white tablecloths and waiters in bow ties and was the sort of joint where judges and gangsters might be spotted in the same room together. It was strictly for the high end of town. Unless a lot had changed since she'd last been there, it wasn't for the likes of kids with baby pompadours and tough-guy aspirations.

Billie got an inkling as to Maurice's reluctance to mention the club. "I'm not here because Adin might have been taking grog, Maurice. And what you imbibe is not my business."

His shoulders dropped a touch. "His old woman doesn't know. She wouldn't like it." He said the words with a shake of his head.

Billie was sure he was right about that. But even if she didn't find it hard to imagine Adin having liquor at his age—plenty of kids not much older than him had been shot to pieces at Normandy or worked to death on the Burma Railway, but a dash of spirits was somehow off-limits—she was having trouble imagining where a kid would get the kind of money needed to get about in a joint like The Dancers. Even if he had a dinner jacket, and a fine one at that, he likely wouldn't have got far at that sort of club.

"Look, it's not my kind of joint, but Adin was keen as mustard. We made it in the door one time, and ended up out on our ears in minutes; we barely got up the stairs, but he was obsessed. Dunno why. He kept wanting to go back in. The doormen knew we didn't have a brass razoo . . . There was no foolin' 'em." He paused. "Well, there was one guy who seemed sympathetic, but it was pointless." He scuffed at the footpath with one loafer. "Yeah, like I said, not my kind of joint."

"Someone was sympathetic?" Billie prompted him.

"One of the doormen. Adin spoke with him."

"What did this doorman look like?"

"Ahhh, long face." Maurice pulled at his chin. "Very skinny young bloke," he stressed. "A wog, I think. About yea high."

"I see," Billie said, ignoring the slur. "Do you know what triggered Adin's interest? A girl, perhaps?"

"Maybe, but like I said, I dunno." He shrugged, and she felt a stab of annoyance. The Dancers had some glamorous acts, but if Adin was interested in someone it was more likely one of the cigarette girls. Perhaps he'd made a connection, or was trying to.

"How long ago was this?" Billie asked.

"Last weekend. I left him to it. Had a bit of a falling out over it, to be honest. I didn't want to keep hanging around there getting snubbed like some lowlife when we could get into the Troc, no worries. I ain't seen him since."

Same with the rest of his friends, Billie thought. But he had gone home, because he'd only been missing two days, not six. "Is it usual for you two to have a 'falling out,' as you call it?"

"It wasn't as bad as all that; I just didn't like being turned out on my ear. Who needs it? Why The Dancers?"

"Why indeed?" she agreed, wondering who or what was so special about the place that would attract the interest of a boy like Adin Brown. "Maurice, can you think of where Adin might be now?"

He shook his head emphatically. "Miss, I don't know."

"If you had to guess his whereabouts, what would your guess be?"

He shrugged again. "I wouldn't like to guess, lady." There was worry behind his eyes and she was inclined to believe him. Some of his bravado had fallen away. Beneath it was a young man anxious about a friend. Again, a set of curtains moved, and he seemed to notice or at least feel the prying eyes. He straightened, not wanting to be seen as soft. "Nah, I don't know nothin'," he declared.

"Is there anything else you can think of? Anything unusual that happened in the past couple of weeks or so?" She watched him as he frowned. "Did he talk about a girl, perhaps? Or something else? Did he act strangely on any occasion?" she ventured.

"Well . . ."

Ah, there is something. "Anything might help," she stressed, and slipped him another shilling. That frown of his eased up a touch, but only a touch.

"Look, it's probably nothin', but there was this thing at the Olympia," he said. "The milk bar. Something with the paper. He went wild when he saw it."

How peculiar, she thought. "What did he see in the paper, precisely?"

Maurice shrugged. "That I don't know, precisely or otherwise. It could be nothin', but somethin' in there sure seemed to set him off." He shook his head.

"But if he went wild he must have told you what it was about." Was the boy fishing for yet more coin? "You don't know, or you won't say?"

"Listen, lady, I honestly don't know. He just went into a fury and ripped the page out of the paper and pocketed it. He didn't show me what it was. Really cut up, he was. I thought it weird at the time."

Now, that could be something, Billie thought. "What did he say? I want every word, if you can recall them."

"Nothing I want to repeat to you."

"I can take it," she said, and gave him another smile. If this kid thought he was more worldly than she was, he had another think coming.

Maurice hesitated, then noted the smile, and his eyes stayed on it for a moment. "Okay, lady," he finally said and let off a long trail of expletives. "Something like that, give or take."

"I see. What day was this? Think hard, now, kid. You've got a pocket full of my coin."

"Maybe Thursday last week, though I can't swear to it." He squinted for a moment, thinking. "Yeah, probably Thursday last week."

"Do you remember which paper it was?"

"The *Truth*, I think. Or *The Sydney Morning Herald*. Not sure."

"This was at the Olympia?" She pointed in the direction of the milk bar at the end of the street. "And he tore the page out, is that right?"

Maurice nodded. Billie thanked him—though he ought to thank her for the shillings he'd collected—and reminded him that he had her card and should contact her if he thought of anything else. She did the smile. He looked her up and down one more time, wagged his chin at her, affecting a cool manner, and turned away, pulling a comb from his pocket to smooth his hair as he walked back toward the house he shared with his mother.

Billie turned on her heel and ventured the extra block down Northumberland Avenue toward Parramatta Road and the Olympia. At last she'd got something.

She stepped out and paused, passed on the corner of Corunna Lane by a smiling man in black, with a stiff white clerical collar, riding a bicycle. He dipped his head to her, and she returned the gesture from her place on the footpath. She watched the cycling rector pass, stepped onto the main road, and focused on the strip of shops and the Olympia Theatre. It wasn't hard to find the milk bar. The local kids were drawn to it as flies were to honey. Several children, some still in school clothes, with scuffed knees and unkempt hair, played around the footpath outside under the awning. The Olympia was famous for its milkshakes, Billie had heard. It would doubtless be a popular place, particularly in summer.

A man with dark hair slicked back from his forehead, wearing slightly shabby but elegant pants and a shirt topped with a white apron, emerged from the milk bar as she approached and shooed the children away from the entrance. "Time to go home," he told them firmly but kindly. "Go on.

"Kids!" The man spoke with a pleasant accent Billie guessed was Greek, and she followed him through the concertina timber doors of the milk bar. A bell tinkled as they crossed the threshold. "Latchkey kids," he added. "Those factories let their parents out too late. After school they all come here." He threw up his hands, a potent gesture that seemed to sum up a widely felt frustration with the ways of the world.

The Olympia was a narrow space, its name proudly picked out in colored terrazzo on the floor just beyond the entry. The ceiling, Billie noted, was made up of ornate paneled plaster. A few neon signs were up on the walls, and a glass-fronted stainless steel counter faced the wooden tables and chairs dotted around the green, red, and yellow tiled floor. It was a cheerful place, colorful and stylish, though it appeared a touch the worse for wear, like much of the rest of the neighborhood. Some of the mirrors and the green vinyl covers of the stools had begun to crack. In places the chrome had lost its polish, though not for lack of care if the busy proprietor was anything to go by. He was already polishing again, his calloused hands pushing a cloth over surfaces, seemingly cleaning up on autopilot while his restless eyes surveyed his domain. He'd have to be eagle-eyed with so many unaccompanied kids trailing in, Billie thought. Bold dares and light fingers were childhood rites of passage.

The sparsely stocked shelves held boxes of chocolates, bright gumballs, and a couple of basic sundries; rationing had made its mark. Billie turned her eyes to the proprietor again. He was working alone and wasn't quite the young soda fountain assistant—or "soda jerk" as the Americans were fond of calling them—you saw in the upscale city joints. His glossed hair was black, but under the lights he looked older than she'd first assumed.

"What can I get you, miss?" he asked.

"I'll have a soda, please," she replied, and slid onto one of the stools. She felt the slightly cracked vinyl fight with the weave of her skirt. "Keep the change," she added as she pushed her money across the counter.

"Soda coming up," the man said and busied himself.

"You're not from around here, are you, miss?" he remarked, and she let that ride for the moment as she spotted a stack of Hollywood and entertainment rags and a single newspaper at the end of the bar. It was today's copy of the *Truth*. She recognized the front page. Her heart sank a little when she couldn't see any other papers, except for the current *Sydney Morning Herald*. She noticed the owner filling her glass with a lot of ice, but that wasn't entirely unwelcome on a warm evening.

"You know that movie *The Killers*?" the proprietor asked, placing the drink in front of her. "I ain't seen it yet myself, but I've seen that actress in all those rags. What is her name? Ava something. You look like her."

Billie knew she was no Ava Gardner—if she were, she sure wouldn't be running a humble Sydney private inquiry agency and watching her mother sell heirlooms to pay the rent—but it was one of those compliments a lot of men fumbling for a pickup line had come up with lately, and she had to admit a fair resemblance was there in her even features and long neck and limbs, and the way she wore her dark hair long and parted on the side, though Billie's locks flared red like a flame when the sun hit them. For a moment she'd thought Maurice was going to go there, too, with his quip about the pictures.

"Thank you kindly," Billie said. From this gentleman, the compliment was sweet.

"She's pretty, isn't she? Now, in my younger days . . ."

Billie cut in before he got too carried away with his nostalgia. "I wonder, would you happen to have any old newspapers out the back? I'm packing up, you see. If you don't need them anymore, I mean. I would be most grateful."

He peered at her. "Moving into the area?" he asked, a touch puzzled. Admittedly she wasn't dressed for packing up a house.

"I'm helping a friend, actually," she responded, lies falling easily from her lips. She could lie about unimportant things, she'd found. That kind of creativity was second nature. Good for the work. She took a sip of her cool soda and again flashed that winning professional smile she'd learned to use years ago.

"Well," he said, "we have some out the back. You're welcome to them, though they might have got a bit damp in the rain last night." He came around the bar and led her to a back door, on the other side of which were heaped boxes, cartons, and a messy pile of newspapers, perhaps two weeks' worth.

"Thank you, that will help a lot," Billie said, and sincerely hoped that would be the case. Checking through the papers would be no cup of tea, but it was worth a shot if what Adin had got steamed up about proved to be relevant. There were worse things than pawing through damp paper.

"Okay, pretty lady. You're welcome to them."

He gave her three brown paper bags to carry them in, then excused himself as the bell tinkled and a customer entered the shop. Billie searched through the papers for those dated from Tuesday the previous week, grabbing about a week's worth in case Maurice was wrong about it being the Thursday, and shoved them into the bags, bundling them to her chest so the papers wouldn't fall out the bottom. She called her thanks to the proprietor, then bobbed and weaved her way around the children still playing on the footpath and made for the tram.

Three

—⌇—

"How did you find out?"

He opened his eyes—at least he thought they were open, but they felt hot and swollen, his eyelids not moving as eyelids normally did, but staying in place, barely lifting despite the urgings of his throbbing brain. He could hardly see, making out only movement and darkness, but he recalled a smile as thin as a knife blade. The smile that went with that voice.

"Who else knows?" the voice came again, heavily accented and menacing.

The voice hit him like a slap with every question, "*Who—else— knows?*" repeating the words with cold, firm precision so close to his ear that his brain seemed to throb with each syllable. He recoiled from the sound each time, pushing back against the creaking chair to which he was tied, until it started to tip backward and an unseen set of hands put it straight again. In a moment of blissful silence, a pause between the words, the sound of something like a whimper came to his ears, and it took a moment to realize that it was coming from his own throat. His stomach ached as if he'd been trodden on, and though he recalled being hit, he could not precisely remember where it had happened or how much time had passed. He knew he'd been in the boot of a motorcar. But when?

Head shaking back and forth, he tried to respond. "I did not tell . . . I did not . . ."

"I grow bored," the voice said, again so close to his ear it felt like a painful touch, and following it came the pressure again, as something, a finger or something colder, pressed into his temple where he'd been injured. Harder, ever harder.

He screamed.

Four

———⌁———

Billie took the small elevator up to the second floor of Cliffside Flats, her home in the leafy suburb of Edgecliff, leaning against her door to balance the bags of newspapers while she fiddled with her keys. Once inside her flat, she dropped the bags to the floor with a sigh of relief and rubbed her aching biceps. She couldn't wait till the blasted petrol rationing was lifted. Her perfectly lovely car was sitting unused in the garage at the base of the building. What a crying shame that was. She hung her trench coat on the hallstand, slipped off her shoes, and noted with a vague sense of fatigue that the big toe on her right foot had begun to push through her stocking.

Blast.

She also noticed a piece of paper, neatly folded down the middle, that must have been slid under her door. She reached down and took it.

I NEED TO SPEAK WITH YOU.

Billie recognized the handwriting as that of one of her valued informants, Shyla. She had an idea of what the note was about, and on that line of inquiry she'd so far come up empty-handed. Instinctively she reopened the door, looked down the hallway in both directions, and closed it again, disappointed. Shyla had not waited around. The problem was, this particular informant couldn't be reached through the telephone exchange, didn't have a card or address of employment that she'd chosen to share with Billie, and had not divulged her personal address. Shyla would reach her again when Shyla was ready, Billie supposed.

Billie padded over to her small kitchen, filled the kettle, struck a match, and lit the stove. Tea would help. Tea always helped.

What was it that enraged Adin? And is it relevant? If there was a page missing from that stack of newspapers, she'd have a pretty good idea, she hoped.

She slid her hatpins out and took off her tilt hat, ruffling her hair. Lost in her thoughts about her new case, Billie absentmindedly removed her ivory blouse, then reached down and undid the smooth button of her skirt and the three little snaps disguised in the fold of the fabric beneath it, slid off her skirt, then sat down to unclip her right stocking. One. Two. Three. Four. Five. Six. So many damned clips, but she supposed the things wouldn't stay on straight otherwise. She carefully rolled the damaged nylon down, undid the ties on the thigh holster for her Colt, and placed the whole thing, little gun and all, gently on the tabletop. Then she undid the left garter clips. One. Two. Three . . .

Mrs. Brown's son is certainly missing and she's certainly distressed about it. That much rings true. But why is he missing? Is there a clue she's leaving out? Billie sensed there was some element Mrs. Brown was withholding. If so, she wouldn't be the first. In the initial meeting, clients often held on to information they perceived to be sensitive or embarrassing. But if this case was anything like previous cases, the truth would out. Often the information would have been helpful to Billie's work if offered at the start, but she knew a bit about human nature and it was not human nature to pour out every bit of detail to a stranger—not unless you thought you'd never see them again. It had been that way during the war: The nearness of death and the constant movement of anxious people far from home could make any meeting an intense and intimate confessional. But once everyone returned to the places they knew and had come from, they tried to make nice and to get on with their mouths shut. There was still gossip, lives were still complicated, but details weren't offered up as easily, not without the lubrication of liquor. It might be something as simple as a now-regretted argument that had triggered Adin's departure, or something unsavory the boy was into that wouldn't reflect well on the family. Or something about the family itself, Billie mused. But there was something, the little woman in her gut told her, some key detail left out. Perhaps a second meeting might see Mrs. Brown more forthcoming. Perhaps her husband would be able to shed more light on the case.

Billie took her tea strong and black, and as the leaves steeped, she gave her other stocking a brief examination and decided it was not in need of mending. Once she had a steaming cup in hand, she made her way toward the front of the flat in her slip, her damaged stocking over her shoulder, and took her place behind a small table in the corner nook. This was the spot with good light. The curtains were open, but there was nothing but the tops of trees to witness her semi-undressed state or the lithe figure it revealed. It was close to sunset now, and the evening sun was pouring in across the woodwork, the spools, the sewing machine, the pincushion, turning everything a lovely rose gold. A rainbow of threads was propped neatly on the little wooden spikes of a rack mounted on the wall behind her. The traffic from the street below seemed distant, as so many tired men returned from work in the city to so many bored wives at home grappling with a changed world after a war that had bid so aggressively, so openly, for their involvement, only to ask them now to return to domestic service behind closed doors.

Certainly there are many Mrs. Browns, but she doesn't look like one, Billie thought, despite the decidedly brown theme of her client's clothes. The name was English, and common. But Billie's new client did not have an English accent. She wondered why it niggled, if it mattered.

Billie pulled her wooden egg-shaped mold from a drawer, ran her fingers over it to check its smoothness, and pulled the foot of her stocking over it. Damned holes. She'd been fortunate enough not to have to go without stockings for too long, but now that nylon stockings were in supply again she'd be damned if she'd let that little hole get any larger. Expensive things, stockings. Damned expensive. And while there'd been plenty of men happy to give them to her, she wasn't happy with their romantic price. As with everything else, she'd buy her own, thank you very much. What a client wanted for his pound was sometimes pretty steep in her business, but what men expected for nylons was something else entirely. She found a fairly well-matched thread in tan, threaded her darning needle, and began to close the small hole. The sun was lower by the time she was finished. Night was coming and her telephone was due to ring.

It was only one minute past eight when it rang. That would be

Sam checking in, right on time. He was to call the office, letting it ring, and if she didn't pick up he was to try her flat. She put down her satisfactorily mended stocking and strode to her black telephone.

"Ms. Walker. What's doing?"

"Sam, how did you go? Have we found our boy?"

"Bad news, I'm afraid," he said to her. "I didn't find anyone with his description. Actually that's not such bad news considering the blokes I did find. Some of them were rather mangled."

She hadn't thought it would be that easy, but it had been worth a shot. "Righto. Change of plans, then. We're going out tonight, Sam," Billie announced. "Will that check okay with your dance card?"

"No problem at all. I have no, er, card."

"It will be in a couple of hours, around ten," she added, glancing at the clock.

"Where shall we meet? The morgue?" he asked.

She laughed. "No, the death house will have to wait." Sam had not yet had occasion to visit the morgue, and Billie in fact preferred to make those visits solo. "We have something more interesting to pursue. And more lively. Meet me back at the office, will you? Ten o'clock sharp? Oh, and wear the jacket."

There was a pause down the line. "The white jacket?"

"Yes, dear Sam. The white jacket. Tonight is black-tie. We'll be mixing with the high end of town."

Billie hung up and reheated some leftover casserole on the stove. It was, at best, below average, and the dirty dishes were depressing to look at afterward, an unfortunate price to pay for something that had tasted pretty lousy. Housework and culinary pursuits had never been Billie's forte, but she managed well enough on her own. For

lack of a wife or maid, or any prospect of either, Billie cooked merely
to sustain herself, treating the work more as a chore than the art form
it could be. She saved her art for other mediums, content to experience great food in restaurants, or when dining with her aristocratic
mother. So it was with mild distaste that Billie slid the empty plate
and cutlery into the sink under some tepid water and promised herself
she'd clean up later. She had, after all, no one to impress but herself,
and the possibilities of her case seemed more important by half. Fortunately she'd managed to purchase a bar of good dark chocolate—it
had been terrifically hard to hunt out during the war—and she sa-
vored a single square in small nibbles, leaning against the kitchen
counter in a kind of temporary ecstasy. Her palate recovered, she tied
her hair up with a scarf and peeled off her remaining silk underthings,
leaving them on her bed. She had started to feel a sticky heat out in
Stanmore, or perhaps it had been all those heavy looks. In the city
she didn't arouse quite so much attention, at least not when wearing
a skirt suit and oxfords.

With a smile Billie showered under a stream of warm, clear water
and washed the day off. Oh, how she'd missed these showers in
Europe. Her flat, like the others in the building, had modern conve-
niences. So many of the places she'd stayed with Jack had been
spartan and lacked hot water, let alone a shower. Some had even
lacked a roof.

Jack.

Billie recalled the first time she'd clapped eyes on the British
correspondent, he with his ever-present Argus camera, her friends in
Paris regaling one another with stories of his recent triumph, surviving a light airplane crash and smuggling film past Nazi German
officers in tubes of toothpaste and shaving cream. He'd covered the

annexation of Austria into Nazi Germany earlier that year, and the recent Nazi march into Sudetenland after Prime Minister Chamberlain's disastrous part in the Munich Agreement. He was relaxed on that first meeting, wine in hand, blushing modestly as the others bragged on his behalf about his exploits, and watching his lean face and those bright hazel eyes, Billie had been hooked. Even now she could see him sitting there across the café table, his shirt slightly undone, his face glowing and almost tanned despite the autumn chill, lips reddened by the wine, head bowed slightly as he squirmed under the weight of their praise and playful teasing. She could see him so vividly in her memories that he was almost there, close enough to touch. He spoke of what he'd witnessed, of wanting to return next to Vienna. When he did go, Billie was with him.

And now she recalled the feeling of his body under hers, those pale chest hairs, the warmth of his skin, her fingers running over him, bodies intertwined. All around them was cold darkness, and in the distance air-raid sirens. It was just him, just Jack and Billie, the rest of the world seeming not to exist in those moments, and in his irresistible accent he would softly say her name, "Billie, Billie . . ."

She swallowed and, closing her eyes, ran a hand down her body, tempted to touch herself. Her fingers caressed her slim, softly rounded belly, her velvety pubic hair. How long had it been? Well over one year. No. Now over two years, in fact, she realized with a kind of horror. Her chest began to ache and she shook herself gently, hand retreating. Where was he? Was he really gone?

Stop.

There was no time for diversions or longing. Frowning now, Billie turned off the tap, toweled herself vigorously, and slipped into a pale peach dressing robe with a nipped waist and long, flowing hem. The silk felt lovely against her bare, clean skin. These were the sensual pleasures she had at her disposal. Simple luxuries. She'd not had this silk robe when she was in Europe, nor Savon de Marseille to soap herself. But she'd had Jack.

Stay on track, Walker. Stay on track.

Her choice of clothing this evening had to be strategic. Billie padded to her bedroom and opened both doors of her generous satin maple wardrobe. She stood on the round Persian rug and pondered what she saw inside, as a surgeon might look over a case file. *The Dancers.* She had not been there for some time, but she recalled the rarified atmosphere. Billie had to fit in, look appropriately glamorous yet not stand out. This was no time for her suits and trench coats, but anything too bold could attract unwanted attention. She needed something fashionable, but something that didn't particularly catch the eye. Nothing overly daring, though a little daring was certainly preferable to gauche. An emerald dress with beading beckoned, and she pulled the hanger out, turned the garment this way and that in the light. No, the beading was too much, the neckline too low now that she'd regained her curves after Europe. With rations finally easing, she'd soon fill it out dramatically. For a date with Jack? Certainly. For tonight, no. She replaced the dress. After some consideration she pulled out a dark ruby dress, silk and cut on the bias. She'd altered it and fitted it with shoulder pads when the fashion came in. It had a neckline that skimmed across the clavicle and a nice V-shaped cutout at the back. It suited low shoes, but really it was too clingy to wear her Colt underneath. It would stand out a country mile. The weapon would go in her handbag. Yes, the outfit would do. She hooked the hanger over the edge of the wardrobe, sat before her mirrored vanity, and started to prepare a convincing evening look.

Billie powdered her face, darkened her lash line a touch, and reached for her small black bottle of Bandit, the perfume designed by one of Paris's finest and most famous perfumers, Germaine Cellier. She swept her dark hair up and applied the leathery, sensual scent to her naked nape. Bandit had sprung up two years earlier, in 1944, launched by the haute couture designer Robert Piguet, his runway stalked by mannequins in dark masks and red lipstick, brandishing knives and revolvers, the whole scene loaded with sexual innuendo and resulting in some considerable controversy. Billie had been dedicated to it ever since. That launch was one of Billie's last memories of Paris, and one of the better ones. Not long after, she'd got word of her father's condition and had flown home to be with him, arriving too late to say good-bye. Jack was still missing and the war came to an end and nothing was the same. Things wouldn't be the same, she reminded herself. Couldn't be the same.

She lifted her stick of Fighting Red to her lips. Some Einstein in marketing was discontinuing the color, she'd heard, so when this stick was gone she'd have to find a new favorite. Jeep Red was not getting near her mouth, as far as she was concerned. Jeep? It brought memories to mind of wounded soldiers and falling shells. The telephone's ring broke her concentration and Billie crossed to the pink bedroom phone on her nightstand. She sat down on the edge of the bed, smoothed her robe, and picked up the receiver. It could be Sam, hopefully not backing out of their evening commitment, but if not, she could guess who it was.

"Darling, I knew you'd be in," the voice on the line said. "There's something I'd like some help with."

Billie took a deep breath and slouched back on the bed. Her eyes darted to the small clock of her pink celluloid vanity dresser set. She wasn't ready for The Dancers yet but didn't need to be either. She supposed she had a little time to spare. "Okay, but I'm not in all night. I'm going out on a job," she stressed. "See you shortly." She hung up.

Billie completed a rushed lipstick job, blotted her lips, scrutinized herself in the mirror, and, reasonably satisfied, pulled on her foundation garments and slipped into the sleek red gown. A turn at the full-length mirror told her she would pass, though her neck was bare and her hair needed work, particularly at the back, before she faced Sydney's top end of town. Anyway, her first task was to talk with Ella. She still had plenty of time to get to the office and meet her assistant, if she could keep the length of this visit to a minimum.

Five

—⁓—

Billie Walker took the stairs to the next level of the building and sauntered down the corridor to the large corner flat. The door was unlocked. Familiar as she was with it, she knocked and entered almost in the same breath and found the Baroness Ella von Hooft in her favorite spot before the large window, her lady's maid, Alma McGuire, pouring her a sherry in a delicate crystal glass with a pair of strong, steady hands.

Alma nodded to Billie with a bob of her curled and neatly pinned silver and strawberry hair, and the ever-elegant Ella turned and spotted her daughter. "Darling, it's been weeks since I saw you," she exclaimed.

"Mother, it's been since Sunday," Billie corrected her. The baroness did have a flair for the dramatic. "And we live in the same building, after all. I'm hardly in Berlin." She walked over to the settee and bent to give her mother a kiss on her scented cheek. As usual, she smelled pleasantly of Chanel No. 5, a staple she clearly had no intention of giving up, no matter her financial circumstances.

"Don't call me that," Ella said with a wave of her manicured hand. "*Mother.* You know how I hate it. It makes me feel old."

Billie sighed.

Tonight Ella wore sequins and silk, her darkly dyed cropped hair set in impeccable marcel waves, tight to the head and curled gently at porcelain cheekbones. One might assume she was dressed this way because she'd come from a lavish dinner, but Billie knew perfectly well that she dressed like this for dinner every night as a matter of course, whether she had company or not. *If you don't take pride in yourself, what is the point in living?* she'd often say. As a once-divorced and now recently widowed Dutch aristocrat, the third of five daughters of Baron von Hooft, a former mayor of Arnhem, Ella had grown up with wealth and had never really let go of her taste for the finer things, even when her situation had become "strained," financially speaking.

Something of a free spirit, Ella had lived a large life, having come to Australia from Holland with her first husband, only to have him take up a rather too public affair. It was then that she'd met Billie's father, Barry Walker, a former cop turned PI, whom she had hired to gain the necessary proof of adultery, which was rather easy, as the story goes. What she hadn't counted on was Barry's gallantry and charm. They'd fallen in love hard and fast. She'd had Billie out of wedlock, something a woman without a title could have barely survived. But Ella had the title and the money to support herself and her little family, and she'd weathered the scandal in the way the upper classes sometimes did. She was a savvy, determined woman. She had done her time as a good girl, and it hadn't paid off, as she saw it, so she'd married the man she wanted, had the baby she craved, and to hell with social expectations. Ella had not changed her name, either, which was just the sort of thing she would dig her heels in about and Billie's dad wouldn't give a toss about. Barry Walker had been a thoroughly modern man, in his way, happy to let Ella be her own woman, an idiosyncratic and passionate "goddess," as he'd liked to call her. They'd been a good match, Barry and Ella. Billie missed her dad keenly, and she knew her mother did, too. Since his death her mother had seemed listless, and a touch more demanding, which wasn't something Billie felt like dealing with tonight.

"Let me have a look at you," Ella von Hooft said to her daughter. "Give us a whirl. Where are you going tonight?"

"I'm not going to give you a whirl. I'm on a case," Billie said, not in the mood for play.

"Being on a case doesn't make you invisible, does it? Certainly not in *that* dress."

Invisibility would be handy sometimes, Billie thought.

"Have a drink with me." Her mother changed tack, patting the seat beside her.

Billie sat next to Ella on the plush emerald-green settee, crammed with jewel-colored cushions of ruby and emerald velvet and silk. Alma poured her a tipple, a quiet smile on her ruddy, weathered face. Against Ella's exciting presence, Alma appeared as calm and solid as the Pyramids of Giza. An Irish immigrant, Alma hadn't family of her own. She'd first come on to help with newborn Billie, and as Billie had grown older, Alma had taught her to sew and mend. She had patience, a steady hand, and a keen eye for details, and she'd soon made herself indispensable. The other staff had been let go over the years, but she was always there. Ella would spend her last shilling to keep Alma, Billie knew, and unlike the other tenants in Cliffside, Ella had her maid live in the flat with her. She had a fair-size room at the east end of the flat as her personal quarters, and

Billie understood it housed a near library-size collection of paperback romance novels and copies of *Talk of the Town* and *True Confessions*, though the part of Alma that indulged in them remained well hidden beneath a sober surface.

There was a shared maids' quarters at the top of the building, with beds side by side and a kitchen where the staff made meals for their various employers, but Ella wouldn't hear of it. In truth the two women were inseparable, particularly since Billie's father had passed on. While Billie and her mother sipped their drinks, Alma walked off to the kitchen to see to something that smelled quite divinely of sweetness and cinnamon. To add to her many talents, the woman was an impressive baker.

Ella had her eyes on Billie, thinking something over. "You know, your line of work shows you the worst of people. It exposes every nasty instinct," she pronounced.

"Isn't that what you found exciting about it?" Billie shot back. She leaned against the cushions and smiled, then took a sip of her sherry. This was a well-worn track for them.

Barry Walker had been charming and, behind his sometimes tough exterior, rather softhearted and compassionate, too, but that probably wasn't all that had appealed to Ella von Hooft. Certainly he was the opposite of her first husband, if the stories were anything to go by, but it was more than that. Billie's first and happiest memories were from the end of the Roaring Twenties, a freer time in many respects, with an aristocratic mother who was more than happy to "slum it"—as others liked to say behind her back—with her dad, the baroness painting the town red each weekend with her PI; insisting on throwing extravagant parties in her two-story home, attended by intellectuals, performers, and artists; and employing a fair-size staff, in keeping with the standards of her Dutch childhood. The fact that the disapproval of others never fazed Ella was just one more reason Billie respected her. She thought Alma, her loyal lady's maid, felt the same, despite what Billie took to be more conservative leanings. Her mother rather had a taste for the gritty, Billie suspected, despite her protestations and fiercely glamorous exterior. She was indeed a woman of contrasts.

"What are you working on at the moment? No peeping, I hope," her mother prodded, not taking the bait.

"A rather clear-cut case, in fact," Billie replied. "Not at all unsavory. A mother hired me to track down her missing son."

"There must be a lot of those at the moment."

"Indeed, but not like this. He's not MIA." Billie thought of Jack again and quickly pushed the thought away. This was getting to be a quite unhelpful habit, thinking of him when her mind should be on her work. "This one was too young to serve," Billie added by way of explanation.

"Dear goddess, tell me it's not like the Lindbergh baby!" Ella exclaimed.

"No. More like a teenage runaway. He's seventeen. Hopefully the boy hasn't got himself hurt somewhere."

"Well, you wouldn't know what to do with one of those, anyway."

Babies. Billie groaned softly into her glass. "As I recall, you had Alma to help you out with me," Billie said loudly enough to include everyone in the flat. From the corner of her eye she spotted Alma's sly grin in the doorway of the kitchen. Her mother liked to rib Billie about her domestic circumstances, or lack thereof, but Billie knew that Ella had hardly embraced the domestic life herself, and it was no accident she'd had but one child. The baroness knew about Marie

Stopes and her family-planning devices and firmly believed in women controlling the fate of their wombs, despite what gray-haired men of religion had to say on the matter.

Billie rose and moved to the window, the red gown holding to her firm curves like liquid.

"That's a lovely dress," her mother said, and Billie thanked her. She had to admit it fitted better now that she was not as thin. Europe had taken the weight off her, and many others besides. The only people who got fat on wars were the ones who weren't really there—weren't on the front lines or in the factories, or starving at home, but were pushing pawns around as on a chessboard, far from the action.

"It's for The Dancers," Billie explained of her attire.

"Ahh," Ella responded, understanding.

Billie looked around her, glass in hand. The baroness had a sweeping view over Edgecliff, Double Bay shimmering in the distance, in what was year by year becoming a rather too sparsely furnished apartment. What was still in place was impressive and in impeccable taste, but the pieces were gradually receding, like a glacier. There was a large space where a Steinway baby grand piano had recently stood, Billie noticed. Not that anyone had played it much since they'd sold the stately house in Potts Point and moved to Cliffside Flats. She took another sip of the sherry. If only things were going a bit better at the agency, she'd be able to support her mother as well as herself. Perhaps in time, she thought.

Her mother was giving her a look. "Where is your mind tonight? You look like you are somewhere else."

"I'm fine."

Ella wasn't going to let it go. "It pains me to see you single like this, Billie my girl. Men throw themselves at you. Surely you see that? Why don't you take one of them up on it?"

Billie put the sherry down, folded her arms, and pulled her brows together. She didn't like this conversation. She had a puzzle to solve and it wasn't this one.

Ella raised her eyebrows. "All I'm saying is take advantage of it, Billie. Enjoy yourself. You only live once and there are plenty of nice young men out there. They certainly notice *you*."

Jack was back at the forefront of Billie's mind now: that smile, that soft mouth, those warm, strong hands. *Billie, wait for me. I want you. I want to be yours.* She hungered for him, for that deep, reassuring voice, that physical chemistry, that touch her body recalled so achingly, so devastatingly well.

Her mother seemed to read her thoughts. "Darling, he's not coming back," she said, as gently as she could. But, of course, there was no way to say it gently. "He may have been a good man, but he's gone."

Billie's whole body erupted in gooseflesh, a feeling of sickness sweeping over her, mingled with unbearable longing. She'd long suspected that Jack and his Argus camera had taken on one too many assignments. If she was truly brave, as he'd often said she was, then he was a step beyond, positively reckless in his pursuit of the Nazis and their war crimes. The two of them had played a small part in turning the tide, but a part nonetheless, Billie's words and his photographs helping to tell a story to the world of cruelty against civilians, against children, in what had been a bold attempt at absolute and total genocide. Together they'd been part of something larger than themselves, Billie and Jack. His last assignment that she knew of had been in Warsaw in '44, when the Polish Home Army, an underground resistance group, had risen against the German occupation forces. It had been risky for a press photographer by then, far riskier than it had been in 1938. He'd sent one letter from Warsaw—and then nothing. Word had come on the wireless that the rebellion had been crushed, the Soviet forces having failed to help. The center of the city had been razed in October of that year, with more than one hundred thousand killed. And no word from Jack. *Nothing.* The British paper he'd worked for had no information on his whereabouts.

He'd vanished only months after he and Billie had married, following a wartime affair of several years, broken up into romantic interludes and stolen weekends of intense intimacy. Then Jack was gone. And Billie had left Paris to return to Australia and her ailing father, arriving too late. In no time at all she had lost not one but the two most important men in her life. It had been more than two years now since she'd seen Jack, she reminded herself again, but time moved strangely after the war.

Billie looked down at the luxurious fabric of her evening gown, finding it surreal against her thoughts of the war. Everything had changed when the war began, and now it was so different again. So little was the same; her whole life before was almost like a dream. Sometimes it was as if she watched her world through the lens of Jack's Argus, distant and somehow disconnected, everything in monochrome.

"Darling, being a spinster suits some, but not you. I know you yearn for something else," her mother was saying.

"I made a vow to Jack," Billie managed in a tight voice. Her mouth felt as dry as the outback. Their vows had to do with each other, but also their common cause. They would do whatever they had to in order to bring the truth of what was happening to the world, and especially to America, where isolationist public sentiment had finally turned, changing the course of the war. Hitler had wanted more than Poland and Austria, more than all of Europe. He had wanted the world reflected in his terrifying image. He had come closer than many cared to admit.

"You may well have done, my girl," Billie's mother said, bringing her back to the moment. "You may well have made a vow to that man, but that was the war. Things are different now. The war is over and you have no ring, no papers, and no husband. There were two witnesses and you haven't seen them since. Such things happened in the Great War, too. No one would begrudge you moving on. He wouldn't."

"You never met him," Billie said softly. It wasn't much of an argument, but it was true. They would have got on, she thought. Both were free spirits in their own ways. Complicated. Stubborn. Exciting.

Love was often more intense in times of war, she knew. But that knowledge didn't change the shape of it, didn't release her from her feelings about Jack Rake, wherever he was, whatever fate he'd faced in Warsaw. It was true their wedding had been makeshift—a borrowed dress, a homemade cake—but that made it no less real to her. Their lovemaking had been real. What was still in her heart was real.

"You need to face facts, Billie. You are a war widow," her mother said.

War widow.

Spoken out loud, the words stung, though it wasn't the first time she'd heard them. Through her work, Billie knew the fate of war widows in Australia—some were objects of pity, others considered a threat. Widows were the common targets of gossip, thieves, and swindlers, men on the prowl, and the suspicions of married women who believed any widow was looking for a new husband and willing to do anything to get one. Society defined women with those two words, and they were stigmatized by it—until they could change their status by marrying again, that is. Though the words might be accurate, they made Billie squirm, extinguishing all hope of Jack's return, and like Mrs. or Miss, defining Billie by her marital status. Further, despite the tireless advocacy of the War Widows' Guild, widows with children received but a pittance, and a young civilian widow of the war, with no children, was not eligible for anything. Their sacrifices during the war were not recognized by the government, and the men in charge believed that what a charming, young childless widow needed was not a pension but another husband. If Billie wanted to remarry, she would need to seek a certificate of presumption of death, but she would have to provide evidence first, and that was not something she had yet.

"But I . . ." Billie began to protest, and her mouth closed again.

If not a war widow, what was she? If Jack was alive she would be within her rights to seek divorce on the grounds of desertion, something she had helped other women attain through her investigation agency. Unless he turned up or she could furnish more information about precisely when and where he was last seen, she could have no way of knowing what had happened to him. She didn't want a divorce. She wanted Jack. Or at least answers.

She swallowed back the bitter taste that had settled on her tongue.

"Let's talk about something else, can we?" Billie pleaded. She stalked off to the kitchen to get herself a glass of water. Alma was there, bent over an open oven. The air coming from it was hot and sweet.

She downed a glass of water and returned to the settee. "What can I do for you tonight? You said there was something you needed help with. Urgent, was it?" Billie watched her mother take a long, slow sip of sherry. "There's not really anything, is there?" Billie looked at the thin watch on her wrist. "Lunch on Sunday? The usual?" She stood impatiently and gave her mother a kiss. "I have to go and fix my hair, Ella. I'm half-dressed."

"I didn't want to say anything," her mother teased.

"Well now, that *is* unlike you." Billie smiled. Some of the tension had dispersed. She just couldn't talk about Jack with her mother. It wasn't helpful.

"Your neck is too bare, my girl. Alma, could you fetch the sapphires? The drop set?" Ella called.

"No, no. I have plenty of adequate costume jewelry," Billie protested, but it was no use. In a few moments her throat and earlobes were decorated by a stunning deep blue sapphire and diamond Art Deco set, which she accepted without further fuss. She caught a glimpse in the mirror of the coat rack at the door and did a double take. Billie had to admit her mother had picked it right. The drop earrings held ten little square sapphires in a vertical line, surrounded by small diamonds. The matching pendant drew attention to her slender clavicles and long neck. A small round diamond hung off the bottom of each earring, swaying gently and catching the light. The blue set off the dress and subtle red hues in her brunette hair perfectly and made her eyes seem larger and more striking. The jury was out on whether Billie's eyes were blue or green, and even Jack hadn't been able to make up his mind.

Billie laughed. "You're right. You win. It's perfect. I'll return these on Sunday when I pick you up for lunch."

"Would you like the car? Alma could drive you."

"No, thank you," she answered. She strode across the flat to give her mother another kiss. "I love you."

Billie left the matriarch with her book and her sherry and Alma's loyal company. As she retreated down the hall toward the stairwell, she heard the soft sounds of the wireless being turned on.

Six

———~~~———

Resplendent in her dark ruby-red silk gown and her mother's shining blue sapphires, Billie returned to her office by taxicab. Despite her mother's diversion, she got there in plenty of time for Sam's arrival and busied herself with paperwork, leaning back in her chair with her stockinged feet up on the desk, the split in her gown falling open to just above her knee. The prospect of an interesting evening ahead made the tedium of her least favorite part of the job bearable.

It was but twenty minutes later when she heard the outer door of the office open, and the little buzzer that alerted her to visitors sounded. Her eyes went to the Bakelite clock. He was very punctual, that Sam. Billie closed her file, pulled her feet down, and slipped them into her shoes. Soon the doorway filled with the outline of one Samuel Baker. He had the kind of shoulders that could plug a doorway handsomely. He was several ax handles across, as the saying went.

"Do I pass?" he asked and turned for her.

She looked him over. "Indeed you do pass muster, Sam. The jacket fits perfectly."

Sam wore a ready smile and Billie sensed this was a part of his job he rather enjoyed. He had on his new white double-breasted shawl-collar dinner jacket, worn over a button-down shirt, black bow tie, and satin-stripe black tuxedo pants. His shoes shone. Yes, he looked the part in his summer whites, and that was precisely why Billie had had the jacket made for him early in his employment with her. A keen amateur seamstress herself, she had good connections with tailors, some of whom owed her favors. She'd had one good day suit and one formal wardrobe made for Sam. This was the first outing for the black-tie ensemble. Far from a luxury, Sam's wardrobe was as vital to his work for Billie as a wrench was to a plumber. They needed to be able to fit in anywhere without raising eyebrows; tonight they had to slide into the top end of town. With freshly combed hair and a sparkling white jacket, Sam looked every bit the leading man, though his gloved hand gave him a slightly dark edge, which was not entirely unwelcome considering where the trade sometimes took them. She pushed back her chair and stood, and he looked her over briefly, keeping his appraisal polite and professional. "Ms. Walker, I must say you look as pretty as a diamond."

"You do have a way with words, Sam." Billie smoothed down her silk dress and caught a glimpse of the shining sapphires at her throat. She dearly hoped her mother would never need to sell them, though she knew her jewelry collection was dwindling as fast as her furniture. "It's balmy out," she said. "Shall we walk?"

"You can walk in that?"

"Watch me." She grabbed her stole and tossed it elegantly around her shoulders.

Billie never sacrificed mobility for style, just as she wouldn't sacrifice style for much of anything. These were practical considerations, after all. If she didn't look the part, she wouldn't get far at their destination, and if she couldn't get far in her shoes, she might miss some vital clues. She shared her mother's belief that attractive shoes needn't be ankle breaking. In fact, the baroness still wore the low 1920s style, which was a bit out of date for Billie's taste. She didn't need to do the Charleston all night; she just needed to walk four level city blocks, and who knew how much farther later on. Her shoes had a two-inch heel, a little satin bow above the toe, and fabric soles. Leather was still quite dear, having been needed for men's boots. But equally, fabric was quiet. Billie liked quiet shoes. Not for her those clanging leather soles that announced your arrival like a marching band.

"What's this about tonight?" Sam asked as they stepped onto the street. It would take little more than ten minutes to hit the theater district.

"Our boy was hanging around The Dancers, apparently, and spoke with a doorman. I'd like to know what he was doing there and what was said," Billie explained.

"Really? Was he looking for a job as a dishwasher?"

"Precisely my first thought, but no. He was trying to get in as a customer, it seems."

Sam's eyebrows went up. "Now, I haven't met the kid, but I reckon he'd have more success tattooing a soap bubble than getting served at The Dancers."

Billie grinned. Sam was absolutely right, but that didn't always stop young men from trying things, particularly if there was a girl involved.

In no time they were upon the George Street theater district, which was in full swing, most of the theaters having just let out. As they crossed Liverpool Street, Billie pushed out the crook of her elbow and Sam linked his arm with hers. A couple of actors on a mission, they walked arm in arm to the narrow Art Deco street entrance of The Dancers on Victory Lane, as the passage off George Street was colloquially known, smiling and looking for all the world like any other couple coming from the shows. A Rolls-Royce was pulling in as they neared the entry, and a uniformed doorman who was as thin as a shadow opened the door to greet a gray-haired gentleman and his somewhat younger platinum-haired female companion. "That might be our doorman," Billie remarked under her breath, and they waited for him to turn but missed the opportunity to talk to him as he escorted the couple inside.

Sam nodded and Billie held on to his arm with imitation intimacy.

They made their way through the portal to a plush emerald-colored carpeted staircase that led to the next level. Sam stayed close at Billie's side as they made their way past the wordless doormen guarding the entry to the main floor. The doormen bowed slightly and white-gloved hands pushed open the white-and-gold doors in well-trained unison, the ballroom opening up before them, almost blindingly white for a moment compared to the darkness of the stairway.

Billie sensed Sam's awe as they entered.

The Dancers was one of those joints that aimed to feel international, and mostly succeeded. The walls were covered with illuminated murals of glamorous cities—Paris, Cairo, Athens—and everything from the waiters' crisp white bow ties and dinner jackets to the palm motifs of the carpet, crockery, and napery conspired to give patrons the impression they were on an expensive holiday.

There was a slightly American feel about the place, Billie thought, not for the first time. It had probably been designed to please the US troops who'd come here with their money after '41. It wasn't a place a lot of Aussie diggers could afford, and the clientele these days seemed mostly to be the types who were too well connected to have seen a front line—judges, barristers, men and women of leisure, and anyone they wanted to impress. The Dancers had a reputation for catering to wealthy gentlemen on the other side of the law, too, including those who claimed to be "legitimate businessmen" despite notorious reputations. The club gave the impression of being exclusive, though as far as Billie could tell that meant they'd let in anyone with enough cash, fame, or glamour to make the place look good. If you dressed well you could get in, but if you behaved badly or didn't like buying drinks, you wouldn't stay long. Little wonder Adin and Maurice never made it past the second set of doors. If she could find out just why this place was of such interest to the missing boy, and imbibe a good champagne cocktail in the process, it would be an evening well spent.

They made their way past the circular dance floor, which was dotted with extravagantly adorned patrons, and came to the long bar on the other side. It seemed The Dancers, despite the name, was not really the place to carve up the dance floor. This was a place for expensive swaying, Billie decided. Or at least it was now that the war had done its work and trimmed down the customer base. She turned her back on the crowd and slid onto a stool at the gleaming bar, her silk dress settling smoothly around her hips and long legs. A crisply uniformed bartender with one of those curiously old-young faces looked to Sam for their order.

"Champagne cocktail, please," Billie cut in before Sam could speak. The bartender tilted his head, taken by surprise, though not at all put out by her ordering her own drink.

"Whatever the lady wants, the lady shall have. And for the gentleman?"

"I'll have a planter's punch," Sam said.

"Oooh, getting adventurous," Billie teased her assistant quietly as the bartender moved away to get the ingredients he'd need.

"I *have* had a cocktail or two, you should know," Sam said, slightly defensive.

She grinned mischievously. Sam was more of a beer kind of guy, but he was acting the part well enough tonight. Swiveling around on their stools, they turned their backs to the bar for a moment to take in the room from their new vantage point. The Dancers had the round dance floor as its focus, with white-clothed circular tables all around it, the majority of them taken. There was a raised stage for live bands along part of one wall to their right, which might be two musicians deep, but the focus was that floor, and when an act came on they walked out there, lit by a spotlight to captivate the room. Billie had seen a show here at the start of the year. It was top-shelf.

Billie surveyed the tables. The ones closer to the middle were especially exclusive. She recognized two judges at one such table. Gray-haired and sitting in that puffed-up way older gentlemen sometimes did, they were very familiar, but she couldn't quite get their names to surface. Not connected with any of her recent cases, thankfully, though her mother would likely know them.

The maître d' was fussing over another central table and drew Billie's eye. Champagne flowed there. The real French drop, no pretenders. A well-fed and smooth customer in tails—the only tails Billie had seen so far in the joint—was brandishing a small, velvet-covered box. On one side of him a lean man wore summer whites, like Sam, but would look more at home in denim and an Akubra, astride a horse. His face was deeply lined, tanned, and weathered, as if being indoors was a habit he avoided. He seemed relaxed, and he appraised the box with faint interest, holding his coupe glass in a rough hand that almost engulfed it. Beside him was a blond woman with a somewhat fussy veil-and-flower combination on her head, reminiscent of the top of a wedding cake. She wore a glass-eyed fox fur over an apricot gown and looked positively taken with whatever was in the rotund man's box. Gems, Billie guessed. The blonde leaned over to the grazier type and said something in his ear. He smiled languidly. A large, glittering ring flashed on her finger. A well-to-do country couple come to town for some solid spending, Billie decided.

Across from the assumed grazier, and on the other side of the tails-wearing, rosy-cheeked gentleman, was his absolute opposite: a tall, slender, pale man with almost iridescent skin and a snow-white head of hair that his body and neck looked a touch too young for. Billie caught the side of his face, and it looked strange, pulled. An honorable war wound, no doubt. A skin graft for airman's burn, she speculated, thinking of the lift operator, John Wilson. Those damned planes had a habit of catching fire on a whim. Perhaps he was one of the lucky, unlucky ones who'd made up Dr. Archibald McIndoe's Guinea Pig Club in Sussex? Maybe it was a plastic job. She'd seen many of those since 1945. Wars provided surgeons with an influx of test subjects and much had changed since the Great War. What a man could survive these days was remarkable. The pale man sat stiffly and sipped from his glass, holding it gently at the base in the French way, so the champagne would not warm in his hand.

Beside him a fifth figure padded out the small table but seemed not to belong. It was a young brunette woman in a violet couture number. Though beautiful, the clothing had the effect of a dress-up. Had that ravishing dress been made for someone else? Billie wondered what her story was. She sat among this interesting circle of characters but looked at none of them, appearing almost bored and wishing she was elsewhere.

"If you were trying to blend in, you shouldn't have worn that dress," Sam commented quietly, pulling Billie's attention back to him.

She turned swiftly, eyebrow arched. "I say, you can be an impudent young man," she scolded playfully. "Except that you may be right. Ella said the same." A few heads at the closer tables were craning their way, possibly drawn to that ruby red. It was better than the beaded option, though. She still felt sure about that.

"I didn't mean—" Sam began sheepishly, and Billie waved her hand as if to change the subject, their drinks arriving just in time to close the conversation. They were still figuring each other out, she and her secretary-cum-assistant. He couldn't always tell when she was teasing.

"Cheers," she said to the barman, and swiveled back to her partner. "Here's to a successful case."

She and Sam clinked glasses, her coupe making a dainty tinkle against his larger, heavier glass. She took a delicate sip of her cocktail, which went down a treat, and soon most of it was gone, before Sam was halfway through his beverage. He raised an eyebrow at her.

"Where'd you learn to drink like that?"

Billie ignored the question, pushing her empty glass aside. "I'm going back downstairs. You hold up the bar, Sam. If I don't come back in fifteen minutes, come and save me, hey?"

He gave her a look, as if to say, "You? Need saving?" and stayed put as she slipped away through the ballroom and down the staircase, a wisp of satiny red drawing the eyes of staff and patrons. In moments she emerged on Victory Lane and took a deep breath of the humid night air, the cocktail providing a pleasant buzz. Here the doormen were helping people out of their cars and letting them in through the beautiful Art Deco doors. She leaned against a brick wall and observed the new arrivals. Yes, everyone let into the place looked extremely well-heeled. What had Adin and Maurice been thinking?

"Miss? May I help you?"

"I just need some air," Billie said and pulled her slim cigarette case from her handbag. The doorman stepped forward with a lighter. Sure enough, he was as lean as a greyhound, with a face almost as long, just as Maurice had described. She removed a fag, tapped the case shut, and placed the cigarette between her red lips. He lit it in a polished move.

"Thank you," Billie said, looking up to make eye contact, sure she had found the right man and the right moment for her purposes. There was a lull in the arrivals.

"Pleasure," he said, locking his deep brown eyes with her green-blue ones.

She reached out with her gloved hand and slid a few shillings into his. He seemed to appreciate the gesture. Tips would be generous at The Dancers, and she seemed to have picked the right amount. In seconds the tip was secreted in his coat, another well-practiced move. He'd barely broken eye contact. "You were here last weekend?" she asked casually, smiling that professional, disarming smile.

"Always am, miss. Six nights a week," he responded cheerfully.

"Isn't that every night they're open here?"

"Indeed it is," he confirmed. His smile made deep lines in his lean young face. "I didn't see *you* here."

"Do you remember a young man, curly hair, perhaps out of his depth, about seventeen?" Billie asked. "He spoke with you, as I understand it. His name is Adin."

At this the doorman stiffened. The smile dropped. "I couldn't say. I meet a lot of people," he replied cautiously.

"Oh, I think you could say. You'd remember this one. He couldn't get in." She smiled some more and took a drag of her cigarette.

The doorman shifted uneasily. "We don't allow minors in the club, miss."

"Precisely." She took another puff and let the smoke drift in the night air. The lane was still quiet, the comings and goings of patrons conveniently halted for the moment. "He spoke with you. I'd be interested in what was said," she pressed and handed him a card. He read it over. It could be that he flushed a little, though it was hard to tell under the lighting of the entryway. She wondered why he was so cagey. If there was nothing to it, he wouldn't respond like this. Could it be that Maurice had given her a good lead?

A shilling was in her hand, but he hesitated this time. "I'd like to help you, miss, but I don't recall," he said in a flat tone, looking away. But he was agitated. He could be swayed.

Sure you don't, she thought. It wasn't the right moment to show him the photograph. This wasn't about that. He recalled. He recalled the boy well. "I can perhaps . . ." she began, but then his focus shifted suddenly. Billie followed his eyes. A man stepped through the front doors and looked at him; it was the round-faced man from the table she'd been watching, and though he only appeared for a moment, the doorman's back went as straight as a board. He moved away from Billie and walked into the club, but not before their eyes met again.

He knew something. And she could get it, but not tonight.

Recognizing temporary defeat, Billie stubbed out her cigarette and sashayed up the staircase to the small ballroom, feeling eyes on her once more. The staff opened the doors for her again with their white gloves, and she spotted Sam still at the bar, surveying the room over a fresh, hefty glass. Three shillings for, on the face of it, a whole lot of nothing. She'd have to do better than that if she hoped to stay afloat. Still, there was something to it, the little woman in her gut told her. The doorman had looked scared when the round-faced man emerged. He must have been afraid of losing his job, Billie thought. She'd make another pass at it, when things cooled down a little. He'd tell her something, she felt sure.

"Sam, are you all right to come into the office at ten tomorrow?" Billie asked, sliding in next to her assistant once more. She looked at her thin gold watch with the tiny mother-of-pearl face. It was not quite eleven thirty, not so late by her standards, but she had to get to the morgue soon if she wanted to get any sleep at all. "I'll have a chore for you," she told him. It wouldn't make for the most pleasant Saturday morning, but it wouldn't be difficult or dangerous.

He nodded. "Of course. Ten it is. You don't need me earlier? But let me drive you home. It's late." She paused, deliberating. "Ah, the death house," he added, remembering. "Let me drive you there, at least."

She considered his proposal. She had a small gift set aside for Mr. Benny, who would be working at the morgue, but it was back at the office. She didn't mind being overdressed, but her silk gown, not to mention the sapphires, was perhaps not best for a visit to Circular Quay West, where the city morgue was located. Or maybe it was the thought of her fabric-soled shoes on those less-than-clean floors that put her off. She'd need to walk back to the office for the gift and then go home to change before heading out again, or else ask Sam to drive her. It was all less than ideal, she had to admit.

She screwed up her even features. "We won't get much further tonight, but I want to come back here. Maybe our fellow will have calmed down a touch by then. I spoke with him, but he's a bit . . . nervous. How about we hit this place a touch earlier tomorrow, and I'll bring what I need for the death house." She swiveled back toward the main floor. "I don't think that's where we'll find this kid, anyway," she murmured under her breath.

It was the little woman in her gut again. Adin Brown was not on a slab somewhere. It was going to be a lot more complicated than that.

Seven

—〜〜—

He woke with a start as ice-cold water hit his sleeping face.

In a flash the boy was scrambling to his feet, his body wet, and crying out with suddenly recalled pain, and now tumbling over as something prevented him from standing upright. He fell forward helplessly and tried to reach out to stop himself but could not bring his hands forward. His shoulder and head hit a rug, barely softening his fall, and he briefly caught sight of wooden bed legs and two pairs of scuffed leather shoes before hands grabbed him by his bare shoulders and hauled him up again. Shaking now, he looked down and twisted around in a half crouch. To his horror he was naked, a long piece of rope connecting his wrists and ankles. This rope was the reason he could not stand fully upright.

His eyes were clearing a little, his memory, too, and he took the opportunity to look around him. It felt like it was very late at night, or perhaps early in the morning, but he could not see the sky, had not seen the outdoors for days, it seemed, but he could not be sure. Having been forced to strip, then grilled again, he had been sleeping on top of a creaking bed laid with unexpectedly fine sheets, in a small, luxuriously appointed room with wooden boards nailed across the window. A Persian rug was at his bare feet. An oil lamp had burned on a rustic table set with pretty objects. It was an odd arrangement and one he hadn't been able to place. A knitted blanket had been on top of his freezing body and now it had slid to the floor. He could see his lean nakedness for the first time since the ordeal began, and what he saw was ruin. His stomach was coming up in dark bruises of maroon, where he now recalled he had been viciously kicked. There was raw skin where the ropes had rubbed him. He was humiliated in his nakedness before these men, though they seemed not to care. They kept their eyes averted, faces hard.

To the boy's surprise there was a bathtub sitting in the odd room, a claw-foot bathtub, and it was filled with water, water he hadn't even heard running. Though he was eager for relief from his wounds, this bath was not inviting.

"*No . . . no . . . no . . .*"

His protests were ignored as he was lifted and carried toward it, struggling weakly. The one with the strange, hard voice and the smile like a knife blade was not there, and the others, the hard-faced men, did not speak to him. They wore shabby suits and one had a flattened nose like a prizefighter, and it occurred to him to fear the fact that he could see them clearly and they knew he could see them, and they seemed not to care. With a sobering jolt he was dumped in the water, and he cried out as he realized it was as cold as the bucket of water that woke him. His wrists were tied behind him and he sat on those, his scraped knees bent, his face and upper chest above the water. He watched as the rope at his ankles was tied to a bar across the tub, and then he was alone, left that way in the cold water, confused and breathing hard.

Time passed. How long, he could not say.

In the low light he could see his body turning a marbled blue, where it was not already purpling with bruises. *So cold,* he thought. *So cold.* The room was odd. The bed. The bathtub. He scanned along the floor for anything he might try to crawl to, anything he might use to unbind himself. The objects on the little table, did they have sharp edges? Beyond the door there were footsteps, and he became still, listening. He heard talking. Was that the voice of a girl? Two girls, talking. He couldn't make out what was said. And then there were heavy footsteps, and the voices fell silent. They were coming back—the men who had left him here. He tensed, unbearably vulnerable in that tub of cold water and afraid of what was to come.

The hard-faced men entered the room. They were with the other one now, the man with the smile like a knife's edge. His face, where he could make it out in the shadows, was hard and angled, as if carved from stone. He came in and took off a coat, as if he had been outside. One of the men took it reverently and disappeared. The man grabbed a wooden chair, pulled it up next to the tub, and sat.

"You know what you must tell us," came that strange, foreign voice.

"I don't—" the boy protested.

With a sudden, unexpected movement, a chain attached to the bar was yanked, and with a jerk he was pulled under the water. Eyes still open, he saw the world through a terrifying prism. He'd swallowed water as he went under, and when he managed to right himself he was spluttering and shocked, coughing hard. Whatever vigor had been restored to him was quickly extinguished. Again and again he was asked the questions, the same questions for which he had the same evidently inadequate answers, and he was pulled under. Exhausted, he wanted it to end, and he tried to drink the water and drown. Life clung weakly to him.

He had not been blindfolded. He knew their faces. They would not let him live.

It seemed no longer to matter.

He welcomed death.

Eight

—⚊⚊—

When Billie arrived at her office on Saturday morning, laden with her bundle of newspapers, Sam was already in. "Good morning, Sam," she chirped. "How are you feeling after last night's adventures?"

"Fresh as spring grass, Ms. Walker," he joked. It had been just past midnight when they'd left The Dancers, not so late by the standards of their trade, but he'd downed a fair few of those planter's punches. Had it been three in the end? Four?

"Well, as promised, I have a pretty tedious job for you this morning," she said. "I can't say it will help a hurting head, though," she teased, and dumped the bag of newspapers on his desk. A stench rose up of wet paper and rotten vegetables. "I need you to find a newspaper with a page torn out of it."

"Which paper?"

"That I can't be sure of, I'm afraid, but the odds are good that it's one of these. I narrowed it to the week. I think it might be the Thursday, but I'd like you to check all of these. Something on the missing page might have triggered Adin to go off on his own and do something rash."

Ever the professional, Sam held back a grimace.

"Sorry, mate," Billie offered. "I'll nip out and grab today's papers. You find me that missing page."

She looked her assistant over. He was a tad less robust-looking than usual, which still made him about five times more robust than any man she'd likely see on the street. "Feeling okay this morning? You need a pie or something to take the edge off?"

"Stop looking at me like that. I'll have you know I can drink like a sailor, Ms. Walker. I only had three in the end. And, besides, it's not pies I'd take to stave off a heavy head—if I had one."

She believed him.

—⁓—

Billie was returning from nearby Central Station with the weekend papers tucked under her arm and was entering Rawson Place when she saw a familiar silhouette near the entrance to Daking House. A dark, small-statured woman was standing by the entryway, wearing a charming navy bow in her short, tightly curled hair, worn flat leather shoes without stockings, and a navy coat that seemed a touch too heavy for the weather. Her posture was impeccable, her head high. A delicate gold crucifix hung around her neck. There was no doubt in Billie's mind whom she was waiting for.

The young woman turned at her approach and looked at her with prematurely world-weary eyes. The sunlight hit them and the eyes turned a warm caramel. "Shyla," Billie greeted her. It had been some weeks since she'd last seen her. "Can I get you some morning tea?" Her other business could wait an hour. Shyla nodded and they set off back toward Central Station.

Billie and Shyla had met outside the big station by chance when Billie returned from Europe in '44, and they had since struck up a friendship and something of a trade in information. Shyla was a young woman of the Wiradjuri—the people of three rivers—and she had been taken from her family by the Aborigines Welfare Board when she was four, along with her older siblings, and sent to the Bomaderry Aboriginal Children's Home, run by Christian missionaries, tasked with assimilating the children into the lowest levels of white society. When she was old enough, Shyla had been trained for domestic service at the Cootamundra Domestic Training Home for Aboriginal Girls, and at fourteen she was sent off to a wealthy family in rural New South Wales, who paid a pittance for her often back-breaking labor. Her brothers had been put into service on sheep and cattle stations, Shyla said, and last Billie had heard she was trying to track them down and make contact, something Billie hoped to help her with. Shyla was a smart young woman and well connected with the other girls who had been put into service. Rich people often chose to overlook just how much their domestic help knew and were witness to, and in the right circumstances that information could be shared. The girls trusted Shyla, and in turn she trusted Billie, meaning Billie could benefit from her insider knowledge.

At the Central Railway Refreshment Room, Billie and Shyla were shown to a table made up with a crisp white tablecloth and neatly set silverware stamped with the railway insignia. A milk jug and sugar bowl sat in the center of the table along with a fresh bouquet of white bougainvillea in a delicate glass vase. The handsome space had a high ceiling and was hemmed with carved wooden partitions and punctuated with structural pillars. Above the table, a metal fan hummed gently, pushing the air around.

Shyla chose one of the wooden chairs and Billie took a seat across from her, stacking the newspapers on one side of the table. She ordered strong black tea for them both.

"You work all the days of the week," Shyla commented, and Billie smiled.

"Sometimes," she responded. "I'm on a case."

"Working for women whose men are running around?" Shyla guessed.

"Thankfully, no, not a divorce case this time." It was pretty much necessary to hire a private inquiry agent to secure grounds for divorce, and it was often ugly work, skulking around bars and dosshouses to obtain proof of adultery. Had her financial situation been better, Billie would have refused such cases absolutely, but the Depression had taken its pound of flesh from the von Hoofts and the Walkers. Her mother might like to deny it, but if Billie didn't get the agency to work—really work as a financial enterprise—her every last pearl and piece of silverware would end up sold. Maybe not this year, maybe not the next, but soon enough. Billie wasn't about to let that happen.

She pushed the menu across the table and watched her quiet companion. "Would you like something to eat?" She wasn't sure of Shyla's age but thought she might have been about eighteen, though at times Billie guessed her as older or younger. Shyla took her navy gloves off, and Billie noticed the rough skin of her hands, and how the gloves she seemed always to wear had been worn in patches and repaired with careful mending. She had a fine hand with a needle.

Shyla informed Billie in a quiet voice that she'd like the made-to-order French cutlets and bacon. It was still well before lunchtime, so Billie ordered a single scone for herself instead of her usual salade Niçoise. A blond waitress delivered their tea and took their order. When she returned to her post, it was obvious that she was talking about the unusual pair with the other server, but Billie couldn't make out what was being said.

Tea steamed in Shyla's cup. After a moment, she sipped it gingerly, seemingly oblivious or resigned to the fuss her presence was causing among the refreshment room staff.

"I got your note," Billie said. "I'm sorry to say that I haven't heard anything yet about your brothers, though there is a cattle station down at Urana that I hope to hear back from soon." Her inquiries into the whereabouts of Shyla's brothers had been surprisingly difficult and frustrating. The system was simply not set up to make it easy for separated Aboriginal parents, children, and siblings to find their families again. For a start, the names of the taken children were routinely changed from those given at birth by their parents to anglicized Christian names like Elizabeth and John.

"I didn't come to speak to you about my brothers," Shyla interjected to Billie's surprise.

She sat up in her seat, then leaned forward conspiratorially. "Tell me, Shyla," Billie prompted in a low voice.

"There's a white fella up at Colo. There's a bad feeling about him. He has some of my mob there—four girls."

"Girls you trained with at Cootamundra?"

Shyla nodded, and her eyes darkened.

"What is the bad feeling about him?" Billie asked. She knew Colo was a town on the northern fringes of the Blue Mountains, but she had not been there. It was a fairly remote area of bushland, a few orchards and farms.

"He came after the war, one year now they say. They say he has no woman, no children, and he has a lot of money. Four girls do the work for him."

"What does he do? Is it a property he has there? Sheep or cattle? Crops?"

"A house only. There are no men working there, only him. He lives alone, except for the girls, and travels in a motorcar, carrying things to Sydney." Shyla took another sip of her tea, seeming to hold on to her cup for comfort. Though she wasn't usually one to be emotional, she was upset about something, beneath her usual reserve. "Since the girls went there to work no one has seen them. It's not good," she said.

Was he a deliveryman of some kind? Billie wondered. Delivering what? Shyla knew a lot of girls in service to different families. She wouldn't have come to see Billie about this man without reason.

"What does he carry? Do you know?"

She shook her head. "I haven't been told."

"It would be good to find that out," Billie said, keeping her voice low. "What is the bad feeling about him? Do they think . . . Does he hurt them?" she asked.

"I can't say," Shyla said, shaking her head slowly. "I think it's not good."

Billie's eyes narrowed. Their food arrived, and she leaned back in her chair. Her scone was warm and she spread a touch of jam on it. She looked up at Shyla. "When you say he came *after* the war, do you mean that you think he might not be Australian?"

"They say he's a foreigner."

"What does he look like? Were you given any description?" Billie asked.

"He's white and big. That's what they told me. Odd-looking face. A big man."

"I see. And he travels alone in a motorcar. Do you know the type?"

"A Packard. A fancy one. It's black."

"Number plate?"

Shyla shook her head. It was a shame about the plate, but there couldn't be too many Packards in Colo, surely? Billie could dig it up.

"Do you want me to check him out, Shyla? What would you like me to do?" Perhaps it was time for some real quid pro quo. Shyla had come to Billie with good information several times, and now perhaps she was coming good on the promise to ask for something more in return than simply some tea and some shillings here and there for her work.

Shyla nodded. "I promised I would do what I can, and you are someone who . . ."

Billie waited, anticipating the next word. "Someone who?"

"Someone who knows things. I know you are good at finding things out."

"So are you," Billie said truthfully. "I will make some inquiries on my end, give you the lowdown on this man; then you decide what's next, okay?"

Shyla paused for a moment, thinking of something, or perhaps someone, then nodded and tucked into her cutlets. She was quiet for a while, but after she'd finished and wiped her mouth with the white napkin, she said simply, "I'm worried, Billie."

"I understand." Billie opened her handbag and passed her a

fountain pen and asked her to write the man's name and address on the corner of the paper. When she got it back there was simply the name "Frank," and "Upper Colo."

Billie looked at it, disappointed. "No address?"

"The big house," Shyla explained, holding her hands apart in a gesture to emphasize the size of the house. "By an orchard. It is easy to find, they say. Not far from the river."

"Okay." It was far less information than Billie would have liked, but she could probably track him down by the car and the big house, if Shyla was correct. "I'll find out whatever I can about this Frank. Would the girls go to the police if they were in danger, do you think?"

"I can't say," Shyla replied, but her head was shaking as she spoke. That was hardly a surprise. A lot of Aboriginal people were suspicious of the police, or gunjies, as Shyla sometimes called them. Through conversations with Shyla, Billie had some of the picture— how contacting the authorities about anything might lead to being arrested for something else, or having the men taken, or having the Aborigines Welfare Board take children away "for their own good." Stuff like that tended to ensure that trust was in short supply. That long and troubled history had not been forgotten and had created understandable tension between Aboriginal communities and the white authorities. That couldn't simply vanish overnight. Much as Billie knew and liked a lot of police officers, she could hardly blame Shyla or her friends if their trust was lacking. Hell, Billie's trust was often lacking, too. She had learned through her father that the New South Wales police force had its corruption issues—there were a lot of decent cops but a fair few rotten eggs to poison the mix. It was one of the reasons he'd given her for retiring and going out on his own.

"I'll see what I can find out about him," Billie repeated. "And I can see if the police want him for anything."

"They don't want any trouble out there," Shyla said, stiffening. "I can tell *you*, but no one else. No police."

Billie got it. "I'll look into who this fellow is however I can and get back to you. If the police need to speak with him about something, so be it, but I'll keep the girls out of it."

"That's the best way," Shyla agreed. "Thank you for the lunch, Billie."

"You're welcome. Anytime. How will I reach you when I have something?" she asked.

"I'll find you," Shyla said, as always. She rose from her chair and walked away, a proud if lonely-looking figure in the room of whispering passengers and staff.

Nine

—∿—

When Billie returned to the office with the weekend papers, her thoughts swirling with speculation about the mysterious "Frank" and the girls Shyla was worried about, she found Sam looking triumphant and a touch fresher for the extra cups of tea he'd made himself.

"Don't tell me. You found our missing page?" Billie guessed.

"*Sydney Morning Herald,* Thursday, November 21, 1946," he said, holding up the newspaper in question. A section was ripped out of a page on the right-hand side.

This narrowed their focus even better than an entire missing page. "This is the only possibility?" she asked.

"Well, this is the only thing ripped out of these papers," he said, his face falling a little, doubtless imagining another tedious run through soggy newspaper.

"Excellent work. And that gels with what the boy Maurice told me about the date. I'll get you to head to the library and find out what was on that page," Billie said.

"I have it here," he said to her surprise. Again, her assistant's smile was triumphant. He held up a wrinkled copy and her eyes widened.

"Nicely done, good sir. What is it? Do tell." She hurried over to his desk.

"It's an advertisement for an auction that's running this weekend. We still had our copy of that edition."

He passed her the paper and she ran her eyes over it. Georges Boucher Auction House. This was not what she had been expecting at all. An auction? "How fascinating. I think we'll have to attend this tomorrow." The advertisement featured photographs of antiques and jewelry. A carved sideboard. Rings. An unusual necklace. It looked like high-end stuff. Why would it interest the boy, let alone enrage him?

"I suppose we ought to look into this George character and his business," Sam said.

Billie laughed softly. "*Georges*," she said, using the correct French pronunciation. "We'll need the library anyway," she decided. "Head there now, please, and research this Georges Boucher. Find out what you can about when he came to Australia and what his story is. I want a physical description, too," she said. "Meanwhile, I'll visit the fur shop. I feel like there's some element missing in the story Mrs. Brown told me."

"Like what?"

"We'll see," she said, leaving it at that.

She bade her assistant adieu and strode into her office, making her way to her modest corner balcony, where she opened the doors, a fresh breeze blowing in with the sounds of the city below. She stepped out and leaned against one of the two Roman-style pillars, gazing out over the top floor of nearby Station House, which was connected to Daking House by a small safety bridge, and the bustling Rawson Place and George Street below. It was humble as balconies went, with barely enough room to turn around, but it was one of only three balconies on the sixth floor, and only half a dozen in the whole building, the rest being on the first floor. It had been a favorite contemplation spot of her father's. Naturally she'd saved this spot for herself when necessity meant subletting the other offices.

Seconds later, Sam appeared among the foot traffic below, strolling along the footpath in his trench coat, soon blending into the moving crowd. In a few minutes she'd take the lift down herself and walk to Brown & Co. Fine Furs shop to see what else her clients could tell her. In the meantime, she continued to watch the moving streetscape, her mind on Shyla's unexpected request, and on the thin doorman and his expression when he'd realized he'd been seen talking with her. It bothered her, that expression. There was something there, she thought. Something.

Far below on George Street, eyes watched her—eyes that did not approve of the woman in her high tower.

—m—

Brown & Co. Fine Furs was located in the grand Strand Arcade building on George Street. The last of the great shopping arcades built in Victorian-era Sydney, it still held appeal after the ravages of the wars it had survived, if the crowds Billie saw milling around were anything to go by.

As Billie stepped inside the arcade, the hustle of the main street fell away and she saw that little had changed since she'd last ventured inside. As always, it was cooler within the arcade than on the street. Patrons strolled slowly on the patterned tile floor, looking in the timber-fronted shop windows at jewelers working with fine tools, at cobblers repairing shoes, at racks of fine clothes, and at milliners arranging tilt hats of the latest style. She picked up the scent of a florist before turning to see a beautiful display of dahlias, gardenias, roses, and little plain daisies in pleasing arrangements. Leaning her head back and holding her brimmed hat, Billie looked up at the vaulted ceiling of tinted glass panes that hung high above the two farther levels of shopping, each level lined with cast-iron balustrades, the shops announced with oval, hand-painted signs propped up on curved Victorian iron posts.

Billie pulled off her round smoked sunglasses and contemplated her surroundings with shrewd eyes. This was a strangely tranquil place. Busy but never bustling. Something about the design, she supposed, or the businesses that set up shop here. The Brown & Co. Fine Furs shop was down a large staircase just in front of her, announced by a tasteful painted timber sign propped up on a stand of swirling ironwork. Yet amid the tranquility she felt eyes drilling into her back—a feeling she was rarely wrong about. She turned the sunglasses in her hands, pretending to clean them with the edge of a scarf in her handbag, and the reflection showed a man who had entered the arcade, his hat pulled low, watching her. She tucked the glasses into her handbag and looked around in one simultaneous movement, but by then he had his back to her, his attention apparently drawn elsewhere. Nonetheless, out of habit she memorized the texture and color of his well-tailored gray suit, his slightly crumpled fedora, his height against the shop-front windows, the black hair above his collar, shot with strands of gray. He was heavyset and moved away before she caught a glimpse of his profile, his face. Then he was gone, just another stranger back on the street outside.

Billie walked down the steps toward Brown & Co. Fine Furs, detecting the distinctive smell of a furrier—that variety of animal odors and tanned skins particular to the trade. Alone, a fur coat did not usually have much of a smell unless it had been cooped up and become musty or rancid. But when several furs were crowded into a shop, there was an undeniable mix of scents, though here, as with other fine fur shops, it was not unpleasant. A vase of deeply scented wild roses added another, sweeter odor to the mix. A bell tinkled to alert the shopkeepers to the presence of a new visitor.

"Mrs. Brown?"

Billie's client was busying herself with a display, and she snapped her head up, as if jolted; her startled doe eyes fixed on Billie. Today the woman wore the same suit, the same fine mink stole, the hairs brushed down and gleaming, but her hair was tucked under a turban of brown and emerald green, knotted at the front and secured with a circular brooch encrusted with diamantes. It suited Mrs. Brown. But despite her show of style, the past day had not been good to her, it seemed. Dark circles were forming under those uncertain brown eyes, and the lines of worry on her face seemed yet deeper.

"Oh, Miss Walker," she said, and scurried over. "Is there any news of our boy?" Her tone was heart-wrenchingly hopeful.

"Nothing yet," Billie replied gently. "We hope today may be fruitful. Perhaps I might speak with you and your husband for a short time?"

"Of course," she said, though with a hint of uncertainty.

Looking around, Billie noticed how widely the garments were spaced on the racks. The Browns were putting up a good front, but it wouldn't surprise her if they didn't have a lot of stock. They certainly wouldn't be alone if that was the case. The importation of luxury goods like fur pelts had been banned in New South Wales in 1942, as was the manufacture of new luxury garments, though Billie believed the ban on general fur manufacture had been relaxed to account for utility items and a shortage of warm clothing. Having previously focused on importing luxury pelts, Sydney's furriers had become creative about using rabbits, goats, sheep, and even water rats, said to loosely resemble mink, to make garments. She recalled her mother commenting on all the curious "new" animals used by the trade, and it was through those eyes that she surveyed the coats on display.

Mrs. Brown seemed to catch her thoughts. "We get new stock in next month in time for Christmas. We're organizing a display with Father Christmas and the reindeer."

"How charming," Billie said.

A man of perhaps fifty emerged through a door at the back of the shop. "This is my husband, Mikhall," Mrs. Brown announced. He walked over and shook hands with Billie. Mr. Brown was perhaps five foot eight, and slim, but with a rounded belly. His hair was curly, what remained of it. His shoulders sloped and he appeared to be shy, his eyes meeting Billie's for just a moment. Next to him, his reserved wife seemed a bold and forthright person.

"I'm sorry, I don't have much English," Mr. Brown said in a heavy accent, perhaps a touch ashamed of the fact. "I try, but it's not so good." His accent was certainly much more pronounced than his wife's, who had clearly worked hard to dampen it. It was a German accent, Billie noted.

As Billie sat with the pair of them in the administration office, it soon became clear why Mrs. Brown had been the one to come to Billie. Her husband was not at all confident conversing in English, even with his wife there to help him along. Mikhall managed to speak of coming to Australia in late 1936, and how grateful they were to escape Europe and what was happening there. He backed up his wife about their only child, saying what a "good boy" Adin was, and how pleased they'd been to get him to safer shores in Australia.

On their shared desk was an array of family photographs, many showing several generations. A faded black-and-white image of a cherubic, curly-haired baby, surrounded by adults, took pride of place in a large frame. "This is Adin?" Billie inquired.

"Yes." Mrs. Brown did not elaborate, though it looked perhaps as if she wanted to. Her eyes welled up as her attention was drawn to the photo, and she turned away, holding back her emotions. "Happier days," she said simply.

"Where was it taken?"

"Europe," Mrs. Brown answered cautiously. She dabbed her eyes.

"And what about this photograph?" One of the small silver frames on the desk was empty, Billie noticed. She picked it up. "Where did this one go?"

The Browns seemed genuinely surprised by this. "I don't know where it went," Mrs. Brown exclaimed. "I hadn't noticed anything missing. Mikhall?"

Her husband shook his head and said something to her in German in a low voice.

"It could have been like that for a time, he says," Mrs. Brown explained.

"Where is *mein Junge?*" Billie thought she heard Mikhall mutter. He was clenching his fists now, evidently overwrought. When he looked up she caught the glittering tears in the corners of his eyes.

Ashamed, he wiped them and looked down again, body hunched and tense.

Billie calmly put the empty silver frame back on the desk. "In peacetime, in places like Australia, most missing persons do turn up," she began. "Most young people run away to a relative, a friend, or, if they're Adin's age, a lover." Adamant headshaking from her clients followed this comment. "I do not judge," Billie stressed. "It's not my job to judge a client, be it someone seeking a divorce or parents looking for their child. Anything you can tell me about Adin—his personality, his interests, anything unusual you might have noticed recently—could help to track him down and return him to you. Was he acting strangely in the past week or so? Did anything seem different? His mood? His routines?"

There was the headshaking again, and when it stopped both of them looked at Billie with vulnerable expressions, eyes hopeful. They wanted her to fix this. They needed her to.

"We are telling you everything we can," Mrs. Brown reiterated. "We just need you to find our son."

Mr. Brown said something to his wife again in a low voice. "Yes, you should mind the shop, Mikhall," she agreed, and he stood up.

"Just one more thing," Billie said as the man got up. "What do you think your son might be doing at a place like The Dancers?"

At that, Mrs. Brown's eyebrows pulled together. Husband and wife exchanged puzzled looks.

"It's an exclusive club off Victory Lane. Quite a high-end joint," Billie added.

"We haven't any idea. It's not the sort of place he would go. We've never been to such a place," she said, as if that would discount his having been present.

"Well, it *is* the sort of place he would go, because he did, but I agree it was not his sort of club under normal circumstances. The doormen saw him out."

"I don't know of this," Mikhall said awkwardly, shrugging. He continued his short journey out of the office, those sloped shoulders and bent head leading the way. The door closed behind him. The women were again alone.

"Mrs. Brown . . . May I call you Netanya?"

Her client nodded. "Nettie is what most people call me."

"Well, Nettie, please call me Billie, if you like." She leaned closer. "*Anything* you can tell me about Adin's life, Nettie, your family life, might help reveal why he was at The Dancers, trying to get in there. Anything. And it stays between us."

"Do you think he got into trouble at this dance club?" Nettie looked stricken. "What was he doing?"

"At this point, I don't know, but I'm doing my best to find out." Billie could see that Nettie was almost at breaking point. "What more can you tell me about your family? Were you involved in the fur trade back in Germany?" Billie prodded.

Nettie's eyes widened as Billie mentioned Germany, and then the tension went out of her and she slumped in her chair. After a beat she closed her eyes and nodded. "Yes. It is as you guess. We are Germans. It's not a secret but we do not like to advertise the fact."

Billie waited for more.

"We came from Berlin in 1936. Adin was quite young then, and I was worried about what I was seeing. I knew we had to leave. Mikhall took some convincing, but not much. He does not adapt so well, as you can see. It wasn't a good time to be Jewish. Not in Germany. Not anywhere in Europe. I was never very religious, but I am a Jew. I will always be a Jew." She smoothed her skirt. "We took everything we could and started the fur company here in Sydney. It was our trade back in Germany, you see. My sister stayed, and my aunt and widowed mother. They shouldn't have," she said sadly. Her face was stoic as she spoke, but her eyes filled at the corners again. She was only just holding herself together.

Billie swallowed. She herself had reported on the infamous Warsaw Ghetto for the Hearst papers. She recalled seeing children as young as six forced to wear the yellow Star of David on their clothing, identifying them as Jewish, which led to bullying and worse. It was no wonder the Browns had wished to save Adin from such a fate. No matter how successful the Browns' fur business in Berlin might have been—and perhaps that was one of the reasons some of the family stayed in Germany—it would eventually have been seized by the Nazis along with all their property. The fate of Nettie's family members in Germany was not difficult to guess.

"You changed your family name?" Billie asked gently.

Mrs. Brown nodded. "Braunstein was our name. We simplified it." She searched Billie's face for judgment, some hint of rejection, but found her unchanged, professional and steady. "Do you think that all this . . . matters?" she finally asked.

"No," Billie said. "The name doesn't matter, so far as your son's situation is concerned, but knowing the family history may prove helpful. You managed to avoid internment, is that right?"

Nettie nodded again. "Yes. We had naturalized. 'Alien nationals,' they called us, but though we were no longer Germans we still had restrictions on our movements. We weren't allowed to travel without notifying the Australian authorities, and we weren't allowed to own a wireless or a camera, even for work. We had to pay someone else to take photographs of the merchandise. It was expensive. A hard time for the business," Nettie reflected.

"I imagine so."

"My husband was too old for conscription, Adin too young," she added. "We registered the factory to offer the manufacture of fur-lined uniforms, to try to do our bit, and we did make several hundred when they were needed. Rabbit, mostly. For a time it looked like Mikhall would be sent to a labor camp, but it did not happen. The rules kept changing," she said.

How terrifying it must have been to flee Germany only to have the government of another country, let alone neighbors and rival business owners, view you with suspicion, Billie reflected. It sounded like the Browns—or Braunsteins—had been luckier than some, and certainly luckier than their loved ones who had remained in Berlin. But Billie could understand now why Nettie had seemed cagey, as if withholding something.

She pushed back memories of the war—and Jack. Him running out from their position to intervene as a young Jewish girl, identified by the compulsory Star of David armband on her dress, was tormented by two older fair-haired boys, the boys pulling at her clothing and slapping her, calling her filthy names like rat and *Judensau* as she wept, terrified. The girl had finally been thrown to the ground, her clothes torn. Jack scooped her up like she was as light as a feather and dried her tears as the boys ran away. They'd been children. Just children. Already taught to hate with such violence.

Jack.

"Do you know why your son might be interested in an auction? Have you heard of Georges Boucher before? The auctioneer?" Billie asked.

At this Nettie appeared utterly baffled. "An auction? What was he thinking?"

"I'm not sure. Does anything in this advertisement ring a bell?" Billie pulled the folded newspaper clipping from her pocket and spread it on the desk.

Nettie barely glanced at the clipping, shaking her head, clearly flabbergasted, then ran a hand over her face, wiping tears that had started to form again. "Where would he get the money to buy things at an auction? Or to go to this Dancers place? What could he have been thinking?" She now raised her hands, palms to the ceiling. "Are you sure you are looking for the right person? My son, Adin?" she demanded.

"Yes, it is him," Billie confirmed, unruffled by her client's tone. "Can you look again?" she pressed, but the woman was shaking her head adamantly. "Do you think it is possible he is in debt of some kind?"

At this Mrs. Brown gasped. "No. How?"

"There's nothing missing from the till?" Billie pressed, folding up the clipping again.

Nettie looked shocked at the suggestion. "I handle the finances, Miss Walker, and I assure you there isn't a shilling out of place," she said indignantly. The strength was back now. She'd have to be a strong woman indeed to get through what she had. And yet more strength was needed now, it seemed. No matter what the fate of her only child was, she would worry terribly until it was known.

Billie hoped there would be an easy, cheerful resolution to the case. She knew only too well the agony of not knowing what had befallen the person closest to your heart.

Ten

—⁓—

"You look lovely," Alma said, opening the door to Billie.

"Thank you," Billie replied. "I'm in a bit of a hurry, I'm afraid. I'm just returning these before I head out." She entered her mother's flat, holding the sparkling blue sapphires in her hands.

The sun was low in the sky, the bay trees outside Cliffside Flats turning gold and amber in the evening light. Ella was sprawled on the settee in her usual pose, sherry in one hand. She turned and gave her only child a quick toe-to-coiffure assessment. "That dress is too dark if you plan to catch anyone's eye," she decided.

Billie smiled, ignoring the criticism. She'd made the dress from a McCall's pattern. It had a Grecian-inspired neckline that flowed over the bust and nipped in snugly at the waist before draping with strategic pleats from one hip, ideal for covering the bulge of her gun in its garter. The layered hem fell into a taper just past the knee but opened up enough for a fair stride, should running be in order. The fabric she'd chosen was darker than she'd originally thought, but dark was fine tonight. While her day had proved reasonably uneventful, she hoped to get some movement on her case tonight. It was early still, the puzzle pieces not yet falling into place, and in truth she did not yet possess enough of them, but time was short in a missing persons case. The clock was ticking. With that in mind, she wasn't going to leave The Dancers this time without getting somewhere, and that might mean a very long night. The ruby dress had been a touch too distracting. Tonight she'd opted for a less eye-catching dress, and frankly she didn't feel like arguing about it.

"I've come to return these," she said simply. "Thank you." She held out the sapphires to her mother.

"Wear them some more, darling. I'm not using them, and the sapphires suit you. They bring out your eyes." Tonight they looked blue, like the sapphires themselves. "Goddess knows you need them if you wear that dress," Ella added. "Is that *black*?"

"Midnight, actually," Billie countered.

"It's pretty black out at midnight," Ella said, deadpan. She did have very good taste, Billie had to admit, even if she was a little more insistent on imparting her opinion than was always comfortable. "Black is bad luck, some say."

Billie resisted an eye roll. "Well, thanks for letting me wear your jewels."

Ella waved her hand dismissively. She hadn't got up from her seat, and Billie bent over her to give her an affectionate hug. "Is that crepe? Matte crepe? Surely a little shine or sparkle would be better? Sequins?"

"Look, I do have to go," Billie explained apologetically. "Sorry to drop in and run. My assistant is meeting me outside the club."

"Oh, that handsome fellow." A hand with a viselike grip took her wrist and Billie found herself suddenly on the settee.

"It's not like that," she managed, recovering herself. She wondered if Ella had learned that move from her late husband. It was something like the judo of Tokugoro Ito's dojo in Los Angeles. Barry had known someone who'd trained there and had taught Billie a few moves, thirdhand. It was all about leverage and balance. He'd obviously also handed on some of the tips to his wife.

"Maybe it *should* be like that," Ella persisted.

"Thank you, but I assure you that when I do decide to find a man, I won't be paying him to spend time with me," Billie retorted and rose, smoothing down the crepe folds of her dress.

"Why not? It worked for me," her mother shot back. A little wicked grin was apparent in the crease of her mouth.

"Just don't keep holding on to the past," Ella added, and on that uncomfortable note Billie extracted herself from the flat and made her way downstairs to prepare for a second evening at The Dancers, trying her best to push aside thoughts of Jack Rake and the larger mystery that haunted her but that she had not yet come even close to solving.

—m—

Billie held her champagne cocktail in gloved fingers and listened to the music as she surveyed the crowd at The Dancers with sparkling eyes the color of her mother's sapphires, which were once again hanging around her neck and dangling from her ears. A five-piece band was playing "As Long as I Live," a Benny Goodman hit she hadn't heard since Europe, and the patrons were doing their expensive swaying. Little appeared to have changed at the club from the night before. A different and yet identical set of wealthy guests had gathered around the central tables in a different set of frocks that were also somehow the same. The same gossip and agendas and romances and social climbing and business deals were unfolding. The old-young-faced barman was the same, the doormen the same. They were peddling the same champagne-soaked fantasy world, just on a different night. The second time around, one was less dazzled, less distracted from the grime under the stools, the drink spills on the carpet. In daylight, The Dancers would not be so pretty, Billie guessed. Still, they put on a good show; she had to give them that.

"What can I get the lovely lady?" the barman asked smoothly, noting she was nearing the end of her glass and no longer making the mistake of looking to her male companion to decide her drink for her.

"I'm fine for now, thank you," she replied.

"Anything for you, miss."

"I'm fine, too," Sam interjected, and the barman gave a subtle nod, barely looking his way. Billie continued to survey the room. "Are we looking for anyone in particular tonight?" Sam asked her, sensing her focus.

"Yes, in fact, we are," she responded. His work at the library had turned up one key detail. Sam had retrieved some solid information on the auction house and its owner, including, in the back pages of a catalog that he, unlike Billie, had not had time to examine, one small photograph of Georges Boucher himself. "It seems he was here in front of us," she explained. The rotund man at the table the night before was almost certainly Boucher, which would explain the little box he'd been brandishing. That country couple had doubtless been clients.

"*Boucher*," Sam whispered. "The penny has dropped, as the Americans say. So, he was the reason the kid wanted to get in, do you think? Or do you still think he was mooning over a girl?"

"I don't much believe in coincidence," Billie replied. In her experience there was no such thing. "I'm going to try the doorman again; you watch the room. Look out for Boucher, okay?"

Taking her time, she sauntered toward the powder room in her inky dress, then slipped past it and continued all the way out of the main room, down the stairs to the street entrance. She was pleased to find the doorman she wanted to speak with still out front, as he had been on their way in. He wasn't busy now. Billie smiled when she saw his bony countenance, but as soon as his eyes clocked her, his long face fell yet farther and he turned away.

"Excuse me, sir," she called, moving fast on her low heels and taking him by one shoulder. She gave her best winning smile. "I can't help but feel you aren't happy to see me."

The smile had no discernible effect, unless the effect was fear. His dark brown eyes were large and almost scared. "No offense, but I have nothing to say to you, lady," he told her flatly, eyes focusing on his feet.

One of Billie's arched eyebrows rose. "I'm sure that isn't so," she said, whispering now. "The boy I'm looking for, Adin Brown, wanted something from Georges Boucher, didn't he? Boucher uses this place as a kind of office for his better clients? He's here every weekend wining and dining them and trying to interest them in auction items or private sales. The kid wanted to speak with him, is that right? Trying to pawn something, perhaps? He was getting nowhere at the auction house so he tried to catch Boucher here? Stop me when I tell you something you don't already know."

The man looked positively stricken. "I don't know anything and I don't want anything to do with it." He looked this way and that, to see if anyone was watching, or perhaps to find an escape point. "I don't know anything about anything," he reiterated, palms up.

Billie was not convinced. "Oh, but you do. And I can make it worth your while," she explained. "And Boucher isn't here yet to see you talk with me this time."

The man hesitated, closed his fingers around the coins she dropped in his hand, and shut his eyes. "You're going to get me into trouble, lady," he said, defeated.

A couple emerged from the main doors and he turned his back and pretended to busy himself while another doorman assisted them. When they were gone, she continued in low, soothing tones. "Just tell me what the conversation was that you had; then I'll be out of here and this will all be over—"

"Not here," he replied, cutting her off and darting his eyes from side to side again. "I can't be seen talking to you. I'm at the People's Palace," he said. The lodging house was named rather ironically, but Billie knew it. "I'll be there at one thirty, after I get off. Room 305." He paused. "Maybe I'll meet you in the lobby. I might have to let you in. I know that's late, but—"

"It's fine," she agreed. The death house could wait another night. "People's Palace, 305. Your name?"

"Con Zervos," he muttered.

Another patron walked out of the ballroom and Billie turned away, pretending to adjust her gloves. When she turned around again, Zervos had already ducked away, as nervous as a greyhound. Billie noticed the staff entrance to the kitchen swing shut. He wanted distance from her, at least while he was here. Fair enough.

She turned on her heel and walked back up the stairs. The doors were opened for her and she stole a look across the main ballroom at Sam, who was doing a fine impression of the kind of man who liked it there. She crossed the dance floor feeling quietly triumphant and slid into the stool beside him without a sound.

"Enjoying yourself?" she queried, and his gaze, which had been fixed on a woman dancing in a low-backed gown, went to her immediately.

"Crikey, how do you do that?" he asked, looking startled by her sudden presence.

Billie just smiled. "Lovely sequin detail on that dress," she said, thinking of her mother's comment. "Really draws the eye."

He appeared to blush.

"I've got a date at one thirty at the Palace. The People's Palace, not the theater." She leaned back and planted her elbows on the edge of the long bar, sliding one leg over the other.

"The doorman?" her assistant queried.

She nodded. "One and the same."

"At one thirty in the morning?" He frowned. "Obviously I'm coming."

"No, you aren't. I don't need any safety net."

"I'm coming."

"And I have a hunch he doesn't want extra company," Billie said in a low voice.

"*Do you think?* I'm coming," Sam said, insistent.

Billie sighed. "I don't want a babysitter, Sam. That's not what I'm paying you for."

"Since when am I a babysitter? *I'm coming.*"

Now it was her turn to frown. "Okay, but you'll have to wait outside." It might be a good idea to have backup, though Con seemed a nice enough fellow, and more nervous by a country mile than she was. She could handle the likes of him; she was sure of that. Sam nodded in agreement and slowly finished his planter's punch while she watched the room. No sign of Boucher yet.

"You think you can last here another hour or so?" she asked him quietly.

"Is that a real question?"

"I see," she said, smiling. Sam was clearly liking this more than the usual doss-house or back alley he had to frequent in their line of work. "Well, we can't hold up the bar forever. I think we'll have to dance," she suggested.

She pulled Sam toward the dance floor, and they inserted themselves among the throng of swaying patrons, standing close to each other and then swaying in time, measuring the moment. This would provide a different, less obvious vantage point for a while. She placed one gloved hand on Sam's right shoulder, which was practically at her eye line; he took her other hand lightly in his leather-gloved one, his thumb pressing gently against her curled fingers, and slid his strong right hand around her waist. She could just make out the feel of the false fingers and the real ones as their hands touched. There was electricity there in the touch between them, taking her off guard. Billie winced, then fought off the feeling with a bite of her lip. Memories. Just memories of Jack. Of intimacy. Had that been the last time she'd danced? Now it was Sam's turn to lead, and she felt his unspoken hesitation. "She is my boss," that hesitation seemed to say, and perhaps he'd felt her inner jolt. *Side, side, rock step, side, side . . .* He was younger and stronger than a lot of the other men on the dance floor, but more tentative. They looked at each other, her head tilted up to meet him, his aquamarine eyes searching her face for the right moves, the right approach. Just then the tempo changed and their gaze broke.

The band was back to its Benny Goodman set list, a new song, a touch faster. Would he be okay with this faster tempo? And could she really dance in this dress? Well, yes. She could run in it, too. She turned back to her dance partner just in time to see his face break into a wide grin as the rhythm quickened. As if in answer to her unspoken question, Sam swung her out from him, guiding her lightly with his gloved hand before pulling her close with his right, his body coming confidently to life. Billie laughed softly as he swung her out again and their clasped hands rose like a steeple. She spun beneath their raised hands, whirling and feeling weightless, the peplum of her dark dress fanning out around her. For a blissful moment her body took over—and that was the beauty of dance, wasn't it?—her body moving to his lead, and her mind for just a little while taking its focus off the purpose of their visit to this place, off the case, off the mystery and the violence in the world. His injured left hand taking her right with surprising ease, Sam spun her out again and she came back, curling into his broad chest. She'd almost forgotten what it was like to dance.

Eyes . . .

There was the feeling again. Billie felt eyes drilling into her, not observing the dance, but *watching* her, just like she'd felt at the arcade. She was pulled from the moment and scanned the dance floor, then the tables beyond, her face dropping as she concentrated.

"Are you okay?" Sam whispered, and Billie saw the question more than heard it. The music had not slowed, and they transitioned into an open hold and moved toward each other, then away in sugar push as Billie nodded that she was fine, but broke again from his gaze to watch the crowd, trying to identify whose stare she felt. Was she being paranoid? Now they were side by side, and Billie followed Sam's backward lock steps, almost in time, and it brought her back to their dance. She had to watch him to anticipate their next move, and that made other preoccupations impossible for the moment. He sent her out in a Lindy whip and she kept her eyes on him, her focus returned, turning, swapping hands, and doing a Texas Tommy. She'd had no idea her assistant could dance like this. He was tall and fluid, yet retained his raw charm; he was naturally elegant but unpolished, never too smooth, never too practiced.

Time flew, and the music's tempo slowed again; the patrons returned to their swaying. Had it been a different crowd, they might have pushed things up a notch to a jitterbug, but not with this set. Billie looked once more for Boucher, for the country couple, the woman in violet, the pale man. None was to be found. She'd spent more time looking at Sam than she'd expected, but the dance had required that.

"I'm impressed. You didn't step on my feet once," Billie quipped.

"And you didn't fall over," he countered, not missing a beat.

She laughed. "Touché." They made their way back to the bar, which was beginning to clear. "My lolly kicks aren't what they ought to be."

"Is that what they call those?"

"I think so," she said. "Barman, can I have some water please?"

"Whatever you want, lovely lady. You dance well," he replied.

Billie smiled at the compliment, though she doubted it was true.

"I haven't danced like that for years," Sam confided, and Billie wondered why. His injury was no real hindrance, she'd noticed. She'd never seen her assistant with his glove off, but he clearly had enough comfort with his thumb and his pinky to guide his partner and keep that hand in play. Surely Eunice would like to dance with him? He was a young man, and dancing was what young people did when they weren't on the front lines, wasn't it? But while other couples had done the Lindy in dance halls, she'd been crawling through bombed-out buildings with Jack, sleeping off long, dangerous nights in strange beds with Jack. Their courtship had involved dancing, but much else as well, not all of it traditional. A photographer and a reporter driven by the same things: The war had brought them together—and ultimately torn them apart, it seemed.

"I'd forgotten what it was like, too," Billie replied. Sam's personal business was his own, and she would do well to forget her personal business in that moment, too. She had to be on the job, not thinking of her husband missing across the seas.

The barman returned with two tumblers of water. Billie took hers, lifted it to her lips, and downed it quickly. Dancing made her thirsty. Sam watched her for a moment, gave her another of his grins, and excused himself to the men's room. Billie watched him go, the white dinner jacket sitting just so on his broad shoulders. She scanned the slowly dissipating crowd. Boucher had been entertaining his guests by this hour the night before. He was unlikely to show now. Perhaps the previous night had been a fluke, or maybe Fridays were his usual routine. His was not a late-night trade. Perhaps it was for the best that he didn't see her again tonight. She wondered what the auction would be like the next day, and if he would be a strong presence there or would prefer to hover out of sight. The real question was why the boy was trying to reach Boucher, if that really was his reason for trying to get into The Dancers.

"Miss . . ." a voice said.

It was the barman. He smoothly delivered a glass of champagne in a delicate coupe, placing it at her gloved fingertips. "Why, thank you, but I didn't order this," Billie protested. She didn't protest too hard.

"This one is on the house," the barman said. "You seem thirsty." His lips curled a bit at the corners, his eyes crinkling. "And it's nearing closing time. It'd be a shame to waste the rest of the bottle, particularly when there's someone like you at the bar."

"You devil," she replied, thinking this wasn't his first time flirting with a customer, and she smiled mischievously in response. "Thank you kindly." She took a sip. The champagne was good. "I was meaning to ask if you knew anything about some boys who came round last weekend, trying to get in. Adin Brown, five foot nine, curly hair? Did you hear anything about that?"

The barman leaned toward her, perhaps closer than was professional. "Like I told your boyfriend, I don't know anything about him. He sounds too young to be coming to this place." It was an honest enough answer, she decided.

"He's not my boyfriend," Billie corrected him, sipping the champagne. It went down beautifully. "And regardless of what you might have to say to anyone else, I was wondering what you thought about it, on the QT. Did those boys cause a bit of a scene? An embarrassment of some sort?"

The barman flicked his eyes to something or someone behind

Billie, and he stiffened, his demeanor switching in an instant. "Look, lovely lady, I wish I could talk to you," he said, "but I have my job to consider. Sorry." He moved away to polish the far end of the bar.

Blast, Billie thought. She turned and scanned the room. She'd thought she had him. Who was it who'd caught his eye?

Sam arrived a beat later, looking cut up about something.

"You didn't give the bartender a cross look, did you?" Billie asked, a touch accusingly.

"No. But guess who I saw in the corridor," he seethed, clearly focused on something else entirely. "That bloody eye-tie."

Billie sighed. This was just what she needed. Sam had what might delicately be called "impatience" with Italians since Tobruk and that AR-4. "You aren't still holding a grudge against the entire population of Italians, are you, Sam?" she responded darkly, and sipped her bubbles.

"Pardon? *You* don't hold anything against them?" Sam snapped angrily. "Against the Japs? The Germans?"

"Look, let's not argue about this. It's late." Of course she had some raw feelings about the Axis powers. Of course she did.

"It takes a nation to support a leader like—"

Billie closed her eyes. "Nazis are a different matter, Sam. Or Mussolini himself. But millions of civilians can't be blamed for wars waged by their leaders. What about those German students, the White Rose resistance, who were hanged, even though they were kids? There were civilians who protested against what their governments were doing, and plenty more who wanted to protest but feared for their lives. Hell, I heard a story today about a Jewish German family . . ." She trailed off, deciding it wasn't important for Sam to know the Browns were a German-born family, not while he was in this state.

"How's that for a betrayal by your own leaders—you aren't worthy of living in your own country because you were born a Jew." After the lead with Con, and some dancing that had unexpectedly made her feel more herself again, the evening was turning to hell, and fast.

"There were plenty of civilians who egged the war on," her assistant said, his body tense as a fist.

"Sam, you're right about that, but it's not that simple." She thought about the pleasurable hours spent with her mother and father in Ciro's Café on Elizabeth Street, Luigi Rosina regaling them with stories between mouthfuls of pasta. She thought of all the Italians she knew in Sydney and how they'd become "enemy aliens," some of them after having fought in the Great War for Australia. Old men, kind men, and their families put into camps. "Thousands of Italians were put in internment camps here after fleeing fascism," she reminded Sam. "Regardless of their age or their health or what they thought of the war, they were put behind barbed wire." She shook her head. "Forget it, Sam. I'll be back," she said, disappointment in her voice.

This was a losing argument. She couldn't blame Sam for the hatred he felt after watching his mates blown to pieces, after what he'd suffered himself. It was far too soon. Or perhaps it would always be too soon. He likely wouldn't be working for her if that Italian thermos bomb hadn't mangled his hand, but still, this wasn't what she wanted in an assistant. *Maybe a black dress is bad luck,* she thought. Or a "midnight" dress.

Not managing to suppress her frown, Billie made for the powder room, where she fixed her Fighting Red and powdered her nose, staring in the large gilt mirror. The person she saw in the reflection was alive with determination: She had a puzzle to solve. There was frustration, yes, but she was alive. It was a bit of the old Billie. The Billie who'd swung into action in Europe. She pulled herself together and found that she knew that face, knew that look. She appeared fresh, despite the hour, and she hoped that by the time she returned to Sam he would have calmed down. She liked her assistant—he was a solid worker and she had no regrets about hiring him—but she didn't want to deal with his Italian issue right now when they ought to be focusing on finding Adin Brown and figuring out his connection with The Dancers.

When Billie returned from the powder room, Sam was not at the bar. She slid back onto her stool and sipped at her champagne, thinking it had perhaps started to go flat. The taste wasn't what it was, and neither was The Dancers. The crowd had almost thinned out entirely; perhaps only a dozen couples were still dancing. Billie took another sip of her drink, swallowed, decided it didn't taste any good, and pushed it away, leaving the last few sips. She and Sam should leave, before they made themselves too obvious, if that ship hadn't already sailed. Had all of the staff been instructed not to speak with her? She thanked the barman from afar, tipped him an extra shilling, leaving it by her near-empty glass, and headed for the door, hoping to pick Sam up along the way.

"We should head out," she said to him when she spotted him loitering near the main doors. She leaned against his arm, her head dipping onto his shoulder. "I got the drinks . . ." She'd slurred her words, she noticed. "I paid up," she tried again, more successfully.

Sam frowned and looked down at her. "Look, I think you might have misunderstood me about the Italian thing . . ." He trailed off. "Billie, I have to say, you look tired."

"Thank you," she replied somewhat sharply, and stood to attention. If he normally had a way with words, it wasn't the case to-night.

"I didn't mean it like that. You just don't seem . . . yourself," he continued, searching her face. "Maybe we should put it off until another night. Or you should let me go instead," he said.

"What are you talking about? Sam, I'm *this* close to finding out why Adin was here before he disappeared." She held her fingers up, an inch apart, to illustrate. "It's the only real lead we have apart from a slip of newspaper. It's something to do with Boooer, I'll bet."

Boooer?

She did feel a bit tired, and a bit unclear, and rather suddenly, too. It was late and it was time to go, but she'd never let a little tiredness dictate when to turn in, or to turn down an opportunity to forward a case. Fresh air would help. That doorman *did* know something. He was nervous and people that nervous often had something to be nervous about.

She'd see him. She'd know something then. And if not, this dress was proving very poor luck indeed.

Eleven

—◊◊◊—

The People's Palace was, suffice to say, not much of a palace. It was a rendered-brick eight-story hotel and lodging house at 400 Pitt Street, boasting VERY MODERATE rooms, in capital letters so it had to be true, with HYGIENICALLY PREPARED MEALS AND TASTEFULLY SERVED FOODS, CLEAN AND COMFORTABLE SLEEPING ROOMS.

For some years the Palace had been under Salvation Army management. Billie was aware that they ran a hostel of sorts out the back, accessed by a different entrance, for those who weren't able to afford the hotel prices. The Victorian-era building had at some time housed a public bath and been a meeting place for swimming teams, thanks to an impressive pool, since filled in and bricked over. Times had changed. There were certainly no athletes meeting here now, and at nearly one thirty on a Saturday night it looked quiet inside, though the streets were still inhabited, mostly with men, some in uniform, evidently trying to find trouble to get into. With so many about, you wouldn't have thought it was already hours after the infamous six-o'clock swill before the public bars closed. In fact, Billie realized she hadn't spotted another woman since they'd left the theater district. The hotel was a mere walk away, not far from Billie's Daking House office and the Central Railway and tramlines. The air was doing her good, even if she didn't care to advertise to Sam that the champagne had really gone to her head, making her feel queer. The idea of her own employee coddling her wasn't acceptable. She was made of stronger stuff than that.

There was a greenish glow to the lighting in the lobby of the Palace, visible through the large front windows as Billie and Sam approached. Billie pushed open one of the main double doors, looked over her shoulder, and caught Sam slipping into the shadows of the street. If she didn't emerge in half an hour he would come up to room 305 to check on her. That was the plan. She knew it was her plan, but her head was starting to ache fiercely, perhaps on account of the hour or that last glass of champagne, and, despite herself, she was starting to regret being there.

Stay sharp, Walker.

The lobby was sparsely furnished with some weathered couches and chairs, a lamp that glowed about as brightly as a single candle, and a table pushed against one wall with what seemed to be brochures propped up on it. There was a sound in an office behind the bell desk, perhaps the stirring of a night watchman who was, at this moment, not doing what Billie would class as a top-notch job. That suited her fine. Otherwise, all was quiet. She looked around one more time with a sweep of her tired eyes, and on realizing that Con Zervos was nowhere in sight she pulled the stairwell door open and started to climb. Her legs ached sharply, and she reminded herself that she just needed to get through the next hour; then she'd be back in her own bed to sleep things off.

Stepping into the corridor on the third level, she encountered yet more quiet, save for the muted sounds of a radio playing in a room nearby and the muffled noises coming from Pitt Street below. The walls weren't cardboard here, she mused; they just didn't sound-proof the new places like this. A light glowed from beneath a door three rooms away. That would be 305, she guessed, but as she approached she saw it was 304. No light showed under the door to 305. Good goddess, she felt tired. So tired. Something was most assuredly not right.

Billie put her hand on the knob of room 305 and the door creaked as it moved. It had not been latched.

A chill went up her spine, and she stepped back, her heavy head clearing instantly with the sense of something being very wrong. Instinctively she reached down, hiked up her dark crepe dress, and pulled the little Colt from her garter. She fixed her finger over the trigger, the mother-of-pearl handle warm from the heat of her thigh. Despite the spinning in her head only moments before, her hands were steady. She put one foot forward and her toe eased the door open.

"Mr. Zervos?" she asked the coal-black room.

There was no answer.

Billie reasoned she might have missed him as he went down to the lobby to wait for her, he going down one set of stairs as she climbed another, but her instincts tossed the notion away. That wasn't what this was. The little woman in her tummy, the little woman who knew things, knew that this was something else entirely. A knowledge that came from every bit of this puzzle that didn't quite fit yet, every observance, every signal. There was a cloying smell in the room that made her feel jumpy, and the heaviness of her head was becoming more distinct, though adrenaline was pushing it back as best it could. She was not safe. What was that smell? It was metallic, like blood or vomit or the sickly sweat of a fever. Someone needed to open a window. She didn't want to walk through that dark doorway, but she needed light.

Billie reached along the wall to her right, her fingers searching like spiders until they found a protruding light switch. She flicked it down. The light came on with a start, illuminating the small single room as a lightning bolt would have done, revealing a diorama of horrors, then going out, plunging her back into darkness, before flickering on again with a faint and steady hum.

Billie did not scream. She did not flinch. She just looked at him.

Con Zervos's uniform was hanging over a chair, but he wasn't in it. He was dressed in a suit with some of the shirt undone, but he was on his back on top of the white bedsheets, his eyes bulging and un-seeing, his tie wrapped tightly around his neck, making everything above it blue. He was looking straight at her, through her, one hand at his neck, the other hanging down at the end of a dangling arm and almost touching the patterned carpet of room 305.

Twelve

———

Waiting for water to boil was nothing on waiting for the police to arrive at two in the morning on a Saturday night at the People's Palace. In the green-lit lobby, Samuel Baker sat next to Billie Walker on one of those threadbare couches she'd spotted earlier and tried from time to time to rouse his boss as she unwillingly drifted off to sleep. The adrenaline had passed and now she felt tired again, and queer, only it was so much worse.

You're going to get me into trouble, lady, Zervos had said. *You're going to get me into trouble.*

Time moved strangely. There were voices, and then nothing, and then she blinked and wondered how much time had passed. The night watchman was confused and sheepish and drifted by at odd moments.

"Lady, we've just been up to 305," someone was saying now. "We don't know what kind of prank you are pulling here but we don't appreciate it one bit."

Billie opened her eyes and focused them with effort. It was a red-haired cop, heavyset and cross, looming over her and staring with green eyes shot with red veins. Watching him was like observing a scene through several layers of foggy glass. She became aware that there were two police officers there. They seemed to have been there for a while.

"Sorry, Officer, what?" Billie replied. Her eyes threatened to close again and Sam elbowed her in the ribs.

"There is no one in room 305 of this hotel," he reiterated curtly. "This Zervos character you're talking about isn't in."

"He's in. He's in all right. He's dead. It's . . . It's terrible. That poor man," she rambled, his anxious words repeating in her mind. *You're going to get me into trouble . . .*

The officer looked at her with utter distaste. "Take her home," he said to Sam, and turned away.

Billie was confused. "I've been waiting for you guys for . . ." She looked at the clock. "Forty-five minutes and you come here and tell me that a dead man has vanished."

"Did you go up there?" The cop was talking to Sam now, ignoring Billie entirely.

"Well, no," he admitted. Billie had instructed him to wait with her downstairs until the police came, though she'd never imagined it would take so long. How many bodies were found in this town on a Saturday night? Scratch that, she didn't want to know.

"There is no one in there. Get her out of my sight," the cop said to Sam, who put his arms under hers and pushed her up. "I suggest you get her to lay off the drink," he added as Sam helped her out of the lobby and into the fresh night air. "It's not good for the ladies. It's biology," she heard him say as the doors swung shut.

Billie was too tired to walk back inside and slap him.

—m—

"Are you sure you don't want me to take you up?" Sam asked at the threshold of Cliffside Flats.

The night air was bracing, Edgecliff quiet. Billie shook her head stubbornly at her assistant's suggestion, though she was swaying on her feet. What a queer feeling she had, the world swimming around her. Sam was frowning and searching her face. "I don't need help. I'm fine," she lied to him, looking away. It was the drink, she was sure now. Those last few sips. They had tasted funny. Something hadn't been right. It was the only way this made sense. Thank goddess she hadn't finished it. But she'd be damned if she let her employee put her to bed, even if it appeared she'd been drugged.

"I'll call you in the morning," he told her, concern in his voice. Billie nodded and let herself into the building, fumbling with the keys, as he watched. The front door shut behind her, locking out Sam and the sounds of the night with him, and her legs burned as she climbed the few stairs to the small lift. She pressed the button and got inside the timber-lined cab, and as the inner door closed she caught a glimpse through the square glass panel of Sam still standing at the front entrance of the building, watching to make sure she got to her floor.

It was half past two in the morning when Billie tossed her keys onto the hallstand and missed. Shaking her head, she began undressing as she approached her bathroom, items of clothing trailing behind her like bread crumbs, first the right shoe, then the left, then an unclipped stocking that her tired brain still couldn't quite leave on the floor. She looked at it with blurry vision. Blasted expensive things. She scooped it up, which took more effort than was comfortable, fishing in the half-light with clumsy fingers. She propped herself against the back of one of the dining chairs to unclip the other stocking and roll it down. The bathroom. She had to get there next. What a horrible night it had been. Horrible and mystifying. And her head felt awful.

Billie removed her makeup haphazardly, her bedtime habits too deeply ingrained to ignore completely. She filled a glass with water and gulped it down, then filled it again. She washed her hands and pulled her cursed crepe dress off before leaving the bathroom. Her head felt leaden, and she was pleased to make herself horizontal on her bed, still wearing her slip and underthings, including her garter belt, its clips dangling around her thighs. Her mother's necklace was heavy on her neck. She tried the clasp and the blasted thing stuck and she gave up, instead pulling the earrings off and putting them both on the nightstand without dropping them. A small triumph. Struggling with the heaviness in her limbs, she shoved her Colt under her pillow, the closest place at hand. It was an effort to climb under the sheet.

She quickly sank into the mattress with a sick heaviness as the room turned darkly under her lids.

Thirteen

—∽—

Dark, dark world.

Through the thin slits of vision his swollen eyelids afforded him, Adin Brown could make out only a mottled film of dark color that shifted and shrank as he tried to focus, the dim light moving as if he were still underwater, still fighting for air, his lungs straining. Yet he could not be in water now; that much he felt sure of. This place was too gritty and dusty, too dry. The air itself hurt his eyes. His body itched and his head throbbed, and under his hand he felt things that were sharp and hard. Was he dead? Was this Sheol, the shadowy land of forgetfulness where he was destined to dwell, or the Hades his grandmama had warned him of? A place without his loved ones, without God?

He ran a hand over his face and found the surface changed, his flesh painful to touch and adorned with grit that fell in clumps. His hands were free, he realized. He was no longer bound; the ropes that had held him were gone and the flesh where they had been was raw. He was no longer in the tub. No longer in that strange room. Had he been freed? Had he really been left to live after seeing the faces of his captors? The face of his interrogator? He turned his body over painfully, stretched out, and kept feeling blindly, reading this new dark place as if by braille. He found something cold like iron, something solid. Did he bring his injuries into death? Should he not be free of pain if he was dead, or was this punishment? As if in answer, ears that had only heard ringing now heard something else—a roar. A deep, powerful roar was building. His hand shrank from the iron and he rolled over, finding more of it with the other hand. Under his body was dirt and planks of wood as well as lengths of iron, he now realized. And something was approaching, something building. The iron under his hand began to vibrate, harder and more urgently. He strained his eyes, catching only faint details. Tracks. Train tracks. He was on train tracks.

And a locomotive was coming.

Fourteen

—◊—

She was right back in the moment.

The cold Vienna sky was red with flames, and they were huddled breathless against a line of low bushes, Jack with his Argus camera, Billie with her notebook and her keen eye, recording every detail. All around them was the violent crashing of glass and crackling of fire, shocking shouts and screams as mobs of civilians and SS soldiers gleefully smashed windows along the street and torched the shops within. All over the city it was the same, ferocious mobs spontaneously joining together—or was it planned, Billie wondered? She'd entered the synagogue briefly, moving with the crowd, Jack at her side, the two of them following the activity when it first began, and, seeing the smashing of the pews and the curtain of the ark torn to pieces, they'd retreated once the mob lit fires and the synagogue had filled with smoke. Now hidden outside, obscured by the row of bushes across the street, they watched as a German soldier in those high leather boots kicked a man of about sixty to the ground just a few feet from where they were hidden. He was in his nightshirt and held his hands aloft, pleading and unarmed, and with horror they watched helplessly, soundlessly, as the man was set upon by angry Austrians, men no fewer than twenty in number, who took turns to viciously kick and stomp, cheered on by the soldier, reducing what had moments before been a human man, wailing and crying out for help, into something Billie had not seen before, something broken and bloody, shattered and pushed into the cobblestones on which they'd stood only minutes before.

She closed her eyes.

Open them. Open your eyes.

Something woke Billie Walker with a start, long before the usual time, long before it was decent for a Sunday morning. It was still dark and the birds were resting their songs. Only the faintest sunlight came into her room. Yet she'd needed to wake. Was it something in her dream? She'd been dreaming of Kristallnacht again, she realized. The Night of Broken Glass.

Billie was no morning person, and on this particular morning her head was heavy, so heavy. Somewhere far off in her mind suspicions were continuing to form about just how tired she was, just how tired she'd been. She could hold her liquor. It wasn't like her to collapse into bed or, conversely, to wake with the dawn. Through the heaviness she detected something out of place, some shift. Breath held, she listened, still prone. Not a sound. Not a movement or creaking floorboard. Something else. She swiveled her head. Her bedroom door had been ajar when her eyes had closed, but the angle was different now, by a few degrees. She grabbed her Colt and sat up, holding it out in front of her. The movement brought a most unpleasant throb to her temples, and, involuntarily, her eyes closed again.

Something . . .

When she forced her eyes open seconds later she found herself awake. A startlingly sober kind of awake, with freight trains running across her nerves. She was not alone. A man was on the floor next to her bed.

With a jump she was up on bare feet, standing over him in her wrinkled slip with her little gun poised in her hands, her finger positioned lightly over the trigger. She was momentarily confused, then lowered the Colt to her side.

Con Zervos, still very much dead, was sprawled on the Persian rug.

Fifteen

—–ᨏᨏ–—

When Billie knocked on the door at the end of the hall one floor up, clad in her peach robe and matching slippers, her hair tousled and the mascara of the night before smudged around one eye, it was Alma who answered. Such was the early hour, the baroness's lady's maid was not yet neatly put together. Her eyes were watery from the rude awakening, and she wore a quilted robin's-egg-blue robe, hastily tied with a sash and buttoned at the neck. Alma's hair was in pin curls, held under a brown net, and her thinly plucked brows were pulled high in surprise.

Billie pushed past her, aware from Alma's expression that her countenance was alarming. She was aware, too, that her hair had not been brushed and had gathered on her head in something like a dark bird's nest. That was unimportant.

"Can you lock the door? I need to see Mum right away," Billie instructed urgently, forgoing niceties. Alma did as requested, unspoken questions on her tongue. "I'll need you, too, I think," Billie added. At this, Alma's already wide-eyed expression exaggerated further. She moved off to Ella's room without a word.

Her mother took some time to be roused. There was little doubt where Billie got her sleeping genes. Billie turned on some lights, then paced around the living room, trying to think the situation over. After what felt like half an hour but was probably closer to five minutes, the baroness emerged in hair scarf and curlers, a satin eye mask pulled up to her forehead and a belted black silk robe embroidered with flowers hanging from her slender form. Her feet were bare, black satin slippers in her hand, and her eyes were unfocused and bloodshot. She had no eyebrows to speak of, having plucked them away when it was the rage.

"Darling, you look a shocker," Ella said automatically, looking her daughter up and down with astonishment and a fair measure of disapproval. Billie resisted returning the compliment. "Really, darling, you look pale as the moon. What time is it?" With a confused expression, she began searching the living room for a clock. "What's all this about? I thought it was lunch we were having. It's practically still dark out. What time is it?" she repeated. "You can't go out like that."

In her days as a war reporter, Billie had seen torn-up soldiers coming out of anesthesia talk with about as much sense as her mother was now. For her part, Alma observed the muddled exchange and walked off to the kitchen. The sound and smell of coffee being ground soon emerged. Wonderful, blessedly clever woman. Though Billie preferred black tea on most occasions, the aroma of strong coffee was quite appealing under the circumstances. She could use a bucket of the stuff at this hour.

"You're wearing the necklace *now*, with . . . that?" It was still around Billie's neck. She distantly remembered having been too tired to manage the clasp at three in the morning. "What do you need your gun for?" Ella continued, now with more clarity, and Billie realized she was still holding the thing at her side, gripped tightly in her right hand. She released her white-knuckled grip and placed the weapon gently on a table.

"Sorry. Mother . . . *Ella* . . . This isn't about lunch today. I have to cancel that anyway. I have to attend an auction, I think . . . Well, never mind that for now." Billie put her hands on her mother's shoulders and looked steadily into her eyes. "There is a . . . problem. I need your help."

"Good goddess, at six in the morning?" Ella broke away from Billie's gaze and rubbed at her eyes. "Alma, coffee, please," she muttered, though Alma could scarcely have heard her from the kitchen and was well ahead of that thought process. "Are you okay?" She looked searchingly at Billie.

"I'm physically unharmed, Mum. Don't worry. I think . . . Well, it looks like I've been set up, and we have scant time to fix the situation. I'm not sure we have time for coffee."

She paused, the reality dawning on her in increments. She'd been drugged at The Dancers. Someone had followed her to the People's Palace, or rather followed poor Con. "Someone is trying very hard to get me out of the way. It must be the new case. Yes, I'm sure of it."

After sharing her life with Billie's father for so many years, Ella was more aware than most—certainly most society women—of the situations people in Billie's line of work might find themselves in. "Set up? How?" she asked, her eyes clearing and that old steely intelligence coming back into them.

"I think you'd better come down and see for yourself," Billie said.

She took her mother by the hand, unlocked the door, peered out, and led her down the staircase toward her flat. As they came out on her floor, she checked the corridor. Everything was unchanged, still dark, still silent, not a neighbor stirring. They crept down the carpeted hall in their slippers. Billie unlocked the door of her flat, looked both ways again, held her breath, and listened. No creaks. No breathing. It was as quiet as a grave. Once satisfied they were alone, she ushered her mother inside and locked the door behind them.

"There is a man in here," she said in a whisper, and moved with her toward her bedroom. They stood at the open door and looked.

"Great Hera!" her mother said simply, eyes riveted to the form on the floor.

"I saw him last night, the same man. Con Zervos is his name. He was just like this, but in his own lodgings over at the People's Palace." The clothes were the same, even his shirt, still partially undone. The main difference was the increasing greenish-blue tinge of his skin. The past few hours had not improved things. "By the time the cops came he was gone and they tried to tell me I'd imagined it," she continued. "Someone must have taken the body before the cops got there. Then I woke up this morning to find him. Someone switched it up so he'd be here in my flat. They moved the body in here while I was sleeping."

She realized what she was saying. Someone had come into her room while she was passed out on her bed in her slip. Billie shivered and wondered fleetingly if she'd ever be able to sleep again.

"You are unharmed?" Ella asked, watching her daughter's face carefully.

"I'm unharmed, just as I was when I fell asleep. Although I was slipped something that knocked me out. No one looted the place, either. Your sapphire earrings are right here . . ." She pointed. "No, they're gone," she realized with another layer of horror. Whoever was here had swiped them, the rat. "I was too tired to get the necklace off. That clasp is tricky . . . but it looks like someone took the earrings. I'm so sorry . . ."

Her mother shot her a look.

"There's no time to worry about that now. We have to worry about *him*."

Even without Alma's coffee, the baroness was now wide-awake. She lifted her chin, her mouth set in a grim line. Her hands went to her hips. "I guess we'd best get rid of him," she said matter-of-factly.

Billie nodded. "Agreed."

"I think we ought to get Alma," the baroness said.

"I think so, too. I'll run up. Don't you touch anything."

The baroness took an exaggerated breath. "Trust me, darling, I have no intention of touching any of . . . *this*," she said, making a circling gesture with an open palm. She backed out of Billie's bedroom.

In a couple of minutes Billie returned to her flat with Alma and a thermos of fresh coffee. Billie poured it into three cups while Alma stared at the corpse on the Persian rug, blanching. Billie had forewarned the dear woman, but the shock made her dry retch and she ran to the bathroom. This was not a good morning for Ella's lady's maid. She liked order and quiet and doubtless didn't like anything about this situation. There wasn't much to like about it in Billie's books, either, especially this close to home.

"Drink this." Billie thrust a steaming cup at her mother. Ella sipped eagerly and seemed to grow a touch taller.

She heard the toilet flush and Alma returned, her face damp and ashen. Billie handed her a cup of black coffee, and after a few sips some color returned. The three women stood in a semicircle looking down at the corpse.

"He seemed a nice man," Billie offered after a short silence. "I only met him twice. I think he was about to tell me something important."

"I'd bet my finest pearls you're right about that," her mother replied. "You've been poking in the right fireplace, my dear."

Billie's initial jolt of adrenaline was subsiding, and now the reality was sinking in. Yes. She had been poking in the right fireplace. Probably the same one Adin Brown had been, which did not bode well for the boy at all. Someone very badly wanted Billie to go down. And they didn't want her to find the boy. It was well past six now. There could be cops here any minute, and if they really wanted to put the nail in her coffin there would be a photographer as well, positioned across the street to catch her humiliating arrest for murder, as she was dragged out of the block of flats at sunup wearing little more than disheveled lingerie while the body of her would-be informant was stretchered out. A very dirty setup. Even if Billie was exonerated by the courts, could prove her innocence, having a corpse show up in her bedroom meant her name would be mud for a long time to come, and there were already too many people who wanted her out of this "man's occupation." Inquiry agents sometimes came across stiffs, of course, but not in their own bedrooms.

"Let's wrap him in the rug," Alma said, breaking Billie's spiraling train of thought. The resourceful woman put her cup down on the floor and got on her knees, her mouth set in concentration. She began to roll the edges of the Persian rug, tucking it around the body like a shroud. After a beat, Ella and Billie knelt down and joined her. "We'll get him to the lift," Alma added.

"Good thinking," Ella said.

They kept rolling.

"He's skinny, at least," Billie said, hoping they'd be able to carry him all the way to the lift and wondering if indeed he would fit inside it cocooned in the rug, which added considerable stiffness and bulk. Her mind churned through the logistics as she worked. She left Alma and Ella to finish the job and roughly made up her bed, put the coffee cups in a cupboard, and tidied things so everything looked as it had the day before, apart from the empty space where the Persian rug had been. There was nothing to do about that, but she supposed anyone who didn't know her flat wouldn't see the difference.

"He looks a lot more like a body rolled in a rug than I was hoping," Ella observed quietly as she and Alma inspected their hand-iwork. "Let's hope we don't run into any neighbors or the next residents' meeting will be hell."

—⁓—

At six thirty on a clear Sunday morning, the three women dragged a suspiciously heavy rolled rug out of the door of Billie's flat, sliding it down the hallway of the second floor, Alma and Billie at the front and Ella taking up the rear.

"Shame," Ella said, panting softly and taking a break from her efforts. "Your father picked up that rug for me at—"

"Not now, Mum. Please. We need all hands," whispered Billie with some urgency.

"Of course," she said and got to work again. "I must say, though, I've seen a dead man before, but I never realized they were so damn heavy."

"Shhh." Deadweight they called it, and it seemed to Billie to be out of all proportion, particularly with this fellow, who for all the world had looked like a featherweight. He'd been pure sinew, muscle, and ribs, the poor man. Billie and Alma were now walking backward. "Mum, you watch the hall behind us; we'll keep an eye behind you. We have to be very, very quiet. No chatting. Okay, it's not too far now. But there's not much time left." They put their backs into it as they moved down the hallway toward the lift. They were but a few feet from their destination when their burden shifted and a foot slipped out the bottom end of the rug.

"Blast!" Ella exclaimed.

"Shhhhh," Billie reminded her. Maybe the stairs would have been wiser? No, too awkward, though the prospect of being seen would possibly be less. "I promise he won't be in your flat long," she whispered, thinking through her plan.

Ella dropped her end again. "*My flat?*"

"Yes," Billie said calmly, in a low voice. "If we go *down* we risk running straight into the cops. We are going *up* . . ." The baroness might not have quite the clout she once did, but Billie felt confident the police wouldn't dare burst into her flat without a very good reason and an ironclad search warrant. Billie, on the other hand, was not protected by a title or her mother's impressive connections.

Ella stared at her daughter, then turned up her nose, closed her eyes, and crouched beside the bundled corpse, evidently having accepted the inevitable. "Do you think your father ever did something like this?" she whispered, stuffing the foot back in.

Billie sidestepped the question. She didn't have an answer to that, though she felt sure her instincts had come at least in part from her father. He'd known a setup when he saw one, and there was zero

possibility he would be sitting around waiting for a knock on the
door after a body showed up in his room.

Reaching the lift, the three women encountered another problem. A horizontal Zervos wouldn't fit in the lift. Billie, Alma, and Ella
were now visibly perspiring, their hair disheveled, and looking suspicious in the extreme.

"We'll have to drag him up the stairs," Alma panted, and her
employer's face dropped.

"But—"

"There's no time to argue," Alma insisted. "We can carry him
together."

"He's too heavy, especially with the rug." Ella stood back,
frowning, and with the back of one elegant hand wiped the space
where her eyebrows should be.

"Wait," Billie said, bending, and unwrapped the rug as if it contained a grim present. She worked to sit the body upright. It was stiff,
rigor mortis having begun, but she could still do it with some effort.
When she was finished, Zervos sat with his back against the wall of
the lift, legs slightly bent, arms unnaturally stiff at his sides. His
mouth was gaping a touch, and the bruises around his neck had
darkened to a deep blue. "There," Billie said, and the doors successfully closed them in. Billie ignored the revulsion of her living companions and pressed the button for her mother's floor. The lift came
to life with a whir of gears. She had never been more grateful that
the building had been designed with an automatic lift, one of the
first blocks of flats to boast such a luxury.

A few agonizing minutes later, the women found themselves in
Baroness von Hooft's flat, breathless and staring at a suspicious-

looking rug with two feet sticking out of it. Bodily decomposition had begun immediately upon death, and this poor soul had passed away at least five hours earlier. Things were not set to improve anytime soon. It wasn't anything like the reek of a field hospital, but the inevitable stench of death was still unpleasant, particularly in such a domestic setting, bringing to mind the rot of putrid flowers and meat. Death, though, had its own distinct odor, and it wasn't something one forgot.

Billie opened all the windows in the flat to let a breeze through, while Alma locked the front door and slid the bolt, then disappeared into the kitchen. Soon Billie was in her mother's boudoir, pocketing the first bottle of perfume she saw and stalking back down the hall. Thankfully, the lift had not moved. She opened the doors, sprayed perfume inside, wafted the air around as much as she could, and closed them again. Truly, there was no dignity in death. She returned to her mother's flat and locked and bolted the door again behind her. Her mother had not moved an inch.

Ella's naked brow was uncharacteristically corrugated, deep lines running up her forehead. Billie offered her an apologetic smile, then accepted a cup of coffee from Alma gratefully, along with a couple of aspirin from the medicine cabinet. After a few minutes she felt the heaviness of her head lifting a little more. A plan began to form. "This will work," she said under her breath.

Her arms were aching, she realized. Her mother and Alma, both much older, would most likely be hellishly sore after that lifting. Had the man been larger, like the portly Georges Boucher, for example, the task might well have been impossible, no matter the necessity.

Georges Boucher. The auction was today. She had to get there.

She couldn't let sleeplessness, or an interrogation with the cops, prevent her.

She moved to the telephone table and was rather surprised when Sam picked up on the fourth ring, sounding quite awake. "I didn't expect you to be up this early," he said when she greeted him down the line. His throat didn't sound the best, but he seemed lucid enough.

"Trust me, neither did I," she replied and cast a sideways glance at her still unmoving mother. She seemed to have frozen in place.

"Are you feeling okay this morning? You seemed a bit . . ." Sam's voice trailed off.

"Yes, I did, didn't I? I'm sorry to do this to you, Sam, but I need you to get dressed again in what you were wearing last night and pick me up in Quambi Place, the street behind Cliffside Flats, in about half an hour."

"Pardon?"

"I'm afraid I need you to dress again and pick me up," she reiterated. "I realize it's inconvenient. I'll spot you when you pull up in Quambi Place and I'll get into the car. Don't bother getting out, and whatever you do don't cruise around the front of the building or down Edgecliff Road, as I think the flats are being watched."

Sam took a moment to absorb her instructions. "Billie, are you okay?" he asked, concerned.

"Can you do it, Sam?" She held her breath while she waited for his answer.

"Well, my jacket is a bit crumpled now. It will take a while to press, and—"

"Don't bother. Crumpled is fine. Just wear it, same as last night.

Can you get here in half an hour, in your car? You know it's important or I wouldn't ask."

There was a pause. "Yeah. I can get there in thirty minutes, or a touch longer."

She had another idea. "Also, do you have a mate you can borrow a motorcar from this afternoon? Someone trustworthy and not prone to gossip?"

"I don't like gossips," Sam said simply, then paused again, evidently thinking. "Stevo isn't driving much on account of having his touch of shell shock. His missus doesn't like him behind the wheel. I could borrow his car, I think."

"Is the car reliable?" Billie ventured.

"Oh yes, his missus drives it. It's solid."

"Good. I'll explain more when I see you."

"Got it, Ms. Walker."

Billie hung up and looked down at herself, then at the clock. "Mum, I'm going to have to borrow some of your clothes. I don't think I ought to go back to my flat now." They'd been lucky to get Zervos out before seven. But if she was right about what her unknown nemesis had in mind, the police would come knocking very soon. They could be there already, searching her place.

The baroness led her daughter into her luxurious, burgundy-painted bedroom. She indicated the double robes with a raised eyebrow, and Billie opened them up. Either from a strong bond with her past or from her current state of relative impecuniosity, Ella's closet was dominated by 1920s haute couture and ready-to-wear fashions. Billie frowned.

"You don't have anything more . . . fashionable?" she asked, somewhat foolishly. She realized her mistake as soon as she'd spoken. "I mean . . . newer?"

Her mother's eyes flared angrily. "That is Schiaparelli, I'll have you know," she said icily, nodding at the exquisite dress Billie had pulled out.

Billie closed her eyes and took a breath. "You're right, Mother. This will be fine." She took off her peach dressing robe and pulled the beaded gown on over her crushed, slept-in slip. The gown did fit beautifully, even if it was a touch shorter on Billie than it was designed to be. It would do.

"Schiaparelli will always be *fine*," Ella retorted.

"I didn't mean it like that, Mum. I meant that it has to look like *my* clothing, not yours."

"And you are more fashionable, I suppose?" Ella responded. "With your mannish clothes and your shoulder pads?"

The baroness crossed her arms tightly as she watched her daughter continue to raid her things. "You know, you used to do this when you were six," she said, softening slightly. Her mother's shoes were a bit tight, but Billie got them on over a pair of dark silk stockings, then assessed her reflection in the mirror. The back of the gown had a lovely plunge. The overall effect with the stockings and slightly tight shoes wasn't perfect, but it would do. She pulled a fox fur over her shoulders.

"I owe you one, Ella. Thank you. You do have the most beautiful wardrobe," Billie said placatingly. She looked around. "I'll need that steamer trunk, too, I think." She indicated the Louis Vuitton double wardrobe trunk stored in a corner alcove.

Ella's eyes followed her daughter's gaze. "Yes, you may borrow it," she said. "But I want it back in good condition," she added primly. Her voice had become a touch stiff and formal, in that irritating way it had sometimes when she had spoken to underlings, back when she'd had them.

"Are you sure?" Billie murmured, deadpan.

Ella gasped, horrified, suddenly comprehending Billie's intention. "Oh no, you don't! You can't put him in there! I've had that trunk for nearly two decades. Haven't you any idea of the value? You could buy first-class passage to London and back for the price of that trunk!"

Billie shrugged, being deliberately naughty now. "We have to get him out of this flat somehow. I suppose we could use your hatboxes, but I dare say it wouldn't be very pleasant. And we'd need to find a saw."

The baroness paled, one delicate hand to her mouth. "You wouldn't really . . ."

"I suppose not," Billie conceded. She had a strong stomach, but, no. She hoped not to add too much more indignity to Zervos's untimely end.

"Okay," Ella said in a resigned voice, looking at the trunk sadly. "Do what you want with the thing. Levi gave it to me. Burn it if you like." Levi had been her first husband. "Thank goddess that poor fellow is skinny," she added.

Billie put a hand on her mother's shoulder, conveyed her gratitude with a look, then got to work.

Sixteen

—⚬—

Billie Walker successfully descended the back fire escape in her mother's beaded dress and fox stole, crossed two property boundaries without soiling her mother's shoes terribly, and was waiting in the shadows of a tree beside a block of flats on Quambi Place, directly behind Cliffside Flats, when her assistant pulled up right on time in his faded blue 1939 Ford utility. She rushed over, yanked the door open, and jumped in.

"Thank you, Sam. I know this is over and above."

Sam put his leather-gloved hand to his forehead. "Oh, you gave me a fright. How do you always manage to do that? I didn't see you."

"That's the general idea." Billie scanned their surrounds. It appeared she truly had been unseen. This was a sleepy Sunday morning for most, and even the keenest folk in the neighborhood were only just beginning to wake up.

Sam took in her appearance, registered the evening clothes and stole, and if he noted her underslept visage he was tactful enough not to comment on it. She had used her mother's makeup and brushes to get herself together, but there was no cure for those bloodshot eyes. Sam, for his part, had dutifully donned his white jacket of the night before, and his formal appearance sat slightly at odds with the rural feel of his vehicle. His clothing did look a touch crumpled, but that didn't matter in the slightest. His large aquamarine eyes searched her face. "Are you okay? What's happening?"

"I don't think anyone is watching us. Kill the engine for a second," Billie instructed, and took a few minutes to get her assistant up to speed with events. He sat listening with rapt attention as she described her groggy head, the discovery of the unfortunate Mr. Zervos in her flat, his removal to her mother's place, and what her plan was. She'd never seen his face darken so angrily.

"Who is this bastard who set you up?" he spat. "And drugged you?"

Was it the bartender who'd spiked her drink? Billie wondered. Surely not. Could someone have walked up to the bar and dropped something in it? And whoever it had been, were they acting alone or following someone else's orders? Had the same person killed Zervos and moved his body?

"I don't know yet, Sam," she answered, "but there is some very dangerous game afoot here. He may be the same person who killed Zervos, and he clearly wants me out of the way, and, by extension, he—or she—wouldn't be keen on you, either. I advise you to watch your back." It was chilling to imagine that a murderer might have been in her room while she slept. A shiver moved up her body from the base of her spine and raised the hairs on the back of her neck. She stifled the desire to physically shake it off and instead pushed her dark hair back and straightened in the seat. External calm often helped muster the internal variety.

"I will watch out. Thank you," Sam responded. He was shaking his head now. "I don't get it . . . Why switch the body to your place? Why not put it where it won't be found for a while?"

"Well, it certainly makes a statement. As a warning to me? To get me tied up with cops and rumors and uncertainty? At least long enough to miss the auction today?" she speculated. "I don't know. Maybe to get me done for murder, but that seems a stretch." She'd been thinking on it but found her faith in the system was not yet so poor that she believed they would actually lock her away. Not for long, anyway. "I mean, what motive would I have?"

"He refused to talk?" Sam suggested.

"So I strangled him? What am I, the Gestapo? No, I'm not convinced a judge would be expected to buy that." She shook her head. "To get the cops to descend and mire me and the case in problems, yes, but an actual conviction? To put me away for murder?"

Was it possible?

"Maybe they had a judge lined up specially for the job?" Sam wondered aloud.

Billie frowned, thinking. Alma's coffee was bubbling away inside her, and she felt sharp with an almost supernatural clarity. The drugs of the night before were no longer filling her mind with that awful mental fog, but it was more than that. The horrifying jolt she'd woken to was still running across her nerves, electrifying her limbs and keeping her heart moving at an unnatural pace. Now her assistant was watching her face, she noticed. "I don't know, Sam," she finally said to him. "At the very least someone wants to warn me off this case, or they want to tie me up with the law so I can't continue working on it."

Yes. A warning. A fear tactic. They thought they could scare her away. Well, they didn't know Billie Walker.

Billie tilted up her chin. "If they think this will put me off, they are dead wrong. I don't know just what we're dealing with yet, Sam, but this is a lot more complicated than we thought. There is something far more interesting and a helluva lot more rotten going on."

—⚌—

When Billie and Sam pulled up in front of Cliffside Flats, the sun was up but most of the residents of Edgecliff were not. Billie could not be sure if anyone was watching, but they made a nice show of their arrival in any event, Sam gallantly pulling up at the curb and walking around to the passenger door of his Ford to help her out with an extended hand.

Soon they saw they were not alone, as a woman who was clearly an early riser—and from the dark looks she was giving Billie, evidently not one to approve of exciting nocturnal activities—walked toward them on the footpath with her miniature schnauzer. She wore a frown as deep as the Grand Canyon. After scowling silently at Billie in her glittering evening clothes, she shook her head and moved along. Sam, it seemed, was not as offensive, as she did not bother to glare in his direction. The diminutive canine took no notice of his master's moral judgments and Billie did her best to follow his lead. She instead made a good performance of wishing Sam a pleasant day in a formal but lighthearted tone before walking up the sloping path toward the entrance of Cliffside Flats.

"Oh, you forgot something!" she called, turning back dramatically before she reached the front door of the building.

Sam shut down the engine, opened the door, and got out of the automobile. "What is it, Billie?" he called, a little more loudly than necessary.

She sashayed back to the street and handed Sam his handkerchief. "Nice work," she whispered. "That should do us well. Thank you." If the cops weren't there to see her arrival, at least it wouldn't have been a performance completely without an audience. It was hardly enough to wake the whole neighborhood, but perhaps some of the more nosy residents of Cliffside would be talking about her over their breakfast. She was already a scandal in their eyes anyway. Billie waved as Sam drove off, presumably to get some overdue sleep rather than to change clothes and start canvassing his friends for a motor vehicle to borrow. She took the opportunity to take one more look around the winding main road, wearing a vague, pleasant smile for the benefit of whoever might be watching her. The birds were becoming louder and the sun was already starting to get hot. There weren't any cops on the street that Billie could detect, not in cop cars in any event, though she didn't recognize all of the parked motorcars. She thought she spotted a dark head in a parked late-thirties Vauxhall, though it could have been a reflection. She walked back to the front door and slipped inside.

When Billie stepped out of the automatic lift a minute later, the constabulary was already standing outside her door, looking about ready to break in. She did hate to be so terribly right about things. At this early hour she was faced with one plainclothes officer and one uniformed constable, both gaping at her as she approached them in her mother's finery. It wasn't the current fashion, wouldn't have been the current fashion just before the war, either, but few men would know the difference—she hoped.

"Good morning, Officers," Billie called, swaying over to them, beads flashing. "That's my door you're knocking on. How may I help you gentlemen?"

Even after two hours of hellish morning it was still before eight. On a normal Sunday she wouldn't be awake until at least nine, and certainly she would have expected to rise later than that after a night out.

Billie smiled at the two men—her even, pretty smile with hidden steel behind the ivory. The heavyset constable, with a long brow and a thin face like the wedge of a hatchet, was someone she vaguely recognized, but the other, taller man had not crossed her path before, she felt sure. He had doffed his hat for her as she appeared in the corridor. A gentlemanly type. He was about six feet in stature, broad-shouldered and rangy, and under other circumstances she would have found him fairly handsome, with his strong jaw and honest face. He had pale eyes and paler lashes and his brown hair was shorn in a neat military cut, short except at the top, where it was smoothed down into a side part. His blue suit was nicely fitted but worn. The suit of a man who thought about other things. The silk tie had a bird pattern in burgundy and ivory, with hints of sky blue. Not bad. His fedora had a welt edge and was held in large but elegant hands. Overall, he was neatly put together and perhaps ten years older than Billie. Either that or the little creases by his eyes had been earned in the war and he was in his early thirties yet. Hatchet Face didn't require much inspection. He was a little over Billie's height but about three times her girth. Sausage fingers. A face set in a permanent frown. Aged in his twenties, he was a tough-guy underling, eager to prove his mettle. A dime a dozen in this town. She was sure she'd already made his acquaintance on some job or other and had not been impressed.

"Miss Walker? We're sorry to disturb you, but I see you are already up," the tall one said without too much sarcasm, which was admirable in the circumstances. "I'm afraid we'll need you to show us your flat."

"It's Ms.," Billie said, sliding past him and unlocking her door.

"Pardon?"

"Ms. Walker. Never mind." Billie stepped into her flat and slid the fox fur off her bare shoulders, noting the way the movement drew their eyes. "May I see your identification please?" she asked, poker-faced. She put one hand out, the other resting on her curved hip.

"Lady, we could have busted your door down if we wanted to," Hatchet Face piped up impatiently.

"Well, I see you did not. I'm most grateful to you," Billie replied and smiled again. "Identification, please."

Both men seemed taken aback, and then the tall one flashed her his wallet without a fuss. She took it, held it, and read. *Detective Inspector Hank Cooper*. She looked him over, head cocked.

"Hank. Is that American?" she asked.

"My mother was American," he replied with a crease in his brow, retrieving his wallet. His pale eyes had grown a touch larger. Were they green? Hazel, with shots of green and yellow, Billie decided.

She took her eyes off his and looked at the constable's ID casually, then handed it back. *Constable Dick Dennison*. "To what do I owe the honor of this visit, Detective Inspector?" she asked the tall one. She considered slipping those blasted tight shoes off but resisted.

"If you could not touch anything, we shouldn't take too much of your time," the inspector said. He was all hard and professional now, as if remembering what he was there for.

"Tea? Coffee?" she offered.

They ignored her and began to look around. The constable

walked into her bedroom. She heard wardrobe doors opening and closing. After a minute he walked back out.

"What brought you here, exactly?" she asked.

"You've been out all night?" It was the tall one asking the question.

"I'm afraid so," she said. It wouldn't be great for her reputation, but the alternative was less appealing, so to hell with appearances. "I don't make a habit of it, but I closed an important case last week and it's taken till now to get the time to celebrate. I was out with my secretary—or I guess you could call him my assistant."

He absorbed that. It was hard to gauge what he thought of it, now that he'd recovered his professional veneer.

"Perhaps you've met him? Samuel Baker. He was one of the Rats of Tobruk: 2/23rd Battalion, 26th Brigade, 9th Division. Where did you serve?"

He sidestepped her question. "You're a private inquiry agent, I take it," he said.

She nodded. Hatchet Face continued his bumbling around in the background. He was in her bathroom now.

"An anonymous call about something, was it?" she pressed.

"Yeah," Hatchet Face replied, emerging. His jaw was pushed out, his eyes small. He wasn't as good at veneers.

"It must have been a trusted source to bring a detective inspector out so early," Billie added casually.

"Yeah," the constable grunted.

"Anonymity isn't what it used to be, I guess," Billie commented.

Silence hung heavy in the air. The inspector stood by the closed front windows, observing the exchange, his hands in his pockets and those pale eyes of his not missing a thing. Hatchet Face began bustling around again, now with even less grace, opening and closing cupboards in the kitchen and making a show of things, as if he hadn't already failed to see what was supposed to be there waiting for them, clear as day.

Billie walked to the large front windows and peered down at the street. Her flat was at the farthest northeastern corner of the building, providing a good vantage point for watching the passing traffic on Edgecliff Road below. A block or so back from the driveway of Cliffside Flats was the parked Vauxhall. Yes, there was someone in that car, she sensed. Perhaps the same person who'd tailed her that day to the Browns' fur shop in the Strand Arcade. How did that fit into the picture? "The Vauxhall down there. He one of yours?" she asked the detective inspector casually.

"The Vauxhall?"

"Yes. I think there's someone watching the building."

"Not one of ours," the inspector said with ease, but she sensed Hatchet Face, who'd returned to the living room, stiffen.

Billie turned a dining room chair around and sat down. "The offer of tea still stands," she said to the inspector. "Or coffee."

"No, thank you, miss," he replied, folding his arms.

"Are you a recent transfer?" she ventured. "I don't believe I've heard your name before. Do you know Special Sergeant Lillian Armfield? Please pass on my regards if you see her. I owe her a call."

Detective Inspector Cooper wasn't biting. He'd closed up like a clam. A polite clam, but a clam nonetheless.

Hatchet Face was scowling and looking flushed. "Didn't you call in a stiff last night?" he asked gruffly.

"That I did, Officer." She threw one arm over the back of the chair and looked at him, wondering where he'd go with it. "At the People's Palace."

"Then you went out on the town after that? Geez, you dames are wacky. Seeing a stiff makes 'em all excited," he said to the other man, as if he needed an audience, all the while laughing at his own joke.

"Don't tell me you never take a drink after coming face-to-face with a stiff?" Billie queried with a level gaze, and the grin dropped from his face like a lead bubble. The inspector exhaled suddenly from his position by the window. She didn't look at him. She kept her gaze on Hatchet Face, but he wouldn't look at her now. His skin had turned beet red and he was clenching his fists harder than a pauper grips a coin. Given different company, one of those fists might have tried landing on her.

"There wasn't anyone there, anyhow," the constable managed after a moment of recovery, his repartee delivered with less confidence now. "This one just *dreams* of stiffs," he announced. That got him chortling to himself again. He was a regular one-man show, and his own audience. The inspector kept watching.

"I did not imagine it, Officer. He was there in his room at the Palace," Billie said earnestly. Her sincerity was wasted on the constable, though the inspector was watching her carefully, in silence. "A dead person is not something one *imagines*."

"What were you doing there, in some man's room, anyway?" It was Hatchet Face again. He really had it in for her. She'd like to know why.

"His name was Zervos," she explained in a professional tone. "Con Zervos. He worked as a doorman at The Dancers on George Street, off Victory Lane, and he wanted to talk with me, just like I told you coppers last night. It was late because it was after he got off work. The Dancers closes at one."

"You accept a lot of invitations up to men's rooms in the middle of the night?"

Billie let that ride. "Are you finished here, or do you want to go through my panty drawer?" she asked him.

"I think we're finished," the inspector said, seeming to have seen and heard quite enough. "Thank you for your time, miss. Sorry to have bothered you."

She stood and handed the inspector her business card. "If you need to ask me any questions, you know where to find me. I'll be here or at my office in Daking House. I was not making up what I saw last night, Inspector. I don't know what brought you here today, but I'd surely like to know."

He turned her card over in long, elegant fingers.

"Helluva thing, a pretty dame like you mixed up in a business like this," Hatchet Face said. He just couldn't shut up. Billie's patience had worn thin. He turned to the inspector and added, "Her pop was a private dick, you know. Barry Walker. He was a copper once, too. Poor bastard would be turning over in his grave right about now," he said, looking at her with small, glinting eyes. "His own little girl . . ."

Billie felt her temper rise, nearly get the better of her. Her face felt warm. A few seconds ticked over while she resisted his bait, resisted her fury. Bringing her late father into it was low. "Well, if you're finished with me, I could use some beauty sleep," she said with an effort, using that professional smile again. She walked to the front door and put her hand on the knob. "Good day."

Once the men were in the hallway she closed her door unceremoniously. The constable knew who'd called the police. Maybe the inspector did, too. She found herself at the window, catching sight of the pair as they made their way down the sloping drive to the road and back to their motorcar. She'd have to pay a visit to that detective inspector, she thought, watching him. To her surprise, he broke away from his partner and approached the Vauxhall parked down the curved street. Before she knew it he was leaning over the driver's side, talking to someone, while Dennison hung back. The constable shook his head and kicked at the footpath, as transparent as a child. After a short exchange, the car door opened and a man got out, reluctantly, it seemed.

Well, well, what do we have here?

Billie Walker recognized him. It was another private inquiry agent. Vincenzo Moretti was his name. He was rumored to be involved with the Black Hand or the Camorra, secretive Italian-Australian criminal gangs known for extortion rackets and violence, a rumor Billie had always found convincing. He had hated Billie's father with a passion and her father had warned her about him. Something about his days as a cop, but she didn't know the details. He had given Moretti some trouble and Moretti never stopped giving it back, it seemed. Rival PIs didn't always get on, naturally enough, but it wasn't as if there was so much dough in the biz that it was worth trying to make trouble for other agencies. No, his hatred for Billie was different, inherited. Something personal. And now here Moretti was, parked outside her flat at eight on a Sunday morning. And what an interesting morning to be there.

Down on the street the conversation had finished. Moretti was getting back into his Vauxhall, his shoulders sloped, and the tall inspector had made his way back to Dennison. Before they slipped out of sight, Inspector Cooper looked up and caught Billie at her window. She couldn't read his face.

—⁓—

It was two hours later when Sam came around in a Ford Prefect with a luggage rack, perfectly suited to the task. As instructed, he was wearing a suit, a pair of round glasses, and a tan cap low on his head, not for all the world the man who had been at the same address just a short time earlier. He disappeared into Cliffside Flats and emerged with a late-middle-aged woman in a cloche and a loose-fitting, drop-waisted light tweed coat. He held her gently at the elbow and helped her into the waiting car before loading her many suitcases. One was a large, heavy trunk.

Twenty-five minutes later, interested onlookers would have noticed Alma McGuire, lady's maid to Baroness von Hooft, entering Cliffside Flats, seemingly returning from a Sunday morning stroll. Only the keenest of observers would have spotted that her walking shoes looked remarkably similar to those worn by the woman with the cloche.

Seventeen

—◦◦◦—

It was the start of an uncertain afternoon, the follow-up to a surreally unpleasant morning, and the street in Paddington where Billie and Sam stood was a visual feast of Rolls-Royce and Cadillac limousine automobiles delivering what to Billie appeared to be Sydney's most wealthy and chic citizens. She observed her surroundings as if through a telescope, at a distance, the display so blue-blooded, so polished and civilized, it hardly seemed to be from the same world she'd woken to. Here the well dressed arrived by way of uniformed chauffeur and were escorted by men in crisp suiting through the open double doors of a two-level historic sandstone building. Billie spotted an understated sign with delicate gold filigree lettering set against a deep black background hanging by the doors, confirming that they had indeed found the location of the auction house mentioned in the advertisement to which Adin Brown had evidently taken such exception.

GEORGES BOUCHER AUCTION HOUSE, it said.

She looked the building over as they approached. Iron gate, presently open. Perfect green hedges. Trimmed topiaries. A modestly sized well-kept garden of traditional English flowers. Like many of Sydney's older establishments, it was tightly nestled between other buildings of a similar vintage. This one had that immaculately kept and tastefully understated look that seemed always to guarantee extortionate prices. Though Billie could handle herself in almost any social circle, she felt more like an interloper than usual, particularly on this day, which had started in so undignified a manner. A nap, several large cups of tea, and a vigorous shower had restored her sufficiently for the afternoon's auction, something she had no intention of missing, particularly if the unfortunate setup that morning had been concocted to ensure that she did not darken the doorway of this particular establishment.

"Well, this is toff central," she heard her assistant mutter under his breath as they strolled arm in arm toward the moneyed throng. "Sorry, Ms. Walker," he apologized almost immediately, doubtless recalling that her mother was a baroness.

"Not at all, Sam. This is, as you say, toff central," she agreed and smiled warmly at her companion, who had today gone well and truly above the call of duty. *I guess I'm half-toff,* she considered, thinking of her socially mismatched yet perfectly romantically compatible parents, and wishing for the moment that her bank account reflected her toff side a touch better. This was the kind of setting where one noticed just how little power and wealth one possessed. But she was far luckier than most and she rarely forgot it, not after all she'd seen. And she was certainly luckier than poor Con Zervos, who deserved so much better than the card he'd been dealt—one she hoped young Adin Brown had not also found himself holding.

Men in expensive tailoring and women in custom-made dresses and fanciful millinery passed them. Lustrous pearls and gems glittered and shone in the sunlight, worn on ears and fingers and over gloves on frail wrists. Shoes were shined and spotless, as if unmarred by anything as lowly as ground or footpath. Sam had parked in the alley at the back, and that seemed particularly prudent considering his Ford utility spoke more of rustic charm than of old money. Billie gave him a nod and they moved between the trimmed hedges and through the open gate toward the crowded entrance of the auction house. They made an attractive pair and were noticeably younger than most of the crowd, many of whom were elegantly silver-haired beneath their homburgs, bowlers, jeweled turbans, and cartwheel hats.

Sam was wearing his good light wool suit of French navy, which she'd had made for him, a complementary necktie of browns, navy, and lighter blues chosen to match his light eyes, and a brown leather belt and brogues, the latter not entirely broken in. The outfit had often been deployed for the courtroom. Between his black tie the night before, the pin-striped suit he wore at the office, his retired army uniform, and what he was wearing today, this was likely close to the entirety of Sam's wardrobe, she reflected.

Billie herself had made particular sartorial effort this afternoon, wearing a square-shouldered but feminine dress in light gray with a shining hunter-green silk edge and carefully tied silk bow at the waist, teamed with matching hunter-green gloves. She'd made it from a Vogue Couturier Design pattern, and as with all her homemade garments, it had been time-consuming, but the resulting fit was immaculate. It fell just below the knee, with an A-line skirt that allowed Billie's desired range of movement without wasting unnecessary fabric coupons. A small raffia and silk topper sat at an angle over her dark wavy hair, a thin black veil covering one eye and skimming her cheekbone, and a pair of round, darkly tinted glasses completed the look, along with a faux-pearl brooch and earrings. The hemline and midheight heel were just right for daywear, but the textures were strategically luxurious. The silk Billie had used was a beautiful weight and had been saved from before the war. Meanwhile, her near-black crepe dress of the night before was relegated to the back of the laundry cupboard, possibly to become dishrags in the near future.

Billie straightened her shoulders. "Into the lion's den?" she suggested playfully.

"Into the lion's den," Sam replied. "And I must say, you look a picture." He tipped his deep brown fedora to her. He looked the part himself. You'd never have thought he'd spent his morning sneaking a dead body around in a trunk.

Up a couple of sandstone steps and they were in, moving across Persian carpets and passing ornate antiques, the air in the auction house cooler than on the street and scented with freshly cut flowers in baroque vases and, beneath that, the aroma of furniture polish. Guests were milling about, exchanging small talk and sipping refreshments. Printed catalogs were offered, and Billie took one. The walls on all sides were draped in heavy velvet curtains, giving the impression they might be drawn back at any time to reveal some unseen marvel. There was a podium on a small raised stage at the front, with perhaps two dozen folding chairs set up to face it. On the stage and all around it were what appeared to be priceless objects of all sizes. Through a door on the left, aproned and white-gloved staff came and went carrying still more treasures. The guests were of at least as much interest as the wares on offer, Billie mused, and it seemed she was not the only one to think so, as several patrons openly looked at her as she discreetly surveyed the assembly. Fleetingly, she wondered how many of this crowd knew one another. It did seem to be quite a clique. Perhaps this was part of what made her presence of interest—she and her companion were not regulars.

Most of the women in the room wore fur of some type, Billie noticed, many favoring imported fox stoles, glass eyes staring out from the creatures' stuffed heads. Would business pick up for the Brown family if the fashion kept up? Rationing and the restrictions on luxury items had evidently not impacted this crowd too greatly. Had any of them shopped at the Browns' shop? Met Adin? Billie took note of faces, filing them in her formidable memory bank.

"Let's sit," she suggested.

They moved to chairs at the end of the fifth row. Billie handed Sam the auction catalog and asked him to look for the items advertised in the clipping Adin had ripped out while she continued to survey the crowd.

In front of them a man in a three-piece suit with bow tie moved to the podium, and the din of the crowd subsided. "Please be seated. The auction will begin shortly," he announced, conducting himself in a sedate and formal manner that wouldn't have been amiss in a mortician.

Sam looked up from the catalog. "Do you want me to get you anything before things get started?" he asked quietly.

She pulled her dark glasses off and locked eyes with him. "I don't think we'll be needing a paddle," she replied. This auction was too rich for her blood, at least on her father's side, but looking at the crowd, only half of whom were carrying paddles, it didn't seem out of place to watch.

"Champagne?" he suggested, nodding toward the servers who were circling with their silver trays.

"Never again," she countered and shifted in her seat. "Well, not this week anyway."

The next ninety minutes passed uneventfully in the numbingly lavish room, the pieces on auction coming and going until they blended together in one decorative procession, unreachable for Billie's bankbook. There was no sign of Adin Brown, even as the carved sideboard that featured in the newspaper advertisement was displayed and sold. The portly Georges Boucher mingled selectively, greeting favored customers, then disappearing into the mysterious realm beyond the black curtains. Billie looked for the couples he'd been with at The Dancers but did not spot them.

Perhaps it was the strange twenty-four hours she'd had, but attending the auction gave Billie strongly conflicting feelings about family, wealth, and property. She couldn't help but speculate that some of the pieces represented the downfall of once-great families, or the passing away of loved ones whose most beloved possessions were no longer valued by the living, except as objects to fetch a price. There was, for instance, the strangely heart-tugging sale of a Victorian writing box embellished with silver and mother-of-pearl inlays and engraved with the name Rose Cox. Within the velvet-lined box was a card inscribed "In Loving Remembrance" of one Rose Hannah Caroline Klimpton, no doubt the girl's married name, who'd "Died September 1, 1897, aged 26." How had this found its way under the hammer? Such occurrences were not rare, Billie supposed, but something about the sadness of the discarded writing box and its once-cherished owner almost compelled Billie to purchase it. Auctions were places of loss or discovery, depending on which end you sat.

"Are you okay?" Sam asked in a low voice. He'd clearly felt, if not actually seen, her tense ruminations.

Billie hoped her mother would not soon be forced here, parting with more of her possessions out of desperation rather than choice. And yet, after the war, what did possessions matter except to feed and to clothe and to ensure a roof over one's head, if even for another day?

Billie was distracted from her reverie by the movement of those heavy velvet curtains. A black-and-white–clad staff member was slipping through a parting in the all-enveloping drapes around the room, and Billie caught a glimpse of an open door beyond, and a man with his back to the door, his hair as white as snow. The heavy fabric slid back into place and the vision disappeared.

"And here we have lot 664," the auctioneer announced.

Sam pointed to the open catalog, and he and Billie exchanged a look. This was one of the other pieces shown in the advertisement, a necklace. The auctioneer described it as a rare Art Nouveau piece by the jeweler Georg Kleemann, crafted in silver and featuring opals, freshwater pearls, blue lapis lazuli, and purple amethyst. What made it stand out most, however, was the batwing shape of the main part of the intricate pendant. Kleemann, the auctioneer explained, had been a well-known figure around the turn of the century, working in Germany in the Jugendstil style. Was this something that had caught Adin Brown's interest? Or was it simply the auction house name, Boucher's name, that he had reacted to? Billie cast another look around the room and strained to look back at the entrance. There was no sign of the boy. If he was present, he was well hidden. But then, it was a room of hidden things. Billie longed to get behind those curtains.

An auction house employee in an apron and white gloves began walking through the audience, showcasing the necklace, which was pinned elegantly within a velvet-lined frame, to anyone who indicated interest. Several people signaled almost invisibly to him and, observant as all auction house staff were trained to be, he moved smoothly over to them. None of them was familiar to Billie, and she felt sure they had not been at The Dancers either of the previous two evenings. The piece shone in the lights as the auctioneer spoke of the luster of the pearls, the glitter of the amethysts, and the estimated vintage of 1907, the Art Nouveau movement's peak. As the employee came down their side of the room, Billie raised a finger and he came over. It was indeed a beautiful, very unusual piece of jewelry, something she could imagine the French actress Sarah Bernhardt might have worn. She asked to see the back, and gloved hands turned it for her. Signed on the reverse were the initials GK in a cartouche and the number 935, signifying sterling silver. Two more people called the man over to inspect the necklace, neither of whom Billie recognized. Paddles were raised, money was bid, then, just like that, it was gone. Twelve hundred pounds. That was enough to kill for, certainly, but was that why Con Zervos had died? Money was, after all, one of the primary motivations for murder—part of the triad completed by jealousy and power. But how did that fit in here? With Adin and Con?

After several further pieces did the rounds—rare mantel clocks and pearl necklaces—the lot of rings from the advertisement came up, recognizable by the large Victorian men's gold ring, set with three round-cut gems—a cognac diamond, a blue sapphire, and a second cognac—that was the advertised showpiece item. Billie called the rings over, examining the Victorian ring and the write-up for it: "One Round Genuine Sapphire weighing approximately .12 cts. and two round Genuine natural brown Cognac Diamonds totaling approximately .20 cts. Total Gem weight approximately .32 cts. Provenance unknown."

Again nothing unusual appeared to be at play. Perhaps the clipping had been a red herring after all?

Nothing fitted. Surely Zervos hadn't had the rings or necklace or, for that matter, the sideboard shown in the advertisement. He hadn't had much at all, and now he was dead, along with whatever he might have been able to tell Billie. Adin didn't seem to be at the auction, either to bid or to steal. No, the puzzle was still moving, the pieces not yet coming to rest in their logical places.

What about Boucher himself? Could his name alone have been enough to set the kid off? Was it an argument over a love interest? The girl in violet who had seemed too young, out of place at Boucher's table the other night? Was it only a coincidence that Boucher had been at The Dancers, a place Adin evidently was desperate to get into?

Eighteen

———※———

"Do you believe in luck, Sam?" Billie asked.

"Luck? Well, I suppose some people have it."

The sun was lowering in the sky as they finally made their way out of the rarified atmosphere of Georges Boucher Auction House, the lengthening shadows turning to cool semidark around them as they rounded the corner into the alley behind the sandstone building where Sam's utility was parked. The experience had not been without interest, but Billie did not consider herself much better informed about the case at hand, and the feeling of all that money clung stiflingly to her. Her quiet inquiries about Adin Brown with the staff after the auction had brought up precisely nothing. Lips were sealed, almost suspiciously so, and any attempt to slip behind the curtains had been thwarted with so many workers around. Somehow, Billie was unsettled by it all. She felt dirty, as if she needed to wash off the place. And she felt deeply, truly exhausted.

"I don't think I believe in luck," she said. "But some days . . ."

Perhaps the inky-hued dress had not been the bearer of bad luck, as her mother had suggested. Perhaps it was Billie herself who was bad luck. This had not been a fine day for B. Walker, Private Inquiries. And in a few short hours her assistant would have the unpleasant job of unpacking that heavily burdened travel trunk so poor Con Zervos could be found by the authorities—but nowhere near the flat of Baroness von Hooft or that of her PI daughter. Billie hadn't asked Sam where he'd stored the trunk while they were at the auction. Perhaps it was still in his mate's car. Hopefully it was somewhere cool, she reflected darkly.

Her mind went to the extreme contrast between that poor doorman, treated little better than vermin and dumped on her rug, and all the wealthy people gathered inside the auction house, treated like royalty and offered refreshments on silver trays as they bid on fine art and sparkling jewels. She pondered their various reasons for wanting the paintings and sculptures and glittering necklaces and rings on show. There were some beautiful things there, some masterpieces even, but also the strong scent of competition. How else could one explain so many people eager to be *seen* buying?

"All that money . . ." Sam muttered under his breath, his mind clearly running over some of the same themes.

He had seemed struck by the immense wealth in the room. Coming from the country, he likely hadn't seen wealth and privilege quite so concentrated before. Billie, on the other hand, had seen it before, albeit in a different setting, and had grown cynical. Where were all those "friends" who had populated her mother's social life before she'd had to sell the Potts Point mansion and move to a flat? Where were they when she lost her PI husband? Where were they now that she'd sold her baby grand to make ends meet? Ella maintained some impressive social contacts, but many had fallen away like rats from the proverbial sinking ship as her fortunes had gone down. And that's what they were. Rats.

"Some people did rather well out of the war," Billie mused. "And all those dead deserved better." She shook her head sadly. The dead were almost invariably the poorest, the ones with the least political and social power. It had always been thus, with powerful men pulling men and boys from their communities and putting them on the front lines while they smoked cigars and made deals and decisions from a safe distance. "I suspect wars wouldn't be nearly so common if no one made money from them," she added, and Sam turned to look at her.

It was hard to know what Sam thought of such a brutally honest statement, considering his great sacrifice. But war could not be separated from the pursuit of power, wealth, and territory. Hitler had his lebensraum push for a Germanic takeover of foreign territory and the annihilation of populations he considered *Untermenschen*. The Allies would have lost everything had he not been defeated, and casualties were devastatingly high, but there were still those who did well out of the whole deadly debacle. Just who they were was not yet clear, but they were out there. There was newfound wealth in America and Switzerland, she'd heard. And there was the rumor that the Australian government was going to call in all existing bank notes and reissue new notes, making the old ones worthless. This would flush out cash that had been hoarded during the war—especially cash made by black-market racketeers. Some of the auction houses would be doing very nicely with all that cash people were so desperate to part with. Just how well was Georges Boucher doing?

"Is that what you mean about luck?" Sam asked, puzzled.

Something caught Billie's eye, distracting her from her thoughts.

"Is that a Packard?" she remarked, recalling Shyla's description of the foreign man's car. She turned and stopped in her tracks. Sam was some paces ahead of her now, aiming to open the door of his car for her, when an arm grabbed her from behind, gripping her waist.

What the . . . A small gleaming knife appeared at her smooth right cheek. A switchblade, held by rough, masculine hands. The nails were dirty, the shirt cuff tattered. She could smell male sweat and feel a heart beating against her shoulder blades. Billie absorbed this sudden turn of events and took a slow, measured breath, shifting gears internally. The world slowed down. She bent forward carefully, tilting her head away from the sharp, shining blade, and pushed her buttocks into the man who held her tightly against him. Having expected her to struggle forward, away from his body and not toward it, the assailant loosened his grip on his blade a touch, his wrist slackening. Billie continued to bend forward and stretched out both hands as her head moved closer to the grubby footpath. Seizing the man's left leg, she wrenched it forcefully off the ground, pulling up and forward, cradling his foot to her chest. She heard a seam of her carefully sewn dress tear, followed by the more satisfying sound of her attacker falling backward with an awkward thrashing movement. She leaped out of the way, letting go and momentarily free before a second assailant grabbed at her leg and she went down on one knee, feeling a stocking tear irreparably. Now she was cross. Very cross indeed.

"This is our way of saying *lay off,*" a gruff voice said, and as Billie lifted her eyes she felt a kick in the ribs, a vicious blow. In that moment, punctuated by pain, she snatched a view of a flabby face, a flattened profile. The two legs beside her were clothed in grubby chocolate-brown slacks with a slightly tattered hem. Not so unlike the pants of the man she'd yanked off balance, but those had been a tatty dark blue. Unremarkable leather shoes, low-end. The grabby man she'd toppled would be getting to his feet soon. And he would be cross, too. "Next time I cut your pretty face," the close one with the flat nose added convincingly, as if he knew a thing or two about how that worked.

Billie elected to stay down, huddling protectively while the screaming in her kicked ribs subsided. She waited for the next move to reveal itself and from the corner of her eye saw Sam, next to his car, catch a strong punch in the kidneys by a second set of assailants. It had all happened so quickly, so unexpectedly. Sam went down swinging, but he went down. "Four of you. Seems a fair fight," Billie managed from her position on the ground, pulling a hatpin from her topper and swinging it at the closest man's ankle, pushing all three inches of it through his unmended black sock into the soft space between his ankle bone and heel and out the other side. He howled like a dingo and doubled over. She withdrew the hatpin and jumped to her feet, her raffia-and-silk tilt hat sliding off.

"You!" he shouted at her lamely, purple with humiliation and grabbing at his wounded ankle. He was so shocked that she had time to kick him roundly in the arse with one heeled foot, and he fell forward between two cars, letting out a string of expletives, trying unsuccessfully to regain his balance. It was one of her less elegant moves, but effective. If this wasn't a time for dirty fighting, she didn't know what was.

Billie turned and glared coldly at the other man, who was ready for his attempt at a comeback. She stood with her feet apart, the hatpin held in her hand like a dagger. While she waved it in front of a scarred face that looked like a piece of meat with two eyes in it, her other hand lifted her torn dress inch by inch. The eyes went from the hatpin to her knee, and then her thigh and the top of her stocking with its pretty lace-edge holster, and then the barrel of her mother-of-pearl-handled Colt, now neatly in her hand and pointed squarely at him. Just above that barrel were her piercing green-blue eyes. He knew better than to move, or even breathe.

"Look, lady, I don't want any more trouble," he managed after a moment.

"What an unfortunate choice of profession you've made in that case," she remarked, her hand still steady on the gun. She got the impression this was a young man, despite the head on him. His suit was shabby and threadbare at the elbows. Like the other one, he looked underfed and overbeaten. This was some nasty line of work he'd chosen. And he wasn't very good at it.

The man who had kicked Billie was up now, standing on one leg like a cowardly flamingo and shuffling artlessly behind his small colleague. How considerate of them to stick together in a neat little cluster of stupidity for her to point her Colt at. They'd picked her as an easy target, clearly, as these two men were thin and about as smart as a pair of spoons. The two boys who had gone to work on her strapping assistant were larger and possibly more capable, though. She didn't want to take her eyes off either of the gormless goons at the end of her gun. From the corner of her eye, however, she saw something large that looked like a sack of potatoes in a bad suit sail through the air into a line of garbage bins with a thundering crash. There were groans and cries and none of them in Sam's voice. Billie felt more than saw that he was now up and in control and could sense the rage coming off him. He was moving quickly, a blur of navy, and now he had someone by the throat, pinned to a brick wall. She risked a glance, her attackers also temporarily distracted by the action on the other side of the alley. Yes, Sam was holding a man up with his injured left hand. It seemed not to be slowing him down, Billie thought. Not one bit. Not in a dance hall or in an alley. His right hand was pulled back, ready to strike. She fancied her own assailants looked a touch awestruck. She watched them over her Colt and heard a crunch as Sam struck again. It must have looked grisly, for their eyes widened and they began backing away.

"How about you fellas tell us about your employer, hey?" Billie said loudly enough to grab their attention and for Sam to hear. They froze in place. Sam looked over his shoulder at her, seemed impressed by what he saw, and let his right hand relax a touch. It was then that she noticed that the man he was holding didn't have his feet on the ground. The body lying among the garbage bins moved a little and there was a groan; then all was still again.

Billie took a step toward her two assailants. "Come on, now, gentlemen. I want to hear some information, fast, or I might find my finger slips and one of you is relieved of something vital." She lowered her gun to the closest man's crotch and his eyes grew yet larger.

The four assailants remained silent in their respective positions.

"I don't know, Sam," Billie called. "I think I might have to—"

There was a terrible noise as the man amid the garbage managed to get up and flee, staggering and holding his injured body like a child holds a toy baby.

"That's it, these two are going to get a bullet in the—"

"Moretti," someone said in a small but clear voice. She didn't catch who it was, though the one with the meat face looked guilty.

Vincenzo bloody Moretti. She'd half expected Boucher's name, but Moretti? He was in this up to the part in his grubby hair. It figured.

"Where is the boy? Where is Adin Brown?" she pressed. "Come on, let's hear it!"

The one with the meaty face shook his head.

"*Where is he?*" She moved up the end of her pistol to sit right between his eyes.

"It's too late for him," came the small, guilty voice. His eyes were averted.

Too late?

Now he turned and ran, moving his body out of the line of sight of her little Colt, his cowardly companion behind him. She lined him up and for one heart-stopping moment watched the man over her little shining barrel, then dropped the gun to her side. She wasn't going to shoot a man in the back. Billie shrugged. She looked across at Sam and gave him a look, one eyebrow raised.

"Where is the boy?" Sam asked the man he was holding off the ground.

"I . . ." came a strangled voice. He clearly couldn't speak. As she watched, Sam slowly released his grip on the man he'd been holding up like a nail to be whacked into the brick, but that other hand of his stayed poised.

"Where is the boy?"

"You're asking the wrong guy," the man said, trembling. "They don't tell me nothin'. They just paid me a few shillings to rough you up, tell you to leave it alone. I don't know nothin' about why."

When Sam finally took a step back, the man bolted.

Moretti. Vincenzo Moretti sent them.

A group of people appeared at the mouth of the alley, perhaps also coming from the auction if their finery was anything to go by. They watched the man running away, puzzled. Sam walked over to Billie, his aquamarine eyes a bit wild. "Geez. I didn't see them, Billie. I'm so sorry." He looked her up and down and seemed not to like what he saw. "Oh geez."

"I didn't, either. Never mind, it wasn't a total loss. But let's get out of here before those people wonder what we've been up to."

Sam opened the car door for her and she slid inside, sore and disheveled. She'd sure feel that in the morning. And that stocking was beyond repair. A shame. "Unless you have good reason to protest, I'm taking you for a drink at my flat," Billie said. "Frankly, I need one desperately and I don't drink alone. And I don't feel in a fit state to be seen publicly in these clothes. Any protest?"

"That's not a real question, is it?" Sam replied, and started his car.

What a day it has been, Billie thought as she sank back into the passenger seat and willed her heart to slow to a more normal pace. She had woken to unexpected deceased company, had a pair of her mother's valuable earrings stolen, faked a party-girl persona for the benefit of a couple of police officers, spent an afternoon among Sydney's most wealthy, and been set upon by thugs in an Eastern Suburbs back alley. The morgue would be next on her dance card, neatly bookending her Sunday with corpses. Even by Billie's standards, this combination was something memorable, particularly now that there were no longer shells falling. And she'd thought the world had become less violent.

—∞—

"Your flat is a real beaut," Sam remarked, standing like a soldier at the window of Billie's living room and looking down over the Moreton Bay fig trees toward the water. The sun was setting, and it gave him a soft golden halo and illuminated his silhouette down to his waist. They had reached Billie's place without anyone else trying to kill them or warn them off, but the adrenaline from their encounter in the alley had not yet subsided.

"I've not seen that kind of excitement since . . ." Sam's voice trailed off.

"Tobruk?" Billie suggested.

Sam nodded. "Yes. And they didn't have anyone like you there."

The encounter seemed to have affected them in a similar way: Their faces were flushed, their cheeks glowing, their eyes alight with excitement. Billie felt acutely alive as she walked over to her walnut Art Deco bar cabinet and cast a look back at her assistant's haloed form. Her breath caught in her throat. Sam had been very impressive in that alley. Very bloody impressive. He'd suggested that he should be the one to get the drinks for them, as seemed to be his way, but he was a guest and she couldn't have that. This wasn't the office. Sam had done quite enough already in the service of their professional work, and his day was not yet over. It was quite possible the worst was yet to come. The state of Con Zervos's remains would not have improved over the last few hours.

A day of bad luck.

"What would you like?" she asked her assistant and bent to open the cabinet's lower set of doors, one of which was sticking slightly. Yes, her ribs were going to bruise; she could feel it. Masking a wince, she saw that she still had some port, a good scotch whisky, her mother's favorite sherry, and a couple of bottles of wine.

"Whatever you're having," Sam said cautiously, still at the window. "Perhaps just one drink . . ."

"Yes, you have a big night ahead. This will ease the way. Scotch on the rocks? I have a good Dewar's White Label."

"On the rocks? Certainly." Sam thanked her, seeming impressed. He waited uncomfortably, looking at the glowing treetops, his large, scarred hands clasped behind his back. How bad was his left hand beneath that glove? Billie wondered. Even with prosthetic fingers, he'd managed those two men exceedingly well. She hoped the effort hadn't damaged his hand further.

"Are you injured?" she inquired. He might have been masking discomfort even more than she was. "That kidney punch looked ugly. And your hand . . ."

He shook his head. "I'm fine."

"Good. We're both fine, then," she declared, pulling the bottle of scotch up onto the bar. "My stocking was the only real casualty," she added with a lighthearted smile, but when she looked down at her legs she frowned. She hadn't the energy to take them off yet, nor her torn dress, and being thrust into this close proximity with Sam in her own place suddenly struck her as more intimate than intended. There was something in the air, some lack of ease that was not a usual mark of their time together. Maybe they shouldn't have danced. And now this reminded her of how long it had been since she'd last entertained, and how long it had been since she'd had a man in her flat—well, one who was alive at the time. That last male visitor would likely have been her father, in fact. Yes. It had been him, before she'd left for Europe, before he'd fallen ill. Having her strapping young assistant here threw him into a different light, and perhaps he felt that unexpected shift, too, as he seemed uncharacteristically stiff. No, she reflected, now was not the time to announce that she was going to slip into something more comfortable. She wanted to get out of her torn things, but that could wait until after his departure. A drink was what was needed. A good, medicinal drink to get the taste of adrenaline out of her mouth and work the smell of death out of her nostrils.

"Please take a seat and relax," Billie urged, grabbing a couple of her nicer crystal glasses from the cabinet and moving off to fetch some ice chips from the kitchen. "I know you have a date tonight. I promise I won't keep you," she called back, and when he turned toward her she thought she caught a slight blush on his cheeks.

She took her sharp ice pick from a drawer and chipped off enough ice to comfortably fill the two crystal glasses.

"Can I help?" Sam called from the next room, and she assured him she was fine. She returned to the living room and saw that he was sitting as instructed. The whisky poured beautifully over the fresh, clear ice and crackled as it settled into the glasses. She handed one to Sam and sat down, careful to leave distance between them.

"Thank you. I wouldn't have liked to have come home alone after that," Billie said. She held up her glass. "Here's to getting through this day. May it end soon and never be repeated."

"Here's to getting through today," Sam returned, locking eyes with her. They clinked glasses, looked away, and sipped. "And last night," he added.

"Indeed."

The whisky burned satisfyingly, with a hint of sweetness and peat smoke behind the fire. She had fancied she could taste her at-

tackers' sweat and smell it in her nostrils, and in one strong swig the
sensation was blissfully obliterated. The burn settled all the way
down into her stomach. She took a deep breath and her shoulders
seemed to drop a full two inches.

"You looked good out there, Sam," Billie said. "I'm impressed.
Hell, I think those thugs were impressed, too." He seemed to blush
again, cradling his drink. "Well done, good man," she said, raising
her glass and taking another sip. She didn't need to ask him where
he'd learned to fight like that. He'd probably had plenty of opportu-
nities to learn in New South Wales, and then in Tobruk. He was
a man you wanted on your side in the trenches; that much was
certain.

"It was nothing," he said dismissively. "You were pretty impressive yourself." He raised his glass to his lips and widened his eyes
as if to punctuate his point.

"It wasn't my first rodeo," she explained a bit blithely, and her
guest choked a little on his whisky. "Though I must say, Sydney has
changed a lot since before I went away."

When she was in Europe for all those years she'd fondly recalled
Australia as peaceful and safe, and she supposed it was, relative to
occupied territories and front lines. But then it might also have been
the effect of the rose-colored glasses one classically dons when pining
for a missed home. What had Johannes Hofer called it? *Nostalgia*, or
"severe homesickness considered as a disease," from the Greek *álgos*—
pain, grief—and *nóstos*—homecoming. Nostalgia was thought to be
a disease of soldiers fighting away from home, but it had proved a
disease of young women war reporters, too, she'd found—if "disease"
was really the right way to view it. She'd missed Australia terribly in
the end. After all her father had shown her of Sydney's underworld

when she was younger, she hadn't been so naïve, and she wasn't easily shocked, exactly, but some fundamental things seemed to have worsened with the war. There seemed to be a dangerous desperation about.

"I didn't know about your Colt," Sam remarked.

"I rarely leave the house without it these days," Billie confided. "Can't remember when I started doing that."

It wasn't right after she returned from Europe, where she'd seen enough of guns and their deadly effects to last several lifetimes, but as the business had become more intense she'd started keeping her sidearm with her with some frequency, and she didn't feel the need to defend that decision, particularly after the day's events. Her instincts had been right, after all. That gun, unfired, had helped them in the alley. They were outnumbered four to two. If Sam asked for an explanation about why a "lady" packed heat, as some men tended to, she'd not like it. She doubted the male PIs were asked about such choices. Thankfully Sam seemed to accept her wisdom when it came to her own personal security. He didn't say a word.

She sipped her drink and gazed toward the window. "You have a piece?" she asked him after a stretch of silence.

"I do," he said to her. "It's a .38. Has a long barrel, though. I've not been wearing it to work as a habit."

"I think you might want to get into the habit of wearing it for the next little while, Sam, just until we find out what's going on," she said. "It's licensed and in good working order?"

He nodded.

"A revolver. Good," she added. If you happened to be wounded in the hand or arm, it would be a bugger to load a pistol. A revolver, like Sam had, was safer to carry around loaded, and easier to load and fire with one good hand. A good choice for him, all things considered. "How long is the barrel?"

"Six inches," he said.

A farm gun, not really for concealment, Billie thought. Guns like that were not usually aimed at humans, but at ill-fated animals. It would not be subtle under a jacket, but Sam was clearly comfortable with it and it was unwise to introduce new weapons just before battle. Four men had brought a knife fight to them in that alley, and you didn't want to get caught bringing a knife to a gunfight, if that was where they took things next.

"Billie . . . I'm so sorry about what happened in the alley. I should have spotted them," Sam said, his eyes wide with apology. "I hold myself responsible."

"Sam, neither of us saw them," she stressed. "It wasn't your fault."

Billie raised her glass, took a sip, felt it burn. She locked eyes with her assistant again for a moment. He was solid, that Sam. So solid. It wasn't just his size or his ability to toss a man around like a rag doll, either. He appeared entirely unfazed by what she was asking him—to pack a gun. To dispose of a body. She was beginning to think he was one in a million. She looked away and sat back in the couch. "And it was the work of Vincenzo Moretti," she mused.

Sam leaned forward, thinking, holding his glass tightly, frowning. "Might explain why he was at The Dancers last night."

Billie could not have been more shocked by this revelation. "What do you mean?" She put her glass down too suddenly on the side table, and the amber liquid nearly washed over the rim. "What do you mean: He was at The Dancers?"

"He was there. I told you." Now the memory emerged, vaguely. Sam had said something about an Italian. They'd got tied up in some pointless conversation about prisoners of war and civilians and the like.

"It was Vincenzo Moretti you saw? Why didn't you say so?"

"I did say so," Sam protested.

"You said you saw an Italian. Not all Italians are Vincenzo Moretti."

In Moretti's case all distrust and animosity were certainly warranted. If the dealings of Georges Boucher Auction House were wrapped up with Vincenzo Moretti somehow, that brought it down several pegs, too, in Billie's eyes. Something always smelled bad when he was around, and that display in the alley was just the sort of shoddy parting committee he'd organize. If he was at The Dancers, he could have been the one who'd spiked her drink, come to think of it. If someone was fast enough and slimy enough they could have spiked it. And in a high-class joint like The Dancers. How galling. And the doorman had ended up staring at death in his own room after work. Beneath all that glitz, the place was rotten. Wasn't that always the way.

Blasted Moretti. "He's been tailing me. I didn't figure it out until I saw him outside this morning. One of the cops who came, a Constable Dennison, knew he was there, I think. I think it was Moretti at the Strand Arcade, too. He's been searching me out all over town," she said, the realization hitting her.

"Bloody Moretti couldn't find a grand piano in a one-room house," Sam snipped.

"Yes, he is rather an idiot," Billie agreed. "But a dangerous one."

More dangerous to her than she'd reckoned. Moretti hadn't faced them himself, of course. He'd sent some low-rent thugs for the job. She almost felt sorry for them. Almost. No, Moretti didn't think much of her; that was evident. What would he make of the story his rent-a-beating boys returned with? Was Moretti behind the dead body switch? Were the two things related? Who was his client? And where was Georges Boucher in all this? Was he the one giving orders, footing the bill? Or was this personal somehow? What would make Moretti go this far?

"I didn't like that answer about the boy," Billie added.

Sam looked up.

"*It's too late for him.* I wonder what he meant by that."

"You don't think . . . ?"

"That Adin Brown is dead? Perhaps. I rather hope not." Billie frowned deeply. "When's your date?" she asked, breaking from her darker ruminations and looking at her wristwatch. Her assistant had the unpleasant task of disposing of Con Zervos beforehand. The sun had set and now the world outside her window was nearly dark. Soon it would be time.

"I'll cancel," he replied.

"No. Don't. Please. I mean, if you can manage it. It would be better for you to go about things as normal after . . ." After disposing of the body. "You should try to take your mind off things tonight. I really do appreciate all you've done. I hope you aren't too sore tomorrow." He had a few reasons to feel that way.

"I'm fine. I'm worried about you, though."

"Well, I can't have that, Sam. I can take care of myself. You'll have to trust me there." The way he'd looked at her with her gun trained on two terrified men told her he was starting to get the idea. "Thanks for joining me for a drink. And thank you for what you'll do tonight. I'll see you tomorrow at the office, yes? You're not thinking twice about the job, are you? I'd understand if you were."

"What?" He looked almost hurt. "No way, Billie. You've got me. If you want me."

She let that sink in.

"I'll do what I have to, and then I'll go out if that's best. You watch your back, okay?" he added.

Billie thrust her whisky forward again and they clinked a second time. They drained their glasses and, with a somewhat less awkward exchange, parted ways. She shut the door behind him and paused. What a day. Billie peeled off her stockings and dress. She should have been positively shattered by the day that was, she reflected, particularly following such a disturbed night, but that electricity seemed to be running over all of her nerves again. There were too many unanswered questions to simply leave it be for the evening, even for something as restoring as rest. Her body needed some tending to with soap and arnica and perhaps another restoring glass of that good scotch, even if she did have to drink it alone. It was medicinal after all. Then she had to go out, too.

Tonight she would visit the death house.

Nineteen

—ᴧᴧ—

Billie ventured to Circular Quay West and stepped into the shadows of the dark-brick- and sandstone-trimmed arches of the morgue on Mill Lane. The night was heavy and warm. It was after midnight.

She was overdue to visit Sydney City Morgue for this case, though the case itself seemed to have been keeping her from whatever it held within its walls. She sincerely hoped the missing boy, Adin Brown, would not be waiting on a slab as an unidentified guest, a tragic end to a calamitous day, sealing her latest case with a sad resolution on top of the growing violence it seemed to spawn. No, she hoped she wouldn't find him here, for his family's sake, but she couldn't keep away no matter how battered she felt. In missing persons cases, such visits had become routine for her, and now, with the words of the meat-faced thug, she had another reason to be there, a reason she could not possibly have anticipated on Friday afternoon when Nettie Brown had first walked through the door of her office with a seemingly simple case of a runaway teenage son. The events that had unfolded since had made Billie restless in her bones and anxious for answers. Sleep seemed far away.

Billie paused, deep in thought, absentmindedly rubbing the bruise on her rib cage through the fabric of her dark clothing.

What did Con have to tell me that was worth killing him over?

Why is Moretti tailing me? And why the thugs outside the auction house?

Is he the one who spiked my drink? Did he kill Con? Why? For whom?

The many puzzle pieces had not come together yet, not by a long shot, but a couple of things were certain—foul play, and a strong desire to keep her away from the case.

Billie leaned against a sandstone arch. The facilities inside the city's morgue were basic, with a receiving room, the main morgue, a postmortem room, and a small laboratory. It was considered a less than hygienic space—notoriously so. During the gravediggers' strike of Christmas 1944, the place had been overflowing with "stinking dead bodies," according to witnesses. Billie believed it. Two years on, the city morgue still lacked refrigeration and anything approaching adequate space, though she understood there were plans for an upgrade. Though still cramped, things here were, at least, an improvement on the prewar setup at the morgue that rather unfortunately had allowed the guests aboard visiting cruise ships coming in and out of Sydney Harbor to see into the building and the bodies stacked there. Not good for tourism, to be sure.

In anticipation of this late visit, Billie had changed out of her ripped ensemble of the afternoon—yet more mending to be done—and donned dark blue cotton pants, an ivory silk blouse, a navy driving coat, and old over-ankle leather-soled boots that could be easily cleaned. She usually preferred the quieter crepe or fabric soles, so the sharp sound of her feet on the stones in the dark had come as a surprise.

Another thought pulled at her, one she couldn't let go of. Was there corrupt police interference in this affair? If so, why?

As death took a rest for no one, the death house operated day and night, but apart from the necessary police identifications made by relatives of the deceased, it didn't welcome living civilian visitors. Billie, however, was an exception. She knocked at the door and was let in, her arrival met with the unabashedly delighted smile of the young man who had been stationed at the desk. Billie had known whom to expect. She'd cultivated a warm welcome in this cold place. Despite the silent company, it could be a lonely sort of place, she imagined, most of all at night.

"Good evening, Mr. Benny," Billie said.

"Oh, call me Donald, Ms. Walker. It's such a pleasure to see you." He did indeed look pleased.

"Or perhaps I should say good morning?" She looked at her delicate watch.

He nodded. "Yes, it's quite late."

Donald Benny was a slim, bent fellow with a complexion nearly as waxen as that of the clients he guarded. He was about Sam's age, twenty-four, but there the similarity ended. Bookish in appearance, he wore round spectacles for his vision, a white collared shirt, and a dark tie visible above a collarless white lab coat. On this occasion it had no noticeable bloodstains or unidentifiable marks on it, which Billie took as a good sign. As usual, Benny appeared entranced by Billie's presence. She smiled warmly at him, having no intention of letting her hold on him go until she was ready to leave.

"I brought you a book," Billie said and reached into her satchel to reveal a paperback detective novel. "A Georgette Heyer." Heyer was better known for her historical romance novels set in the regency and Georgian eras, but she'd written some fine detective books.

Benny's cheeks had colored, she noticed. With his anemic complexion, his every private emotion sat on the surface. His eyes went to the book, then wandered to her hand and its long, elegant fingers, and wandered farther up to her neck, which was exposed on one side with her dark hair cascading down the other. "*Death in the Stocks,*" he said, reading the title of the book aloud once he was able to bring his eyes back to it.

"You haven't read it, have you?" she inquired.

"Oh, no, I haven't. How do you always seem to know which ones I haven't read?"

She simply smiled again. "I was wondering if I might have a little look in at your guests tonight? Is there anyone unidentified at the moment?"

His face became serious, a show of professionalism against the almost giddy welcome. "Two unidentified," he said, avoiding the word *stiffs,* though Billie could see it was on the tip of his tongue.

"May I . . . ?" she ventured, looking at the open door to the morgue's main room.

Benny tore his attention from her to look around at the quiet office, as he always did, then nodded, as he always did. Billie didn't know what he expected to find when he silently questioned the room each time, but as the dead did not protest, he led her quietly through the door into the main morgue. She followed close behind him, hands in her coat pockets.

"Have you a handkerchief?" he asked.

She nodded and pulled one from her pocket. In a quick motion she soaked the cloth with tea-tree oil from a small vial she kept for this purpose. Though Billie knew what to expect, the room still had a most unpleasant smell—the same smell that had greeted her upon waking. Something like rotten leaves, or animal meat, but not exactly the same as either. The tea-tree oil reduced the pungency but could not stop that distinctive smell from taking hold somewhere deep within her. She hoped that when it came her time, she'd be bathed in French perfume and buried fast, before too many people had taken a gander or a whiff. Billie did not fear death, but she did have some unsettling feelings about how her body might be handled once she could no longer protect it. Death could be terribly undignified, she knew. It was something to come to terms with, she supposed.

"You haven't had an Adin Brown through here? A boy of about seventeen? Five foot nine, curly hair, no identifying marks?" she inquired, sweeping her eyes across the room and bringing the handkerchief to her face.

It's too late. The words kept cycling in her mind. *Too late.*

Billie's eyes stung a little from the sharp waft of tea-tree oil. There were about a dozen deceased guests, of a variety of ages, sexes, and shapes—slim, plump, male, female, old as the hills and as young as Adin. Death did not appear picky tonight.

Benny stopped by the first of the corpses and thought for a moment, bringing a thin finger to his lips. "No. I'm sure no one of that name has been through recently, and neither of the unidentified men has been of that age."

That was a small relief. Benny's memory was good, and Adin would have been a quite recent arrival. There wasn't much risk he'd been here. That didn't mean, of course, he was still alive.

Her guide began to move again, and Billie took a step forward to follow her host, then realized with horror that she was looking down at the skinny doorman, Con Zervos, his face but inches from her right hip. A chill went up her spine as if he'd reached up and touched her. His eyes were mercifully closed now, but somehow he was still looking at her as he had in his hotel room, strangled by his own necktie.

She gasped.

"Ms. Walker?"

"Sorry," she said. "I ate the wrong thing for dinner. Seafood. It's unsettled my tummy."

"Would you like some tea?"

"I'm fine," she assured him. She tried to smile again, but it wouldn't form.

This was hardly the first dead body she'd seen—the war had taken care of that, as had multiple trips to the morgue—but it was the first she'd woken up with, the first violently taken civilian in peacetime that she'd walked in on unawares, and as such the death of Con Zervos had shaken her. Her guard had not been up when she'd walked into room 305. She hoped the grisly discovery would be an isolated incident. She blinked and brought her body back into line, doing her best to remain calm. Con Zervos was no longer a man but a hollow, human-shaped cast, as lifeless as a dressmaker's dummy. The face was shrinking back, eyes falling deeper into the skull, the whole of his flesh abandoned utterly by the life-force that had filled it at The Dancers. The sight of it, of what had been him—so wiry and nervous and alive—made her heart thud beneath her blouse, despite the fact that she'd expected to find him here already, if Sam had done his job well. In fact, this was what she had hoped. Nothing could be done to breathe life back into him, but now that he had been collected, he would be cared for by Benny, and his family could be informed of his fate.

"Are you okay?" Benny asked suddenly. She must have paled.

"What's his story?" Billie managed, running a hand over her hair.

"Sorry, it's a bit gruesome, this one."

"You know I can handle it." She tried another smile, and this time her cheeks worked, and his confidence in her appeared to return. She hoped he hadn't heard the story of her claiming to have found his body in room 305.

"You are one of a kind, Ms. Walker," he told her admiringly, then turned and regarded the corpse. "This poor fellow was found out the back of the People's Palace tonight. Strangled, he was. They do get some rough trade. The night watchman identified him. Some Greek immigrant who came out here for a new life, and this is what he got for his troubles."

She swallowed. The night watchman. She wondered what he thought of all the confusion with the police on Saturday night, and now this.

"Isn't that a temperance hotel?" she asked, trying to strike a normal conversational note.

"Fat lot of good it did this fellow," Benny remarked.

"Indeed."

Billie told herself to resist the urge to chat. It was easy to begin talking needlessly when you were nervous and keeping secrets, and then those secrets had a way of tangling you up. It wasn't every day you woke with a corpse. If the police did find out, it would do her no favors. Had the force been less corrupt, she might have trusted them with her innocence, but her father had taught her better than that. Silence was best. Silence or brevity. Reg, the city coroner, would likely give young Con Zervos an autopsy the next day, if budgets allowed. How long would it take his family back in Greece to find out his fate? She walked on, fighting the impulse to look back at Zervos or ask further questions about him.

"Sorry your kid isn't here," Benny said, a welcome change of topic.

"I'm not sorry," she said, and was sincere. "I still hope to find him alive."

It's too late. Too late . . .

"Of course," Benny said. "I didn't mean . . ."

"I'm reading one of those American detective novels where they go out and bury the body in the desert," Billie said, changing the subject as they returned to the front desk. "The desert around Vegas is full of bodies, apparently." She noted his interest. "I was wondering, where would someone do something like that around here? Hide a body, I mean."

"Why, the Blue Mountains, of course." His answer was immediate.

"Is that so?"

"If you don't have time to drive all the way into the outback— and that's risky, you know, the longer you have the body with you. I mean, you could be pulled over, your automobile could break down, all kinds of things could go wrong. So if you don't go all the way to the outback, you go to the Blue Mountains. It happens all the time. Better than the country, where the locals and their dogs pick things up and know what's about. No, you'd settle for the mountains and all those wild areas. It's hard to tell a murder from an accident after a couple of weeks under a cliff," he added matter-of-factly. "Or a suicide. The roads must be backed up with all the poor souls heading up there to take a walk off the Blue Mountains escarpments. It's a damned shame."

"I never thought of that," she said. He had given her an idea.

"Otherwise it's the harbor."

She had thought of that. "Then they would end up here, wouldn't they?"

"Eventually," he said. "If they were found at all."

—✺—

When Billie arrived home she walked through her rooms with her Colt drawn and, once satisfied, double-checked the lock on her door and closed and locked her windows. She undressed, pulled the freshly washed sheets on her bed back, and sat on the edge. After a moment she rose again, walked to the kitchen, and pulled some old newspapers from the lower cupboard. She padded back to her bedroom and closed the door behind her. One by one she pulled the newspaper sheets out, crumpling them in her hands and scattering them in a large arc around her bedroom floor, like a circle of protection in some novel about the occult.

No one, but no one, was going to creep up on her again.

She did not sleep well, but she did sleep. And that was something.

Twenty

———ฌ———

It was just past nine thirty, the pen pushers already well into their workday, when Billie strode into Daking House in a cinched rayon dress of navy blue printed with flights of delicate white birds, her little loaded Colt holstered beneath her slip, its outline visible only to those with the most keen and suspicious eye.

She could really have used more sleep, but there was, as her father used to say, plenty of time to sleep when you're dead. Today there was much to do.

Billie wore her trusty fabric-soled oxfords—those of the satisfyingly soundless soles she'd so missed the night before—her dark navy driving coat slung over one arm and her hair wrapped neatly in a shining silk scarf of navy patterned with the soft shapes of cherry-red and white abstract flowers. A small tilt hat in navy completed her ensemble, her sunglasses round and impenetrable, her smile steady and painted as always with her last stick of Fighting Red. She felt optimistic, determined, wrapped in her clothes as if in armor. Her mind had been ticking over, and she had a plan.

Straight-backed and quiet, she was delivered to the sixth floor by John Wilson, who seemed, as always, enlivened by her presence. He looked sidelong at her finely sculpted profile without seeming to realize she could see him doing so, fooled as he was by her smoked glasses and the effect of her wrapped hair and hat, which made her look somehow like a fashion mannequin come to life. She slipped him a shilling, flashed him a wide ivory smile, and told him she would require him again presently.

Let this be the day, she thought, stepping into her office.

"Good morning, Ms. Walker." Her assistant stood at attention behind his desk as she entered, looking slightly surprised by the relatively early hour of her arrival. Sam's trench coat was already hanging on the coat rack; the newspapers were open across his desk. Despite the trials of the weekend, he looked no worse for wear. His eyes were clear and bright, his posture not at all that of a man who had been punched by cowardly assailants the afternoon before. He had probably expected that Billie would sleep in, and it was gratifying for her to know that he still got to work on time regardless of the strong likelihood that she would not walk in until close to eleven.

"Good morning, Sam," Billie replied. She pulled off her round sun cheaters and ignored his move to help her with her coat. The waiting room was again empty, the magazines and journals untouched. No clients. But if she played this right, that might change—and many other things besides.

"There was a note slipped into the mail this morning," Sam said. "Just a piece of paper among the letters slid under the door. I thought you might want to take a look right away. It could be something important."

Billie wrinkled her brow. A note? She didn't know whether to expect a death threat or an invitation to tea, such was her professional life at the moment. She accepted the plain piece of notepaper. "Did you go okay last night?" she asked, and watched his expression carefully.

Sam nodded. "Yes. No one could have seen me. It's done."

"You did well, Sam," she reassured him. "Con has been identified and his family in Greece are possibly by now being informed so they can make arrangements and grieve. It was a rotten thing, what was done to him. Rotten and unfair and I hope to make someone pay very dearly for it."

Sam looked relieved, though the corners of his mouth were turned down. "It was hard leaving him there."

He didn't seem to want to talk about it. Fair enough. An ugly business, it was. Billie unfolded the piece of paper, revealing a short series of numbers and letters: *XR-001*.

She recognized Shyla's distinctive hand. "A license plate number," she declared, pleased. It was for a recently registered car, she noted, which fitted with what Shyla had told her about the man Frank being new to the country. Since Saturday the clever young woman had elicited the information and delivered it on a page with no other clues, so only Billie was likely to know the significance. Perhaps a trip to Upper Colo was in order, once other pressing matters were resolved? But it would have to wait at least another day. For now, she had a boy to find, and she wanted a hell of a lot of answers.

"Another matter," she said to Sam, pocketing the piece of paper. "I made it to the morgue," she went on. "That's how I know about Zervos. But our boy Adin wasn't there, and no one of his description has been through. One piece of good news, at least." She checked his expression and saw that he still looked a touch glum, brows pinched. Billie changed the subject. "On another note, how was the rest of your night? Did your date with Eunice work out? You were feeling up for it?"

Sam flinched and a strange look came over him.

"I mean . . . up for a night out, after the incident in the alley," she clarified, wondering about his sensitivity.

"We went to the late session of *The Bells of St. Mary's*, thank you, Ms. Walker," Sam said rather stiffly.

Something about his night had not worked out well, but she decided it was best not to inquire further. "Are you up for a trip?" she asked. "A drive to the Blue Mountains?"

"Always," he said, brightening. "I've only been there once . . . saw the Three Sisters. I'm parked not far away, unless you want the train?"

"No need," Billie said to him, smiling. "It's now December. A new month with new petrol coupons. I've brought out the roadster and filled her up already." The opportunity to cruise the open road for a few hours was not one she would pass up. Following her chat with Donald Benny at the morgue, she had hopes for the case, which she didn't yet want to reveal to Sam, in case they fell through, but even if things led nowhere on this Monday, at least they would enjoy a scenic drive and some mountain air. They deserved that, at least, after their record-breakingly awful weekend. "Let's lock up here and hit the road."

Her two-seater Willys 77 roadster was waiting near the entrance of Daking House, its top down, black paint gleaming in the morning sun and red leather interior beckoning. Billie thought she saw Sam actually lick his lips when he spotted the automobile. It gave the impression of being as much animal as machine, part black steed, or perhaps panther. It had few miles on the clock for its age, as it had waited patiently for its mistress while she was away reporting in Europe. The roadster had been a twenty-first-birthday present from Baroness von Hooft, who had so far given her only child a fast sewing machine, a faster motorcar, and a small Colt, in that order. All three appeared to have been chosen because the baroness recognized the power of the skills associated with them, even if she was not adept at those skills herself, and probably never would be—having no ability to sew or drive or shoot or, for that matter, cook. At least that Billie was aware of. Ella had been a modern woman for her time and her station, but her daughter, Billie, was of an altogether different era, and thanks to those gifts she could go anywhere, make anything she needed to wear, and protect herself in the unique line of work she had chosen.

On the bonnet of the roadster, leading the charge as it were, was the winged goddess Victory, or Nike, her head tilted back and nestled into her wings and long, wavy hair in what Billie fancied was a pose of pleasure. The ancient Greeks had worshipped Nike because they believed she could grant them immortality and the strength and speed to be victorious in any task, making her an appropriate ornament, to be certain, though Billie didn't want to test the immortality theory too vigorously. No further than the dial could take them, anyway.

Sam strode forward and opened the driver's-side door for his boss. Billie slid behind the wheel, inside the lush red interior. There was no question of her car being driven by anyone else. She pulled black leather driving gloves out of the glove box and eased them over her soft white hands as Sam got in the passenger side. He watched silently, seemingly a touch overcome by the automobile. She'd not had reason to take him out in it since his employment began.

With a grin she pumped the accelerator and pressed the starter button with her foot, and the engine cranked over, she felt it fire, and the beast that was her automobile began to warm to their presence. Driving was, to Billie's mind, something every woman should experience, and often, though such possibilities were limited until petrol rationing ceased. For now, the restrictions prevented her from enjoying her beloved car quite as much as she'd like, but being behind the wheel on the open road was the kind of rare thrill that didn't leave one with a hangover, social embarrassment, unwanted male attachments, or diseases, and who could argue with virtues such as those?

"You'll want to hold on tight, Sam," she said.

—⁓—

After nearly three hours of pleasant motoring, Billie pulled her roadster onto Woodlands Road, found a parking spot near Katoomba cemetery—cemeteries always being unnervingly close to hospitals—pulled off her leather driving gloves, and walked toward Katoomba's Blue Mountains District ANZAC Memorial Hospital, her seemingly unrattled passenger trailing behind her.

The drive had been in turns relaxing and thrilling, the landscape shifting as the buildings gradually slipped away, until the dense bush and the air of the mountains seemed to turn blue, the oil from eucalyptus trees mingling with dust particles and water droplets to give the region its color and name. She and Sam had talked as much as the engine's roar had allowed, which wasn't much. The higher they'd driven, the more the bustle of the city had fallen away, and now here in Katoomba the atmosphere was decidedly tranquil. In the gaps between the roar of motorcars on the main highway, birdcalls and the deep, living quiet of nature prevailed. There was something magnificent about it, and it made Billie stop and take a deep breath.

Sam had not asked why Billie had decided to drive out to the mountains, and he did not ask why they were walking toward a hospital. Whether it was his nature or his army training, Billie did not know. But the fact that Sam trusted her judgment . . . well, it was strangely comforting. Allies like that were rare.

"It may seem odd that we've come all this way," Billie began. "I did some ringing around and I think I have a lead. If not . . ." She hesitated. "If I'm wrong, Sam, we deserve a drive out of the city regardless. We'll have afternoon tea and visit the Hydro Majestic, or the Paragon," she said, and his eyes lit up at the suggestion.

"I don't feel I should be paid for *that*," he said.

"You will be paid, regardless of what we find here. Which may be nothing. You have gone above and beyond. I don't want you to think I don't realize that, because I do, Sam."

He met her eyes and said nothing. Then there was a slight nod. *Good.* They understood each other.

They walked up the few stairs to the entry porch of the hospital, a gabled single-story building with a central arch on which the name of the establishment was announced, then pushed through the beveled glass doors into the cool interior. The walls inside were stretcher bond brickwork, marble memorial plaques off to one side and Roll of Life Member plaques to the other. It smelled of disinfectant and starch.

The nurse at the reception desk nodded when Billie explained their business, her face suddenly and unexpectedly opening up. "I spoke to you on the telephone!" she said, her blue eyes wide. "That poor boy. Please come. He's this way. Follow me."

The nurse spoke about the boy being brought in, how no one knew who he was, how he had a head injury and was barely conscious, still unable to speak, how everyone was terribly concerned. Billie got the feeling the mystery boy had become quite a focus in the hospital. Had there really been no one else to visit him except the local constabulary to take down his description? She and Sam followed the woman into the men's ward, where fewer than half of the beds were occupied. The nurse led them all the way to one end of the ward, where a boy lay, bandaged and bruised. The moment Billie caught sight of the curly hair sticking up between bandages, her heart leaped. *Yes, this could be him. This really could.*

"He speaks sometimes," the nurse said, "but it's mostly nonsense. He seems to have lost his memory. We haven't been able to find out his name or where he's from."

"I understand," Billie said.

"Do you think this is . . . who you were hoping to find? Oh, we so hope we can find the boy's poor family."

At this, Billie pulled the small photograph from her pocket. She held it up next to him, feeling her stomach tighten. She pocketed the image her client had given her, then knelt next to the boy, gathering herself. His eyes were shut tight with swelling, but his hair was a giveaway.

"Adin Brown? I'm Billie Walker," Billie whispered into the boy's ear, though he did not answer. She resisted the urge to check his pulse and temperature. He was in good hands now, but where had he been? What had happened to him? Her gaze went to the raw red marks on his wrists. *Rope?* Still kneeling, she turned and asked the nurse, "Can you tell me where exactly he was found and when? How did he come in?"

"Oh, it was a terrible thing, miss. Some hikers were coming back from one of those big walks and were headed for a train, and they saw a body at the bottom of this little cliff down at Wentworth Falls, right next to the line. They thought it was something that had fallen out of a train, at first. Then when they approached, they thought it was a dead body, but when they got there he was breathing. He was badly hurt and dehydrated, but alive. Miraculous, really. He stank of alcohol. Poor dear must have been drinking and . . ." She trailed off. "He could have been hit by a train, he was that close."

"When was this?"

"Yesterday morning," she said.

"So he was found near the tracks. Does it seem that he possibly jumped from a train? Or had a fall?" Billie asked.

"Every month people come here to end their lives, you know," the nurse reflected, shaking her head. Billie listened with a neutral expression. "But usually they leave their motorcar by the top, or their things. Shoes and a note, that sort of thing. He didn't seem to have anything with him but the clothes on his back. We don't know if he jumped or fell; he might have gone wandering after leaving a pub and slipped, poor dear. Some of those places have quite a sharp edge." She paused, and her next words indicated, perhaps, what she really thought. "And so young, too."

Samuel had been standing silently behind Billie, and now he spoke. "His family will be so pleased he is alive. Thank you for what you've done."

Billie wondered if she perhaps could get further. She put on her most trustworthy smile and said, "I think it may be who we're looking for, but I'm not sure. Were there any personal effects on him? A wallet?" she asked, though she was quite certain she'd found her man. She wanted to see everything.

"No wallet, or we'd have known who he was right away," the nurse responded.

"Of course."

"Do come this way, I'll show you his things. I surely hope it helps. I've been worried sick about this lad."

"Thank you," Billie said. She looked over her shoulder at Sam, motioning to him to stay put.

She and the nurse entered another area of the hospital, and the uniformed woman opened a locker and removed two labeled parcels wrapped in brown paper. An awful smell of liquor hit her nose as soon as they were opened. Inside one parcel was a pair of black leather men's shoes. The other held some folded clothing, which struck Billie immediately as unusual. It looked like a formal outfit. This perhaps explained the nurse's belief that the boy had come to die in the Blue Mountains. He had not been out hiking, that much was certain.

The nurse placed the items on a table for Billie to peruse, and she did a quick inventory. The leather shoes were fairly plain oxfords in a worn black. The label showed they were size eight, which fitted roughly with what she'd expect, considering Adin's height. They were "prescription shoes," but that only meant they had arch support. There was no way to track a man's name down with a pair of shoes so standard. And the clothes: a pair of good black pants, rather the worse for wear. A crumpled and stained white shirt, smelling of gin, and a cheap gin if her nose was correct. Could he really have spilled so much of it on himself? A similarly crumpled and torn dinner jacket. Billie surmised the jacket was tailor-made, but not recently. It might even have been from before the war, perhaps when things were going well at the fur company. It reminded her of Mrs. Brown's suits—they were prewar. But if it was made before the war, it wouldn't have been made for Adin. Was this Adin's father's jacket? Billie wondered if Mikhall had given it to him, or if it was missing and hadn't been noticed. She went through the garments carefully, finding no identifying labels or tags, and nothing of note until she discovered an inside coat pocket and felt something small and flat inside. It was creased and a touch thicker than paper. *A photograph.* She took only a moment to glance at it before secreting it so swiftly in her driving coat pocket that the nurse did not register that anything had been there at all. It was possible that whoever had inflicted the injuries on him had stripped him of his identification but missed this small item.

Billie had brought the *Sydney Morning Herald* clipping with her in case Adin could be interviewed, and she had fleetingly hoped to find his own torn copy in the pockets of the dinner jacket or pants, perhaps with something of note circled or written on it that explained his interest. Still, no wonder he was a no-show at the auction. At the time it was held, he was in this very hospital, semiconscious. The photograph, whatever it was of, was the only clue among his things as to what he might have been up to, apart from the fact that whatever had happened to him had likely happened at night, given he'd been dressed for The Dancers or a similarly formal environment.

"I'll give a detailed description of these clothes to my client. I am hopeful," Billie told the nurse. "There was nothing else? No bottle?"

The nurse shook her head.

"Will he recover, do you think?" Billie asked.

"I hope so," the nurse answered. "We don't have a doctor on staff here, but our local doctor has come to look at him. He'll be back to see him soon. He's taken quite an interest."

They walked back to the ward where Sam was waiting, watching the boy with troubled eyes.

"Here's the doctor now," the nurse said, spotting the man at the same time Billie did. He was a white-coated man of about fifty with side-parted hair, a reassuringly healthy complexion considering his occupation, and a look of concern. The nurse introduced him as Dr. Worthington.

"Dr. Worthington, my name is Billie Walker," Billie said and extended a hand. "A pleasure to make your acquaintance. This is my colleague, Samuel Baker," she said, gesturing to Sam.

The doctor looked at the patient and back to them. "Are you family?" he asked.

"We were hired by his family to find him."

Billie was worried he might toss them out, but instead the doctor's face brightened. "What a relief!" he exclaimed. "So you believe you can identify this boy? We don't think he's a local. He's been here for more than a day now. We informed the police when he was found, but they've come up with nothing. He was in an awful state . . ."

"I see you have given him good care. In your opinion, will he recover, Doctor? I mean his memory, and his injuries?"

"The prognosis is good, but things will take some time. He's been through an ordeal, the poor boy. He shouldn't be moved until he is more fully recovered; then he can perhaps be transferred to a bigger hospital. He has a back injury, which will improve with rehabilitation. And there is a strong chance his memory will come back fully, though I can't be sure."

Billie thanked the doctor and she and Sam made their way out of the ward. She appeared serene, but beneath her rayon dress her heart was pounding. The photograph. It was about the size of the empty frame back at the fur shop, Billie thought. How interesting. And those wrists. Those raw red wrists. Adin Brown had not had an easy time of things since he left the family house. No, Adin had not done this to himself. There was a lot she didn't yet understand about the boy and this case, but attempted suicide was not the missing piece of the puzzle. He wasn't some drunk youth out wandering alone, either. However Adin had ended up here, he was alive. He was alive, and there was a chance he would talk again.

Billie, for one, was deeply interested in what the young man would have to say.

Twenty-one

———m———

"Are you *sure* it's him?" Nettie Brown asked down the crackling telephone line. "Are you *really sure*?"

Billie took a moment to answer her client. She was sure, the little woman in her gut was sure, and that curly hair was uncannily like that in the photograph, but it was best to exercise caution when it came to something like this. "I am very confident it is your son, Mrs. Brown," she replied, "but I can't positively confirm it. Only you or your husband can do that. The boy fits Adin's description, but the timing of his being taken to the hospital is right only if he spent some days elsewhere before being found."

"Elsewhere?"

"That's correct," Billie said, and did not elaborate. She looked around the nurses' station. The staff was giving her space, but the nurse who had helped her caught her eye, her blue eyes shining with hope. Billie gave her a smile and a nod and cradled the receiver close to her ear again.

"But where?" Mrs. Brown pressed, and Billie did not answer.

"He's in and out in terms of his memory, the doctor says. Try not to be too upset if he does not recognize you right away," she told her client in a low voice. "He's been through a lot, I suspect. A concussion, some abrasions and cuts, and a back injury, though the doctor thinks he will recover in time. But he can't be moved, Mrs. Brown. Not yet."

There were no words now, the line crackling.

Then Billie detected a wet, indecipherable sound. Her client was sobbing, she realized, and a part of Billie went to pieces at the sound of the dignified and reserved woman's raw emotion. When she'd recovered herself, Mrs. Brown vowed to leave work immediately and drive up to identify her son at the hospital. Billie had allowed room for some doubt as to the boy's identity, but she felt very confident indeed that they had their young man. This was a great outcome, as long as he recovered from his ordeal.

"Just one thing, Mrs. Brown," Billie added, cupping her hand around the mouthpiece and speaking in a low voice. "I want you to listen to me carefully. Perhaps you should consider keeping fairly quiet about Adin's identity and condition, until we know what happened to him."

There was a pause. "What do you mean? The case is closed, isn't it? You found him."

"I believe so. But what we don't know is—"

"I want the case closed if you found him. That is final."

Billie had thought this might happen. "I understand. I'm off the clock now, Mrs. Brown, if that is what you want," she reassured her. The Browns didn't want any surprise expenses, she appreciated that. Her fee would be forty pounds, representing four days' work, but she suspected the Browns were barely holding on financially. "Unless you want more from me or the courts come calling, my work is finished. I'm confident I have found your son, but if you find otherwise I want you to let me know. However, I daresay there may be a criminal element at work here, and the police could be interested once your son is able to recall what happened to him. For the moment, at least, I would advise that you reveal his condition and location to only those who absolutely must know," she warned.

"But we've been so worried. Everyone knows we are looking for him . . ."

"I recognize that, Mrs. Brown. Nonetheless, that is my advice."

Again, the line was quiet. Billie waited patiently. This turn of events would be a lot for Mrs. Brown, or any person, to absorb. "You think he is in danger of some kind, don't you?"

Billie believed that was possible, but she didn't want to alarm the woman needlessly. "Can I wait for you here?" she responded cautiously.

"Thank you, there is no need."

"Are you certain, Mrs. Brown? It's no problem for us to stay here for a few more hours. It would be good to see—"

"My husband and I will be there soon. Thank you for finding our son. We are very grateful, but your work is done now." Mrs. Brown's tone was firm. "We just want our son back."

Billie nodded and gave Sam a knowing look. "I understand. Good luck, Mrs. Brown." Billie meant it. Thoughtfully, she hung up the telephone.

Twenty-two

—◆—

The Hydro Majestic hotel was as majestic a sight as its name would suggest. Painted in a pleasing pale green and cream, it had been built by the retail magnate Mark Foy at Medlow Bath on the thrilling edge of a sheer cliff overlooking the Megalong Valley. The Hydro had opened its doors in 1904 and been the site of salubrious health spas, fine restaurants, and royal visits since, with a pause in 1942 when it was taken over by the US Defense Department and turned into a hospital for American servicemen wounded in the South Pacific. The place was now a hotel once more and a new wing had recently been opened.

Billie Walker wanted to see it. She had some celebrating to do.

The main dining room of the Hydro was closed on a Monday afternoon, Billie and Sam discovered, but Cat's Alley, entered through the richly decorated Salon du Thé, suited them nicely and offered cream tea and beverages. The narrow space, adorned with several spectacular paintings on its rear wall, boasted jaw-dropping views of the lush Megalong Valley, which stretched out at the base of the drop just beyond the hotel's grounds and extended as far as the eye could see.

Sam pulled out a chair for Billie, beating the waiter to it, and she stared longingly at the spot on the menu where Veuve Clicquot was offered at a price of three pounds per bottle. *Three pounds.* That was a touch extravagant, considering they'd only managed four days of paid work. Circumstances were different now than when she'd last visited and drunk that lovely drop with her mother. Still, it was a case closed, another happy client. She was supposed to celebrate.

Her assistant had been taking in the décor when his gaze landed on hers and he seemed to catch her mood. "Is something wrong?"

"Absolutely nothing is wrong," she replied. "This day has quite changed my view of Mondays."

"You were rather cagey about the boy's identity on the telephone. You do think it's Adin Brown?"

"I'm positive," she assured him, ignoring the unhelpful thoughts niggling at the back of her brain. She looked around for the waiter. "Excuse me, *garçon.* Could we have two glasses of your Veuve Clicquot? *Merci.*" It was a sensible compromise, she thought, as long as she could limit herself to one glass. It wasn't every week you woke up with dead bodies, got pummeled in alleyways, and found a missing youth in the Blue Mountains for a client. She also ordered scones and cream for two, and in quick order the waiter returned with a chilled bottle, already opened, and carefully poured them each a glass.

"To another case closed," Billie said, watching the bubbles rise.

They clinked glasses and sipped. "To another case closed," Sam repeated.

The bubbles danced delightfully on her tongue before going down all the way to the base of her stomach. She realized she'd barely eaten and it was past lunchtime now. She felt a slight warmth in her cheeks, and her brain relaxed a touch.

"I thought you were off champagne," Sam remarked, evidently in response to her obvious pleasure.

"It seems not." Billie smiled.

"Well, this really is the drop," Sam declared.

They looked out at the view and let the champagne do its work, but in no time Billie's mind wandered to Vincenzo Moretti and she felt herself tense. There would be time enough to figure out his game, she tried to assure herself. For now, she was at the Hydro Majestic sipping good champagne after a win, and with an assistant who had more than proved his mettle. It was definitely a win, even if she didn't have all the hows and whys answered. It was a win because the client said so, and that was how the private inquiry agent game worked. If no one wanted you to seek more answers, it wasn't your job to. Still . . .

"I never did tell you why I answered your advertisement for a secretary-cum-assistant," her companion said suddenly.

Billie put her glass down and regarded Sam. His cheeks were flushed, she noticed. He was unused to champagne and it seemed to have loosened him up a touch.

"My father worked with your father, Barry, for a spell, before he returned to country policing. Robert Baker was his name."

Billie leaned forward, interested. She knew Sam's father was a cop, and Sam had told her he might well have pursued that career had the war not got in his way, and had he not subsequently been declared unfit for duties thanks to his injuries. But this detail was something new.

"I was applying for jobs when I recognized the name in your

advertisement and wondered what I would find," Sam continued, absentmindedly rubbing something that bothered him on his gloved left hand. It was a habit he seemed not to notice. "When I applied, I didn't expect to find . . . you," he finished.

"You mean you expected someone else?"

He exhaled with a laugh. "You could say that."

"But you found you didn't mind working for a woman after all?" she ventured, getting his meaning.

"Oh no, not at all. Some of the strongest people in my life have been women. I have four sisters, and my mother, well, she could lead an army." He raised his glass to his lips. Yes, his cheeks were flushed all right.

"I'm surprised you haven't mentioned the connection before," Billie said, taking a sip of her drink.

"I didn't want it to be a reason for you to hire me, not that you would have necessarily. I didn't want you to think that I expected it would help me, particularly considering . . ." He looked down at his gloved hand with its wooden prosthetics hidden beneath the leather. "And after you hired me, when I thought I might mention it in passing, well, by then I knew how much you missed your father, and I guess I didn't want to . . ."

"Upset me?"

"I guess. It just never felt like the right moment." His eyebrows pulled together a touch, his blue eyes large.

"It takes a fair bit to upset me, Sam, but I understand what you mean. Thanks for telling me." It seemed he'd been holding on to that one for a while. "How is your father now?"

His face dropped. "He died during the war. An accident."

"Oh, how awful. I am so sorry to hear that. My condolences."

She took a breath. A lump had formed in her throat. Discussing her late father still had that effect on her. "Well, there is another thing we have in common." She raised her glass. "To our fathers, taken from us too soon."

"To our fathers," Sam said, clinking his glass with hers.

The waiter returned with their scones and cream, and Sam dug in somewhat inelegantly, like a ravenous sportsman after a grueling day of training. Billie watched him for a minute, amused, before partaking herself. He did try to fit in, to behave with decorum, and for the most part he succeeded, but in moments like this, with his guard down, she saw the boy he had once been in rural New South Wales. She wondered whether he and his siblings had fought over helpings of food in his household. Hunger and rationing would do that. Sam finished his scones, dabbed his mouth, and took another sip of champagne, possibly unaware of how furiously he'd eaten everything up, while Billie was still working through her serving with delicate bites, her lipstick unsmudged.

"Things didn't go so well with Eunice last night," Sam let slip, and then looked like he regretted it.

Billie cocked her head, one brow arched. Her assistant had a lot to share this afternoon.

Sam seemed a bit unsure of himself, romantically speaking. To add insult to his war injuries, his girlfriend of some years' standing had jilted him while he was fighting overseas, her head turned by a handsome American GI, from what Billie had gathered. She'd only caught the story in bits and pieces, not wishing to pry. With their dashing uniforms and Hollywood accents, nylon stockings and greenbacks, the Americans had cut quite a swathe through the locals. But Sam was young enough to get over any lingering heartache once he found his footing again. She knew that Eunice was a newish girlfriend for him. Was it a good match? It was hard to tell, as Billie hadn't met her and he didn't talk about her much.

"We had a . . . quarrel," he admitted.

"Is that so? What about?"

He seemed about to answer, then reconsidered.

"Oh dear, it's not something to do with me, with our work, is it?" Billie hoped not. His silence announced that indeed it was. "You didn't tell her about . . ." She tried again. "Sam, you didn't tell her about the trunk, did you?" she asked in a hushed voice.

At this Sam shook his head adamantly, putting his champagne glass down. "Heavens no, Ms. Walker. I'm sworn to confidentiality in all of my work with you." He sounded sober now, despite the flushed cheeks. "I wouldn't break that trust for anyone. No, it was nothing like that."

Billie relaxed and leaned back in her seat, then sat upright as she thought of something else. "Eunice doesn't think . . . ?" It had occurred to her that Sam's girlfriend might wonder about Billie telephoning him at all hours. She awkwardly pointed a finger at her chest and then his and he got her meaning.

"No, it's not that, either," he said, shaking his head. "She says you're not . . ."

"Do go on," she prompted him, when he seemed to think better of whatever he'd been about to say.

"Errr . . . *proper.*"

She restrained herself from laughing out loud. Not proper? Well, she has an argument there, Billie thought. The usually reticent

Samuel Baker seemed to have taken to champagne like some kind of truth serum, the poor fellow.

Billie considered for a moment whether it was best to press for further details and found she couldn't help herself. "In what way am I not proper, dare I ask?" she inquired. There were so many reasons to choose from. Which would it be? The hours she kept? The places she frequented? The company she kept? The clothes she wore? Her swearing or smoking or the fact that she seemed to have misplaced a husband?

"She said . . ." This looked almost painful for him now. "She said that ladies ought not to be in your line of work. They ought to leave the work for men who need it."

Billie blinked. "I see. And what of women who need work, too? Where are they to get their money? Did she have views on that?"

He swallowed. "She didn't say." He was blushing vigorously now and had trouble meeting her eyes. She felt perhaps she'd gone too far, but Billie did genuinely wonder if Eunice gave thought to where Sam got the money he used to take her out. The stuff did not grow on trees, as they say.

They fell silent as Billie finished her last scone with a lovely berry jam that seemed a perfect complement to the bubbles on her tongue. Nothing was going to turn that to acid. She'd been judged before and she would be again.

"I'm sorry, I'm not sure why I told you that," Sam said. "It doesn't matter."

"You told me, dear Sam, because I rather insisted," Billie reminded him. "Never mind, there are plenty of others who feel that way. Your Eunice is no orphan there. But today we have a very satisfied client. It was a strange case, not entirely explained, but it's closed now, and the client is happy. Perhaps we ought to focus on that."

She tried to feel elevated again, but it was curdling in her belly now—the champagne, the scones, the whole thing. The finding of Adin Brown had in no way diminished her interest in what had happened to Con Zervos, or the whereabouts of her mother's sapphire earrings, or just who had crept into her bedroom in the night. There was something rotten all right, and she found she couldn't relax despite her best efforts. Her mind kept ruminating on the Browns: on them closing up shop and driving up to the mountains, excited by the prospect of their son returned to them. All that might attract some attention. What if it hadn't been her being tailed in the Strand Arcade, but them?

Stop it, Billie. She took another sip of champagne. The part of her that did the books knew the case was closed, and that was it. That was *supposed* to be it. Mrs. Brown had been insistent. But she could feel the puzzle pieces pulling at her, demanding her attention.

As Sam finished his champagne, Billie pulled out the small photograph she'd pinched from the boy's pocket. She'd almost forgotten she'd taken it. At a glance she'd thought it was an old image, a family portrait of some description, and on examination both impressions proved correct, the hairstyles indicating it had been taken in the late twenties or early thirties. The print was bent but still clear enough. It showed two adults—presumably a husband and wife—and three children, ranging in age from about one to eight. Every one of them, save the man, wore fur, in the form of either a stole or a small coat. This was of interest, naturally, but more startling was a shape on the woman's chest. She stood looking impassively at the lens, backed by a portrait photographer's drapery, wearing a dark dress with a corsage and an extraordinary necklace. It had a most distinctive shape—like a bat's wings.

"Oh hell," Billie exclaimed.

"Pardon? Billie, what is it?"

She sighed. "I've had a nice little celebration here, and you sure deserved a celebratory drink, but I think, well, I think I want to stick around," she said, looking over her shoulder for the waiter. "I'll drop you to a train, if you like."

Her assistant looked aghast. "What are you talking about?" he replied.

"I'm really sorry. I'd drive you back, but I can't afford the time. The train journey is quite pleasant, I'm told. I will make it up to you, Sam."

"Stop right there," he insisted. "What are you doing?"

"I played it safe at the hospital," she told him. "But now Mrs. Brown knows we've found her son and is coming up with her husband, and, well, before too long word could get out that the boy is alive. I worry that . . . Well, I've been tailed, but I was tailed near their shop and I can't be sure if it was me being followed or them . . ." *Or both now.* What if the parents were being watched? Or their phone was tapped? It took resources to do that, but it could be done for a price. Could what the boy was up to be so important? The stakes that high? She thought of the red marks on his wrists. He couldn't have done that to himself, and it certainly wasn't from some bar fight.

She pushed the photograph across the table. "And then there's this portrait. See? It's the necklace." She took a deep breath. "I think this is the photograph that was missing from their office and I think the boy took it because he recognized that the necklace this woman is wearing was to be offered at the auction. If he was wrong and it was a coincidence, he'd have been thrown out on his ear, told he was mad and a troublemaker. But if he was right . . ."

Sam looked down at the image. "You think someone might still come for the boy," he said.

"Look what happened to him," she said. "Yes . . . I do think it's possible."

Twenty-three

—◁ᎲᏇ▷—

The Veuve Clicquot had well and truly worn off as Billie parked outside the hospital in Katoomba, having driven there with some speed. Sam had hung on in the passenger seat uncomplainingly, having refused to return to Sydney and leave her to face potential danger alone.

By the time she sprang out of the roadster, Billie was feeling even more uneasy than when they'd departed the Hydro Majestic. She told herself the feeling could be illogical. Today had been a success. Her informed gamble about Adin Brown's whereabouts, thanks to her conversation with Mr. Benny at the morgue, had paid off. She had found him alive, if not quite well, and that was not yet three hours ago. She should enjoy the success of another puzzle solved, another closed case. But the little woman in her stomach was not happy. There was an unmistakable cold dread there. The photograph, the auction, the doorman, the thugs. Those red marks on the boy's wrists. It could be that she was conflating separate elements here, but the end result was fear for the boy, and she couldn't shake it.

She hurried to the hospital building with Sam at her heels.

"I'm back," she announced at the reception desk, slightly breathless and forcing a smile. The same helpful nurse was on duty. "My client is on her way," Billie offered by way of explanation. "She should be here any moment, probably with her husband. Their name is Brown."

The nurse looked confused. "Some friends of Mr. Brown arrived just a minute ago," she said.

Either Nettie Brown drove a lot faster than Billie had imagined, or something else was going on. Her heart sped up. "Can we see him again now please?" she declared more than asked, and even as she said it she was running to the men's ward where Adin Brown was laid up, the nurse striding quickly after her, clearly sensing something was wrong. Sam kept pace, and she saw his hand linger near his jacket, where his long-barreled revolver waited. He, too, knew what was at stake.

The scene in the ward as they entered was one of confusion. Adin Brown was not in his bed. He was on the hospital floor, or at least Billie thought that was him, as she could only see a blur of moving legs and arms. A man was crouched over the thrashing limbs. A patient several beds down began screaming. Others were staring and still others appeared sedated beyond consciousness, oblivious to the excitement. Billie felt eyes on her and looked up from the struggle on the floor to see one of the weedy thugs who had helped her tear her nice stocking in the alley behind the Georges Boucher Auction House. *The same bloody thugs are here.* Billie cursed in a decidedly improper manner and lunged toward the figure on the floor, who was still kicking out, fighting for life. The man crouched over Adin, for Billie could now see it was him, looked up and rolled away from the boy, then leaped to his feet. With his accomplice, he made for the door at the other end of the ward, hitting the nurse and nearly knocking her over in his rush to escape.

Adin was coughing and spluttering on the ward floor, his pillow next to him. They'd tried to smother him, Billie realized, and knew with certainty the men had not been sent as a warning; they'd been there to kill. There'd been no messing around. They'd outrun even the boy's parents. Adin was out of breath but otherwise seemed to be relatively unscathed, and without delay Billie took off after the men, pushing past the nurse, who was calling for help.

"He needs medical attention!" Billie shouted, catching the woman's wide eyes as she tore past. "And call the police!"

Sam was already ahead of her, pursuing the men and pulling the long-barreled revolver from his jacket.

"Call the police!" Billie shouted again as she ran toward the main entry doors, streaking past the administration desk.

Sam drew his gun as he reached the hospital entry and she heard two shots, coming from somewhere out of sight. Billie was hoping to get these two alive but was feeling rapidly less stuck on the idea. There was another shot, and Sam pulled himself back against the brick wall, part of which exploded with a small puff of white dust. He aimed his revolver and steadied it over his gloved hand. He pulled the trigger once, twice, the resulting noise so much louder than seemed possible. There was a cry as a shot made contact with one of the men. Billie, now beside Sam, saw the taller one grab at his leg, then continue across the street, dragging his injured limb. Still, he was moving. He was getting away.

"Careful!" Sam urged, and put an arm out as if to warn the hospital staff away from the under-fire main doors. Further shots were exchanged, and then the firing halted as the men concentrated on their escape by car. The second man zigzagged across the road and the two threw themselves into a battered tan-and-brown two-door Oldsmobile Sloper coupe that looked like it had seen better days. The engine was loud but uneven and the car's tapered backside gave the impression of a scared brown dog running away with its tail tucked between its legs. Billie broke away from the protection of the hospital entry and ran full tilt toward her roadster, not for one moment accepting that these two could slip from her grasp. Sam bounded forward on his long limbs and was by her side as she flung open her door.

"Let's go," she said a little breathlessly, and he was seated in a flash.

Billie fancied that she saw Mr. and Mrs. Brown talking beside their car, not far from the hospital, oblivious to what was happening, as she threw the roadster into gear, the engine coming to life with a roar. The mad timing of it all! The road curved like the trap of a sink drain between the hospital and the highway, and she confidently pointed the car along the curves with speed. They were only a few lengths behind the Oldsmobile, and she noticed with some pleasure the surprising amount of traffic traveling down the mountain ahead. Automobiles were backed up bumper to bumper, presumably as the result of a prang below, or a flood of traffic let out of the level crossing up the hill, and Billie thought, *I have them, yes,* before blinking as the tan-and-brown car failed to stop and instead careened across the two lanes of waiting vehicles, clipping the front of a passenger bus and resulting in much pantomimed rage by the occupants of the waiting cars. Horns honked. Bumper bars crunched. Bus passengers stared. *What do they think they're doing?* Billie wondered for an instant, but of course she knew. She knew they would do anything to escape and knew she had a chase on her hands as the driver took the Oldsmobile straight over the divider to the other side of the road and with a screech and a change of gears began roaring up the mountain.

"Hang on, Sam," Billie said, a thrill in her veins. The traffic farther down the mountain had started to flow again, she could see, but automobiles on the nearest side of the road had not yet shifted, their outraged drivers too busy rubbernecking at the errant vehicle. Without hesitation, she took advantage of the brief opportunity to dart though the narrow path in the Oldsmobile's wake, setting off another round of shouting she could barely hear above the roadster's engine and the honking of horns. She made it through the gap expertly, not even scratching a corner of her beautiful motorcar, and soon the low divider went under them like a rock, and the black roadster was narrowly missed by speeding cars coming up the other side. Billie turned sharply with a deft spin of the wheel and joined the flow of traffic going up the mountain. She felt the stares—including Sam's—but did not acknowledge them. She had other things to focus on. Billie shifted gears, put the pedal down, and set to catching up with the men who had made the grave mistake of first ripping her stocking in a crude alley brawl and now attempting to hurt—no, kill—her client's injured son while he lay helpless in a hospital bed. For these men, evidently no bar was set too low, and this was an error in judgment they would keenly regret if Billie had anything to do with it.

Sam, evidently not as thrown by events as she had thought, had the presence of mind to reach into the glove box and pull out Billie's leather driving gloves for her, which she managed to wriggle her hands into one at a time, not once taking her eyes off their target. Yes, she would need them.

"Good thinking, Sam," she said, and used both hands again to weave around a bus full of schoolchildren, the leather providing an excellent grip on the wheel.

The drivers on the Great Western Highway were by now well aware of the sudden and alarming presence of the tan-and-brown Oldsmobile, which moved erratically as the driver and his passenger turned around repeatedly to mark the progress of Billie's roadster. Her car was a faster one, lighter and with a larger engine, and Billie knew it to be in far superior condition, despite its age. Both vehicles wove around the traffic, speeding up from thirty-five miles per hour to forty. By the time they approached Medlow Bath they were doing near to fifty, dodging around cars, using the shoulder as the road narrowed. The Hydro Majestic hotel, where they'd triumphantly spent much of their afternoon, flew past. If the thugs wanted a chase, they had it.

"The roads are becoming less familiar. They'll try to lose us along here," Billie predicted. "We can't let that happen."

One of the two small sloping rear windshields of the Oldsmobile shattered with a bang as they sped through the intersection at Blackheath and passed Gardners Inn, scattering glass over the road outside the pub, where three men were perched on wooden benches, enjoying an afternoon beverage. Two of them stood with a start, shouting and waving their arms, and in a flash were far behind them. They certainly had the attention of the locals. Now the armed passenger in the motorcar ahead sat low, wind whipping his hair, the muzzle of his weapon falling temporarily from view.

"Keep the gun down when we go through the villages . . . if you can," Billie shouted. "The cops are bound to catch up." Though she wondered if that was true, considering the speeds they were hitting. This was not Sydney, where the police might meet them from any direction. "They shot out that window so they can hit us next," she warned, watching one of the men crawling toward the back. "We have to stop them, fast." They came around a bend, buildings falling away and the bush taking over. "Try the tires now!" Billie shouted above the roar of the wind and the engine. If Sam could get one wheel, they would end up on the side of the road and this reckless chase would be over. As they passed between a railway line and an old cemetery, Sam shot once, twice, the Oldsmobile swerving in front of them. No hits.

"I'm out!" he shouted with frustration. His Smith & Wesson revolver was a five-shooter, and there wasn't time to reload now, even if he had the bullets. He held up his gun helplessly next to her.

"Take mine," Billie said and pushed her left thigh toward him, flipping back her hem with one hand. "It's in my garter."

Sam hesitated. Her gun garter was a few inches wide and she had fashioned it to sit over the top of her stocking, and the effect, with the strip of lace and the delicate ribbon ties like the back of a corset, was pleasing as well as practical, she thought. But the sight of it strapped to her thigh evidently gave her assistant some pause, which was, at this moment, quite inconvenient.

"*Sam, take it now,*" Billie urged. The wind rushing through the car pushed up the hem of her dress yet farther and the little mother-of-pearl grip of the gun flashed.

Sam extracted the Colt.

By now the traffic had thinned considerably; for the moment it was just them and the Oldsmobile, which frustratingly had not slowed. They'd passed the intersection at Mount Victoria with the old hotel and the railway, the last spot Billie knew, and were heading west into unfamiliar territory. Now dense bush and loosely tended agricultural land hugged the road, the odd weatherboard house sagging into its foundations the only sign of human habitation. The barrel of a gun revealed itself, gleaming and deadly, from the back window of the motorcar ahead. "Look out!" she called, and a shot was fired, missing them narrowly. Billie steered in deliberate arcs along the road, making them a tougher target, her dark roadster holding the road expertly. And then the road opened up dramatically to reveal a precipitous descent into a valley awash with afternoon sunlight. The road turned left, winding downward in wide curves through a cutting, a convict-built rock wall on one side, the valley beyond. Having seen the descent, Billie braked gently, feeling the roadster pull forward to the right. In seconds it came back under her control. The pair ahead had stopped shooting, and now that Sam had Billie's gun, he seemed ready to use it. But not here. Not now. It was too steep. Too much curve.

The Oldsmobile wobbled and veered left, a rear tire moving unsteadily, and the old motorcar swung dangerously, inexorably, past the edge of the lane, then onward, bursting through the timber guardrails.

In a plume of dust and shattered timber, the thugs were careering over the cliff, plummeting some three hundred feet to the valley below.

Twenty-four

—∽∾—

"Tell me again what happened," the fresh-faced officer said, watching Billie carefully and with a somewhat puzzled expression, brows knitted together and head cocked. "*You* were driving the automobile, you say?"

Billie and Sam sat in Katoomba Police Station, a combination sandstone lockup, police station, and sergeant's residence at the rear of the Katoomba courthouse. Her black roadster, now a dusty gray from the chase, was parked outside the back entrance. The sun had set on both the day and Billie's patience. The adrenaline of the pursuit had subsided, leaving little energy for strained diplomacy.

"Yes, *I* was driving *my* motorcar," she answered with emphasis. She had endured a far too tedious interrogation already, and her professional smile—usually so handy—did not quite work, and settled into a scowl. She pushed back a wavy lock of dark hair that insisted on falling into her eyes, tried to tuck it under her hair wrap, but, not finding a hairpin where she thought she might, let the curl fall again, all the better to obscure her interrogator. She crossed her arms. "I went to the hospital to see my clients—" she began again but was interrupted.

"Your clients?" the officer echoed, as if she hadn't painstakingly explained the situation already.

Billie watched the uniformed constable from beneath her uncooperative locks. Sandy-haired and fit, he had the glowing but prematurely weathered skin and bright eyes of an outdoorsman. She imagined him scaling the local cliffs in his time off. He might have seen many things in his work with the Katoomba police, but it seemed that gunfights and women PIs driving fast automobiles did not fit into his framework of understanding about the world.

"Yes, my clients," Billie enunciated clearly, with deliberate slowness. "I am a private inquiry agent, as I mentioned, and this gentleman is my assistant." She gestured toward Sam as a schoolteacher might indicate a blackboard with a simple math equation written on it, then cleared her throat and paused, trying to maintain whatever scant composure she still possessed. "My clients had almost arrived at the hospital when two men attacked their son in his hospital bed, then fled on being interrupted. It was at that time we made chase, as I mentioned," she said, stretching out her thinning patience as one would stretch a stick of chewing gum to the moon.

There was a knock on the door and another officer entered, not quite as young, but with the same weathered, glowing skin as his colleague. "Mate, the crocodile . . ." He paused. "Pardon me," he said, looking at the elegantly windswept woman and her partner, who looked somewhat like Alan Ladd, clearly believing the pair had already departed. "Um, Constable, there's been another spotting of the crocodile."

Billie's eyebrows shot up. "A crocodile? Out here?"

"Escaped from the traveling circus, it did. Been eluding us for weeks," the second officer said. He removed himself from the room, and Billie sincerely hoped that the sighting of the crocodile would precipitate the end of the interrogation.

"And the shooting?" the constable continued, evidently not finished yet, despite the bizarre news of a crocodile stalking the streets of his jurisdiction. "Why did you chase these armed men?" he asked, for what might have been the fourth time. "That was dangerous, wasn't it?"

Billie willed herself to stay calm. *Because* they were armed men, *shooting at people*, she wanted to say, but refrained. "We felt it was our civic duty to alert the police, protect the vulnerable citizens at the hospital, and hold the men until you arrived. Sadly, we could not reach them in time and they drove off the pass."

"Right," the constable said. "I'll get my superior."

Billie felt like slapping him.

—⁂—

It was dark before Sam and Billie were released and found themselves back at Katoomba's ANZAC Memorial Hospital, finally alone with Nettie and Mikhall Brown, and provided with tea and Anzac biscuits. It was a blessing, to Billie's mind, that the Browns had missed the struggle and the shooting, and had not seen their son pinned to the ground with a pillow forced over his face.

"Do you recognize this photograph?" Billie asked, putting down her tea and extending the small portrait first to Nettie Brown, then to Mikhall.

"Well, yes," Nettie responded, surprised. "That is my aunt, Margarethe, and her family. Where did you find this?"

Adin's great-aunt. The one who stayed in Berlin. It was as Billie had suspected.

"This was tucked away in Adin's clothing. Do you think it could be the photograph taken from the frame in your office?"

Husband and wife looked at each other. There was nodding. "Yes, I think so," Nettie said.

"I must ask you again, does anything about this advertisement look familiar or ring a bell of any kind?" Billie smoothed out the folded clipping on the tabletop, between the plate of biscuits and the pot of tea.

"Well . . ." Nettie blinked and bent closer. "My goodness. That looks like the same necklace, doesn't it?"

"Yes, it does appear to be the same necklace," Billie agreed, and watched her. The Kleemann design was quite distinctive. Those bat-wing shapes. Surely there couldn't be too many like it?

"I . . . I guess I wasn't paying enough attention. What would he have to do with an auction?" Nettie asked, shaking her head. Billie recalled her frustration when she'd first been presented with the clipping, her inability to accept a connection. "But it is impossible. This was made by Georg Kleemann in Pforzheim, far from here. It was a prized possession of Margarethe's. How could it be the same one?"

Billie thought she knew how. And she thought Adin knew, too.

Twenty-five

———~m~———

Billie was stationed at the small corner balcony of her sixth-floor office, leaning against one of the Roman-style pillars, smoking a Lucky Strike and sipping Sam's perfect tea as if it held the key to her restoration—and perhaps it did—when she heard the telephone ring. Today was a smoking day, she'd decided. She kept her eyes on Sydney city, on the miniaturized people coming and going on the streets below, on the morning sunlight falling on the tall buildings, as her assistant answered the call. After a moment Sam filled the doorway with a look of concern in his baby blues.

"There's a telephone call for you, Billie," he said. "It's the police."

Billie strolled back inside, cigarette dangling from her Fighting Red. They'd spent a few too many hours with the police in Katoomba, but it wasn't over yet, she felt sure. Between their overjoyed client, the less-than-overjoyed police, and the shocked hospital staff, it had been quite the evening. She put her empty teacup on the edge of her desk, then sat in her chair and picked up the receiver. "Billie Walker speaking. How may I help you?" She leaned back, put her oxford-clad feet up, and cast her eyes over the front page of *The Sydney Morning Herald* again, with its dramatic artist's impression of the Oldsmobile flying off Victoria Pass.

"This is Detective Inspector Cooper," said a deep voice down the line. "Our colleagues in Katoomba informed me about yesterday's events."

And the papers, too, Billie thought. He couldn't have missed the part where it said: "Lady Inquiry Agent Billie Walker, daughter of the late former detective Barry Walker, was reportedly involved in what witnesses described as a 'shootout' and 'dramatic car chase' that led to the double fatality." It featured a clear photograph of her in a nipped-skirt suit and tilt hat, leaving Central Court on a divorce matter she had assisted with earlier in the year. They'd only just fallen short of giving out her number and office hours.

"I'd like you to come down to the station today, if possible," the inspector said.

Billie cocked her head and adjusted a stocking seam. This was no real surprise, though the deaths of those two men did seem to be somewhat outside what she imagined the detective inspector's usual jurisdiction would be. "Of course, Inspector. I can be there soon, if that suits," she replied. She took another drag of her smoldering cigarette, felt the smoke fill her lungs, felt her shoulders drop. If she was in any real trouble they would be at her door, taking her to the station. The inspector's approach implied that this would not be an interrogation with both barrels, as it were.

"Yes. I'm at Central Police Station. I'll wait," the inspector said and hung up.

Billie placed the telephone receiver back in its cradle. She took another puff of her cigarette, a rare second one, then held it between her fingers, thinking. The gesture reminded her of her father, she realized. She was becoming more like him each day. She smiled her very best serene smile. "Sam, I need to head to the police station. Will you hold the fort?"

Her assistant nodded. "Absolutely. I hope everything will be—"

"It will be fine," she assured him. He was worried about having brandished a gun in front of witnesses, but he needn't have been. The mountain cops seemed more suspicious of her driving than of this returned soldier's attempts to bring down a couple of criminals with his long-barreled farm gun. Men shot guns. That was easy enough to fathom. But women like Billie driving cars and whatnot? She turned and checked her hat in the oval mirror near her desk and, satisfied, slipped on her smoked glasses, cigarette dangling from her lips again. She took it out to touch up her Fighting Red, then replaced it. Blast. It was almost down to a stub. She placed it embers down in Sam's ashtray. He pulled one from his pack and silently offered it, and she nodded.

Yes, today is a smoking day.

"I should be back in an hour or so; otherwise, I will telephone," Billie said, grabbing her handbag. "Oh, and if a flood of clients pours in waving ten-pound notes around, get them all some very good tea and don't let them leave," she said dryly. "Our rate is now twelve pounds per day."

—⁓—

Billie knew Central Police Station well. Her father had worked there in his days as a detective before she was born, and his work had brought him back there plenty of times in her youth. The Walkers and this place went way back. The three-story police station building was a short walk up George Street from her office, and Billie chose to take the stroll rather than waste the precious petrol coupons she so enjoyed using on drives in the country—recent notorious events notwithstanding.

The station got its name from both its location and its purpose. The inner-city sandstone building had long acted as central police headquarters. The station housed the criminal investigation offices and other special branches, and backed onto the Central Police Court in Liverpool Street. Belowground the buildings were connected, allowing prisoners to be taken to court and back through a maze of dark corridors and holding cells filled with stinking, dangerous men—and the occasional deadly woman. At least that was how Billie remembered it from her father's vivid stories when she was younger. But while the courthouse on Liverpool Street had the impressive frontage one expected of a civic building, the public entrance to Central Police Station, with its grand masonry arch, was incongruously on narrow Central Street, in reality more lane than street, as if the city had collectively decided not to look at the police station or think about Sydney's underbelly of drunks, brawlers, thieves, rapists, petty criminals, and crime bosses. It was the architectural equivalent of being swept under the carpet.

There weren't a lot of women walking in or out of Sydney's Central Police Station on a Tuesday morning. At this hour there wasn't even the common presence of women and children in the waiting room that Billie routinely saw on weekends, or worst of all during the holidays, when tensions at home tended to go off the rails into violence. In fact, there was only Billie, and her distinctly female presence did not go unnoticed. Billie felt the heads turn as she walked beneath the masonry arch in her nipped suit with its relatively modest hem, her stacked-heel oxfords, and seamed stockings, dozens of male eyes clocking her movements as she walked past the waiting room on the left and the charge room on the right and stopped at the main receiving desk. The stares at her back were as palpable as hands. She could almost smell the testosterone. Not a terrible scent, but certainly distinctive, and in this context, almost overpowering.

This was what happened when you excluded an entire sex from a line of work for far too many decades, she supposed. If you placed all the private inquiry agents in Sydney in one building, it would be much the same.

It was with some relief that Billie spotted the welcoming face of Constable Annabelle Primrose behind the reception desk. She was a resourceful young woman of about twenty-two with a stocky, athletic build, a square and determined jaw, curly blond hair, and the brightest blue eyes Billie had ever seen. Her skin shone with wholesome radiance. She was from the country, somewhere out west, Billie recalled, and Billie fancied she played a set of tennis, rode a trick pony, and ran to work, all before breakfast. The police force had parked her at a desk job, as it had a lot of other women who'd joined up, assuming that the girls would get married and be forced to resign before long. Primrose could have wrestled bank robbers with one arm, if only they'd let her.

"Good morning," Billie said and looked round. "Quite the atmosphere in here today." The stares were only slowly easing.

The constable nodded. "Oh, Ms. Billie, it is good to see you."

"I understand Detective Inspector Cooper wants a word," Billie said. The inspector would be on the third floor, in the offices of the Criminal Investigation Branch, she imagined.

"Yes. I heard what happened yesterday," the younger woman said with wide eyes. "And it's all over the papers. You're famous. I'll let him know you're here."

Primrose made the call, explaining that the detective inspector's visitor would soon be on the way up with a lift operator, but Billie had a favor to ask of Constable Primrose first. It wasn't for the whole headquarters to know about, though. Aware she was being observed, Billie began a banal conversation about picnic weather with her young friend. This was a code, of sorts, as anyone who knew her well enough knew she was about as likely to chat about a picnic as a poet was to write about the stock market. Constable Primrose nodded, understanding. Such was the atmosphere at headquarters, they'd been through this before. "Really, I do hope it will be clear that day," Primrose agreed. The listening ears zoned out of the conversation with an almost audible click.

While Billie continued to talk about the forecast highs and lows and a possible stormy weekend, she surreptitiously scratched XR-001 on a piece of paper and pushed it toward the young woman.

"I would be much obliged if by any stroke of luck I could find out more about this before I move forward with planning," Billie said clearly; then, like a magician practicing the technique of distraction that aided sleight of hand, she bent at the waist and pretended to straighten the seams of her stockings. Well, one was askew, actually, snaking slightly to the right, and she took the opportunity to fix it. If everyone wanted to stare for a while, it gave her the opportunity for a quick whispered chat as she leaned close to Primrose. "I promise I'll drop the guy who owns the car in the lap of the police if I can," she murmured. "I don't think you have anything on him yet, though if you do, I'd surely like to know what. He's known to his house staff as Frank. The families of some young girls in his employ are worried," she finished.

Billie straightened, having said her piece, and the two women locked eyes. It was an agreement. Constable Primrose was frowning, clearly worried about what this Frank character might be up to. The piece of paper had disappeared into her pocket. Billie knew that determined jaw. Constable Primrose would help if she in any way could.

"I do hope the weather improves for your picnic," the constable said brightly, resuming the coded conversation.

"You know how I love a picnic," Billie replied, and her smile was sly.

She was just saying her farewell before heading upstairs when another woman's voice cut in. "I see you are busy, as always," the voice said rather pointedly, making Billie start.

It was Lillian Armfield. The legendary special sergeant had short hair curled back from a stern, watchful face and lips held as straight as a ruler. Hers was the countenance of a woman who had seen it all in her time as a nurse, and now famously as a detective. Her penetrating light brown eyes were fixed on Billie, and she suspected Armfield had seen her pass the number-plate details over to the constable, while the male officers were either fascinated by her stocking seams or minding their own business.

"Wasn't I right about my young constable here?" Armfield said, breaking the tension by patting Constable Primrose's arm. "She'll go far."

Billie let out a breath. Lillian generally approved of her schemes, so even if she knew the constable was helping her with something, she was unlikely to cause trouble. "I believe you're right," Billie said, recovering. "Right as always."

Constable Primrose looked at Billie and then Armfield and appeared to relax a touch, though the older detective was of formidable reputation and her proximity was enough to give any young police officer the jitters. But Armfield's attention was fully focused on Billie again, and those light brown eyes were giving her a familiar look. "We need more women in the force. Have you been considering it? Your father was very good in his day, you know."

Billie smiled, then recalled his reasons for quitting. There were a few bad eggs giving the force an unsavory reputation, which Barry Walker had wanted no part of. Even after her father's time as a cop, there had been a spate of police corruption in the twenties and thirties, which Armfield herself had been more than acquainted with as she famously battled the brutal razor gangs, as well as the brothel madam and "Queen of Woolloomooloo," Tilly Devine, and her nemesis, sly grogger Kate Leigh, the "Queen of Surry Hills." Had the police corruption corrected itself, the bad eggs been tossed out? It seemed a bit too optimistic. Yet Lillian was playing her part to cleanse the force, determined that new blood was needed, and particularly a better balance of women, who were clearly still few and far between.

"It's more satisfying than divorce work," Armfield added with an acidulous touch, knowing perfectly well the professional demand for proof of adultery in the private inquiry trade, and the often distasteful scenarios that entailed. Billie, on principle, never set men up with paid women to get what she needed as proof, though that was a common practice. But she had followed cheating spouses to catch them in compromising moments. It could be an ugly job, but the scenarios were real, at least. No frames. Billie did not enjoy that work, but she didn't want to have to sublet the last of her father's offices and acknowledge professional defeat. Her father had handled hundreds of divorce cases—after all, that was how he'd met her mother—and if it was good enough for him . . . If Billie earned a bit of a reputation—a good one, or at least an exciting one—she might attract more clients, and then she could leave the divorce work to someone else and focus on the trickier cases, like this business with the Brown family. A puzzle like this was more satisfying, though it was proving a lot more dangerous, too. It was yet to be seen how the unexpected publicity today would affect things professionally.

"Barry had the utmost respect for you, Lillian," Billie said by way of response. She nodded and gave a look that told the older woman that an immense respect for her was very much shared by Barry's daughter.

"I know a brick wall when I see one," Armfield replied. She said it warmly, but with some regret. "Strong heads suit women," she added to no one in particular and stalked out of the station, passing Detective Inspector Hank Cooper, who evidently had come down from his office, tired of waiting for Billie to seek him out.

Cooper was near the lift watching Billie—with a look of what was it? Surprise? Amusement? Curiosity?—and he turned his head to watch Armfield as she disappeared through the archway onto Central Street. When he shifted his attention back to the reception desk, Constable Primrose was a picture of dutiful professionalism. Billie ventured a playful wave at the detective inspector.

"You seem to be unavoidable at the moment, Miss Walker," he said, striding over on those rangy limbs of his. His tone was even.

"Trouble comes to me, Detective Inspector, not the other way around," Billie replied, straight-faced. She followed him to the lift. "And it's Ms.," she reminded him. "Besides, you asked me here today."

Cooper waved her into the lift. "How could I not?" he asked. "You're all over the papers." He didn't look convinced about her relationship with trouble, and she couldn't really blame him for that.

"Indeed, I do seem to be," she said as the doors were closed and they began their ascent. "Or rather, those unfortunate fellows are. I'm afraid I can't compete with that display." The men had picked quite a spot to lose control of the Oldsmobile, and *The Sydney Morning Herald*'s artist had made the most of it.

The inspector led her to his office, a small private room that smelled of cigarette smoke, frustration, and more of the testosterone she'd detected downstairs. Of the three, she didn't mind the last one a bit, owing to her personal preferences, but the first two in this small space were just on the edge of objectionable. Central Police Station was becoming cramped and like so many government buildings was in need of a revamp.

Billie watched the inspector from the corner of her eye, trying to anticipate his next move. Was this meeting to be combative or friendly? she wondered. Would he throw his weight around?

He offered her a wooden chair, then walked to the window and hefted it open. Good manners, Billie thought. She thanked him. He closed the office door and they were alone.

"When were you transferred here?" Billie asked. She was aware of the comings and goings at the station, and this man had not been part of the equation the last time she was on the third floor. She would have remembered him. "Or perhaps you've been in Europe?" she queried.

"I served in the 2/8th Battalion in North Africa and New Guinea," the inspector replied, almost automatically. "Before being recruited to . . . a special unit," he added. Few men who served were cagey about where they'd done so. It was the great divide in Australia and elsewhere—those who had served and those who had not. It wasn't a conversation one could avoid during the war, or even now, with 1947 already close at hand.

Billie watched the inspector's face carefully, considering his reply. "Z Special Unit perhaps?" she guessed, cocking her head. "Military intelligence?"

His expression replied with a possible yes, but he quickly closed down again, hauling himself into that clamshell she'd detected back at her flat. "I'll ask the questions, thank you," he told her tersely.

Billie sighed openly. "I have no doubt your war record is impeccable, Inspector," she clarified. "I worked as a war reporter myself, until I came back here when my father was ill. But I do know some of the goings-on in this office. You're welcome to ask me questions, of course, and I fully expect you to, but in truth I think we could help each other if we shared a bit of information. I consider us to be on the same side, if that hasn't been clear before now."

He gazed at her, temporarily unreadable. "I thought you weren't interested in being a police officer," he said.

"You have good hearing," she replied.

"I'm paid to, Ms. Walker." He pronounced the title correctly and carefully, and she didn't detect sarcasm. *Progress. Good.*

Their eyes locked, the two sizing each other up across the battered desk, sitting tall and unmoving in their respective chairs. After a stretch of silence, neither of them looking away, it seemed something indefinable had been settled between them.

Billie crossed her stockinged legs and leaned back a touch. She'd had the impression back at her flat that this inspector might turn out to be a rather fine detective, and helpful, though it didn't take much to get him to close up. Still, she was here in his office and he wasn't making it formal, and hadn't brought in the detestable Constable Dick Dennison, Hatchet Face. By now the inspector would surely know that her father had been a cop and had worked in this very branch, and perhaps he would know the reasons her father had resigned from that employ, making enemies of those who didn't want any changes to the corrupt status quo of the time. Not waiting for the inspector to lead her, Billie explained the essentials of the case she had been working on, leaving very little out except Mrs. Brown's private family matters and, most notably, the unexpected arrival of Con Zervos in her bedroom and his mode of departure by travel trunk. Her clients expected privacy, of course, but that horse had bolted when a couple of thugs walked into the hospital, threatening a boy's life and attracting an array of witnesses. She stressed her feeling that her client's son, Adin Brown, was not yet safe. Anything but. On that score, she hoped this detective inspector could help.

"I must impress on you how important this is," Billie said, leaning forward again. "I think it would be wise to move him to another hospital as soon as he is well enough—somewhere closer to his parents—under an assumed name. I may have found him for my client, and as of yesterday I am off the clock officially speaking, but it's not over for them yet, I fear. Adin Brown is not safe, despite the death of those men yesterday." The little woman in her gut was rarely wrong about matters of safety. "I'm hoping his memory will come back soon. That should be quite revealing."

The inspector watched her closely, giving little away. He'd listened to her story without interruption. "You're certain the men who had the accident were after him specifically? It wasn't an opportunistic robbery gone wrong?"

"Quite certain," she said with a level, unblinking gaze. It was not quite enough to turn a man to stone, Medusa-style, but it had been known to have a strong, chilling effect.

"I see," he said. The inspector did not seem to doubt her words.

"And I'm quite certain they attacked me and my assistant, Samuel Baker, outside Georges Boucher's auction house on Sunday," Billie added.

His eyebrows raised just perceptibly. "Did you report this?"

"No. If I reported every time someone attempted to rough me up to put me off my work, I'd be in here every day," she said matter-of-factly. It was the truth. "Besides, they didn't have much luck," she added, recalling the satisfying feeling of her hatpin penetrating one of her attacker's ankles. "And no guns were drawn." *By the assailants,* she distinctly failed to specify. She had drawn her own Colt, but there was no need to bring that into it. It was licensed and had not been fired. She didn't feel like losing that license, if, say, this agent of the law happened to take exception to women carrying guns. She felt they were on the same side, but there was no point playing with fire.

Billie watched the detective inspector's reaction. His eyes were hazel like Jack's, she realized, but paler. She'd seen those eyes soften the morning she'd woken up with a body in her bedroom, but he was all business now. She recognized a brick wall as well as Lillian could.

"I understand there were shots fired at the hospital," he continued.

"Shots fired at us and anyone else trying to intervene with the would-be killers' plans, yes. Naturally we had to defend ourselves."

"Witnesses say your . . . secretary, is he? He fired."

Billie nodded. "As I said, we had to defend ourselves, and protect others. The shots were fired outside the hospital, however, and no one was hit, as far as I am aware."

"Indeed. And tell me, why did you follow after them when they left the hospital grounds?"

Ah, this had been a sticking point for the constable in the mountains as well. Why did she pursue a couple of would-be killers?

"I had some questions for them," Billie said, knowing full well that self-defense was hard to argue once the assailants were fleeing. "And they might have returned to finish the job." She wanted to know who they were, and the police hadn't furnished her with that information yet. The only clue she had was that they were associates of Moretti, who was next on her list of people to visit. "They had tried to kill the boy, the boy my client paid me to locate, a badly injured kid, so I took the matter rather seriously."

The inspector contemplated her, his eyes steely beneath lashes the color of tall summer hay. It was a gaze she met calmly. He broke away first. "You have a license for your sidearm, I presume?"

"I do. It is rather standard for most in my profession. Self-defense is sometimes necessary, though of course that did not play into the tragic events at Victoria Pass yesterday. My sidearm remains unfired."

There was a long pause. "We are waiting on the coroner's report."

"Of course. They were definitely the same two men, Inspector, thugs for hire, that type, who attacked me and Mr. Baker on Sunday afternoon, and they had two other companions on that occasion. I believe they were working for Vincenzo Moretti, the private inquiry agent. You may remember him. He was sitting in a Vauxhall outside my flat on Sunday morning."

"Moretti? Why do you say that?"

"Well, because I made one of them tell me," she explained. "I can be persuasive when required."

Now his eyes widened a touch. He did not ask how she had made the man tell her, though he looked awfully intrigued.

"I looked into this Moretti character."

Now it was Billie's turn to be surprised. "Do go on."

He flipped through a few pages of a notepad and landed on what he was looking for. "The Morettis fled Italy following the Milan bread riots of 1898, settled in Sydney. Vincenzo Moretti, born in July 1900, now aged forty-six, works as a private inquiry agent. He has prior arrests, most notably for an attempt to bribe a witness for the purpose of suppressing evidence. Let's see . . ." He trailed off for a moment, turning a page. "Ah yes. He was further charged with attempting to pervert the due course of justice by unlawfully conspiring to dissuade a witness from giving true testimony, for which he did a short stint behind bars. The officer whom he attempted to bribe, and who brought the case to court, has a familiar last name—Walker. Detective Barry Walker, since resigned."

"And regretfully deceased," Billie added, though her voice was smaller than intended, the words shrinking in her throat.

"My condolences, Ms. Walker." He looked at her with those hazel eyes, impenetrable but sympathetic. "This man was outside your flat on Sunday, as you pointed out. Does he do that often?"

"Not that I'm aware of," Billie said, and swallowed. Had he been the one in her room as she slept?

"Now two men who may have been colleagues of Mr. Moretti have ended up at the bottom of a cliff."

"That appears to be the case, yes." She shifted in the hard

wooden chair. "You'll note I reported the incident immediately," she added. "I didn't think they had much chance, careening off the road like that, but we called for an ambulance. They were shooting out of their car at us. Did the Katoomba police tell you that? These men were quite reckless."

Silence crept between them, and Billie considered her father and his history with Moretti. She'd known Moretti hated him for something, something personal. So Moretti was convicted of trying to bribe an officer of the law? That figured.

The inspector appeared to make a decision. "I want you to show me exactly what happened," he said.

"Am I of interest?" He did not seem about to arrest her, but it was worth asking.

"Not at this stage," he replied, poker-faced.

"Well then, I guess we can still be friends," she said with a smile, eliciting a twitch of the lips from the inspector. There was a long pause, during which his eyes softened again, just a touch.

Billie stood up, smoothing down her skirt. "Shall we take a drive, then?" she suggested. "I have my roadster parked only a couple of blocks away. She's a fine automobile. I can take you with me."

"No need, Ms. Walker. There is a police automobile available," he said. He came around to the door to let her out.

"I'll meet you at Victoria Pass, then?" She resisted daring him to a race to get there first.

"Your secretary, Mr. Baker, was also a witness," he noted. "He is available?"

Her heart sank a touch. "You need us both? Surely not. I'll have to close the office if no one is there to man the desk. And the police do have his statement." Today was not a day to leave the telephones unanswered, considering the free publicity the newspapers had provided.

"Very well." The inspector looked at his wristwatch. It was old but handsomely designed, with rectangular gold detail on a worn leather strap. "I'll meet you at the spot where you pull off just after the pass, if you don't want a lift. Will two o'clock suit?" he asked.

Two o'clock. That gave them just over three and a half hours to drive there, she calculated. "Oh yes. I'd prefer to drive myself, thank you. That is, if I'm not under arrest. And that should give me time for a spot of tea first," she replied a little naughtily.

He did a double take as he collected his jacket. "Just don't run anyone off the road this time," he advised, and she flashed him a grin in return, fairly sure she'd heard him make his first joke.

Twenty-six

—⁓—

"Ms. Walker, a note arrived for you while you were out," the lift operator, John Wilson, said.

Billie was on her way back down to the street level of Daking
House, having instructed Sam to hold the fort and take messages,
when she was handed an envelope. She took it from Wilson and
turned it over in her hands. The plain envelope had her name on it
in familiar bold letters, no address or stamp, and it didn't feel like
there was much inside. She slit it open with her nail and read the
slip of paper that confirmed the identity of her correspondent. There
were only seven words:

I GOT A JOB IN THE HOUSE

Billie paled. *Shyla*. "When did this arrive?"

"Just a minute ago. I was on my way up to give it to you when you
ordered the lift," Wilson told her.

"I have to catch her," Billie said, and when the cab arrived on the ground level she sprinted out, forgetting her usual thank-you. She burst out of the front door of Daking House and stood on the footpath of Rawson Place looking to her left and right. Traffic filled the streets around Central Station, with plenty of pedestrians on the footpaths. Which way would Shyla have gone? A dark-haired woman in a dark coat was walking across the road toward Central, visible in a parting of taller pedestrians, and Billie ran after her, weaving through the crowd and grabbing the woman's shoulder. She turned. The brown-eyed woman gave Billie a shocked frown, shook off her hand, and walked on.

"Sorry . . ." Billie began, but the stranger was already gone.

A tram passed and a boy of no more than fifteen wolf-whistled at her. Billie heard it in the distance, as if it were happening in another, parallel dimension. *Damn it, Shyla*, she thought. If that man, Frank, was detaining or harming the girls in some way, Shyla could be putting herself in serious danger. Billie still didn't have an address, but a big homestead in Upper Colo near an orchard couldn't be too hard to find if she could spot that distinctive Packard, and now she had the number plate, too. That was assuming the automobile was parked in the open, or the man wasn't off transporting whatever things he left the homestead to deliver. *Blast*. She'd have to get out there and see what was going on, and soon. But she wanted to hear first from Constable Primrose, with details: a full name, an address, a record of some kind. When had "Frank" arrived in the country? Was he known to police?

She wondered when Shyla's job would be starting; did she have a few days up her sleeve? She wanted, too, to pay a visit to Moretti. She wanted to be sure Adin Brown was okay. She wanted to speak to his parents again. There was much she wanted, but for now she had a detective inspector to satisfy.

Her heart slowing to a normal pace, Billie walked toward her motorcar, uncurling tense fists that had left the faint crescents of fingernail marks in her palms. The roadster was parked by Station House like a waiting steed, and putting the top down and climbing in allowed Billie's shoulders to drop a touch. The vehicle was still a bit dirty and roughed up from the previous day, but it seemed not to diminish her glory. Here Billie was in the driver's seat of something she could control. It had been an eventful few days, and now she was increasingly worried about Adin's immediate safety and Shyla's as well. She needed to clear her mind to get it to function at its best, and for Billie driving at high speed was just the tonic. She placed her handbag on the passenger seat, pulled on her leather driving gloves, and patted the dashboard as if the machine were a large and beloved mare of great power and elegance. The engine warmed admirably, and as she waited for the right moment to pull out into the traffic she considered Sam's response to the news that she would be driving back up the mountain. He'd initially looked disappointed not to be going with her, but had covered that up commendably. The telephone had been ringing—thanks to the press—and she needed him in the office. *Steady Sam. Unquestioning Sam.* She might not have made it through the weekend without him.

Engine warm and ready, Billie pulled smoothly away from the curb and was immediately pleased to detect that the previous day's incident had done nothing whatsoever to sour her desire for the road. This was to be her second trip to the Blue Mountains in as many days, and at this rate she'd run out of petrol coupons mid-month, but no matter. The proximity of death taught you that you only had this moment. Only now. She wasn't going to sit in any cop's car when she could be at the wheel.

The speedometer needle moved higher in its round dial; the wind pushed harder. The exquisite freedom of the road had not been lost to her, and though she was unaware of it, Billie's red lips wore a soft smile, mirroring that of winged Victory just feet ahead of her on the roadster's purring bonnet.

Twenty-seven

—⁜—

Detective Inspector Hank Cooper from Sydney's Central Police and Private Inquiry Agent Billie Walker were both somewhat outside their usual jurisdictions as they stood on the edge of Victoria Pass in the Blue Mountains, the afternoon wind tugging at their hair and clothing. A roped-off area of broken timber railing marked where the Oldsmobile had forged a deadly path to the final resting place of two men on unforgiving rocks hundreds of feet below.

"This was an 'unfortunate accident,'" the detective inspector commented after a long silence, peering over the edge and quoting Billie from the police report. "Is that what I am to believe?"

"Well, one can hardly call it fortunate," Billie noted.

They stood several feet away from the path of destruction, and though all was quiet now save for the rustling of summer wind through the bush and up the steep embankment, and the intermittent roar of the occasional passing vehicle, the aftermath of the plummeting motorcar had left a kind of psychic path that could still be felt. Billie thought she could almost hear the sickening sound of the splintering rail and the crash far below.

"One can't help the bad driving of others," she added, wrapping her dark navy driving coat around her, wind whipping the hem. "Locals die on this bend every year, I'm told, and I suspect the driver did not know these roads as a local would." She paused. "I slowed. They did not."

"You have an answer for everything, don't you?" Cooper said, turning to her and holding on to his hat.

"Do I?" She had theories but she didn't have a sure answer for why those men had wanted Adin Brown's silence, or who had sent them to ensure it. Moretti? And who was *he* working for exactly? Was this part of a grudge against her dad and by extension her? That seemed a stretch after so many years. No, she didn't have all the answers. Billie didn't have a sure answer for why she'd been pummeled in an alley or why Con Zervos was dead and had been planted in her bedroom. Theories were forming, a cast of characters assembling, clues knitting together—but answers? No.

The inspector asked her to describe once again the chain of events, the path of the cars. She complied patiently, shouting from time to time when the wind came up.

Cooper heard her out, took some notes, and without a word led her back down the road, away from the pass with its spectacular view of the Megalong Valley on one side and Hartley Valley on the other, toward where they'd left their motorcars. Unless they wished to rappel down to the fatal collection of rocks, they could not get closer to the mangled hunk of metal from which two bodies had been extracted and which a crane would soon remove from the otherwise picturesque landscape.

"It was unwise to pursue them," the inspector said once they reached their vehicles.

"I don't plan to make a habit of it, Detective Inspector," Billie replied, leaning against the roadster's driver's-side door and wondering fleetingly if she'd have been called unwise or heroic if she'd been her father. "I do wish, though, we could firmly establish who hired them, and their reasons."

"I'll look into it," he said.

"Will you?" she asked, watching him. "You have to admit it's quite a coincidence that Moretti was outside my flat on Sunday and those thugs, who said they worked for him, attacked Adin Brown the next day."

"Yes. It is interesting," he said cautiously.

They would head to the hospital next, and Billie hoped that Adin was recovering well and would have something to say, if not his entire memory restored. She felt the inspector knew more than she did about the whole affair, including, probably, the identities of the dead men. But just what that was remained to be seen.

—⁓—

Billie's arrival at Katoomba Hospital with the tall inspector did not go unnoticed by patients and staff.

As they made their way toward the arched sandstone entrance, Billie noticed a flurry of activity behind the windows on either side. The nurse from the previous day was once again at the front admissions desk, even more wide-eyed and happy to assist, and nearby Billie spotted a copy of the day's newspaper. It appeared to have been hastily put to one side, as if to give the impression that the incident and its coverage had somehow not been a major topic of conver-

sation. Uniformed staff watched them move through the halls,
turning and whispering, leaving a buzz of low voices in their wake as
they headed to an area Billie was unfamiliar with. To her relief, they
had moved Adin Brown out of the men's ward to a private room west
of the main entrance, usually reserved for quarantine cases. He also
now had a police guard, she noted. The local constable from the
previous day—he of the circular questions and outdoorsman glow—
was sitting outside the private room, looking catastrophically bored,
and it was with some pleasure that Billie watched him register her
approach, then stand and put on an air of officiousness, only to have
Cooper flash a badge and put him back in his place several ranks
below.

"Detective Inspector Cooper, Central Police. Ms. Walker is assisting with our inquiries," the inspector said. The constable's goldfish-
like gaping stretched on for a moment and then ceased, his athletic
complexion paling. The nurse opened the door into the room and
Billie gave him a saccharine smile as she moved inside, Detective
Inspector Cooper shutting the door behind them for privacy.

They found themselves in a modest room with a single bed and
a barred window that afforded some natural light. It smelled of
bleach and some kind of disinfectant they'd presumably used on the
boy's wounds. Adin was propped up, which was encouraging, but
when he turned to look in her direction Billie was shocked by the
swollen appearance of his eyes. He had been beaten around the head
with some enthusiasm, that much was evident, and it now made a
great deal of sense that he was having difficulty with recollection.
His parents were with him, his father holding his hand tenderly.
With the inspector and Billie inside the room, there wasn't a lot of
space. A vase with some bright cerise bougainvillea added some

cheer to a setting that might have been somber, except for the palpable relief felt by Mikhall and Nettie Brown.

"Oh, Billie!" Nettie exclaimed, leaping up and embracing her, all
reserve and formality having fallen away. "Thank you for finding our
boy, our dear, dear boy." Fresh tears were running down her face and
so fierce was her embrace that Billie felt she might injure a rib, or
perhaps she was still bruised and tender from the alley attack. Trapped
for a moment in the woman's arms, Billie exchanged a look with the
inspector, who was observing the emotional scene without comment.
Now her client—her former client—was not concerned about what
it had cost to find her son. Now that she had her boy back, it seemed
she felt only pure relief.

Billie waited until the squeeze eased before she spoke. "I can't
take all the credit, I'm afraid, Mrs. Brown. The people who found
Adin near the railway tracks and brought him here should really be
thanked. And the nurses and doctor. I'm just glad he is getting proper
care now and will be safe." She looked around the room again. Yes,
there was no way in except through that door, and anyone trying to
get to the boy would have to get past the police guard.

"There are boot prints on him . . . boot prints on my boy; they
hurt him so badly," Nettie said, sobbing quietly into Billie's ear. They
remained entwined for a moment, Billie reassuring her that Adin
was in good hands.

The nurse had already informed them that the boy's back was
injured but not broken—a relief—but his head injuries were a major
concern, along with some internal bleeding. He would recover in
time. He needed rest, a lot of rest. Billie suspected it would not be a
quick or easy process to elicit memories from Adin Brown.

Once released, she pulled up a chair beside the narrow hospital bed and turned to the patient. "Adin," she began, "my name is Billie Walker. I visited you yesterday, but you likely don't remember." She took his hand in hers and shook it gently, her eyes drawn once more to the raw red lines across his wrists. Ligature marks.

Red-rimmed eyes met hers. "I remember," he said simply, his voice small but determined. "Thank you."

She nodded that she understood. "This is Detective Inspector Cooper from the city. He is here to learn about what happened to you, if you can recall anything," she said, and turned to the inspector, who seemed not to mind that she had taken the initiative. Nettie's display would have put at rest any questions about her connection with the family.

Adin worked hard to pull out recollections for the inspector, and several times apologized and said he was trying to remember. He appeared frustrated that the memories would not come. The inspector, for his part, was more gentle and patient than Billie had expected. When asked, the boy swore he had not been drinking and could not account for the smell on his clothing when he was found. He remembered pulling himself from the train tracks, but he didn't know how he got there, or to the hospital.

The space became stiflingly small as time stretched on, and after twenty minutes or so a nurse entered, bringing tea and refreshments for the patient, his family, and the police visitors. Billie took Cooper aside as Nettie and Mikhall and the nurse fussed over Adin, and told him she'd like to show Adin something that might prompt his memory. Cooper agreed, pressing her for fewer details than she might have expected, perhaps trusting her and her connection with the family to help loosen up the line of inquiry. Not every inspector would do that, she knew, desiring to be seen in control as men in his position often did. Once the refreshments were cleared away Billie took a seat next to the boy and showed Adin the auction house advertisement she had brought with her. The effect was riveting. His painfully swollen eyes widened and he struggled up from his pillow.

"Yes, I saw this advertisement and recognized my great-aunt's necklace," Adin said, sitting up as straight as he could and holding the newspaper clipping with the kind of intensity with which one might hold a lifeline. "I saw this at the milk bar. This advertisement." That fitted with what Adin's friend Maurice had told Billie. The inspector eagerly wrote notes as the boy continued. "That necklace belonged to my great-aunt and they took that from her, took everything from her."

"Who is they?"

"The auction house people. I don't know how exactly . . ."

"How can you be sure it is the same necklace?" the inspector asked.

"I am sure," the boy said.

"It does appear to be the same necklace the woman is wearing in this photograph," Billie said, handing the small, creased image to the inspector.

"Where did you get this?"

"It belongs to the boy," was all Billie said, looking away, not happy to answer questions about its acquisition.

The inspector narrowed his eyes but said nothing to her. For now. "I'd like to keep this, thank you," he said to the Browns, and they nodded their assent.

"I looked up the auction house and contacted them to find out where they got it," Adin said, his memory becoming clearer, the words now tumbling out. "The owner wouldn't speak with me, and they wouldn't let me in the place. But I had to talk with him. Everyone knows Georges Boucher frequents The Dancers, so I tried to talk to him there. I figured I could walk straight up to him and confront him. Then he'd *have* to listen to me."

"And did you speak with him?" the inspector asked.

"No." Adin frowned. "I was thrown out before I could, and then before I knew it someone had grabbed me."

"Were there any witnesses to this?" Cooper asked.

"No," he said. Then he pulled his brows further together. "Actually, one of the doormen. I'd spoken to him earlier. He saw what happened, I think."

Con Zervos. He saw the boy abducted.

"You were alone when this happened? Not with friends?" the inspector asked, noting everything down.

The boy nodded.

"I thought it was the doormen at first. It's a high-class place. But then they were playing real rough. I think I . . . I think I blacked out. I was taken somewhere, and . . ." His breathing sped up, the blood draining from his face. "They . . ." Billie noticed his hands begin to shake.

"Take it easy, kid. You're all right now," the inspector said. "Just breathe. That's it . . ." Slowly, the boy calmed and his chest began to move again at a more normal rate. "Would you recognize any of the people who attacked you?"

"Oh yes . . . I would, I think. They didn't hide from me at all. They . . ." He trailed off again, sweat appearing suddenly on his pale brow where the bandages did not cover him. He balled his hands into fists, and pressed them to his temples. He cried out, startling Billie and the others in the room.

In no time the door opened and a nurse appeared, the constable looking over her shoulder from outside. The cry had been heard. "That's enough for now," the woman said, pushing Adin gently back down into his bed. "You must rest."

The nurse ushered all of them out of the room, even Mr. and Mrs. Brown, and as they assembled in the hallway outside, the inspector protested.

"The patient must rest. You've got your orders and I've got mine. That is enough for one day." Even in the face of Cooper's authority, the steely nurse wouldn't back down.

Billie walked away from the small room in a near trance, head swirling with thoughts, barely aware of the inspector trailing behind her. She could see it clearly now—the boy beaten nearly to death, then doused with alcohol and left for dead on the train tracks. An accident, end of story. The train would explain the injuries sustained by his beatings—if there had been much of a body left to examine at all.

They let him see them, Billie thought. They expected it wouldn't matter, because they expected him to be dead.

Twenty-eight

—⚬—

It was nearing five o'clock when Billie made it back to her roadster and put the top up against a gale that had begun in the late afternoon, a summer wind whipping up from the valley. In the far distance a smoky haze rose into the sky, silhouetting Katoomba in ombré tones from blue to charcoal. A faint scent of cinders carried across the miles. Hot, windy days were a bushfire hazard in these parts. It was perhaps too much to hope for rain, she decided, noticing the clouds were white and moving fast across an otherwise blue sky. The grass beside the road was dry, waiting to ignite. Things had moved so fast the day before, she'd barely noticed.

Detective Inspector Cooper crossed the road, having finished his discussions with the hospital staff, and she noted the length of his stride and his military bearing. His motorcar was parked just behind hers and he joined her, helping her fasten the roadster's roof.

"Thank you for assisting with our inquiries," the inspector said, speaking first. He slid his hands into his trench coat pockets.

It had been a long but profitable day for his active investigation and her closed one, puzzle pieces coming together thanks to the boy's gradual recovery and efforts to recall what had happened to him. The auction house had not been a red herring, after all. But where had he been taken? To what end and by whom? Moretti himself? It was clear Adin's captors had not expected him to live, and it was a stroke of luck that hikers saw him before he perished of his wounds or exposure. The inscrutable inspector knew more than he was telling her, Billie was sure of it, and she watched him with a mind to unlocking that invisible wall of his, the wall that seemed to come up at the slightest nudge.

"I think I'll have some refreshments before the long drive back," she said casually, holding her tilt hat against the rising summer wind. "Would you care to join me, Inspector?"

He took a step forward, as if he might lean past her and open her door for her, perhaps, or, she thought fleetingly, kiss her. She didn't move. They locked eyes, she tilting her head up slightly to match his gaze. Billie's green-blue eyes were steady, his hazel eyes warm and liquid for a moment, then unreadable again.

"I should head back," he said, breaking away to look down at his polished, well-worn leather shoes. After a long silence, he added, "Off the record, you seem to have saved me a lot of trouble, Ms. Walker. Those two are unlikely to be missed. Everyone in that hospital seems to have witnessed the attack. If they'd got away . . ."

"They'd still be a menace," she commented, and he nodded. "It's a long drive back," she added, giving it one more try. "Can't I tempt you with some refreshments first? You do need sustenance, surely?" She wasn't about to let him go if she could help it, now that she had him away from his desk, away from the likes of Dennison, and the discussion with Adin Brown had been so productive. Trust was building between them. If she could keep him open . . .

"I'm afraid I'll have to decline," he responded, and gave her a look she couldn't read. "Thank you for your assistance today, especially with the boy." He paused and she did not interject, instead waiting the silence out. He had not walked back to his motorcar, had not forced the issue by opening her door.

She crossed one ankle over the other, and leaned back against her black motorcar.

"The local police haven't seen such excitement for a while," he finally added. "As you may know, one of the men has been positively identified, but the other is so badly mangled it will take a while longer to confirm." She hadn't known, in fact. She waited for more. "But they think we have an ID as they were a pair who always worked together. Known to police," he went on. "And yes, they were known to consort with Moretti, among others."

"Ah," she said, victorious at last, smiling. He'd have known that information back in his office, and he hadn't let on. She'd thought it unlikely that one of them had lied when faced with the working end of her pistol. Why pull Moretti's name into it if he wasn't the one who'd hired them? That wouldn't make sense. So Vincenzo Moretti or whoever he was working for didn't want Adin Brown talking. Where was Moretti now? And where were the other two men from the alley? Not at the bottom of the escarpment. Somewhere else, possibly still with orders to put an end to Adin's memories of what had happened to him.

"You think the boy is safe now, in there?" Billie asked, pointing across the street. "If Moretti or others want him dead?"

"He has a police guard," the inspector said.

"Would he best be moved?" she pressed.

"Possibly," he admitted.

"Is there anything that can be done about it?"

"Possibly," he said again. "I'll look into it."

"And the auction house?"

"It's not come across my radar before, but it might be of some interest now." He looked down at his shoes again, his chest rising with one deep breath. "I should head back. If you learn anything more, please feel free to contact me. This is my private number," he said, handing a card to her. He'd written the number in pen on the back. The writing was fresh. A corner of it had smudged.

Billie took the card, sensing that it was unusual for him to offer his private number. "Thank you, Detective Inspector Cooper," she said, and they exchanged a look of unexpected intensity. She held it as long as she could before he broke away.

"And thank you again for your assistance today," the inspector said again, a touch awkwardly.

"Of course. I'm happy to assist. You know where to find me," Billie told him.

They shook hands, a courteous if formal gesture after the intimacy of Adin's tiny hospital room, and she opened her driver's-side door and slid inside. He closed it for her, having been robbed of the opportunity to chivalrously help her into her motorcar himself, and stalked off. Blast, she thought, having hoped to hold him longer. Before she pulled away she watched him drive past, headed for Sydney's Central Street and his cramped office. She leaned back in her red leather seat and sighed. Cooper might have had more to tell her if she'd been persuasive enough. She was losing her touch.

—m—

Billie had plenty of time to consider the inspector, and how to best approach him when they next met, as she ate a light meal in the Hydro Majestic's Salon du Thé, served by the same waiter who had been in Cat's Alley just the day before. If he had seen the paper and recognized her, he was professional enough not to let on. The establishment appeared busier today, with several gray-haired men gathered around one table, taking tea and appearing to discuss business.

What a full and eventful twenty-four hours it had been since her last visit. And she would have a big week ahead, searching for Shyla, now that the boy was in good hands and under police guard, but for now she was spent. She could do worse than relax at a scenic table at the Hydro, and on a day that was still reasonably clear, despite the growing haze of smoke farther down the mountain. She ordered no champagne this time, but washed down her repast with black tea. Drinking alone, to her mind, was a slippery slope and a common downfall of a private inquiry agent, and she'd seen it plenty of times. Finally, refreshed, and with a full belly, she left the salon, noting that the wind had not died down. The sun was still high—it was barely three weeks off the summer solstice—so she wouldn't have to drive home in total darkness. She had her eyes on the Great Western Highway, holding her hat and contemplating the long journey back to Cliffside Flats, when she walked past a dark motorcar parked near the hotel's curved entrance.

She stopped and turned, then froze.

A black Packard stood beside the arches of the main building of the Hydro Majestic. Billie blinked, checked the number plate against her memory, and looked around for its owner. There was no one stepping out of the hotel just yet, no one standing nearby. She turned on her stacked heels and made her way quickly to her roadster, parked on the Great Western Highway, and, after some consideration, reversed it and parked by the new, imposing Belgravia building, where she could watch the main entrance from her seat. She pulled her French-made Lumière binoculars out of the glove box, adjusted the lenses, and waited. As it turned out, she didn't need to wait long.

There he is.

Even from a distance equivalent to a short city block, she was struck by the appearance of the driver when he stepped out of the hotel and was bade farewell by a uniformed staff member. Through the round lenses of her binoculars she caught a thin smile before he turned and walked to his fine automobile. Billie knew perfectly well, with a sickening turn of her stomach, that the man she had her lenses trained on would walk to that Packard, not to any other car. The man was tall and slim and wore a suit of palest blue, perhaps linen, and wrinkled somewhat from the drive. His hair was as white as snow and cut short at the back and sides in the military style, smoothed down at the front. She couldn't catch much more, as his head was tilted away from her, toward the far end of the hotel and the highway beyond. He got into his motorcar and pulled out along the driveway.

Shyla had said the man was "white," but that had meant more than Billie realized. It was the man with the snow-white hair. The man with the airman's burn, or the plastic job. The man from that table with Georges Boucher at The Dancers. Hadn't she also seen someone with snow-white hair at the auction house? Yes, and the Packard, before they were set upon in the alley. What a nasty little circle this was. Any fleeting question of whether she should follow the Packard quickly vanished. Billie had to know who he was.

Billie ignited her engine and followed the Packard, heart thumping. The big car turned left out of the driveway, in the direction of Blackheath and Lithgow. Billie stayed two cars back, a good distance. There was no reason for the man to think she would be there, she reminded herself. No reason for him to think he was being followed. Still, she was grateful for the flow of local traffic that helped her to blend in. She ran through the scene inside the Salon du Thé. No, he had not been among the businessmen dining there. What had brought him up this way? she wondered. Had he, too, taken an interest in the boy in isolation in Katoomba Hospital?

The Packard wound its way along the highway and passed through Blackheath, through the intersection where the shattered rear windshield of the ill-fated Oldsmobile had since been swept up. The grand motorcar went on, not slowing, past the old cemetery, then continued through bush and agricultural land dotted with the occasional homestead and weatherboard house. Many properties were overgrown, suggesting a boom between wars, now quashed by the lack of able-bodied men to work the land. The powers that be had done a fine job of cutting down the generations. And still the black Packard drove on, away from the city, and to what destination? All the way to Colo? If so, there would be no time to get information from Constable Primrose, no time to figure out who he was.

The motorcar finally slowed at Mount Victoria, right at the top of the mountains, and turned off the Great Western Highway at the main intersection. Billie slowed, happy that one of the two vehicles ahead of her was also making the same turn. They passed the famed two-story Hotel Imperial, Australia's oldest tourist hotel, sitting pale and regal on the corner, its parapets decorated with medieval-style detail. Billie had taken tea there once with her parents, seemingly a lifetime ago. The pale driver did not stop, instead heading out toward Mount Tomah and Bilpin. A country automobile with a flat back pulled onto the road in front of Billie, an extra buffer between the two black cars, her roadster and the Packard. For nearly an hour Billie followed the Packard along Bell's Line Road, hanging back behind the truck and the other car, just far enough to avoid being noticed. Or at least she hoped so. It depended somewhat on the Packard's driver, but in Billie's experience most people did not check to see if they were being followed, even those who really ought to know better.

Who is Frank? Was he a confident man? Suspicious?

The sun was beginning to set when the big black car finally slowed and pulled up outside the Kurrajong Heights hotel, a huge timber building with, Billie guessed, a spectacular view over the valley. She was forced to drive past, knowing that pulling off the road suddenly would attract the man's attention. She followed the farm vehicle and the other car down the road until the hotel was out of sight, then circled back and managed to drive around the closer side, up a second driveway, to park next to a large truck that concealed the roadster from the hotel entrance. She switched off her head-lamps and waited, not knowing whether to get out. Now that she knew "Frank" was the man from The Dancers, she realized that he might recognize her by sight, as clearly as she had recognized him. Was he stopping for refreshments? The telephone? Would he stay for the night? She ran over what she knew about him in her mind as she waited, deliberating whether to enter the hotel or try to spy through the windows to see what he was up to.

Thankfully, only a few minutes later he was striding back to his car, his blanched hair and complexion standing out with a ghostly glow in the gathering dark, exaggerating his almost alien foreignness. Had he spoken with someone? Delivered something? His mood seemed not to have changed, his body language speaking of a confident man, a man who perhaps even felt superior to those surrounding him, a man who did not appear suspicious and afraid he was being followed. He started up the Packard and pulled away, not even bothering to look around him. *He . . . travels in a motorcar, carrying things to Sydney*, Shyla had said. What things, exactly? He'd visited the Hydro Majestic and now this hotel, both places with good reputations. As the Packard's taillights faded down the road, Billie eased the roadster into life and followed again with extra care. By the time he turned off the road onto a smaller dirt road signposted COLO, there was no one between them to provide a convenient buffer, and little light to speak of. In the country, headlamps announced you once the sun was down, but so, too, did the dusty road telegraph your direction. Billie found it easy to follow far back in the Packard's dusty wake as it passed small settlements and isolated homesteads. Eventually there were no settlements, no houses. A kangaroo hopped across the roadster's path and Billie slowed just in time, the other roos in the troop blinking at her in the darkness just beyond. Past the remote Upper Colo church and cemetery, she caught his headlamps as he turned right far ahead.

Windows down and headlamps off, Billie drifted along the narrow moonlit road, feeling the summer air and taking in the scents of eucalyptus, citrus orchards, and the wildness of the bush. She sensed the damp proximity of water, the Colo River, she supposed, probably slow-moving and low in the summer heat. In gaps through the trees to her left she made out a silvery shimmer. *Good goddess, I hope this isn't a trap*, she thought, feeling the isolation of the place. Her Colt was strapped to her thigh. She might well need it.

When she rounded a tree-lined bend, creeping slowly, a homestead by an old orchard of citrus trees came into view. Was this the place Shyla had mentioned? It was the only source of light in the area apart from the moon. Billie stopped, then reversed until it was almost out of sight again. Yes, the Packard was driving up to the main building, having entered through a wooden gate. Her eyes had adjusted to the dark and she could make out that it was a surprisingly grand single-level house in colonial style, elevated on short footings, with a long verandah running from end to end. The house was flanked by various outbuildings and backed by a rugged natural ridge of some height, providing cover from the rear. The area of roadside where Billie had stopped was too unprotected for her to remain on, so she pulled away, headlamps still off, and circled back until the bush became dense again and she could conceal the roadster from both the homestead and the road. It would not do to have the man expecting her, after all her careful tailing.

She decided to approach the place on foot and see what she could from the protection of the bush. Reaching into the glove box, Billie grabbed her binoculars and a battered Rayovac torch that looked like it had seen two world wars, not one. Made hyperalert by the unfamiliar and increasingly heavy rural darkness around her, Billie stepped out of the roadster onto the unlit country road, clicked her door shut quietly, and looked around with the watchful presence of a rabbit, straining for sound or movement. Again, she was reassured by the weight of the mother-of-pearl-handled Colt strapped to her thigh.

Her mother had always said you could never tell where the day would take you, and now with Billie's only leads being a familiar face, a license plate number, and a conversation with Shyla that felt like a lifetime ago, she found herself in quiet moonlit bushland, far from home, far from any police station or even another house, and without much of an idea of what she might find, or even what she might be looking for. What was the precise nature of the concerns about the girls working in the house? Why hadn't anyone heard from them? Were they okay? And how was this white-haired man, "Frank," connected to it all? Was it mere coincidence that he'd been at The Dancers and the auction house? The little woman in her gut knew the answer to that. There were no coincidences here, just a nasty little circle—one she was about to become more deeply drawn into.

Moving cautiously up the road, Billie replayed what she was able to recall of the conversation with Shyla.

There's a bad feeling about him. He has some of my mob there—four girls . . . I'm worried, Billie.

Billie swept her eyes from side to side through the darkness and moved steadily along the uneven roadway toward the wooden gate, relying on the light of the moon and not daring to use her torch in case it was visible from the house. She'd worn her quiet, trusty oxfords, and they managed the unsteady terrain with little difficulty, falling soundlessly on dark pebbles and churned-up earth that was a deep maroon in the soft moonlight. She reached the surprisingly dilapidated wooden gate, where two tire tracks led like a driveway to the house, then started at the sight of a huge, skull-like face.

Death.

Billie brought a hand to her chest.

No, not Death. This was a large, hunching sooty owl, staring at her, its face white, its dark and penetrating eyes almost comically oversize. For its part, the owl said nothing of curiosity and the cat, or of women who wandered to strange places alone in the dark, but flew off, leaving her to it.

The gate was now locked with a chain and padlock, Billie noticed. It clearly broadcast the man's desire not to be disturbed, but it was little more than a bar for vehicles, as the fencing was so eroded on either side that she could walk straight through it. The big Packard had vanished, doubtless now garaged in one of the sheds.

Was this a trap? Billie wondered again. But what were the chances that the man was expecting her in the mountains that day? Expecting her to follow him? On the other hand, what did she think she would find in this place? The specter of abuse, particularly against young women, was something Billie did not wish to encounter again after all she'd seen during the war. Despite all the talk of Britain's "finest moment," the war had seemed to bring out both the best and the worst of humanity, and even the Allies had not been without blemish in that respect. The vulnerable women and children freed from concentration camps had been abused by their Soviet liberators, Billie had heard. Yes, war brought out the worst, and as her mother pointed out, Billie's work showed it all to her, the worst of human instincts and behavior. She had seen and heard enough unnecessary suffering and abuse of power for several lifetimes, and her stomach tightened at the thought of encountering more of humankind's worst, but so also did her focus sharpen.

Step by step she moved up the side of the dirt drive, staying in the shadows of the trees and bushes as much as possible. Lights were on at both ends of the homestead, and as she neared it, she could see that the dwelling was old and not terribly well kept, the verandah sloping to one side, paint peeling. Not quite as grand as it had first appeared. The grounds, too, had been neglected, bush creeping up to the house on three sides.

Now close to the house, picking her way around the unruly bushes and the remains of what might have once been a garden, Billie sensed movement in one of the rooms and dropped into a crouch, her driving coat sweeping the ground. She listened intently. It sounded like footsteps on a wooden floor. One set of shoes. They sounded too light to belong to the tall, white-haired man. Billie rose a touch to try to see what was happening, but bushy tendrils like clawed fingers clutched at her coat, snagging her. Turning and cutting a hand, she cursed the surrounding *Acacia horrida*. Some genius had imported it, evidently unconvinced that Australia was sufficiently furnished with things that could claw, stab, or bite you. With some effort she unhooked herself, and sucked on her pricked and lightly bleeding hand.

As the sound of footsteps faded, Billie eased slowly to her full height. The window opened onto a sitting room illuminated with candles and a kerosene lamp, and next to it a second window revealed a dining room, darkened and empty, lined with odd shapes. *Curious.* Billie moved closer to the glass and cupped her hands around her eyes to get a better look, then immediately leaped back as a pair of bright, slanted eyes met hers. Again she brought a hand to her chest, and stifled a laugh. These were not living eyes, but eyes carved of shell. Out of place in this rustic setting, a pair of imposing carved wooden figures, one facing her at the window, the other turned away at an angle, stood as tall as Billie, the closest one rather unnervingly meeting her eye to eye. She again cupped her hands against the glass to better see. What were they? Satyrs? No, it was Satan and his wife, and it was Mrs. Satan's shell-inlaid eyes that glittered in the moonlight and seemed to follow Billie's movements. The sharp wooden face was set at a downward angle, the mouth upturned in a dark grin. Billie could not see Satan's face, but his long hand was held out to support a silver dish, in which calling cards could be placed. What exquisite, if unnerving, carvings they were. And how odd to stumble across them in Upper Colo, in this rather ramshackle homestead. She'd seen such a pair in Europe once and had been told they were Italian and all but priceless.

Next to the Mephistophelian pair were smaller objects, Billie now noticed, of perhaps similar value. A gold candelabra. A china figurine of a woman and a fawn. A small ornate chest. This odd arrangement of valuables was juxtaposed against an assortment of rustic, even rudimentary, pieces of furniture. The dining table, though laid with good silver, appeared to have been knocked together using wood from the property. The surface was uneven. A cabinet in the corner, stacked with more small figurines, looked to have been repurposed from work in a kitchen. The legs were sawn down and Billie noticed small hooks screwed into the shelves from which teacups or mugs would once have hung.

A figure moved past the open doorway, rousing Billie from her speculation. She slipped back into the darkness and moved carefully through the bush, silently cursing as sharp twigs and thorny vegetation tore her stockings and scratched at her hands.

Now she could see more clearly into the sitting room. It was large, with a fireplace stacked with firewood but unlit this summer evening, though the temperatures here would drop dramatically overnight, she guessed. The figure moved past again, walking into the light, and Billie stiffened.

Shyla!

Shyla, who had asked her to find out about this place. Shyla, who had warned her about the white man who was a foreigner, and no good. Shyla, who'd said she was getting a job in the house. She was already here. Billie drew a breath. It might not have been her who had given the note to John Wilson, then. It could have been someone passing information along a chain. Or maybe she had arrived but a short time ago? Either way, she was inside. Billie bent and picked up a small pebble, and moved to throw it at the window, then paused. It was too risky, the house too quiet. They might be heard. Carefully, Billie moved around the perimeter of the building. Where was Frank? Where were the other girls?

The Packard now came into sight, peeking out from behind a shed, gleaming in the moonlight. Wouldn't you want to protect such a costly motorcar, out here in the bush? Billie mused. If that fine motorcar wasn't in the shed, it meant something else was.

Torch still off, Billie looked over one shoulder, then the other, and strained to hear the slightest sound. Slowly, she approached the closest of the two run-down sheds. Like the front gate, its door was secured with a basic padlock, English made and the likes of which Billie had picked many times before. She pulled a long, sharp pin from her hat, examined the ornamental pearl on the end, decided she liked it too much, replaced it, and pulled out another. She took the chosen pin in hand and with some force bent the end until it formed an L shape about the depth of the lock, then inserted the end into the keyhole. In relative darkness and going by feel, she spent a moment listening for the lever inside the padlock. *Come on . . . Got it!* She lifted the lever and the padlock fell away. Billie pocketed the hatpin, regretting that it was probably never going to sit quite right again, and quietly pulled the shed door, stepping into the deep darkness, then closed it behind her, shutting out all light.

A strange, musty smell hit her nostrils, and even in the blackness she could tell the shed was tightly packed. There was barely any space to move. Her shoe hit a box or drum of some sort. She took a breath and switched on her torch.

Paintings?

Billie had not been sure what to expect, but this was not it. The shed was packed with oil paintings—portraits, landscapes—and objects of all kinds, some concealed by drop cloths. Some of the paintings appeared quite old. If they were cataloged or arranged in any way, she could not tell. They seemed simply to be stacked for storage. Billie was no art collector, but her mother had been at one point, and some of these looked to be quite good. A stack of frames sat on top of a cluster of oil drums next to her. So that was what she had bumped into. There were a lot of similar drums stored in the shed, she realized, finding the combination of oil and paintings curious. They were not traditionally a good mix. Billie's torch illuminated a surprising assemblage of dusty objects made of china, of bronze, of gold. Cherubs. A ballerina. An elaborate candle holder. A menorah. *How odd to leave these treasures in a shed like this*, she thought. So impressive was the array that Billie marveled that the paintings and objects were not behind glass, proudly displayed for envious acquaintances to admire—and that brought to mind another location: Georges Boucher's auction house, with all those valuables slipping through the heavy curtains to be gazed at and coveted and bid upon by Sydney's wealthy set. If this man had come after the war, he had brought a lot with him. That in itself was highly unusual. So many came with barely a suitcase, or only the clothes on their backs.

And then she knew. The little woman in Billie's belly knew precisely, with horror, what she was gazing at, how it all fit.

Billie found a crowbar on the ground next to one of the drums, cleared the frames away from it, and pried the top off without much effort, suggesting that the drum had been opened recently. It was not filled with oil or with liquid of another kind, and when her torch revealed the contents, she was not even surprised. The sense of familiarity was like déjà vu. Like a nightmare she'd had many times before. *Gold*. The oil drum was filled with gold. She reached in and pulled a piece out. It was about the size of . . .

She dropped it.

A gold tooth.

Billie swallowed. The space seemed to get smaller, the shed's walls closing in. This was an oil drum filled with gold teeth and fillings. Billie's stomach, which had already twisted as the realization first struck, knotted further. She dry retched once, twice, and brought a hand to her mouth. Quickly, she switched her torch off and rushed out of the shed and into the moonlight, welcoming the night air on her face as a world of abstract color burst behind her eyes, her lids closed tight. She could almost feel Jack's hand in hers, feel the cold dread that had seized her that day back in Vienna when she'd first seen with her own eyes, first really realized what they were dealing with.

But now she wasn't in Vienna. She was in Australia and the war wasn't over. The war had come to her.

A sobbing cry rose in the air and Billie stiffened, pulled from her memories. She held her breath, listening in the darkness. In this quiet, remote place, there had been crying. Then, as quickly as the cry had reached her there was a murmur of voices, and all was quiet once more. The night was still again. She heard the owl in the distance. A rustle of wind in the bushes. It had not been her imagination, her memory of Vienna; it had come from the house. The distinct sound of sobbing had come from one of the rooms at this end.

It was a room with no curtains, she realized. It was a room boarded shut from the outside.

Twenty-nine

———✦———

"Cooper," the deep voice answered. If Detective Inspector Hank Cooper was tired or had been sleeping, this was not detectable in his voice. It had taken what seemed like ages to drive back to the Kurrajong Heights hotel, get access to their telephone, and secure an operator on the exchange. It was late, but Billie was not tired. She had never been so awake in her life.

"Detective Inspector, this is Billie Walker," she told the voice.

"Ms. Walker?"

"Thank you for your private number. I didn't expect to call you so soon, or at this hour." She looked at her watch. It was after eleven now. "It's an emergency," she said.

"Where are you?" His voice was now firm and direct.

"I'm at the Kurrajong Heights hotel, but the emergency is not here. There is a remote homestead at Upper Colo where five young women, girls really, may be trapped, and I believe . . ." She considered her words carefully. "I believe a war criminal is living there. I discovered an oil drum full of gold teeth. I believe the man has been selling the belongings of deceased prisoners of war, concentration camp victims, through the Georges Boucher Auction House, and perhaps elsewhere. The homestead and outbuildings are full of European paintings, sculptures, and objets d'art. He must have good contacts here and in Europe to have brought so much over." She swallowed. "These girls with him . . . I think they are in grave danger."

"A war criminal? A Nazi, you mean? Are you certain?"

The Nuremberg trials had only ended in October. Over more than a year Billie had read about the former Nazi leaders being tried by an international military tribunal for crimes against humanity and other war crimes. The evidence against them was chilling. One key element was the requisition of the belongings of civilians, particularly Jews and others considered enemies of the state. Silverware, jewelry, paintings—anything of value was taken as war loot. Gold fillings were taken from the living and the dead, and even hair was collected and sold to create textiles after being shaved off the victims.

She took a breath. "Dead certain," she said to the inspector.

"And an oil drum with gold teeth? And some girls are trapped, you say?"

"Yes, their families have been worried, unable to reach them, and after investigating I believe the situation is worse than they thought," she said with emphasis. "And, yes, I found gold teeth and fillings in a shed on the property. Hundreds of them, at least. I held one in my own hand. That's what they did at the camps. They pulled out the teeth to melt the fillings down. It's . . ." *Horrifying.* "It's what Adin Brown happened across when he recognized his great-aunt's necklace. There is no doubt that boy was right, though I don't think he realized the scale of what he'd discovered. Some chain of people, some group, are bringing the stolen property of war victims here to Australia,

probably through the docks, and stashing it in this remote homestead. Maybe in other places, too. Adin got too close for comfort
when he recognized that bat-shaped necklace of his great-aunt, and
he was nearly killed for it. Please trust me, Inspector. I wouldn't be
calling you at this hour if I was not absolutely sure. I know you would
be putting yourself on the line a bit, but if I am right, and I am bloody
sure I am, you'll be responsible for bringing in a war criminal."

There were no sounds save for the crackling of the line as the
inspector absorbed what she was telling him. If they really had
formed some sort of a bond of trust, this was the moment it was to
be tested. The silence stretched and stretched. Billie worried that
the line had been cut off.

She could not walk away from this. Shyla was in there, and it
was highly likely she did not know she was in there with a Nazi. A
killer, probably. There could be no other explanation for a man
living so far from the city with a homestead full of treasures and his
house staff practically held captive. He was paying for his lifestyle
with the belongings of murdered Jews and political prisoners.

"How did you get there? Were you seen?"

"It's a long story, and I'll explain later, but a friend of mine tipped
me off. No, I wasn't seen." She stopped there, not wanting to involve
Shyla more than Shyla might wish. *She is inside the homestead and I
am worried about her,* she wanted to say. She was worried about Shyla
and she was worried about what that sobbing meant. Who had it
been? Shyla, or one of the girls she'd been anxious about? "I have
reason to believe there may be underage girls in the house, possibly
being held against their will, though I have not seen them with my
own eyes." Not yet.

"You got a tip-off about a Nazi war criminal and went in there yourself?"

"Not quite," she replied. "I didn't realize how serious it was until I saw it myself." Did Shyla know what was in the sheds? Did the other girls know? "I'll explain when I see you, just trust me. I am not mistaken about this," she insisted. Her hand holding the receiver was so tense the knuckles had whitened.

"I'll have to get a warrant," Cooper replied after a spell, evidently taking her word. "I'll pull some strings, but it will take a few hours. I could be out there by . . ." Billie did the math. It was perhaps a two-and-a-half-hour drive from the city to the homestead. Her heart sank just thinking about the time it would take. "I could get there by, say, six, soon after sunrise, with a warrant. The magistrate won't like me waking him . . ." he said. "But I'll be there."

Blast, Billie thought. Of course Cooper would have to play it by the book. She thought of calling Sam for backup. But would that help? Could he get there much faster? Could the two of them get the girls out safely—that is, if the other girls were there at all? The little woman in her gut told her the girls were there, and the situation was bad, very bad indeed. Thinking of Shyla shut in that house with a Nazi made Billie's guts churn.

"The girls may be in danger. I know one of them. And I heard . . . sobbing, coming from a room that is boarded up from the outside." Her arms came up in gooseflesh as she recalled the haunting sound. "I don't like them being left there until morning," she explained. "Is there any way of getting to the man sooner?" *Just to be sure,* she told herself. *Just to be sure they are unharmed and he can't get away.*

The line was silent for a beat. "I have someone I trust at

Richmond station. They're only an hour or so away. I'll call and get him to come and pick up the girls."

"No," she said instinctively. The man could get spooked and it was all backward, the girls being taken away and not the man who was living off the contents of that horrible drum. "They're young Aboriginal girls, Inspector. From what I can tell they would not want to go with the police if they can avoid it. Can you get the man on suspicion and have him held? Can he be picked up, considering what is in the sheds?"

"I'll still need the warrant."

"I didn't imagine it, Inspector."

"I don't doubt you, Ms. Walker."

Billie ran it through in her mind. "If police come for the girls, and they have no warrant and can't hold him, I worry what could happen." She'd been unnerved by the contents of the shed and what she'd heard. She'd have to quiet the uneasiness in her belly and wait. "You get your warrant."

"I will, Ms. Walker. I give you my word."

"You can call me Billie," she told him.

"Billie," he said, "I hope you know what you're doing."

She described the homestead and its location in detail, gave the specifics of the motorcar and its license plate, and Cooper signed off to set the wheels in motion. She hung up and leaned against the wooden partition of the telephone box with her eyes closed.

She hoped she knew what she was doing, too.

Thirty

Shortly after midnight, Billie moved swiftly along the shoulder of the dark road in her quiet oxfords, having parked her roadster at a safe distance from the Colo homestead.

The quiet before the storm.

The homestead revealed itself against the night. Billie swallowed. Lights were still on, even at this hour. She wished for a sympathetic magistrate and wings under the inspector's feet. She had alerted the authorities and could not do much else for now, but she had to see that Shyla was safe. And she needed to be there when the police descended. Shyla did not like police, did not trust them, and she had her reasons for that, reasons Billie thought she understood. But what else could she do? In any event, she could not sit this one out. For some reason Billie trusted Hank Cooper, she realized. At least as much as she trusted any cop she'd only just met. She believed he would come. She believed him, and, Great Hera, she hoped she was right to. She hoped he had believed her when she'd explained the significance of what was in that shed. She could not have been mistaken about what she'd seen.

The orchard across the road from the homestead was undisturbed, rotting fruit dotting the ground like a crop of small, openmouthed jack-o'-lanterns, blackened and malformed with decay. Billie crept past and spotted the sooty owl, now perched on a piece of broken fencing, still staring at her with that skull-shaped face. This time it did not fly off. It was staying to watch the show.

Wait.

The gate at the driveway had been unlocked since her departure. Had Cooper telephoned the Richmond police after all? Could they have beaten her here? That seemed unlikely given the distance to Richmond and the sense of quiet at the property. Her heart eased a little at the second possibility her mind grasped on to. Had Frank left the property again? With another lot of goods for Georges Boucher, perhaps? Could she whisk Shyla and the other girls away in his absence? But as she made her way toward the ridge to approach the homestead from the south, hopping the rotting fence and creeping up through a disused paddock, she spotted the moonlight glinting off an unfamiliar motorcar parked beside the Packard outside the shed.

He is not alone.

Who was this visitor? A danger to Shyla and the other girls? Billie made for the shelter of the outer shed and waited. Satisfied there was no one in either automobile or outside the homestead, she approached the vehicle and noted its number plate. It had a distinctive fluted radiator grille. A *Daimler?* Yes, a midthirties Daimler Light. It was a fine car, as the Packard was, and equally out of place in the rural surrounds.

There was movement at the house, at the rear, close to the out-house, and a light came on. Billie stayed low and sprinted the short distance to crouch beneath the lit window. There were no curtains here, just as there hadn't been in the dining room. With such a remote property, perhaps privacy was ensured, and this man, Frank, did not worry about being watched. That was the reason he'd come to this place. To ensure his privacy, to ensure his freedom. What uninvited guest would bother him here, where even the fruit was left to rot?

Footsteps moved toward the window, and Billie flattened herself against the side of the house. A few clicks, and the sound of a bolt or lock, and then the window swung open on its hinge. Billie held her breath, then exhaled when Shyla's face appeared, dark and res-olute, gazing into the night and haloed by the light of a kerosene lamp inside.

"Pssst. Shyla, it's me."

A gasp, then: "You're here. You found him," in a whisper.

"You found him before me," Billie replied, also in a low voice. She stood up and the two women were face-to-face at the window, Billie in darkness and Shyla silhouetted by the soft light from within. Billie's hands were balled in fists, she noticed, and she uncurled them. "Shyla, are you all right? What about the other girls . . . are they here? Has Frank hurt them? Does he prevent them leaving, contacting their families? Is it as you feared?"

Shyla appeared to consider her words carefully. It was probably only a few seconds before she spoke, but to Billie it felt much longer as she stood outside in the dark bush by the window, wary, unsure, and utterly alone. "One girl, Ruthie, she has more freedom," Shyla told Billie. "She makes the meals. She showed me the book, did

Ruthie. I took it for safekeeping." The young woman reached into her undergarments and pulled something out, then handed a small notebook through the window. Billie took it, puzzled. Shyla spoke again, very softly, after looking cautiously over her shoulder. "The others are locked up. There are two girls, just kids they are, Ruthie says, and locked up for the men he deals with. She doesn't see them, except to deliver meals. I have not seen them, only emptied the pans."

The blood in Billie's veins seemed to freeze. There was a lot to absorb in what Shyla was telling her, and she took a moment to recover herself and push back the bile rising in her throat. The sobbing she'd heard. It had been one of the girls. "How long have you been here, Shyla?" she asked. "Has he tried to . . ." She tried to form the words.

"I came two days ago for domestic service work. I told him I am twelve," she said. "He's ignored me so far."

"He bought that?" Shyla was clearly older, perhaps eighteen, maybe even in her early twenties.

"His arrogance makes him blind," Shyla said. Her clever caramel eyes flashed. "I can make myself seem simple, to a certain kind of person."

Whoever this Frank was, he was bold enough to think he could come to Australia and do what he wanted, in the isolation of the bush, using young, even underage, Aboriginal girls to do his bidding, for whatever purpose he had decided upon. Shyla had infiltrated the house in a way only she could have. But it was risky, potentially downright dangerous, especially so far from any help. Billie was impressed, but deeply worried. Shyla must have read the concern on her face, because she added, "My mob are here. I'll get them out with you or without you."

If she anticipated some protest from Billie, she didn't get it.

"I'm with you," Billie said in a firm whisper, deciding that now was not the time to talk about the horrifying significance of what was in those sheds. "It sounds like those girls need out and need help. Is Frank armed? Is he alone or are there others with him? Do you have a weapon?" She looked around. Apart from the quiet rustlings of some small animal in the deep bush behind her, nothing stirred outside the house.

"He has a pistol," Shyla said. "At least one, but he doesn't always wear it. I brought no weapon, but it wouldn't be hard to find things here to use. Knives, all these heavy statues. And I think I could get his gun if I needed to."

Billie allowed a grin to turn up the corners of her mouth. She'd underestimated this young woman, and clearly Frank was vastly underestimating her, and Shyla knew how to use that to her advantage.

"Other men who come here call him Franz."

Franz. A German name. "Where is he now? Is he still awake? And who arrived in the Daimler?"

"He's at the other end of the house with the visitor, an older man," Shyla said. "You should keep that," she added, pointing at the small book she'd given Billie. "Keep it safe. He will find it in time if I keep it on me. It's better with you."

Billie looked around. Satisfied they were not about to be interrupted, she opened the leather-bound notebook. Not daring to use her torch, she angled it so the light of the sitting room fell upon the pages. There were some neat scrawls in German, but the small book was not in code. It was, in fact, too horribly plain. In the upper-left corner was written the word *Klient*, in pen, and below it, in pencil, *gin jockeys* in quotation marks, as if this offensive colloquial term

had been added at a later date as a curiosity of language. Billie's
stomach churned. Aboriginal women were sometimes derisively
called *gins*. It was a derogatory and sexually humiliating term. *Jockeys*
were the men who consorted with them, the term seeming to imply
their mastery, their superiority. Billie's face was hot. It was worse than
she'd imagined. Perhaps worse than Shyla had first believed. She
flipped through the notebook's pages. It looked like a list of transac-
tions, yet it did not list monetary amounts. There were just the names,
along with dates. Some had several entries beneath their names.
She didn't recognize most of them, but *Georges Boucher* stood out a
mile.

"Is this . . . what I think it is?" Billie asked. Names and dates.
That awful slur.

"I did not know until I came," Shyla said. "We must get the girls
out, Billie. I must go now or he will suspect something."

Billie's fists were clenched again. She was holding in her hand a
little black book detailing the indecent assault of the girls here. The
girls had been sent to do domestic work but were being held against
their will and horribly abused as some sort of power play by the
owner of this book. His notekeeping would come back to bite him,
she hoped.

"When he realizes the book is gone, you'll all be in danger,"
Billie said.

"We are already in danger," Shyla replied simply. It was hard to
argue against that. "Take the book. Keep it safe."

Billie nodded, stuffing it under her driving coat. It was evidence.
"Yes, I'll keep it safe," she assured her friend. Cooper, perhaps, was
the right cop for this. If not, she'd take it straight to Lillian Armfield,

and if that didn't get something done, well, those names would find their way to someone who would extract justice.

Shyla turned to leave, then turned back and pointed at the book, her face dark with anger. "Not *gin jockey*." She spat the words out. "*Rapists*." Her rage was palpable.

Billie had let Shyla down by not investgating this man sooner. Three days had been lost since she came to Billie, but she'd had so little information and there'd been no way of knowing it was so urgent. And now Shyla herself was inside the house, and though Billie had her Colt, she couldn't know what she would find if she went in, gun blazing. The girls might get hurt. He might use them as hostages. They already *were* hostages.

How long could the situation hold?

"Does he suspect you?" Billie whispered.

Shyla shook her head. "I think no. I should go back," she said again, pulling away.

"Wait . . . I went to get help," Billie admitted, reaching out and touching the young woman's shoulder. "I didn't want anything happening to you. There are police coming. When they do, stay down and let them take the man. He is . . . he's a war criminal."

"Gunjies?" Shyla said urgently in a distressed whisper. "You brought coppers?" Her eyes widened with a stricken expression—the expression of someone betrayed.

"I know some cops I can trust," Billie tried to assure her, thinking of Cooper. Constable Primrose, too, though she didn't wield the same power, yet. This was too big to keep under wraps, even if Billie wanted to. "We can't keep this from the police." She patted the book of names through her coat. "They're already on their way."

Shyla narrowed her eyes, as if regretting having asked for Billie's help.

"Please trust me," Billie said. "This book is valuable, and with the right cops we can get him. There is more evidence against him in those sheds, and the cops need all of it. There is no telephone here, right?" she asked.

Shyla shook her head. "Nowhere near these parts. Richmond Railway Station is the closest, I think."

"What happened to the other girl—you told me in Sydney there were four?" Billie thought to ask.

"She ran."

Billie nodded. They'd have to see if they could track her down as a witness. "Have you seen what's in the sheds, Shyla?"

"No. He won't let us near them. They're locked."

And little wonder, she thought. "You just have to trust me," Billie said, racked with anxiety and guilt, even though she believed she had done the right thing in calling Cooper. Or at least she hoped.

"Will you last another few hours?" Billie asked her.

"I've lasted almost two days here," Shyla said, as if insulted.

"Okay." Billie felt suitably chastened. She knew the cops would be a mixed blessing for Shyla. They would end this madness, but what else might they bring? "I'll stay nearby and watch until the right moment," she promised. "I'll be in the bush, out there." She pointed. "I'm sorry about the police, Shyla. I truly am. But there is no other way." She pulled back from the window and slipped away from the house.

A noise grabbed her attention—a grunt?—and she turned. There was a rush of movement in the darkened room, shadows whirling, and Billie frantically retraced her steps.

They'd been discovered.

Shyla was struggling with someone. A man. Billie made out his rounded silhouette. It wasn't the pale man, but someone shorter, heavier, older. Georges Boucher? That would be his Daimler out the back, Billie realized, and he must have heard the two of them and come through the door silently while they were talking. Fortunately Shyla had not secured the window, and Billie hauled herself up onto the sill, just in time to see her friend hit squarely in the face. Rather than crumbling, Shyla scooted backward, escaping his grasp. Billie pulled her Colt out, but Boucher, filled with rage, ran at Shyla, grabbing her by the throat, while she held a hand over his mouth, preventing him from calling out. It was too tough to get a clear shot. Billie rushed to help her friend, but in a blink Shyla reached behind her and took something in her hand. She hit Boucher with it across the side of his head, and the body that had set upon her with violence jerked and crumpled, landing with a sickening thud on a Persian rug. A vase of flowers on the table next to the object in Shyla's hands swayed once, twice, and crashed to the floor, showering the rug with glass and water and native flowers.

For one stretched-out moment everything was quiet and still.

Billie lowered her gun, her mind focused and as sharp as crystal. Shyla stood firm, holding a small bronze bust of Captain James Cook in her hand. Time seemed to have stopped. Could the commotion have been heard by Franz?

"Can we get some more light?" Billie ventured quietly, and stepped forward to close the room off from the rest of the house, shutting the door carefully. Shyla pointed to the kerosene lamp that was sitting on the table, and soon the whole grisly scene was illuminated before them. Both women were still again, not saying a word. Georges Boucher was still on the floor. His chest did not move.

Slowly, Billie knelt next to Boucher, placing her unfired pistol in the waistband of her skirt. She checked Boucher's wrist for a pulse. Nothing. She checked his neck. It was warm, but also without a pulse. His eyes were unseeing. She didn't need to touch his head to know it would be warm, wet, and soft where the heavy bronze bust had connected with it. He was dead.

Billie stood up and gently took the statuette from Shyla's hands, then stepped out of her silk half-slip and wiped the statuette clean of prints, leaving the small mess of blood and hair that was centered on the bust's base. She placed it carefully beside Boucher's body, then stepped back and considered the scene. Could Boucher feasibly have fallen onto the bust? After a beat, she moved the table the bust and vase had stood on forward a touch, so it was closer to the body. She pushed at the rug, rippling its surface, and then observed the arrangement again. It would have to do. She picked up her blood-stained slip and, disgusted with it, balled it up and stuffed it into the pocket of her driving coat, as one would a large silk handkerchief.

"How does it look?" Shyla asked, anxiety in her voice.

"That depends on who's looking," Billie replied honestly, in a low whisper. "He tripped over the rug and hit his head. When the police ask, and they will doubtless ask, I will be a witness. I entered the premises and he saw me and panicked, ran away, and slipped on the rug. There are no prints on the bust anymore. It was an accident."

Shyla, normally so collected, was shaking her head back and

forth, melting into panic. "The coppers won't believe me, Billie. They don't believe us."

"It will be okay, Shyla," Billie tried to reassure her, placing a hand on the young woman's shoulder. "You won't have to be the one to explain this. You weren't in the room. It was only me. You didn't even see it happen," she told her. "If that comes up in a bruise," she said, pointing at her neck, "Franz did that in another room. Or Boucher did. Not here, not now."

Billie felt eyes on them and they both turned. Another girl was watching silently from the doorway, a hand to her mouth. She'd opened the door a hair and they'd been so absorbed they hadn't even noticed. Now it swung farther open on its hinges, revealing the small figure. This would be one of the girls Shyla had spoken about. Ruthie, Billie guessed.

"He fell. He can't hurt you now," Billie said to the girl quietly. "My name is Billie. Billie Walker. But we have to stay quiet. Franz is still awake, isn't he?"

The girl nodded, large, dark eyes riveted to the dead man on the floor, and something passed behind them—fear? relief?—and she looked to Shyla. After a beat Shyla nodded, as if to say this white woman was all right, could be trusted, at least for now. Billie was struck by how young the girl was. To see all this, to be trapped in a place like this, so young . . .

"I'm Ruthie," the girl said finally. She was diminutive, no older than fifteen, Billie guessed. Her hair was pulled back under a cap, her dress was worn, and her wool cardigan was buttoned to the top. A cross hung around her neck and glinted in the light of the kerosene lamp. Although her eyes kept going to the body of Boucher, lifeless on the floor, she did not scream, did not say a word about it.

"Can we get the two other girls out?" Billie asked. "I have a car down the road, around the bend. I can drive us out of here to safety."

Ruthie looked up at Billie, eyes brighter. "No, he keeps the keys," she said.

At this, Shyla came to life again. "I'll wash my hands in the kitchen and check on him."

"Be careful. Take off your shoes. Clean them in the kitchen if necessary," Billie instructed her in a soft, even voice, her eyes taking in the scene impassively, looking for the kind of evidence the police would be searching for. She was grateful for her clarity in these moments. It wasn't until you saw a dead body for the first time, or had a bullet fly just past your ear, that you realized what kind of person you really were—the kind who panics in a life-or-death emergency, or the kind who becomes strangely calm, everything shifting into hyperreal focus. She was pleased that Shyla and Ruthie had both assumed a sort of surreal calmness.

They would get out of this. They would.

"Where are the other girls now?" Billie asked Ruthie.

"Down the corridor," Ruthie said, and moved into the hall to point the way, then folded her arms and stepped back. She clearly did not want to accompany Billie. One room Ruthie indicated had what looked like a padlock securing the door. The other might not be locked, Billie thought hopefully.

She pulled her Colt from her waistband, heartbeat steady, and moved forward, keeping it ahead of her as one might shine a torch into the darkness. Behind her, Ruthie slipped away, and Billie was alone.

She decided to go for the door without the padlock first. If she couldn't open the padlock easily with a hatpin, she'd have to shoot at it and that would alert Franz.

Billie became conscious of the oddest thing as she moved slowly in the darkness, eyeing the light glowing under the two closed doors. *Perfume. Cologne.* Yes, it smelled good. *French.* Billie liked French perfume, had developed a real taste for it in Paris, though this was not her favored scent, Bandit. In this context, a fine French scent was jarring, peculiar. Everything was jarring here, the masterpieces and the rustic furniture and the death's-head owl and the cologne. This strange place, this house, was its own world, had its own rules. She kept her right hand on her Colt, and her left reached out for the doorknob, slowly . . .

And it turned.

It turned before she reached it.

Billie scurried back, holding her breath, and pressed herself against the wall of the corridor. The door creaked open in front of her, shielding her from the person on the other side. She heard steps. Heavy steps.

"Georges?" a voice queried. A male voice. He was moving down the hallway, toward the room where Boucher's body lay. *Blast.* Billie flicked the door back with her heel and extended her gun. It made contact with his upper back.

"*Was ist das?*" The pale head turned. It was him, the tall white-haired man.

"Raise your hands," Billie said. "Back into the room," she ordered him, and slowly walked him backward into the room from which he had emerged. It was a bedroom, the bed made up with fine sheets and pillows. A claw-foot bathtub sat in one corner of the room, a metal bar and chain hanging from it. Billie frowned at the strangeness of it. There was a Persian rug at her feet covering some of the uneven wooden flooring. A finely carved wooden chair. On a round, polished antique table a lamp was glowing, providing a circle of soft light that illuminated pretty china figurines and an ashtray. The windows were covered with panels of wood, nailed shut. It was a luxurious prison cell.

The prisoner was still there. She looked up. She did not scream or cry out.

"I'm going to help you. You're okay now," Billie said.

The girl was perhaps twelve, no older. Billie felt such rage, such white-hot anger, that she hit the man with the butt of her small pistol.

"Can you help me tie him up?" Billie asked. "Find some rope?" The girl just watched her, unable to move or speak, it seemed. "The other man is gone; he can't hurt you now," Billie added. "Can you find Ruthie and Shyla and bring them here?" Again, this revelation had no effect. The girl stayed on the far corner of the bed, watching Billie with wide, empty eyes.

"Shyla!" Billie called. "Ruthie!"

The two girls appeared in the doorway, saw the pale man with his hands raised.

"Help this girl," Billie said. "And I need something to hold the man with."

At this the man turned and glared at her with eerily blue eyes.

"Who do you think you are? You think you will get away with this?" His voice was heavily accented, but his English was good.

"Get any ideas and get shot," Billie countered. "I'm not likely to miss at this range and I have no qualms. You won't be the first Nazi I've shot."

His mouth quivered. He kept his hands up. Ruthie ran to the young girl and coaxed her off the bed, the small, delicate figure moving as if in a trance. She was led across the creaking floor and out of the room. In a waft of fresh air, Shyla appeared with a length of coarse rope, stained in places as if it had been put to agricultural use in a former life. It felt cool to the touch. She'd got it from outside.

"In the chair, Franz," Billie ordered, and the man moved slowly to the carved wooden chair in the corner of the stifling room. "Sit." He hesitated. "*Sit!*" He did as he was instructed and while Billie kept her Colt trained on the man, Shyla secured his ankles and wrists, running the rope around him and through the rungs of the chair until he could not stand, could not run. The lamp illuminated one side of his face, the pulled side, where burns or wounds had healed into white scars. In the low light it looked like a mask with glinting, evil eyes peering out, so different from John Wilson, with his warmth and his honorable war wounds.

"Here," Billie said, handing her Colt to Shyla. "Keep it on him. I'll see if I can find the other girl."

Shyla held the gun admirably, her hands steady.

It will be interesting when the cops arrive, Billie thought. But there was no time to worry about that now. She stepped back into the hall and positioned herself in front of the locked door, down on one knee. She pulled out her bent hatpin and inserted it into the padlock. As she felt for the lever she could detect a presence behind the door, just on the other side.

"Who is it?" a soft voice asked.

"My name is Billie Walker. I'm going to get you out. Just stay calm," she said to the voice on the other side and continued to work away at the lock. *Come on . . . come on.* The padlock wouldn't give. *Blast.* It was a different make from the one at the shed. Billie removed the bent hatpin and tried to bend it at a different angle to suit the lock.

"Billie! *Billie!*" Shyla's voice, urgent and forceful, came from the other room. Billie stood bolt upright.

"I'll be back," she promised the presence behind the door, then sprinted for the other room. It was bright inside, far too bright, and Billie realized with a jolt of horror that this was because the kerosene lamp had crashed to the floor. The table next to the pale man was upended. Flames were spreading rapidly across the floor, catching the fabrics on the bed, on the cushions. As Billie watched, one side of the bedroom was already alight, the curtains against the boards on the window running with fire. Franz was struggling on the floor, facedown, the wooden chair still woven with rope and tangled around him. He'd freed his legs but knocked over the kerosene lamp.

"He kicked over the table," Shyla yelled, still pointing the gun at him. "I couldn't stop him, he did it so quick. Ruthie! Quick! Water!" she called.

Now the other side of the curtains caught. The room would go up fast. The timber here was old, dry. A thick black smoke began filling the room. Billie crouched low and dragged Shyla down with her. "Stay down, out of the smoke," she said, and looked toward the hallway. It was already beginning to fill with the smoke that billowed out of the room in dark plumes. The fire was shocking in its speed, its power.

"We have to get out," Shyla cried. "It's too late for water. It will go up fast."

Billie nodded. She was right. "That poor girl, she's still in the room. I couldn't get the lock." Blasted thing! "Help me with Franz here; I don't want him slipping away. We have to check that Ruthie and the other young girl get out . . . I don't even know her name, then we'll get the one who's still locked in there, maybe out through the window. There's still time."

Billie raced back to the door of the locked room. "Shove something against the gap at the bottom of the door," she shouted. "There is a fire. You need to block the smoke. Don't be afraid. We'll get you out. Block the door and stay down low. Stay away from the door and away from the window."

Not a word came from the room, but Billie heard movement and the glow from under the door was blacked out as the girl plugged the gap as instructed.

Shyla had secured Franz more tightly and she and Billie hauled him up and pulled him from the smoke-filled bedroom and down the hall, his arms secured behind him. His haughty demeanor had dissolved in the face of the emergency he had created, his chalky face now red and pulled into a mask of fear, his mouth stretched. Coughing and spluttering, they made it onto the grass outside, near the shed, Franz falling to his knees. Shyla ran behind the shed and appeared a moment later with a large ax in her hands. She gripped the wooden handle strongly, the ax looking near as big as her, and in no time she was throwing the blade into the boards across the second girl's window like a man twice her size, shards of glass and slivers of wood flying.

Billie ran to the front of the house, where she was relieved to see

Ruthie and the young girl. They sprinted into the paddock, Ruthie holding the young barefoot girl by the hand, the pair lit golden by the glowing building as it went up. The fire had already spread with shocking speed down the corridor. The second bedroom, even with the door shut, would not hold much longer, Billie realized. She tore back to the window, where Shyla was pulling at the broken boards with desperate hands. There was smoke inside already, black and heavy, and the fresh air caused flames on the far side of the room to jump and dance. Billie flung herself through the jagged gap, feeling her clothes catch on the glass, to find the girl hiding under the bed, curled into the fetal position, hands over her ears. Billie pulled at her, dragging her out and begging her to stand, not sure if she was strong enough to lift the small, shaking body alone.

"Come on, we've got you. You're going to be okay," Billie said to the girl, pulling off her driving coat and wrapping it around her. She put her hands under the girl's arms and managed to lift her onto the bed. Now she had to get her out through the broken glass of the window.

"Come with us, it's okay," Shyla coaxed her, and Billie half pushed, half handed the girl to her, first covering her face with the coat, forcing her past the sharp glass and the broken boards, and she was out. Behind Billie the angry flames spat viciously, as if in protest, and she realized her lungs had filled with the lethal fumes. Her head felt light. Her eyes stung, burning.

Out. Get out, now or never . . .

Billie threw herself through the opening and landed on the grass on her side, lungs screaming. Bright flames licked the broken gap she had emerged through. The house itself was roaring now, as if with objection, having lost its human sacrifices. It moaned and cried in the darkness.

Billie lurched to her feet, not sure how fast their party could move. The motorcars? Perhaps she could start one of them and drive them out of this mess, together? As if in answer, angry flames danced across the dry grass, light, swift, and deadly, snaking with speed to the rear of the nearest shed. The shed she had been inside. It lit like a pack of matchsticks, as if it had been waiting for this moment. The Packard and the Daimler would be surrounded or even engulfed before they had time to find the keys or force them to start. Billie watched as the fire raced over the treetops and lit the hill behind the homestead. Her own automobile was down the road, fifteen or so minutes away by foot, but less if they ran. If the roadway remained clear they could reach it, but the fire was already moving at a terrifying rate, devouring the dry summer grasses and spreading toward the roadside. She didn't like their chances with the girls in tow and a struggling Franz.

"To the river," Shyla said, "it's our only chance," and she pointed the way.

Together, the five women and girls, with Franz as their captive, struggled down a dusty path, bent over and moving their feet as fast as they could. Billie's lungs protested and she spluttered and coughed but kept on, her suit streaked and torn, her hands and arms scratched and grazed. Behind them, the wrathful fire was rising, the wind shifting and starting to blow harder, creating a roar of the kind Billie had only ever heard during bombing campaigns in the war. Shyla lifted one of the young girls into her arms, carrying her and running forward with impossible strength for someone her size.

"*Feuer, Feuer . . .*" someone was saying as they ran and stumbled down the track toward the river.

It was Franz, the man who was to blame for all this. The man who had forced the girls into those prison rooms, who had started the fire. He stopped, crouching and whimpering, as terrified as a small child, the roles now reversed. He repeated the same word again and again. "*Feuer, feuer.*"

Fire.

He was terrified of the flames, Billie realized, now sure that he had tried to free himself from the ropes but had not counted on the lamp spilling, had not counted on the dry Australian bush, which came alive with terrifying flame at the slightest opportunity. Not counting on the drought and the hot Australian summer. The bush here loved to burn; the burning was part of its nature, part of the cycle of life and death. And he'd triggered it.

"*Feuer,*" he cried again. He was wailing now, trying to cover his head.

Shyla put down the girl she was carrying and told Billie to get her to the river. Billie took the girl's hand, urging her onward, Ruthie and the other girl running in front of them. Shyla grabbed the ropes binding Franz and hauled him through the paddock like a bull. "You won't get far in Darug Country," Billie heard her say to him as she yanked at him fiercely.

They pushed through a thicket of thorny bush, Billie cutting her hand, tearing her stockings, her suit, and then they were through a fringe of trees and jumping down to the level of the river, where beige sand glowed in the moonlight. Here was water, slow, lazy water, enough to keep them from the flames. They waded in, submerging themselves to the thighs. The two younger girls were immersed to the waist, and Ruthie was with them, slightly taller, cradling them maternally. The water, cool and welcoming, brought tears to Billie's eyes, making tracks down her soot-covered face. Shyla reached them, dragging their prisoner by his ropes. He collapsed onto the sand.

The sky was red with flames, embers rising like fireflies and falling again like black snow. The fire was like thunder now, like a freight train, the taste of smoke on their tongues, the air itself filling with falling ash.

Without words, Billie opened her arms and Shyla joined her, then Ruthie and the other girls, too. The five women and girls formed a circle in the slow river, arms locked protectively around one another.

"I'm Eleanor," the smallest one said, in a child's voice that tore at the part of Billie that was just barely hanging on.

"I'm Ida," the other girl said.

The five of them huddled together in the cool water of the Colo River, heads close. Behind them, the white-haired man was curled on the sand of the riverbank, shaking as the world around them roared and danced with flames.

Thirty-one

—⟊—

The Upper Colo homestead in the early morning light was a vision to behold.

The wooden footings that had held up the homestead had collapsed under the flames, and the blackened walls sprawled out across the scorched grass as if the building had burst its stitching and come apart at the seams. Only two brick chimneys sat in their original places, proud and intact, the rest of the homestead having fallen away. And standing like sentinels from a surreal apocalyptic tale, Mr. and Mrs. Satan were almost untouched: blackened and charred, but their posture unchanged, their glittering eyes feasting on the scene.

The East Kurrajong Bush Fire Brigade had arrived in the dead of night in a single battered red Ford truck with a pump, alerted by a watchful farmer in the hills to the growing inferno at Upper Colo. It was a motley crew of brave locals with firefighting knapsacks on their backs who had erupted out of the truck, six in all, and without pause had begun their work against the raging flames, barely noticing at first the huddle of women and the strange man cowering at the side of the river. With something like awe, Billie had stood up on the riverbank and watched them contain the blaze after a battle that had lasted hours. The areas beyond the road and river were saved; the evil house and its contents stood not a chance.

The firefighters, all volunteers, had beaten Inspector Cooper in his race from the city. But at five in the morning, fully an hour earlier than he had promised her, Cooper and his colleagues had arrived and the white-haired man known as Franz was placed in irons and driven to the Richmond lockup, while Billie, Shyla, and the girls were ordered to stay put and await questioning. There wasn't a vehicle big enough for them all.

Shyla, Ruthie, Ida, and Eleanor were huddled together on the wool blankets provided by the firefighters, talking in low voices and sipping from shared cups and a thermos. Young Eleanor was still in something of a trance since she'd been taken from her prison room by Ruthie, Billie had noticed. Those wide dark eyes remained blank, empty with shock. She was the youngest, Billie guessed, and she'd done well to get to the river at all in her state. Ida, who was barely older from what Billie could tell, was more animated, but also showing signs of shock, hands clammy and pupils enlarged. All of the girls needed medical attention, Billie thought. She had left them when the inspector silently signaled for her attention, but even as she stood with him she watched the group in their semicircle, clothes torn and wet, and wondered about their futures.

Now Detective Inspector Hank Cooper was beside Billie Walker, steady and tall, concern written all over his face. "Billie, I got here as fast as I could," he said to her. "I hope you know that."

Billie was almost unrecognizable, covered in streaks of soot, her suit filthy and ruined, a wool blanket wrapped around her and a steaming cup of black tea in her hand. Her muddy oxfords were drying, so a spare pair of oversize boots, volunteered by the firefighters, covered her feet. Her tilt hat had been lost somewhere, probably engulfed in the house, and her curls were unrestrained. Unruly locks framed her streaked face like a mane. Her eyes were bloodshot, her elegant hands scratched and bruised.

"I know you did, Inspector," Billie replied softly.

The firefighters were walking over the paddocks now, putting out small spot fires. Parts of the homestead still smoldered, walls crackling and glowing orange. Above them, the air was heavy and dark, a smoky cloud hanging over the scene even as the early morning sunlight fought against it, the eternal battle between night and day playing out more violently than usual.

"Please call me Hank."

Billie looked up at Cooper and nodded, and he put an arm around her shoulders, closing the blanket gently across her with his other broad hand. They stood in silence for a while, watching the scene, she cocooned in the blanket and in him. "I'm sorry I didn't get here earlier," he said again.

Her shivering stopped. She hadn't even realized she was doing it. "I know, Hank," Billie said again. "I know."

Thirty-two

—⁙—

"Seeing as you don't like to drink alone," Sam remarked, and grinned all the way up to the corners of his aquamarine eyes. They clinked beer mugs and Billie smiled back across the table at him as he downed another large mug of foaming ale.

It was Friday, two and a half exhausting days since the fire and the discovery of the shed, and it was time to put the whole sordid affair to rest, time to somehow move on. In aid of that idea, Billie and her assistant had come downstairs to let off some tension in the billiards room in the basement of Daking House. Billie, true to her personal rule, was not drinking alone. Indeed, on this occasion she was in some wonderful company.

"Your father would be proud," Baroness Ella von Hooft said, and instead of raising a glass she turned and loudly tried to order a bottle of champagne for the table for the second time. For the second time she was informed that the billiards room did not have any champagne. They didn't have a waiter, either.

"Good goddess, can't you just sip what's in front of you?" Billie implored her mother. This wasn't The Dancers, but under the circumstances that didn't feel like a downgrade. Alma clinked her mug with Billie's, and they each took generous sips, leaving Ella to crossly watch them from beneath her penciled brows and flawless marcel waves.

"I don't think the waiting room will be empty again for a while," Sam said to everyone at the table. "Clients are lining up." He took another swig.

That appeared to be true. While Billie had been in the Blue Mountains with Inspector Cooper and, later, had crept around Upper Colo, her assistant had fielded calls and visitors. The past two days had not slowed down, either. Word had spread about the spectacular fire and her uncovering of possible Nazi loot, and that along with the front-page coverage of the car chase had now attracted new clients. She'd not been entirely sure whether the publicity would scare people away or draw them in, but it had proved better than taking out an advertisement. In a way it was odd. Clients always wanted everything on the down low and hush-hush, yet with her sudden notoriety she had new cases lined up for weeks. The turn of events, professionally speaking, was cause for celebration, even if she hoped she wouldn't need to investigate a similar case to keep Sydney calling on her little inquiry agency.

She looked around the party of revelers packed like canned sardines in a cozy booth in the basement billiards joint. It was an eclectic group, rounded out by Shyla and Constable Primrose, who was downing the off-license ale as fast as Sam could. Billie suspected such a group might never assemble in quite the same way again.

Shyla, who did not drink alcohol, raised her glass of Cherry Cheer courteously. "Another?" Billie suggested, and she shook her head. For someone who could kill a rapist stone dead with one swing, she was very quiet, at least in this company. Franz, and indeed the late Georges Boucher, had massively underestimated her. Perhaps Billie had, too. It was a quality that would come in handy in the trade, if she could convince Shyla to join the agency. So far, Shyla had refused. One thing they were in agreement on, however, was that it was a relief that news about the young girls had not hit the newspapers. Not yet anyway. The last thing they needed was the lack of privacy that would bring. Cooper had done well, if indeed it was him who had managed it. The Upper Colo fire and the discoveries at the house had attracted a lot of speculation. Ruthie had already found a new placement, but as for Ida and Eleanor, Billie knew only that they were in hospital being treated for shock and minor injuries, and Shyla would update her when she could.

"To victory!" Sam said in an overly loud voice, bringing to mind the cry of 1945 and the end of the war, so recent and yet a lifetime ago.

"To victory," the rest of them said in surprising harmony, even Shyla joining in.

They clinked glasses again and she smiled, trying to enjoy the moment of triumph.

Victory, in reality, was a mixed affair, not quite the glorious beast the posters and the songs so fondly announced it to be. It was the end of something, yes, a victory over some things, but it was also a time to take stock, a time to bury the dead. There was Con Zervos, who might still be breathing had Billie not come asking questions of him. There was what Adin Brown had been through, and what those young girls Ida and Eleanor had endured, things no shout of victory could erase. The police weren't finished with them all, either. There was the matter of Boucher's demise, and how that might appear once the dust settled. Billie hoped it would be put down to panic in the fire, but he'd been a powerful man and that could spell trouble for a while, trouble she hoped she would be equal to. And there was the matter of identifying just who the man Franz was, and from whom he'd had help to acquire and ship so many precious things into Australia without attracting the attention of the authorities. And there was the matter of Moretti. Yes, Moretti. She had a word or two for him. Was Franz the one paying him? How much had he known? Billie was going to see to it that he came to justice for his part in all this if it was the last thing she did.

"I have something for you," Constable Primrose said, putting down her empty glass.

Billie raised a brow. She was presented with a small package emblazoned with the word *Tussy*. "You didn't . . ."

"I did. I found one of the last sticks of Fighting Red." The constable smiled widely, her curls bouncing in her enthusiasm.

"How?"

She just smiled knowingly. Yes, she was a resourceful one, that Primrose. And she'd come through with the information on the owner of the car with plate XR-001, albeit too late as the drama unfolded in remote Upper Colo.

"Pardon me, Billie. I should go," Shyla said, pulling Billie from her thoughts.

Billie looked into the young woman's deep caramel eyes, and they exchanged an unspoken understanding. "Thank you for coming. And *thank you*." She paused. "I will do what I can to keep searching for your brothers."

Shyla nodded. "Ruthie says hello. Things are better for her now," she said quietly.

That could only be an understatement. The young woman had not been able to release the two girls herself in that isolated and violent place, but she'd alerted contacts of Shyla's, and Shyla had in turn reached out to Billie. However Ruthie had managed it, she took a risk. She'd been brave. Franz was armed and had doubtless threatened them with severe consequences if they stepped out of line. If Ruthie hadn't taken that chance, who knew how much longer they would have been trapped there? There was no way to undo what those girls had been through, but it was at an end now. The man responsible was in custody, and Boucher was no longer able to hurt anyone, either. The rest of the men in that notebook? Well, there was a reckoning still to come.

Constable Primrose was also making moves to leave. She flashed a toothy, gleaming smile. "Enjoy the lipstick. It's good on you. I'm supposed to be off for the day, but I get the feeling Inspector Cooper might want some assistance. It's a heck of a pickle, this whole thing, and having had him behind bars at Richmond." She blew some air out of her mouth, a silent whistle, then grabbed her things, gave Billie a hearty squeeze, and went to follow Shyla up the stairs.

"Wait. A *pickle?*" Billie echoed, confused.

Primrose bit her pink lower lip. "I've spoken out of turn," she said. "I'll speak to you soon, I'm sure. Billie, you really aced it. I'm so pleased for the Brown family. Sock it to those Nazi bastards," she added enthusiastically, punching the air, her blond curls bouncing once more.

"Indeed . . . but what did you mean by it all being a pickle?" Billie pressed, feeling anxiety building in her gut. Primrose was not forthcoming, bidding her friend adieu and clattering up the staircase.

Billie exhaled heavily and moved closer to her mother on the bench, feeling the tension of the past few days sliding back in. Now she worried that there was something she wasn't being told.

"What is it?" Sam asked her.

In lieu of answering, she picked up her beer mug and examined its state of unacceptable emptiness with an exaggeratedly arched brow, and her assistant dutifully filled it again. He seemed to glean what was needed by way of osmosis, yet another quality to recommend him. Ella raised a penciled eyebrow at Billie, then glanced meaningfully at Sam. Alma, catching the exchange, shook her head ruefully and clinked glasses with Billie, who chose to ignore her mother's pointed signals.

"I could sleep for a week," Billie remarked, and meant it.

The celebration was winding down when the door to the street opened once more. Billie was surprised when Detective Inspector Hank Cooper appeared in front of their booth and offered a good-natured if restrained greeting to the dwindling group.

"I didn't think you'd come," Billie said, sliding out from the bench seat. The ale had gone to her head, and that didn't seem to be a terrible thing for the moment. She'd been thinking over her plans for the night. Would she go home, or try to coax the inspector out for a meal? He'd refused her in the Blue Mountains, but perhaps he wouldn't now.

"I'm sorry I can't stay," Cooper said, and remained standing. Billie frowned. Something in his expression made her excuse herself from the table and go to his side. This wasn't a social visit, evidently. Perhaps this was about the charred body of Georges Boucher, if they had identified him. She was quietly pleased at Shyla's timing, not wanting her around when the subject inevitably came up.

Billie and the inspector made their way over to an unoccupied pool table, and she fished a cool ball out of the recesses of a corner netting. An eight ball. "I could be mistaken, but I got an inkling from Constable Primrose that something might be wrong," she said in her most restrained voice, holding the black ball and considering its meaning. Cooper did not answer her, which did not help the sense she had that all was not well.

Instead, the inspector reached into his overcoat and removed a piece of paper bearing an image. "This man look familiar?" he asked.

Billie considered Cooper's guarded expression and his veneer of formality, sighed with frustration at this part of his character, and looked at what was on offer. It was a photograph, or a copy of some sort, and it showed a man in perhaps his forties, or even his thirties, with extremely pale hair. He was wearing a crisp Nazi uniform, his cap at a slight angle, and on it Billie could see the crest of the eagle atop a swastika, and below that, the *Totenkopf*, the distinctive skull and crossbones worn by Nazi officers. The uniform suited him the way a black hood suited an executioner. The man's lips were thin and his eyes bright. Across one side of his face were lines of scars, the skin pulled.

Billie contained a shudder. "Yes, that's him all right. The girls knew him as Franz or Frank."

"His name is Franz Hessmann," Cooper said in a low voice, pocketing the image. "He was charged in absentia in Hamburg, in the British zone, and sentenced to death. They say he was quite high up at the Ravensbrück camp."

Billie felt a chill rise slowly up her spine. *The Ravensbrück trials*. Ravensbrück was the dedicated women's camp set up by the Nazis north of Berlin where Jewish and Romany women, and women and girls accused of "prostitution" or poor moral standing, were sent during the war. She'd heard that thousands of women from occupied nations were also inmates there—Soviets, Dutch and French women, Poles, and many more. Few survived. Often the women arrived with children, most of whom died of starvation along with their mothers, thanks to the gradually decreasing rations. Conditions were said to have been extraordinarily brutal. The female auxiliary SS guards at Ravensbrück, including Irma "the Hyena" Grese, later transferred to Auschwitz and since sentenced to death, and another guard known as the Beast of Ravensbrück, were infamous. The guards literally worked the women inmates to death with slave labor and, from what Billie had heard, had devised strange tortures and power games, perhaps hoping to impress the Third Reich establishment with their commitment to destroying the will of the prisoners in their care. Eventually, as the Final Solution was put in place, gas chambers had been installed to speed up the killing, and when the end of the war neared, the killing had accelerated yet further, the guards not willing to let their prisoners survive to tell what they had witnessed and endured.

Yes, Billie knew of it.

"He wasn't one of the doctors?" she asked, feeling suddenly as sober as a judge. In addition to the female guards, the place was notorious for the experiments performed on the prisoners—amputations, removing bones and attempting transplants. Cutting the women and infecting the wounds with germs to see what would happen. Introducing dirt and glass into their bodies and refusing to administer pain medication. And when the women succumbed, the Nazis took what was left, of course. Their shoes. Their wedding rings. Their gold fillings. Hessmann had a barrel full to melt down and live off.

Cooper shook his head. "No, I don't think so. He was a camp

administrator. A major in the Waffen-SS and, later, camp commandant."

The camp commandant. Billie swore under her breath. A Nazi
camp commandant, here in Australia? It was almost unbelievable.

"And the airman's burn? Did he do time with the Luftwaffe? Or
was it something else?" she speculated, remembering his reaction to
the fire, the extreme fear in a man who had otherwise seemed devoid
of emotion. It was as if the fire had triggered something, shocked him
psychologically.

Again, Cooper shook his head. "The scarring, you mean? Apparently he earned that in the camp from some prisoners in one of
the factories. Saboteurs."

The Ravensbrück women had been pressed into different types of
slave labor, depending on their physical strength and abilities, forced
to aid the German war machine against their will. Some worked in
textiles, some made parts for Daimler-Benz or electrical components
for the Siemens electric company, and some were involved in making
Hitler's V-2 rocket, among other tasks. Some were made to pull a huge
roller to pave the streets. Billie had seen a photograph of the roller
after liberation. It was a terrifying image—the roller huge and looking
like it needed twelve horses to pull it, not human women. There were
incredible stories of defiance. Even the women who had been forced
to sew, many of them elderly and increasingly frail, used to rig the
German soldiers' socks so they'd get blisters, Billie had heard. A
thousand small rebellions in the face of torture and death.

"A group of the women sabotaged some rocket components for
the Siemens company and there was an explosion and fire at the
factory. Hessmann was there at the time and got out with just the
facial burns, I guess."

Billie thought on that. The bravery of it.

"You do agree it's him?" she asked. "I don't think I can be mistaken. He's quite distinctive-looking with that hair. I mean, you've seen him with your own eyes?" Cooper looked down at his shoes, and Billie's heart leaped into her throat. Her chest felt constricted, as if someone was sitting on it. "Tell me everything is okay, Inspector," she demanded. "Constable Primrose didn't tell me anything particular, but I got the feeling . . . Well, I got the feeling it wasn't all good news. What is it I'm not being told?"

At this, Cooper took a deep breath and appeared to steel himself, which did nothing for Billie's gut. "There was something of a . . . mix-up," he finally answered. "There was a constable on duty at Richmond and he let Hessmann go."

Billie's lips moved to form words, but none came. Stunned, she regarded Cooper silently. She felt the urge to strike him, strike anything, but he was not the one she was angry with.

"Constable Howard says he was faced with a solicitor who was persuasive, and he appears to have panicked and agreed to release Hessmann. He didn't know all the details, of course, only knew about the claims made by the Aboriginal girls. He said there wasn't enough to keep him. The sergeant was not there. It never would have happened on his watch. He . . ." The inspector trailed off, seeing her expression.

The *claims* of the girls. *Claims*.

Billie brought a hand to her face, and she pulled it down slowly over her eyes, her nose, and stopped it over her mouth. The floor seemed to be moving beneath her feet. "This isn't some kind of . . . joke?" she managed.

Cooper shook his head.

"So, we had a commandant from goddamn Ravensbrück, wanted for war crimes and now imprisoning and abusing girls here in Australia, on our watch, and he's gone? And we have witnesses as to what he was doing here, and he was let go? We have Adin and the girls and their testimony . . ." She shuddered, thinking of how Shyla and the girls would feel when they found out a police officer had willingly let the man go, knowing they were prepared to testify. What a betrayal. What an utter betrayal by a system Shyla herself had said they didn't trust because they'd been let down before. And Adin would have been able to identify him. Adin had agreed to testify.

"We have witnesses, Inspector. We have that horrific book of dates and names. We have the surviving oil drums in that shed." A couple of people at the billiards tables looked in her direction, and a game on the other side of the room stopped. She seemed to be speaking more loudly than she'd realized.

"Yes, I believe we have identified him," the inspector said carefully, "and we are still sorting through what survived the fire. I'm trying to convince my superiors—"

"Your superiors aren't convinced?" She slammed her fist down on the billiards table and it stung where the skin had been grazed and torn.

Cooper didn't answer. Billie wondered where Hessmann was now. Where would he go? Did he have enough connections to stay on the run? For how long? Could he leave the country unnoticed?

"Inspector, what am I supposed to tell Shyla, Ruthie, Eleanor, and Ida? And Adin? Adin's family?" she demanded, keeping her voice lower this time.

Cooper reached out and placed his hand gently on hers. Billie looked down at it and, surprising herself, decided not to pull hers away. The large male hand dwarfed the scratched and more delicate one she'd been leaning on the table, his fingers so much larger than hers. She raised her eyes from his hand to his face and waited, eyes unflinchingly on his.

"Please call me Hank," he said to her again in the face of her terrific glare, and though he moved his hand away, that unreadable formality he so often seemed to slip into was dissolving, she could see. His hands slipped into his pockets. "I cannot . . ." he began. "Billie, I cannot begin to convey the disappointment I feel. I believe there is more to this than meets the eye. Hessmann had help; that much is certain. Suffice it to say it is my top priority to locate him and his associates and investigate each of the men listed in that book. You have to believe me. I give you my word."

Billie waited for more.

"He can't get far," Cooper went on. "He'll try to flee to another state, probably another country. South America, perhaps. He may have connections, but we won't let him get far. We're looking for him at every port."

How hard would it be to hide a face like his? It seemed he hadn't even tried. He must have thought Australia was safe for the likes of him. And it certainly had been, until Ruthie and Shyla and Adin.

Billie contemplated the sad certainty that Adin's great-aunt had perished at Ravensbrück under unspeakably inhumane conditions, one of the majority of the women who did not survive the camp. And her necklace had ended up coming to Australia with the camp commandant to be auctioned off to help pay for his life on the run from the war crimes tribunal. Margarethe was the connection, the reason her great-nephew had searched for those associated with the auction house selling the necklace he recognized and remembered.

She might have perished, but she and her great-nephew had helped to lift the lid on a fleeing war criminal. They'd come close, so close, to being the cause of his capture.

"The constable at Richmond has voluntarily resigned from his position," Cooper said. "The sergeant wants to apologize to you personally."

"What good will that do?" Billie replied, folding her arms. "And it's not me he ought to apologize to," she added. "Does the constable have any connection to this Hessmann? Is that possible? What about the man who helped set him free? The solicitor?"

The inspector shook his head, his mouth turned down. "We can't be confident he even was a solicitor. The details he gave were false. I have an alert out at every port," he repeated. He lowered his voice and locked his eyes with hers. "We don't think Hessmann was acting alone—I mean in addition to the auction house, and the solicitor. There has been some investigation into the possibility of Nazi activity in Australia since the war, but it wasn't . . ."

"Taken very seriously?"

"Yes."

"And now you have a singed house full of evidence."

"Exactly. What's left of it, anyway."

"Have you checked the names in the book for whoever might have helped him at Richmond?" she asked.

"We're working on it. Hessmann appears to have used that book for blackmail, writing the details of those who . . ." He stopped.

"I know what they did," she said, sparing him. Hessmann had shipped his stolen goods to Australia, where he thought he could get away with it, and was selling them off one by one. He was living on the final pieces of the broken lives of the women and children he'd helped to murder. And he'd used the girls at his homestead to cement Boucher's loyalty and the loyalty of whoever else was in that book. His dirty little black book was a record of blackmail and assault and it would not reflect well on the wealthy clients who'd purchased the goods Hessmann had to sell. It ensured their silence.

"Hessmann was apparently known for that sort of thing. That kind of blackmail and depravity. It had worked for him in Berlin. One of the ways he kept loyalty was to promise . . . access to certain prisoners, and then he would keep evidence. The men involved wouldn't want their wives knowing. He also kept other paperwork and a diary. Fragments survived the flames. It's being translated now, which will take some time, but it already seems that his diary will provide some leads and . . ." Again the inspector hesitated. "Detail," he finally said.

"That must make some pretty bedside reading," Billie said darkly. "Surely your superiors can't doubt his identity."

"The official line is that his identity is yet to be established."

Billie licked her lips. Her mouth had become dry, and inside her was an unhealthy anger, a simmering rage she thought she'd left in Europe. "Have you a cigarette?" she asked, shaking a little.

Cooper took her request in his stride, pulling a pack of tobacco and some paper from his coat pocket. He assembled a cigarette with the quick precision of a soldier who'd performed the same ritual in countless trenches and in the windows of abandoned, bombed-out buildings on late-night watches. "I didn't think you smoked," he said finally, and handed it to her. Billie placed it between her red lips, and he leaned close and lit the tip with a battered Ronson lighter. She caught sight of something scratched into the side but wasn't able to make it out before he pocketed it again.

"It's a smoking day," Billie replied simply, and took a deep drag. She stifled a cough, her lungs still sore from the smoke of the fire. "Let me get this straight, just so we are absolutely clear. Your superiors don't want it to look like they let a Nazi go. One who was high up in command. Is that it?"

"Without his blackmail book and without those treasures, he won't have so much power now," Cooper said, sidestepping the question.

But that didn't necessarily mean Hessmann was on his own, if there was a network of some kind he could draw support from. And that seemed to be the suggestion. Did he have access to funds to get him out of the country? On one of the ships leaving soon, perhaps? That must have been how he'd got his Nazi loot to Australia to begin with—some amenable connections at the docks. Someone, or a few someones, happy to look the other way. He could stow away if he didn't want to risk more official passage. He would disappear back into the woodwork, to emerge again—where? South America? Hong Kong? Canada? He'd lost a great deal of his war loot in the Australian bush, but it was impossible to know how much more he might have access to.

"I want you to know that we have Vincenzo Moretti in for questioning, right now," Cooper went on. "Though we haven't any evidence against him at this stage, and he claims to know nothing about any of this."

"Of course he'd say that," Billie retorted. A bitter laugh escaped her throat. "I could have told you that for free." She took another drag of the cigarette, felt the burn, the smoke in her lungs. "Moretti is involved. I haven't a shred of doubt." But there would be time enough for Moretti. He was deep in this, and there was no way she was going to let him walk away from it after all that had happened. His men had tried to mess her up, they'd assaulted her assistant as well as her client's boy, and they'd made a fair effort of shooting her off the road. "If you want any help interrogating him, I'll have a word or two to say," she added darkly.

"Just one more thing," Cooper said.

"Do go on."

"There were remains found at the Colo homestead. From a motorcar found at the scene, it seems the body may be that of Georges Boucher, originally hailing from Vichy, France."

Vichy. How fitting, Billie thought. Vichy France, or the Régime de Vichy, had been an authoritarian administration of infamous Nazi collaborators and enablers.

"I think his is the auction house where Hessmann was selling some of his more valuable wares. Seems a nice business." Billie's voice was cutting.

"You wouldn't know anything about what happened to Boucher, would you? He is . . . implicated in the activities recorded in Hessmann's notebook."

"What an unpleasant person," Billie said, as if this was news to her. "I can't enlighten you about his passing, though I will say that the fire was sudden and quite fierce. It's a miracle any of us managed to get out."

"Death by misadventure, then?" the inspector suggested. "Another unfortunate accident?"

"Fires can be terribly lethal."

"And roads."

"Indeed," she said, and caught his eye, daring him to accuse her.

Cooper watched her carefully. Her expression was steady. He said nothing.

"Thanks for keeping me informed about Hessmann," Billie finally said, knowing full well that he didn't have to, and neatly changing the subject. She'd be damned if Shyla or those exploited girls would see any negative repercussions after what had happened. Death was far too good for the likes of Boucher. "And thanks for the cigarette."

"You'll do the same, if you uncover anything?" Cooper asked. "I mean, you'll keep me informed?"

"You know I will, Hank," Billie said, though she was still seething inside. "I told you in your office that we can be of better use to each other if we share information. I meant it."

They shook hands, much as they had up in the mountains. A formal gesture, perhaps overly formal considering the events of the past week. He'd held her, as wet, trembling, and exhausted, she'd surveyed the ruins of the Upper Colo homestead. She'd felt a touch vulnerable then. She didn't now. Rage strengthened her anew. When they withdrew their palms they exchanged a look of unspoken understanding. It lasted just a few seconds but felt like longer, the air around them electric with something ineffable but powerful. She hadn't felt that since Europe. Yes, Jack Rake, wherever he was, would approve of what had transpired—her part in it, at least. He would approve of her determination not to let it go now, either, not that she needed approval from him, or any man, dead or alive as the case might be. This wasn't the end of it. Every man in that book deserved the attention of the law. And Hessmann had better not get far. She'd go to the papers if she had to. Everyone would know that face.

"I have to get back," Cooper said. The dark circles under his eyes spoke of sleepless nights, and he was not likely to see a day off soon. "Sorry to have broken up your party," he added, and she noticed that Sam, Ella, and Alma were standing, and a young woman was next to Sam now, pulling at his hand. Ah, this would be Eunice. Billie had been so engrossed in her conversation with Cooper that she hadn't seen her come in. The celebrations, however brief, were indeed over.

"Thank you for telling me," Billie said once more, and Cooper walked away, pausing on the stairs to incline his head to her. She returned the gesture, and in moments he had slipped out the door onto Rawson Place, the din of the traffic outside filling the space and then receding as the door shut behind him.

"Ms. Walker, this is Eunice." Sam's voice pulled her back to the moment. He was standing with a fair-haired woman of about twenty. She had a chocolate-box prettiness and a tightly closed mouth.

"Pleasure to finally meet you," Billie said to her, and Eunice nodded awkwardly.

"We have to go," Sam said reluctantly.

"Of course," Billie said. "See you in the office tomorrow?"

"Naturally," he replied, and nodded to her.

The pair slipped away and Billie turned to Ella and Alma.

"A lift home?" Alma suggested, and Billie shook her head.

"Thanks, but no. I think I'll head back upstairs for an hour or two. The agency won't run itself." The truth was, there was no relaxing for her now. If she went home to her empty flat, she might go insane. She needed to sit at her father's desk and think. And perhaps break her rule about drinking alone.

Thirty-three

———

Animated by anger, Billie Walker strode through the doors of Daking House. Her latest case was closed. The Browns had their boy back, and she hoped they would soon get Margarethe's necklace back, too. The mystery was solved. She had new clients lining up for the first time. She'd felt that a sense of doing something that mattered wasn't strictly a thing of the past, wasn't confined to her career as a wartime reporter. She had been truly optimistic for the first time in months—that was before she got the news from Detective Inspector Cooper that Franz Hessmann had been released from Richmond Police Station and was now who knew where. There were now enough loose ends to keep her mind occupied for months. She would help in whatever way she could in the hunt for Hessmann and his associates, and was determined to take Moretti down, whatever it took. He must have been working for Hessmann, or perhaps Boucher, as she'd first thought.

Yes, there was work to do.

"John, hold the lift?" Billie called and picked up her pace as she crossed the foyer.

The lift operator smiled in his lopsided way through the grille of the outer door and pulled it back, making his other customers, two men, wait. "Of course, Ms. Walker," he said fondly.

Billie slid inside, noting that one of the two men was familiar— an older man with spectacles and ink-stained fingers, in a striped suit. One of the accountants. A pleasant enough fellow. He tipped his hat to her. The second was taller and had badly dyed brown hair just visible under a fedora. John Wilson pulled the second door closed and worked the lever, the lift starting up with a shuffling hum.

"Second floor, Mr. Peters," he announced, and the accountant lumbered out with a smile and a thank-you.

Wilson closed the doors again and started the lift. "Both for floor number six."

Billie swallowed. The little woman in her gut told her something was wrong, very wrong, and in a heartbeat the man in the fedora was behind her left shoulder and she felt the sharp sting of a blade in her lower back, pressing into her shirtwaist dress and pointing at her kidney.

"How is work, Ms. Walker?" Wilson inquired, his back to them as he faced the lift's controls.

Billie took a steady breath and kept her body still, her voice even. "Work is busy," she replied, tensing despite her best efforts. "How is your lovely wife, Wendy, doing? She felt rather down very suddenly, didn't she, after that bout of, what was it?"

The knife dug a touch deeper.

"Ah, just a cold, it was," Wilson said, after an almost imperceptible pause. Billie's heart lifted a touch.

"Here we are," the lift operator said as the carriage slowed. "Sixth floor."

Billie prepared for what she hoped would happen next, her body tense, her feet firm. When Wilson reversed the controls suddenly and let go of the handle, the dead man switch kicked in, the carriage taking air for a brief moment before jerking violently, and she threw herself forward, turning away from the blade, intentionally falling on her sore open palms and kicking backward like a mule with her heeled oxfords into the man's stomach. He crumpled against the wall, the knife tumbling out of his grasp, and before she could right herself, Wilson, unarmed and with only one upper extremity to work with, had thrown the man forward and pinned him to the floor with both knees, his left arm pressing against the back of his neck.

"Dear God, I do hope that's what you wanted me to do," he said, a little breathless. "When you called June by the wrong name and said what you said, I knew it was a code of sorts."

"Yes, John," Billie said. "You did well. Bloody well." In seconds she had the Colt in her hand, having shamelessly flashed her silk knickers and stocking tops to the lift operator and his loathsome quarry. She steadied her hands on the gun, swaying a little with the speed of it all. "I have him now."

"I thought something was suspicious when I asked him where he'd served and he didn't answer. That war wound."

That war wound one might mistake for airman's burn, just like John's, but was not. That burn inflicted by the man's victims in one final brave act of rebellion.

Wilson unpinned the man and rose, straightening his uniform and the empty sleeve of his jacket's right arm. He started the lift up again and jogged it up and down until they lined up with the sixth floor.

"Thank you. Doors please, John," Billie said, ignoring the angry mutterings coming out of Hessmann's mouth.

Wilson opened the inner door and slid the grille back, revealing the sixth-floor entryway.

"Thank you, again," Billie said. "I do owe you one. And I'll explain later." She urged her prisoner out of the lift. "Call the police straightaway, John, if you would. Ask for Detective Inspector Cooper. He's at Central, just up the way. And Constable Primrose. Tell them I have Franz Hessmann. Tell them to bring as much backup as they see fit, and to make it quick if they expect me to keep this fellow alive. My patience isn't what it used to be."

Thirty-four

Staring into the face of a mass murderer was an enlightening experience, Billie Walker found.

The thing that struck her most forcibly was the sheer ordinariness of this brutal killer. This man who tortured and maimed and raped and killed had the same features, the same kind of flesh and blood and human traits, as the next person. Eyelashes. Teeth. His veins presumably held blood, like the next person. He'd once been a baby, the offspring of some unsuspecting union. A pulse moved beneath his skin, just as it did in Billie. The thing was, she had not spotted him in a crowd. She could not in all reality say she had looked at him at The Dancers and thought, *That one. That one is the killer of thousands, hundreds of thousands.*

Yet here before her was Franz Hessmann, he of the shocking white hair, his one truly standout physical quality in a world now peopled with scarred and injured returned soldiers. Had he earned that hair in the war? she speculated. In the fire that had scarred him? Or had it always been part of him? That hair had dyed badly when he'd finally deigned to cover it, no longer so confident of his ability to hide in plain sight around the high end of Sydney, surrounded by a set of people he'd so successfully gained the support of, through wealth and fine art and the grubbiest forms of blackmail. His hairline was artificial looking and harsh against his pale Aryan skin, the dye sitting strangely. She'd noticed it at a glance, though it had taken a few seconds longer to place just what it meant. Only a few seconds, but that had almost been enough—*would have* been enough, if not for John, the lift operator, and his understanding of her coded words. Hessmann had been on his way up to her office to kill her. That showed a personal dislike, she felt. He would have been safer staying away from her, disappearing and staying gone, but now he was in her father's creaking wooden chair in what had once been her father's office, and she had a loaded 1908 Colt trained at that badly dyed head of his, and truthfully Billie's trigger finger felt itchy.

"Who helped you out at Richmond, Hessmann? It must have been someone persuasive."

He kept his thin mouth shut.

"What did you like to do to help people to talk? Something about a bathtub, I hear. Was that your thing? If I had some of your techniques, maybe you'd furnish me with some information now."

Again, nothing.

The rage in Billie, a warranted but unhealthy rage, was pressing at her skin from the inside, making her feel she might burst. What would she have done if this were eighteen months earlier? Would she wait for the cavalry to arrive? She'd never killed a man, not face-to-face anyway—she'd been bluffing about that—but there was always a first time.

"I heard how those women got you at the camp. Earned you

those burns," she said, pointing at his face. "Hardly an honorable
war wound, unlike so many others. That must have really upset you,
having to walk around with the evidence of their victory written on
your face."

Ah, she was getting to him now. That chalky face of his was
tinged with red.

"Yes, they really got you, didn't they, those women?" Billie went
on. "And the boy here, he figured it out, didn't he? Did you know
who the boy was? His significance?"

Her captive frowned.

"The boy you beat and nearly succeeded in killing, did you know
who he was?"

"*Judensau,*" he seethed in his heavy accent. *Jew pig.* Billie felt her
temper rise yet further.

It's tempting, but no, she told herself. She didn't want him ruining
the rust carpet. He was much better in the dock here in Sydney or
in Berlin or at Nuremberg facing his brave victims than splattered
in her nice office where she would have to return each day and remember him, or at least the stains he'd left behind.

"I don't think much of you, Hessmann. You and your kind aren't
worth the carpet I walk on and that's the only reason I'm holding
back from pulling this trigger right now and ruining this little patch
of rug beneath you. I find myself feeling a bit sentimental about the
rug, but hey, if you really want to change my mind, do go on," she
dared him.

"*Verräterische hure!*" he said and spat on her father's rust carpet.
Treacherous whore.

Billie took a step back to contain herself. *Wait for the cops. Hank
won't be long,* she thought. *Lot of good that did last time,* came the

second half of that thought. The inspector seemed to be doing the best he could; he'd done what he promised when she'd called on him—but that hadn't been enough. Her eye caught Jack's photograph, that blurry, candid grin, and the air shifted, the soft sound of movement alerting her, and Hessmann, moving swiftly, bounded toward the small balcony, its door left open to catch the breeze. Yes, he was going for the balcony, where she'd often lingered to watch the setting sun, or smoke one of her Lucky Strikes on smoking days. It was curious; he had nowhere to flee to. She moved fast, just a beat behind him, and just as she thought he was cornered, Hessmann was over the edge. Billie waited for screams from below and the sound of his body hitting the footpath. Another Nazi escaping justice by his own hand, like his Führer in his bunker.

But no.

Billie leaned over the balcony railing and saw that Hessmann was on the edge of the moldings, clinging to the building, far above the entrance to the billiards room where she had been celebrating so recently. A fire exit, made up of a narrow metal bridge connecting Daking House to its neighbor, Station House, sat high above the laneway, and Billie was aware of its having been used in years past by the panicked workers in the top stories of the adjoining building when fire had broken out. The fire escape was old and considered unsafe, but Hessmann was inching toward it and soon would have it in reach.

Billie trained her Colt on him. "Stop!" she yelled, leaning out over the balcony, steadying herself against one of the solid pillars, and when he didn't stop, did not even pause, she fired her weapon without hesitation, the bullet ricocheting off the metal of the bridge. She heard a gasp from below, as if it were coming from another place, perhaps over a telephone line or from a picture film. She stayed focused on Hessmann, and in no time he was on top of the narrow bridge, crouching low as a spider, pulling his way across the grille toward Station House. She fired again, aiming at his lower body, as the rest of him was protected by the grille. This time he paused, but only briefly. She had not missed him, she realized, seeing a trail of blood as the Nazi war criminal once more dragged himself forward. Now the metal grille was in the way of a clear shot.

"*Blast. Blast!*" There was no one below to help, no one in Station House that she could see. The cops had not yet arrived. The building's windows were open for summer. It would be too easy for him to disappear into one of them. Billie slid the Colt into the belt at the cinched waist of her dress and with only a moment's hesitation pulled herself over the edge of the balcony. The moldings were just wide enough to cling to, but it was perilous. She began to slip and threw herself sideways, catching the bridge with both hands, and with effort lifted herself up and was on the fire escape with Hessmann only feet ahead. The rails were not solid, the bridge swayed, and she crawled forward, catching Hessmann's ankle on one side.

"*Hure!*" he cursed for the second time, trying to shake her off.

"I'm no one's whore, thank you very much," Billie returned with vicious politeness, and calmly pressed the muzzle of her Colt into the bullet wound in his leg. He cried out and stopped trying to pull himself forward. When he was still again she released the pressure. "I don't recommend you move, Hessmann," she said. "Unless you want more of that." The wound poured blood where the bullet had hit him. He couldn't run now, not on that leg. He'd stopped, and so had she. She had him. She finally had him. She would not let Hessmann out of her sight. Not for anyone.

"Don't move!" a voice was calling from below, unexpectedly mirroring her sentiment. She looked down over the lip of the narrow bridge and recognized Hank Cooper's face turned up at her. "We have the fire department coming. They have a net," he shouted, his voice uncharacteristically strained.

Only now, Billie realized they were drawing quite a crowd, perching on the bridge, several stories above the cold, hard pavement. Commuters heading to Central Station and the tramlines after work had stopped to stare. Constable Primrose was beside Hank Cooper, and the lift operator, John Wilson, was with them, looking as white as a spirit. Just ahead, at the top of Station House, two police officers appeared in the window, the glass surreally reflecting Billie's precarious position back at her. Someone in clerical vestments arrived in haste down Rawson Lane, crossed himself, and began praying. The moment stretched out, the sky turning gold around them, the sun lowering slowly in the summer sky.

Hessmann must know now that he was surrounded, that he had no chance of escape. Not this time.

"*Für das Tausendjähriges Reich!*" he yelled suddenly and threw his weight forward, his legs falling downward first and slowly dragging his torso over the bridge. Billie grabbed for him, then let go, realizing she had no firm hold on the bridge, pulling herself backward on her bottom and hands, out of the way of his grasp as he now scrabbled for a hold, either to take her with him or as a final, instinctive bid for survival. The bridge lurched, rusted screws giving way. One white hand reached her right ankle and took it firmly, its grip as tight as a python, pulling Billie sideways in a violent jerk. The bridge shook again, making a terrible noise. Billie slid helplessly to the edge, her movement punctuated by a collective cry from below. She found the slimmest foothold for her left shoe and meshed the fingers of one hand through the grille. They stayed poised there, Billie gripping the bridge and Hessmann hanging by one arm, his entire weight now on her right ankle. The screams from below sounded strangely distant in Billie's ears under the din of her adrenaline, which throbbed loudly in her skull. Her twisting leg screamed out in pain, but her own lips were silent, pulled back in a grimace as white as her knuckles as she desperately held on.

Billie's fine stockings were smooth, slippery, and she felt Hessmann's grasp sliding lower as they tore under the weight of his body, and then he was balanced from the toe of her oxford shoe, her foot twisting. Her shoe began to unlace itself, the heel coming free, bit by bit slipping slowly, as time stretched out like a soldier's minute—every action, every breath extended—nothing before, nothing after, just this moment. One more breath, another, and then her oxford was free, and so was Franz Hessmann.

Now weightless, Billie's right leg pulled upward and she instinctively cradled her knee, scraping it on the metal grille suspending her, and through the mesh she caught a glimpse of the white face, now a twisted mask of rage and fear, retreating below her, growing smaller, eyes round with panic and looking right into her, one hand still stretching up, reaching. She closed her eyes and heard the sickening thud as he landed, her shoe hitting the ground after him with something like a ping. The bridge rocked again and everything seemed to go silent, even the hammering of Billie's heart seeming for a moment to stop.

And then, in the distance, a siren.

The fire department was arriving with its safety net.

ACKNOWLEDGMENTS

———

This novel is a work of fiction set in a historical period still in living memory for a fading few, a time of great personal importance for my family and many others. Billie and her story were born from a mix of real life and fantasy, of family stories of World War II, my fascination with the 1940s and women's postwar history, my love of the great noir and hard-boiled fiction of the period, and my love of action and the great women who made their mark on that time. There is no way to do full justice to the heroes and heroines of this period.

The War Widow took more than two years to research and write and many more years to conceive as I busied myself with nonfiction writing projects. During this time my family were incredibly patient, and my publishers were, too. I am indebted. My sincere thanks go to Lindsey Rose and the team at Dutton, and Jennifer Lambert and Harper Canada, for their support for Billie Walker and *The War Widow*, and HarperCollins Publishers Australia for twenty years of support through several genres since my first novel was published with them in 1999. Thanks also to the wonderful Chris Bucci, Paige

Sisley, and the team at CookeMcDermid Literary Agency and Cooke International, and my Australian literary agent, Selwa Anthony.

I owe thanks to researcher Chrys Stevenson, for her tireless assistance as I went down the rabbit hole of historical period details for more than two years, double-checking every elevator, street, and building in 1940s Sydney; the Australian Sewing Guild, for all they have taught me as patron and student and in turn taught the fictional Billie with her sewing and mending skills; fashion historians Hilary Davidson and Nicole Jenkins for their expertise; consultant Dr. Sandra Phillips, Larissa Behrendt, professor of Indigenous Research and director of research at the Jumbunna Institute for Indigeonous Education and Research at the University of Technology Sydney, which launched the book in Australia, and Raema Behrendt, for their knowledge and research assistance into the history of Aboriginal women's experiences in Australia; Daking House YHA, for access to Daking House and their historical and architectural plans; Joe Abboud, for information about the historical block of flats I have renamed Cliffside for the purposes of this book; Bob Waddilove, for his knowledge of the Willys 77 roadster; and former police prosecutor Sergeant Patrick Schmidt, for his assistance.

The characters in this book are fictional, with the exception of Special Sergeant (First Class) Lillian Armfield, who I hope would approve of her brief inclusions, a crime writer's way of drawing attention to her pioneering work in policing. The reprehensible Franz Hessmann is a fictional character, though Ravensbrück concentration camp was a real place where an estimated 132,000 women and children were incarcerated under extreme conditions, including famine, slave labor (yes, the private companies mentioned were involved as employers of this slave labor), inhumane medical experimentation, and sterilizations performed without consent. Very few survived. Specific elements have been inspired by the brave testimony of Holocaust survivors including Simone Lagrange, who testified against the Nazi Klaus Barbie about her torture in a bathtub while just thirteen in 1944. It is said that the women forced to work at Ravensbrück, among other things, used their skills in sewing to make soldiers' socks, adjusting the machines to make the fabric thin at the heel and the toes, causing the socks to wear prematurely when the German soldiers marched, giving the soldiers sore feet. That story appears to be true, and there were real saboteurs at the rocket factory, women who risked all to rebel and keep their spirits alive in unspeakable, cruel, and dehumanizing conditions. I grew up with my *opa*, to whom this book is dedicated along with my *oma*, recalling stories of his escape and of sabotaging bombs in the munitions factory in Berlin he was forced to work in against his will, along with many other able-bodied Dutch men, when Holland was occupied.

I use the term "disfigurement" in this book for period-accurate terminology around facial difference, which was a particular challenge for a larger than previous number of soldiers returning from battles from World War I onward, as weaponry became more advanced, but so, too, did battlefield medical response and advancements in plastic surgery. I've endeavored to make elements of this book as period accurate as possible, even down to Bell's Line Road, which is now known as Bells Line of Road, Rawson Lane, since renamed St. Laurence Lane, and the escaped circus crocodile from 1946 (the timeline moved forward by just a few weeks for the purposes of this novel, as was the timeline for the Australian release of the film *The Killers*), but in the case of The Dancers, historians will note that the club is made up. Hard-boiled fans will recognize the name as an homage to Raymond Chandler's LA and *The Long Goodbye*, the white-haired man in this case having anything but an honorable war wound.

Thank you to my family for their love and support—most of all Berndt and Sapphira, and Jackie, Wayne, Annelies, Dad and Lou, Nik and Dorothy, Auntie Linda, and my dear friends who have been there through thick and thin.

Here's to the thousands of brave rebellions by everyday people.

Billie Walker's story continues in

THE GHOSTS OF PARIS,

coming soon from Dutton.

Turn the page for a preview.

Prologue

————

Wola, Poland, 1944

He pressed back against brick and stone, arms over his head, shielding himself as the buildings shook and the earth beneath him rumbled.

When the blast subsided and he opened his eyes, the square was obscured in white dust and ash, a sight both curiously beautiful and chilling, as tiny fragments of the town and the people in it spread like unearthly snow all round. This was not destruction from a single grenade, that comparatively tiny, violent blast of resistance, nor was this from the Nazi's devastating "Goliath" tracked mines. For days the west of the city had been raided and torched, residents shot on the spot or tortured for information, and so he knew this ash was not only building and concrete, not only the form of the village square, but also those who had perished within it during days of tireless massacre. The *Verbrennungskommando*, "the burning detachment," was destroying evidence of the massacre here, and so his photographs, if he could smuggle them out, would matter all the more. He tried not to breathe in the ash, not to let it inside him. Over the past two days he had not eaten, had barely found a sip of water, and he was almost glad somehow, as the stench in the air and that deathly "snow" would surely make him retch.

There had been shouting and movement, a grenade blast, and now the noises stopped, a kind of respite to match the eerie, slowly falling ash. He wiped his face, raised his camera.

Crouching, he moved forward on one knee. It was not safe. None of this was safe. Just a few more shots, and he would retreat to the makeshift shelter inside the bombed-out building behind him, the building that for now obscured his presence, him and his ever-present camera. But he would have to find another, safer place before the dogs came, let loose to find survivors to be killed. Already half of his focus was caught in escape with his photographs. He had been in tight situations before, smuggling film out in emptied-out cans of toothpaste, but this, he feared, was yet more serious. How would he do it? The conflict had quickly revealed itself to be a homegrown uprising of Polish rebels against a well-planned and resourced Nazi mission of outright extermination. They were killing all citizens, all witnesses. If he was found by the German soldiers they would not let him live. That, he knew.

Makeshift barricades constructed of torn-up and shattered flagstones had been manned by several young boys with rifles and homemade grenades and bombs—one of which, no doubt, had caused the latest blast—and as the dust cleared he noticed the brave boys were nowhere to be seen, their modest supply against the Wehrmacht, Dirlewanger Brigade "Black Hunters," and SS Police Battalions doubtless spent. He seemed alone in the bloody square as the haze settled, though he doubted if that could be true. Had the resistance—such as they were after five years of occupation and days of nonstop intense fighting—retreated to where they had a better stronghold, the square now ceded? The dusty air that had been alive with bullets, boots, and ash moments before had now settled, slowly clearing, it seemed, to make way for something greater, something slow and menacing. He heard the heavy crunch of tracks moving over the ground and knew instantly what it was. There was shouting in German, but he could not make out the words. From somewhere came a woman's screams, disturbingly urgent and clear in the temporary quiet. A new rumbling grew louder.

Something was coming.

A German tank moved into the square, gun first. It was mighty Tiger II, weighing nearly 70 tons, moving right into the line of sight of his Argus. The massive machine, with its brutal gun turret, thundered steadily into the square, toward the makeshift barricades, lumbering inelegantly over each bump but overtaking, always, like a great impenetrable beast, a gollum so much larger than Shelley wrote of. No barricade would be equal to it. He pushed his back into the dusty building again and his shutter clicked, clicked again, and stopped. He brought the camera down from his face.

No, he was not mistaken. There was something hanging on the front of the tank. Something tied there.

Not something, *someone.*

A woman.

It was her screams he had heard. A woman in civilian dress was tethered by the wrists to the huge gun, her petite body dwarfed by its size and stretched out behind her, legs pulled back and secured by the ankles to either side of the front. Her dress was dirty and torn, her white face twisted in horror and framed by brown, lanky hair.

Petite and terrified, she might have been fourteen or forty, a mother or a child. All he saw was primal terror in her large, dark eyes. Again, her screams filled the square, far above the din of the tank's infernal rumbling.

The sound proved too much.

Before he'd even begun to comprehend his actions, to form a plan, he foolishly rushed forward, hands outstretched, his Argus camera left to swing awkwardly at his side, momentarily forgotten. He crossed the square in seconds and leaped on to the front of the massive slow-moving monolith—which would not pause for him, not for anyone save its master at the helm. Caught in a kind of temporary madness, he tore at the ropes that bound the struggling woman, with a singular focus. Once he had freed her left ankle she twisted in place and gestured to her other ankle. "Tamten!" she shouted in Polish. *That one!* He had to get the other next or she could fall facefirst before the tank and be crushed under it. He tore at the binds, and heard the great hull opening, and a soldier shouting.

There was no time, the soldier was climbing out and reaching for his pistol.

From the corner of his eye he caught the movement as the terrified woman—she was indeed an adult woman, perhaps in her twenties, he realized—both of her ankles now freed, swung herself nimbly upward onto the huge gun with a grunt of effort, and locked her dirt-streaked legs around it. She was hanging upside down beneath the mammoth gun, and despite the urgency of his own dangerous position, he watched, as if mesmerized, as she inched herself forward with surprising speed and a survivor's will, as nimble as any acrobatic performer, until her secured wrists slipped off the end of the giant gun and she fell backward, swimming in the air, dress and hair hanging, suspended by her legs, the ropes now loose and no longer binding her. With a mechanical grinding the gun turret moved to the left, taking her with it, and she let go with her dirt-streaked limbs and threw herself from the giant tank, disappearing from view.

There was a pistol shot, then another, and reality came back to him with a crash, as he realized how exposed he was, the precariousness of his position on the enemy tank. He had been foolish. He turned to jump but was not fast enough, the Nazi soldier was faster, and as he hurled himself off the tank's side he was caught across the neck, body jerking back and upward, killing all breath, a sick gurgling sound in his ears. He hung like a rag doll from the side of the tank by his own leather camera strap, and the mighty Tiger II continued through the square, gun roving, the great beast not halting, not even slowing.

Desperately, he clutched the strap at his neck, frantic for air, and saw blood on his fingers, his hands. It was his own, he realized. The strap of his camera was cutting in, his neck opened up. There was shouting in German, another pistol shot, and the world went black. . . .

One

———

Sydney, Australia, 1947

On May Day, the client walked into the offices of B. Walker Private
Inquiries, announced by a faint buzzer. Billie Walker heard this from
her position at her small sixth-floor balcony, where she'd been
smoking a Lucky Strike and regarding the safety bridge that connected Daking House to Station House with a well-honed emotional
distance. She heard the door, heard the little buzzer, heard her
secretary-cum-assistant welcome the stranger, their voices muffled
by the closed connecting door, and took a long drag. On the slow
exhale, smoke floated from Billie's red lips, creating a temporary haze
across her view, the city streets ringed in smoke.

   Cigarette dangling, Billie turned, closed the balcony doors
behind her, and walked to the oval mirror on the wall inside her
office. She checked her emerald tilt hat and red lipstick in one quick
and practiced movement, regarded the steady blue-green eyes staring
back at her in the reflection, and satisfied, made for the corner of her

wide wooden desk and stubbed out the last of her cigarette. Smoke drifted upward, settling in the air. The Bakelite clock above her door informed her that this potential client was right on time. This one had made an appointment, though Billie had not been furnished with any information regarding the nature of her query, complaint, or troubles, only a surname. Things having improved at Billie's humble agency in recent months, Ms. Walker—the B of B. Walker Private Inquiries and the principle agent—no longer had to wait out long days for the phone to ring or a knock at the door, and for the moment at least, did not need to contemplate the empty walnut chairs in the small waiting room and find odd jobs for her secretary to do. Business was booming for Sydney's most famous—or was it infamous?—female inquiry agent.

Billie smoothed down her skirt suit, opened the connecting door, and leaned against the open doorframe to take in the stranger who had entered her waiting room. She did so hope this wasn't another divorce job.

"Ah, here she is now. May I present Ms. Billie Walker," Samuel Baker, her tall secretary-cum-assistant announced, right on cue. "Ms. Walker, this is Mrs. Richard Montgomery," Sam said.

She still had no first name of her own, Billie thought. Shame.

Amusingly, the woman's gaze was distracted by Billie's secretary in his lightly pin-striped suit and a flattering tie of burgundy and sky-blue that brought out his baby blues. A flirtatious smile played on the older woman's painted lips as she regarded him. To be true, Sam was a pleasing sight. He was a strapping Australian lad whose experience of the war had left him changed, most notably his injured left hand, which was always covered in a leather glove, lending him a touch of mystery. That hand had come up against an Italian thermos bomb and was now missing a few fingers, replaced by wooden prosthetics. Sam had already proved himself invaluable on numerous occasions, so if Billie had his injury to thank for the fact he was happy to work for her, well, the army's loss was her gain. He didn't mind taking orders from a woman—far too rare a trait, in her opinion—and his trigger hand was as whole and steady as you could ask for. It was a bonus that he was something like Alan Ladd in appearance, though far taller, and built several axe handles across, as the saying went.

As Samuel provided a handsome distraction, Billie took in the red-haired woman's appearance quickly and efficiently, observing cues drilled into her from work as an inquiry agent and before that as a war reporter, and a childhood spent listening to her father, Barry Walker, the police man–turned–private investigator who had inhabited these very offices, sitting at that wide wooden desk and smoking on that same small balcony where his only child now spent her moments of contemplation. *Always look at the shoes,* he would say. The fit and quality of the suit. The time piece. The hat. Look at the eyes. *Each detail tells a story.* Indeed it did.

At a trained glance this woman's story looked like one of style and apparent luxury—not something one saw in great abundance since the war. The suede burgundy shoes were new and well crafted, the stockings nylon and without flaw (Billie suspected this woman had never had to stoop to painting a line up the back of her leg with gravy to create the illusion of stockings, as so many had). The Akoya pearl set she wore was delicate and quite real, Billie was sure, that particularly desirable luster not being possible in the new fakes. Her navy skirt suit was notable for being of the latest style, echoing the scandalously feminine silhouette of Christian Dior's "New Look" that had taken the fashion world by storm just months before—softly rounded shoulders, nipped waist, a slightly fuller skirt falling mid-calf—not quite full enough to cause outrage on the streets of Sydney, rationing still being in place, but enough to set this woman apart as a specimen of fashion, a local doyenne of the Parisian trend. Yes, it set her apart, as did the genuine, high-quality glass-eyed fox stole she wore around her shoulders. This was no prewar throwback.

Mrs. Montgomery somehow had her finger on the pulse of international fashion trends and had money and the tailors to pull it off for her. Billie rather wanted to get a name. One thing was for certain, this was a woman of means, and that impression was confirmed by the crowning glory of her engagement ring, which was over a carat, Billie's trained eye told her, and dwarfed the comparatively simple wedding ring worn with it.

"Pleased to make your acquaintance, Mrs. Montgomery," Billie said, and meant it, pleased she was attracting the kind of clientele whose cheques were unlikely to bounce like rubber. She lifted her shoulder off the door frame where she'd been leaning, and smiled, locking eyes with the Joan Crawford–esque beauty. Mrs. Montgomery had large eyes in a strong, rectangular face, her gaze direct and framed by dyed red hair worn short across the forehead and swept back in a center part beneath a flat, tilted navy hat. It was the face of a strong-willed woman of high standards, perhaps unused to inquiry agents and their less-than-luxurious offices.

"Won't you come into my office?" Billie said, and turned on her stacked oxford heel. She disappeared inside and the woman followed in the investigator's wake, her posture erect and proud, eyes flicking back to Samuel Baker, who was trailing just behind. If he was bothered by the woman's flirtatious gaze, he didn't let on. He cut an attractive shadow, happy to let the women lead the way.

The office Billie Walker welcomed this fashionable stranger into was not the kind of surrounds where Mrs. Montgomery would seem, under normal circumstances, to belong. Though Billie was not exactly unglamorous herself, with her contrast of dark hair and pale skin, and her Tussy's Fighting Red lipstick, the utilitarian office suited her like a battered trench coat, or well-travelled uniform. It was a place of action, with Billie herself a devotee of action, as the war years and more recent events as an investigator attested. Fashion was something she enjoyed and employed in her profession to gain entry to all echelons of society, but her office had very few frills about it, and her aristocratic mother, if she ever again deigned to lower herself enough to grace those four walls, would complain the place "lacked a woman's touch," despite the space now being occupied by Billie and her so-far-exclusively-female clientele. It had been left much the same as when her late father had operated his agency, and the decor still bore his touches. The carpets were rust red, the filing cabinets a fading hunter green, the desk wide and wooden and appropriately scarred, all of it imbued with the sense of his presence, now further layered by this new generation of Walker investigator but by no means extinguished by her presence. The only concessions to its new occupant were the placement of the small and handy mirror, a small bottle of Bandit perfume on a shelf, some personal photographs, and the additions of a few of the more fashionable women's journals in the waiting room. The place suited Billie well, as if her late father had lovingly worn it in for her.

Samuel plugged the doorway to the office, waiting, and knowing the next part of this client ritual well.

"Would you care for tea, Mrs. Montgomery?" Billie asked the woman once she was comfortably seated across the desk in the chair she reserved for clients.

"Thank you kindly," the woman replied, and broad-shouldered Sam disappeared, gently closing the door behind him with a barely audible click. She'd seen him throw full-grown men across an alley with his good hand, but he played down his physical size and strength in such situations as this, his strategic invisibility well practiced.

Mrs. Montgomery—who had taken the time to watch Sam go—was now surveying the space around her. Such imperfect and roughly finished spaces did not seem her natural habitat, but she showed no signs of disappointment. Perhaps, if she'd been living as a bird in the proverbial gilded cage—as was one theory Billie was forming—more gilded surrounds would not be comforting in this moment. Something had brought her out of her natural habitat and into Billie's.

"Are you the only woman investigator in Sydney?" Mrs. Montgomery asked.

"Sometimes," Billie said, and leaned one elbow on the wooden desk. One of her competition was currently in jail for some petty matter, nothing to do with Billie of course. Her main competitors were male investigators, however. They dominated the trade, and always had. In fact, much of her post still arrived for Mr. B Walker, as if the fact of her obvious femininity were not quite enough to overcome the assumption that the principle at a private inquiry agency would be a grizzled gentleman gumshoe.

"How may I be of assistance today?" Billie asked.

"You assisted a friend of mine, Nettie Brown, if you may recall," the woman began.

Billie did recall. That had been late 1946, almost six eventful months before, and had begun as a seemingly routine missing person's case, a search for Nettie's seventeen-year-old son, and evolved into something far larger and more sinister. She resisted looking again toward her smoking balcony even while a vivid image of the Nazi who had flung himself over it flashed across her memory. Yes, she did indeed recall the case. A fair bit of Sydney did, also.

"Nettie was quite impressed by you. She recommended you rather highly," the woman went on.

"That is pleasing to hear."

Billie's eyes went to the glass-eyed fox around Mrs. Montgomery's shoulders, as if it could tell her it had been purchased at the Brown family fur shop at Strand Arcade. Her muscles had tensed at the memory of the case, she noticed. There had been a good outcome, but not without shots fired, and lives altered and lost. But then, she and trouble knew each other rather intimately. No reason the end of the war would stop such a seemingly natural pairing, she supposed.

"I understand you spoke with her a few months ago?" Mrs. Montgomery continued.

"Yes," Billie replied.

She had, in fact, run into Mrs. Nettie Brown in the literal sense—under quite the most extraordinary circumstances on New Year's Day. It had been a frightfully humid day, and just as Billie was having her semi-regular afternoon tea with her informant Shyla at the Central Railway Refreshment Rooms, a freak hailstorm had hit, assaulting Sydney from the skies with considerable violence. The clock face above the station was smashed, and the skylight along the entire main assembly platform had been decimated, raining shards of glass on those below. Fortunately, most of the waiting commuters had only recently been whisked away on various journeys. Miraculously, no one died, though hundreds across the city had been treated for head wounds and cuts from flying glass. Tram windows and sky-lights were shattered. Haymarket turned into a torrent of swirling water as pipes and infrastructure broke. The glass roof of the Aus-tralian Museum nearby was taken apart by hail crashing through a stout iron-mesh partition. People were found bleeding in doorways around the city. The *Sydney Morning Herald* had next day run a most dramatic front-page spread: *Ice Storm Lashes City and Suburbs*, it read, but it hadn't sounded like an ice storm at all, not when you were in it. To Billie it had sounded like a squadron of bombers. Those who had been there could be forgiven for thinking it the return of the Blitz.

In the midst of this maelstrom, Billie sprinted to determine the cause of the thunderous crashing—always the type to run toward chaos and not away from it—and Nettie Brown had run straight into her, head on. After a moment of shocked recognition the women had sheltered together by the Central concourse until the storm passed. Their somewhat bruising meeting had felt peculiarly like foreshadowing at the time. The case for the Brown family was offi-cially closed, but loose ends niggled at Billie, never quite letting her go despite the passing months, and it seemed the powers that be weren't keen on releasing her, either. She only hoped those loose ends weren't weaving themselves into a noose, for her or for someone else.

Nineteen forty-seven had announced itself with a bang. Billie had almost been waiting for this follow-up.

"The case quickly faded from the headlines, which was small miracle," Mrs. Montgomery continued when Billie offered nothing more. The Browns would not have liked the publicity.

"Yes, though I'm afraid I can't claim responsibility for such miracles. I'm not that powerful," Billie remarked.

Mrs. Montgomery frowned. "Nettie assured me you can be discreet."

"Discretion I *can* guarantee, Mrs. Montgomery. Discretion is an important aspect of my work. Had I had it my way, the case never would have made the papers at all, but once a Nazi war criminal is involved there's no holding the papers back."

"He's the one who . . ." She trailed off, lifting a manicured hand toward the now closed balcony doors, one finger extended for a moment, before curling back, as if the gesture might have been too vulgar.

Billie nodded.

The Bakelite clock above the doorway ticked. Billie's prospective client shifted in her chair and seemed for a moment to hug the deceased fox wrapped around her shoulders, as if it could comfort her. It seemed a performative gesture.

"The public's appetite for a grizzly story is always ripe," Billie said, offering that morsel of truth to ease an uncomfortable silence. "But they move on. There's always something else to catch the attention. I can't claim any credit for steering them away from their interest." The case had rather steered new cases to Billie's agency, however. The women of Sydney had come knocking, and now here she was, gainfully employed for the first time since the war. For many, it had been a time that had first provided the independence of a proper wage, modest or otherwise. Billie's winning streak was not guaranteed to continue, though—not that it appeared Mrs. Montgomery would be able to relate about the financial concern of single working women. Billie was becoming rather concerned that she would soon run out of disgruntled wives, having aided so many through her offices. How many more could there be in one city?

"I am at your service, Mrs. Montgomery, and you have my discretion. Nothing you tell me will leave this room with your blessing," she said, hoping to move things along.

"It gives me no pleasure to be here, you understand," Mrs. Montgomery admitted. "Oh, no offense."

"None taken. Like dentists, perhaps, few revel in our professional presence, but we are a necessary evil, you could say." *If you don't want the rotting tooth, or rotten marriage, to take the whole patient.*

There was a gentle knock on the door, and Samuel appeared with a tray, upon which two teacups and the necessary accoutrements were neatly assembled. This felt like good timing. The woman had still not given a single clue as to the reason for her appointment, and Billie was starting to become impatient. In her experience there were two types of clients: the kind who came in with a rush of tears and stories rolling off the tongue, and this type, reticent or hard to read. Anything might be on Mrs. Richard Montgomery's mind, though the impression of the bird in the gilded cage still clung to this woman. What had made her fly the coop, if that's what this was? Was there a job, or not? Billie had been busy, but there was a worrying hole in her calendar coming up. She could use a touch more security from well-heeled clients such as this.

"Sugar?" Billie offered, and the woman nodded. She prepared a cup and pushed it across. "Now, if you will, how may I be of service?"

The Joan Crawford jaw flexed, relaxed. The woman took a sip of her tea, decided something, and those bright, glinting eyes fell on Billie with a different intensity. "It's a delicate matter. You see my husband is a very wealthy man, and he . . . Well, he likes his little adventures."

"I see." *A divorce case then.*

Some part of Billie shrank, but then again, she was the one who had decided to reopen her father's inquiry agency. Divorce work came with the turf.

"You are perhaps wondering where his adventures have led him?" Billie suggested gently. This was a frequent complaint for the clients who entered Billie's office. "There is another woman."

"Undoubtedly," Mrs. Montgomery replied. "Perhaps several. Or there *was*."

"Was?" *Past tense.*

"Miss Walker, my husband hasn't been heard from in almost two years. That is an awfully long time."

"Indeed it is," Billie agreed.

"You see, he's an advertising man, quite successful, and some government department—what do they call it again?—the Department of Information, well, they got him to help them out with their war efforts and so on."

Billie had heard of the department, though she didn't know a great deal about it. They helped in the promotion and advertisement of war bonds, government propaganda, and censorship of information.

"There was this exposition in Paris, you see, and nothing would have it but they needed to send him all the way over for that. It was the jewel in the crown of the department, this exposition, and he was—or is—one of their top men. He arrived in Paris, wrote to me from the hotel there—the Ritz Paris, a very fine hotel. He seems to have done his work for them and then just . . . vanished. After that letter nothing else came, and there was no word of his return. I was not alarmed at first, but it is unlike him to not send *any* letters at all, so when there was no second letter, and time stretched on, I became concerned. I have contacts in Paris"—Billie had guessed this, and now she nodded—"but they tell me they have not heard from him. Naturally, I contacted the Department of Information, which wasn't altogether as easy as I'd expected, and they said he didn't work for them. I mean, *really*," she said, aghast. "It was quite galling. The firm he works for said he was working for the department and round and round it went."

"The Department of Information denied that he worked with them?" Billie asked, intrigued.

"They told me my Richard had completed his employment and he no longer worked for them. The firm said he'd left them to work for the department."

"I see. And how long ago was this?"

"A few months after the exposition. At first I thought he was . . . well, just being Richard. But I did become concerned."

"Of course."

Mrs. Montgomery watched Billie from the corners of her eyes. "You mustn't judge me, Miss Walker," she said. "My Richard is a lovely man, a good man of sterling reputation. He works hard, and naturally a man of Richard's status and demanding workload deserves a certain amount of . . . freedom. So, you see that although some may find my attitude shocking, it is the only way to ensure harmony in our marriage. We had an understanding."

Billie nodded and leaned forward, meeting the woman's large eyes. "You do not need to defend yourself or your marriage to me, I can assure you of that." If there was one thing Billie had learned in life, and certainly in the course of her work, it was that marriages took many different forms. "Judgment is not my job, and I don't trouble myself with it. My job is to find your husband, if you choose to employ my services for the purpose."

The shoulders dropped beneath the rounded shoulders of the woman's tailored suit. "Thank you," she said simply.

"Did he make any of these apparent plans to end his employment known to you?" she said, steering them back on subject. "Or the date he would complete his work with the Department of Information?"

"No. I assumed he would still be working for the department after the exposition in Paris. He never discussed quitting, or any such thing with me. He was one of their top men. Why would he quit, or . . . ?"

Curious. Billie leaned back and thought for a moment. "How much did your husband discuss the scope of his employment with you? The aim of his work at the exposition, his day-to-day, and that sort of thing?"

"We never discussed work or financial matters," Mrs. Montgomery replied, shaking her head adamantly, as if this noncommunication on issues of finance were a wifely virtue. "Richard was the man of the house. That was his role. His work was his own affair. He was a good provider, Miss Walker."

Billie had no reason to disbelieve her. "Have you any employment, Mrs. Montgomery? Any—"

"Certainly not," she shot back before Billie could finish. The idea seemed to offend her.

"Of course." Billie replied, keeping her expression even. This view was commonplace—if a woman like this worked, it was thought it would be because her husband was not an adequate provider, not for reasons of need, independence, or personal fulfillment.

Mrs. Montgomery paused, perhaps realizing the implication of her views. "No offense," she added, looking around Billie's office. "Some women are *forced* to work, I understand."

Billie reserved comment on the subject. After all, she couldn't claim she didn't have to work, but it hadn't always been simply for necessity. Puzzles enlivened her, and the work she did during the war as a reporter . . . Well. She was proud of what she'd achieved.

"If your husband returned to Australia, as seemed to originally be the plan, in your opinion is there any possibility he could have entered the country without your being aware? For instance, could any of your mutual friends be unaware of his return, or would they have reason to keep it from you?" She did her best to read this potential client, who she hoped would not also be offended by this suggestion. "Please understand this question is one of logistics," she decided to add. "I am not casting aspersions as to your relationship with your husband, or your friends, mutual or otherwise."

Mrs. Montgomery appeared to consider this. "I think I understand what you mean." She took a sip of her tea, frowning, and contemplated something. "The fact is, my Richard never liked to keep a low profile, so I'd say yes, I would simply have to know if he was in Australia this whole time. Yes, absolutely." The Crawford jaw flexed as she considered her errant husband. "I don't believe my Richard could return to Australia without my knowing, certainly not for this long, and certainly not to Sydney. And he wouldn't have any reasons to. I never kept him on a tight leash. It just wasn't like that." She shook her head for good measure. "No, he simply doesn't know how to keep a low profile, even if he were motivated to."

And was he motivated to? Billie wondered. Many men had returned from the war in secret, to live out solitary lives in the Australian bush, too psychologically damaged by war to face society or the lives they had once known, or unwilling or unable to face the uncomfortable staring of neighbors and pointing of children at scars and war wounds they could not hide. But again, this woman's husband had gone missing *after* the end of the war. He wasn't involved in combat that they were aware of, and there was unlikely to be a great deal of danger in his work. It didn't fit.

"And what have you done in the intervening years?" Billie asked gently.

"I won't mince words, Miss Walker. I have been fairly comfortable, if bothered by the mystery of it." She paused, and Billie considered her impression, that this woman's pride was somewhat more injured than her heart, but then, after so long, one had to find ways to cope. Billie knew that more intimately than she'd like to.

"It did me no favors socially, I can say, as he seemed to have deserted," the woman added. "However, in time most seemed to have assumed he had passed on, as so many men did. It became accepted that I might be a widow, and I guess part of me accepted that, too."

"Is that what you believe?" Billie asked.

"Well, I don't quite know what to believe," she replied, and on face value Billie believed she was being honest about that. "After a time, I went to the usual agencies, naturally, but I'm afraid it hasn't been much help. Well, it hasn't been any help at all, frankly, and the whole thing is such a frustration, especially now. Without some evidence of his adultery, or a certificate of death . . ."

"You will remain married and unable to move on. Should you wish to," Billie added.

Mrs. Montgomery nodded. She seemed a determined woman who knew what she wanted, and often got it, Billie wagered. Forced to remain married while abandoned would be an unsuitable status quo for such a woman, particularly one who considered a wage beneath her, or a sign of failure. That gilded cage may have been fine for a while, but it had surely tarnished with time. It would be getting lonely in there.

Billie leaned back, and quite inconveniently cast her eyes over one of the photographs on her wooden desk. It was *that* photograph—the one in the small frame. It had been an unconscious impulse to look at it; the image she had taken of Jack Rake in Vienna. In the photograph Jack was smiling, and his smile was intoxicating, eyes alive with the irresistible chemistry that had erupted between them like a bright flame. This was the weekend they'd fallen in love, before the world had been irretrievably altered, before the war had begun, and long before their makeshift wedding, and her father's sudden passing that followed, taking her far from him and their work together. Her husband was just as he looked in those flashes that haunted her each time she closed her eyes. That smile. Those hazel eyes. That lean, tanned face. And those lips she had kissed for untold stolen hours, locked in embraces in bombed-out buildings, hearing shells in the distance.

Sitting up, Billie averted her eyes and swallowed. It was only the tiniest movement of her throat, a subtle sign that this conversation was a touch close to home. Someone who knew her well might have caught it—her mother would have—but not this stranger, who was quite understandably caught in her own thoughts about her marital troubles. Billie's bread and butter was missing husbands and cheating husbands. That Billie's own husband was missing was something she hardly needed reminding of. With all the war had done, there was something of an influx of missing men. Professionally, she was adept at looking for missing husbands, but in time she'd all but given up on her own.

Or had she?

Mrs. Montgomery was still talking, oblivious to the gooseflesh that had come up Billie's legs, and her words returned suddenly to Billie's ears, like a radio turned back on. ". . . and between us, I can't access more finances unless, he, well, unless there is some resolution . . ." She paused. "You see, I can't remarry unless I divorce Richard."

"Indeed. I see your predicament," Billie replied smoothly. The money—which must have been substantial—was running lower than was comfortable, along with this woman's patience for answers. This was understandable. Even in the event that finances were not a pressing concern, and that was indeed rare, the social suspicions cast upon unmarried women were not something widows were spared, particularly not if they appeared eligible, as this well-turned-out woman did. It was assumed that such a woman wanted a man, and there were certainly fewer going around these days. Single women had long been considered threatening—one reason daughters were routinely married off while still barely children—and a woman who was not attached to a man was viewed with suspicion by many, with no male hand to guide her, rein her in, and keep her from seducing unsuspecting husbands. Billie knew this too well.

"It must be terribly hard for you, not knowing."

Mrs. Montgomery nodded, and something glittered in her eyes. Finally, a hint of emotion, of vulnerability.

"Sadly, I see these sorts of cases far too often," Billie continued. She understood there were millions of missing persons in the International Red Cross' Missing Persons Bureau in Geneva. Just how many of those stories would have happy endings was increasingly slim as the years wore on. "You have my sympathies, but I'll be frank, Mrs. Montgomery. If you are sure your husband is not in the Antipodes, I fear I can't be of much help."

With this the arms crossed, and Billie caught a better look at the glittering wedding ring—a central large solitaire diamond surrounded by two cascading swirling tiers of round brilliant-cut diamonds and glittering baguette diamonds. It was well and good to have clients from the high end of town walking into Billie's office, but not if she couldn't help them. It seemed a shame to turn her away.

"Nettie said you were the one to come to, that for missing persons you are second to none. What is your rate for this kind of case?" Mrs. Montgomery pressed, ignoring Billie's observation, as if it hadn't been raised.

"It the same as it is for all of my work," Billie explained calmly, having already decided this was going nowhere. "We charge fourteen pounds a day plus expenses." Her rate had gone up recently, with her higher profile after the complicated Brown family case. "We dedicate ourselves entirely to our clients for the duration. There is no guarantee of how long any individual case may take. Some are resolved in just a couple of days and some take far longer. I have found many a husband," Billie said without false modesty. "However, as I mentioned, I fear we are not suitable for your particular needs, given the likelihood your husband did not return to this country. We can certainly explore any local connections, but it does seem you likely need an inquiry agent in Paris, and possibly London as well. Sadly, I don't believe I have contacts on hand to offer you, though I could look into it for you, if that would help?"

She tried her professional smile, hoping to ease the woman's disappointment.

"But you do have contacts," Mrs. Montgomery returned, to Billie's surprise. "Did you not work there yourself during the war? You will go to Paris for me on the next available flight and you will find out what happened to my Richard."

Billie was caught without words for a moment. Since returning in '44 and reopening her late father's agency, she'd worked in Sydney and surrounds, as he had before her. The possibility of traveling for the work had not occurred to her.

"Oh, I had you checked out, naturally," Mrs. Montgomery added, while Billie searched for a response. "I wanted to know who I was hiring. You were a reporter, weren't you?" Billie nodded. She missed that work, though not the war. The newsrooms of Sydney were not so keen on women reporters once the men returned. "You must understand, you couldn't get me on one of those beastly deathtraps . . . airplanes, for all the tea in China," Mrs. Montgomery continued. "My aunt died in one of those cursed machines and Richard never could convince me to get in one. No, I am not going over there, and I am quite determined to have you do it. I will pay handsomely."

Billie could certainly see that determination was real. There was no doubting it. But though she was not the type to dissuade a clearly well-heeled client from hiring her, she wasn't prepared for this, and the idea set off a series of conflicting thoughts and feelings for her.

"I'll admit it is an intriguing idea," she replied cautiously, but it would come with some considerable expenses, you understand." She watched the woman's response, but this idea did not seem to faze her. Could she be the only woman in Sydney not to feel the pinch of the war years? "I can't guarantee my assistant will be available," Billie continued. "I'll have to consult with him on that, and look into our calendar." She must have appeared uncertain, because what Mrs. Montgomery said next sealed the deal.

"Naturally, Miss Walker. I'll pay double your usual rate."

Having seen a fair bit in her years—particularly since '39—it was rare for anyone or anything to raise Billie Walker's brow, but Mrs. Montgomery had succeeded.

"It's a day rate, isn't it, I think Nettie said?" Ms. Montgomery added. "I'll double your fourteen-dollar day rate when you are outside the country, all expenses paid. *Reasonable expenses*, of course," she specified. Those eyes focused on Billie with an unusual directness. "I want this done, Miss Walker. I've waited quite long enough and I won't take no for an answer." The square jaw was set.

And with that the woman slid two hundred pounds across the battered wooden desk and handed Billie a formal card, embellished tastefully with an illustrated spray of flowers.

MRS VERA MONTGOMERY

Vera. She had her own name after all.